"Sunny, will thee be my wife and go west with me?"

Noah's hand was large and rough but so gentle, and his touch warmed her. Then she did something she had barely learned to do—she prayed. *Dear Father, should I marry Noah Whitmore?*

She waited, wondering if the Inner Light the Quakers believed in would come to her now, when she needed it so. She glanced up into Noah's eyes and his loneliness beckoned her, spoke to her own lonesome heart. "Yes," she whispered, shocking herself. Her words pushed goose bumps up along her arms.

"May God bless your union with a love as rich and long as Eve's and mine," Solomon said. The elderly man's words were emphasized by the tender look he turned to his spouse, who beamed at him in turn.

Oh, to be loved that way. Sunny turned to Noah and glimpsed stark anguish flickering in his dark, dark eyes. Maybe Noah, born and raised among these gentle people, would be capable of love like that.

But what could I possibly have to offer in the way of love?

USA TODAY Bestselling Author

Lyn Cote

Their Frontier Family
&
The Baby Bequest

LOVE INSPIRED
INSPIRATIONAL ROMANCE

LOVE INSPIRED®
INSPIRATIONAL ROMANCE

ISBN-13: 978-1-335-47440-7

Recycling programs for this product may not exist in your area.

Their Frontier Family & The Baby Bequest

Copyright © 2020 by Harlequin Books S.A.

Their Frontier Family
First published in 2012. This edition published in 2020.
Copyright © 2012 by Lyn Cote

The Baby Bequest
First published in 2013. This edition published in 2020.
Copyright © 2013 by Lyn Cote

This edition published by arrangement with Harlequin Books S.A.

For questions and comments about the quality of this book, please contact us at CustomerService@Harlequin.com.

Love Inspired
22 Adelaide St. West, 40th Floor
Toronto, Ontario M5H 4E3, Canada
www.Harlequin.com

Printed in U.S.A.

CONTENTS

A *USA TODAY* bestselling author of over forty novels, **Lyn Cote** lives in the north woods of Wisconsin with her husband in a lakeside cottage. She knits, loves cats (and dogs), likes to cook (and eat), never misses *Wheel of Fortune* and enjoys hearing from her readers. Visit her website, booksbylyncote.com, to learn more about her books that feature "Strong Women, Brave Stories."

Books by Lyn Cote

Love Inspired Historical

Wilderness Brides

Their Frontier Family
The Baby Bequest
Heartland Courtship
Frontier Want Ad Bride
Suddenly a Frontier Father

The Gabriel Sisters

Her Captain's Heart
Her Patchwork Family
Her Healing Ways

Visit the Author Profile page
at Harlequin.com for more titles.

THEIR FRONTIER
FAMILY

As far as the east is from the west,
so far hath he removed our transgressions from us.
—*Psalms* 103:12

Therefore if any man be in Christ,
he is a new creature: old things are passed away;
behold, all things are become new.
—*2 Corinthians* 5:17

To my hard-working and insightful editor, Tina James

Chapter One

Pennsylvania, April 1869

"Harlot."

Sunny Adams heard the harsh whisper across the nearly empty general store, knowing she was meant to hear it. Her heart clenched so tightly that she thought she might pass out. Two women at the door looked at her, lifted their noses, then turned and left the store, rudely jangling the little bell above.

She bowed her head, praying that she wouldn't reveal the waves of shame coursing through her. Though she wore the plain clothing of the Quakers, a simple unruffled gray dress and bonnet, she hadn't fooled anyone. They all saw through her mask.

A man cleared his throat. The storekeeper wanted her out. Could she blame him? While she shopped here, no "decent" woman would enter. She set down the bolt of blue calico she'd been admiring, hiding the trembling of her hands.

Feeling as if she were slogging through a cold, rushing flood, she moved toward the storekeeper. "I think that will be…all." She opened her purse, paid for the items Mrs. Gabriel had sent her into town to purchase. Outwardly, she kept her head lowered. Inwardly, she dragged up her composure like a shield around her. Trying to avoid further slights, she hurried across the muddy street to the wagon. Approaching hooves sounded behind her but she didn't look over her shoulder.

Just as she reached the wagon, a man stepped out of the shadows. "Let me help you up," he said.

She backed away. This wasn't the first time he'd approached her, and she had no trouble in identifying what he really wanted from her. "I don't need your help." She made her voice hard and firm. "Please do not accost me like this. I will tell Adam Gabriel—"

"He's a Quaker," the man sneered. "Won't do anything to me. Just tell me to seek God or something."

And with that, he managed to touch her inappropriately.

She stifled a scream. Because who would come to her aid if she called for help? A prostitute—even a reformed one—had no protectors.

"I'm a Quaker," a man said from behind Sunny, "but I'll do more than tell thee to seek God."

Sunny spun around to see Noah Whitmore getting off his horse. Though she'd seen him at the Quaker meeting house earlier this year, she'd never spoken to him.

The man who'd accosted her took a step back. "I thought when you came back from the war, you repented and got all 'turn the other cheek' again."

Noah folded his arms. "Thee ever hear the story about Samson using the jawbone of a jackass to slaughter Philistines?" Noah's expression announced that he was in the mood to follow Samson's example here and now.

Sunny's heart pounded. Should she speak or remain silent?

The rude man began backing away. "She isn't the first doxy the Gabriel family's taken in *to help.*" The last two words taunted her. "Where's the father of her brat? She's not foolin' anybody. She can dress up like a Quaker but she isn't one. And we all know it."

Noah took a menacing step forward and the man turned and bolted between stores toward the alley. Noah removed his hat politely. "I'm sorry," he said simply.

"You have nothing to apologize for," she whispered. "Thank you."

His pant legs were spattered with mud. He looked as if he had just now gotten back from the journey that had taken him away for the past few months. She'd noticed his absence—after all, it was a small church.

But honesty prompted her to admit that Noah had always caught her attention, right from the beginning.

Noah wasn't handsome in the way of a charming gambler in a fancy vest. He was good-looking in a real way, and something about the bleak look in his eyes, the grim set of his face, always tugged at her, made her want to go to him and touch his cheek.

A foolish thing I could never do.

"Is thee happy here?" Noah asked her. The unexpected question startled her. She struggled to find a polite reply.

He waved a hand as if wiping the question off a chalkboard.

She was relieved. *Happy* was a word she rarely thought of in connection with her life.

She forced down the emotions bubbling up, churning inside her. She knew that Mrs. Gabriel sent her to town as a little change in the everyday routine of the farm, a boon, not an ordeal. *I should tell her how it always is for me in town.*

But Sunny hadn't been able to bring herself to speak of the insults, snubs and liberties she faced during each trip to town—not to the sweet unsullied Quaker woman, Constance Gabriel. The woman who'd taken her in just before Christmas last year and treated her like a daughter.

Sunny then realized that Noah was waiting to help her up into the wagon and that she hadn't answered his question. She hastily offered him her hand. "Yes, the Gabriels have been very good to me."

Two women halted on the boardwalk and stared at the two of them with searing intensity and disapproval. Sunny felt herself blush. "I'd better go. Mrs. Gabriel will be wondering where I am," Sunny said.

Noah frowned but then courteously helped her up onto the wagon seat. "If thee doesn't mind, since I'm going thy way, I'll ride alongside thee."

What could she say? He wasn't a child. He must know what associating with her would cost him socially. She slapped the reins and the wagon started forward. Noah swung up into his saddle and caught up to her.

Behind them both women made loud huffing sounds of disapproval.

"Don't let them bother thee," Noah said, leaning so she could hear his low voice. "People around here don't think much of Quakers. We're misfits."

Sunny wondered if he might be partially right. Though she was sure the women were judging her, maybe they were judging him, too. Certainly Quakers dressed, talked and believed differently than any people she'd ever met before. She recalled now what she'd heard before, that Noah had gone to war. For some reason this had grieved his family and his church.

"You went to war," slipped out before she could stop herself.

His mouth became a hard line. "Yes, I went to war."

She'd said the wrong thing. "But you're home now."

Noah didn't respond.

She didn't know what to say so she fell silent, as well.

Twice wagons passed hers as she rode beside a pensive Noah Whitmore on the main road. The people in the wagons gawked at seeing the two of them together. Several times along the way she thought Noah was going to say more to her, but he didn't. He looked troubled, too. She wanted to ask him what was bothering him, but she didn't feel comfortable speaking to him like a friend. Except for the Gabriels, she had no friends here.

Finally when she could stand the silence no longer, she said, "You've been away recently." He could take that as a question or a comment and treat it any way he wanted.

"I've been searching for a place of my own. I plan to homestead in Wisconsin."

His reply unsettled her further. Why, she couldn't say. "I see."

"Has thee ever thought about leaving here?"

"Where would I go?" she said without waiting to think about how she should reply. She hadn't learned to hold her quick tongue—unfortunately.

He nodded. "That's what I thought."

And what would I do? She had no way to support herself—except to go back to the saloon. Sudden revulsion gagged her.

Did those women in town think she'd chosen to be a prostitute? Did they think her mother had chosen to be one? A saloon was where a woman went when she had nowhere else to go. It wasn't a choice; it was a life sentence.

As they reached the lane to the Whitmore family's farm, Noah pulled at the brim of his hat. "Sunny, I'll leave thee here. Thanks for thy company. After weeks alone it was nice to speak to thee."

We didn't say much—or rather, you didn't. But Sunny smiled and nodded, her tongue tied by his kindness. He'd actually been polite to her in public. At the saloon, men were often polite but only inside. Outside they didn't even look at her, the lowest of the low.

With a nod, Noah rode down the lane.

Sunny drove on in turmoil. A mile from home she stopped the wagon and bent her head, praying for self-control as she often did on her return trip from town. If she appeared upset, she would have to explain the cause of her distress to Constance Gabriel. And she didn't want to do that. She owed the Gabriel family much. She'd met Mercy Gabriel, M.D., the eldest Gabriel daughter, in Idaho Territory. Dr. Mercy had delivered Sunny's baby last year and then made the arrangements for Sunny to come here to her parents, Constance and Adam, and try for a new start.

But she couldn't stay in this town for the rest of her life, no matter how kind the Gabriels had been.

"I have to get away from here. Start fresh." Without warning the words she'd long held back were spoken aloud into the quiet daylight. But she had no plan. No place to go. No way to earn a living—except the way she had in the past.

She choked back a sob, not for herself but for her daughter. What if the type of public humiliation she'd suffered today happened a few years from now when her baby girl could understand what was being said about her mother?

Noah's questions came back to her, and she felt a stab of envy that the man was free to simply pick up and start again somewhere new on his own. Sunny did not have that luxury. *What am I going to do?*

Noah slowly led his horse up the familiar lane, to the place he called home, but which really wasn't home anymore. Sunny's face lingered in his mind—so pretty and somehow still graced with a tinge of innocence.

Ahead, he saw his father and two of his brothers. His brothers stopped unloading the wagon and headed toward him. Not his father. He stared at Noah and then turned his back and stalked to the barn.

This galled Noah, but he pushed it down. Then he recalled how that man on Main Street had touched Sunny without any fear. It galled him to his core, too. She had no one to protect her. The man had been right; the Gabriels would not fight for her. The idea that had played through his mind over the past few months pushed forward again.

His eldest brother reached him first. "You came back." He gripped Noah's hand.

"I'm home." *For now.* His other brothers shook his hand in welcome, none of them asking about his trip, afraid of what he'd say, no doubt.

"Don't take it personally," his eldest brother said, apologizing for their father's lack of welcome with a nod toward the barn.

"It is meant personally," Noah replied. "He will never forgive me for disagreeing with him and going to war." Noah held up his hand. "Don't make excuses for him. He's not going to change."

His brothers shifted uncomfortably on their feet, not willing to agree or disagree. They were caught in the middle.

But not for long. Meeting Sunny in town exactly when he'd come home and seeing her shamed in public had solidified his purpose. She needed his protection and he could provide it. But would she accept him?

Feeling like a counterfeit, Sunny perched on the backless bench in the quiet Quaker meeting for another Sunday morning of worship she didn't understand. She sat near the back on the women's side beside Constance Gabriel, who had taught Sunny to be still here and let the Inner Light lead her.

But how did that feel? Was she supposed to be feeling something besides bone-aching hopelessness?

Little Dawn stirred in her arms and Sunny patted her six-month-old daughter, soothing her to be quiet. *I've brought this shame upon my daughter as surely as my mother brought it onto me.* She pushed the tormenting thought back, rocking slightly on the hard bench not just to comfort Dawn, but herself, as well.

The door behind her opened, the sound magnified by the silence within. Even the devout turned their heads to glimpse who'd broken their peace.

He came. Awareness whispered through Sunny as

Noah Whitmore stalked to the men's side and sat down near, but still a bit apart from, his father and five older brothers. Today he was wearing his Sunday best like everyone else. His expression was stormy, determined.

Dawn woke in her arms and yawned. She was a sweet-tempered child, and as pretty as anything with reddish-blond hair and big blue eyes. As Sunny smiled down at her, an old, heartbreaking thought stung her. *I don't even know who your father is.* Sunny closed her eyes and absorbed the full weight of her wretchedness, thankful no one could hear what was in her mind.

Noah Whitmore rose. This was not uncommon— the Quaker worship consisted of people rising to recite, discuss or quote scripture. However, in her time here, Noah had never risen. The stillness around Sunny became alert, sharp. Everyone looked at him. Unaccountably reluctant to meet his gaze, she lowered her eyes.

"You all know that I've been away," Noah said, his voice growing firmer with each word. The congregation palpably absorbed this unexpected, unconventional announcement. In any other church, whispering might have broken out. Here, though, only shuttered glances and even keener concentration followed.

Sunny looked up and found that Noah Whitmore was looking straight at her. His intent gaze electrified her and she had to look away again.

"I'm making this announcement because I've staked a homestead claim in Wisconsin but must accumulate what's necessary and return there while there is still time to put in a crop." Still focusing on her, he paused and his jaw worked. "And I have chosen a woman who I hope will become a wife."

A wife? Sunny sensed the conspicuous yet silent reaction Noah's announcement was garnering. And since Noah was staring at her, everyone was now studying her, too. *He couldn't...no, he—*

"Adam Gabriel," Noah said, his voice suddenly gruffer, "I want to ask for thy foster daughter Sunny's hand in marriage. And I want us to be married now, here, today."

Ice shot through Sunny. She heard herself gasp. And she was not the only one. She couldn't think straight. Noah wanted to marry *her?*

I couldn't have heard that right.

Adam Gabriel and Noah's father, Boaz, surged to their feet, both looking shocked, upset. A few other men rose and turned toward Noah.

White-haired Solomon Love, the most elderly and respected man at the gathering, stood. He raised his gnarled hands and gestured for the two fathers and the others to retake their seats. Adam sat first and then, grudgingly, Noah's father.

Sunny could do nothing but stare at the floor, frozen in shock as Noah's impossible words rang in her head.

Noah inhaled, trying to remember to breathe. Though this was the reaction he'd expected, his emotions raced like a runaway train.

Solomon moved to the aisle and faced Noah. "I understand why thee is in a hurry to get thy crop in, yet taking a wife is an important decision. It cannot be made lightly, hurriedly." The man's calm voice seemed to lower the tension in the room.

"This isn't a hasty decision," Noah said, finding he was having trouble getting his words out.

"When did thee court Sunny?" Solomon asked politely.

Sunny tilted her head, as if asking the same question.

Noah looked down. Everyone here knew that the woman he'd courted over a decade ago—and who had rejected him when he went off to war—sat in this very room, now the wife of another man. And how could he explain how Sunny had attracted him from the first time he'd seen her here at Christmas last year? She'd drawn him because he sensed another soul that had lived far beyond this safe haven.

The war had never penetrated the peace here. An image of soldiers, both blue and gray, lying in their own blood flashed in his mind. The gorge in his throat rose. He made himself focus on here. On now. On her.

"I haven't approached Sunny," Noah continued, keeping his voice steady. "In her circumstances…" His voice faded. Then he looked Sunny straight in the eye. She still looked stunned. He hoped she wasn't going to resent this public declaration. After meeting her in town upon arriving home, he'd thought this over carefully. He'd decided the best way to spike scurrilous, misguided gossip was to propose publicly.

He cleared his throat and chose his words with care. "I didn't want her to take my interest wrongly." That much was true. He'd first seen the way she was treated in town long before he'd left for Wisconsin. "But I think she'll make me a good wife. And I'll try to make her a good husband."

Noah turned his gaze to Solomon Love, wanting to give all his reasons. "I could have just gone to Adam Gabriel's house later to ask, then taken her to the justice of the peace." Noah paused and bent his head toward her as if acknowledging he would have needed her agreement. "But I didn't want to do it like that. I didn't want to do this the world's way, or away from the meeting."

"Like last time? When thee ran away and enlisted?" his father retorted, obviously unable to keep his ire undercover—even here.

Noah stood his ground with a lift of his chin. His father wasn't going to ruin Noah's plans. Or hurt Sunny's feelings.

Solomon cleared his throat. "Marrying should be about thee and the woman thee wishes to marry. 'Therefore shall a man leave his father and his mother, and shall cleave unto his wife,'" Solomon said in a tone that effectively capped a lid on any further public cleaning of the Whitmore family closet.

Boaz glared at Noah still, but shut his mouth tightly.

Noah didn't relax. He glanced at Sunny. She still looked frozen. He hoped he hadn't done this all wrong. Concern tightened into a ball in his midsection.

Solomon's wife, Eve, a little silver-haired sparrow of a woman, rose and leaned on her cane. "I think we should all pray about this now. And, Solomon, we are old and forget the passion of youth. There is no reason to prevent Sunny and Noah from marrying today and leaving for Wisconsin tomorrow with the blessing of this meeting. As long as this is what *the two wish*. And if they have sought God's will and have become clear, we should not try to prevent this marriage. Which I believe," Eve said, her quavering voice firming, "would be of benefit to both."

"Good counsel, wife, as usual." Solomon beamed at her. "Noah, will thee sit and let us pray for thee and Sunny that thee both have clearness about this?"

"I will." Noah sat, suddenly very weary. He glanced at his father, who still managed to bristle though he neither moved nor spoke.

Every head bowed, so Noah lowered his and waited… He hadn't kept track of how much time had passed until he heard Sunny's baby stirring and whimpering. Then he realized that the service had gone on much longer than usual. Others were also becoming restless. Noah tried to sit as if he were at peace, but his nerves jittered. Homesteading he'd seen proved hard enough for a man with a wife. He needed Sunny even though he hadn't thought of marriage after the war. He was offering her a fair deal. He needed a wife and she needed the protection a husband could provide. If Sunny refused him, he'd be forced to go alone.

Solomon stood again, his joints creaking. "We are past our time. Noah Whitmore and Sunny, if it meets with thy approval, my wife and I will meet with thee here at two this afternoon to seek clearness about this."

Noah rose. "I'm willing and I thank thee."

All eyes turned to Sunny. She flushed scarlet.

Constance touched Sunny's arm. "Is thee willing to meet for clearness?"

Sunny nodded, her eyes downcast.

Constance stood. "Our foster daughter is willing."

Noah nodded his thanks.

Then, as if released from a spell, the congregation broke up. They would head home to eat a cold dinner with no doubt a heated discussion of Noah Whitmore proposing to the latest soiled dove the Gabriels had taken in. Noah wished he could change that, but he'd discovered that human nature could rarely be denied.

Outside the meetinghouse Noah approached Sunny,

his broad-brimmed Quaker hat in hand. "I know my proposal shocked thee. If thee is not interested in marrying me, just say so."

She looked up at him and then glanced around pointedly, obviously letting him know that too many people hovered nearby. "I am unsure. I will come at two."

He bowed his head and backed away. "At two." Just then the woman he'd loved walked past him. She nodded and gave him an unreadable look. He felt nothing for her now. She didn't understand him. She hadn't understood why he'd gone to war. And he certainly was no longer the man she'd contemplated marrying ten years ago.

He turned his gaze to Sunny. She was so pretty and so quiet. He didn't know what had caused her to become a prostitute, but she wanted to change, wanted a new start, just like he did. They were well suited in that regard.

Solomon's Bible quote repeated in Noah's mind. *Therefore shall a man leave his father and his mother, and shall cleave unto his wife: and they shall be one flesh.* Declaring his proposal had sharpened his need for Sunny to go with him.

He could only hope that she would seize her chance to start anew. And in the process, possibly save him— from himself.

Sunny paused on the step. She'd never entered the meetinghouse by herself. April sunshine had been tempered by the cool breeze from the west. She pulled her shawl tighter.

Dawn had lain down for her long afternoon nap so Sunny had come with empty arms here—to make a decision that would change both their lives forever. Should she accept Noah's proposal? The thought of marrying chilled her, robbing her of breath.

She couldn't think why he would want to marry her. Why *any* man would want to marry her.

She opened the double door and stepped inside. There in the middle of the Quaker meetinghouse on two benches facing each other sat Eve and Solomon Love, and Noah Whitmore, the man who had said in front of everybody that he thought she would make a good wife.

Fresh shock tingled through her. His thrilling words slid from her mind into her heart and left her quaking. *What do I know about being a wife?*

Sunny tried to conceal her trembling, the trembling that had begun this morning. She walked as calmly as she could manage toward the bench where Noah sat. Without looking directly at him, she lowered herself onto the same bench as he.

Sitting so near him stirred her—and that alarmed her. She had never felt attraction to any man. Was Noah's recent kindness to her the cause? She faced the Loves, who had been good enough to speak to her since she'd come here. Very few of the Quakers—or Friends, as they called themselves—had made the effort to get to know her. They'd been kind but distant. She couldn't blame them for avoiding her. They were holy, she was stained.

Eve smiled at her and, reaching across the divide, patted her hand. "Sunny, thee does not know about the clearness meeting. It is how Friends try to clear their thinking and make sure that they are within God's will."

Unsure of what she should say, Sunny merely nodded. She concealed her left hand in the folds of her gray skirt. In the hours since this morning she'd chafed the flesh beneath one thumb from fretting, a childhood habit. She'd been forbidden to suck her thumb or chew her nails, so when upset, she'd taken to scratching, worrying at her hand. She resisted the need to do it now.

"Noah," Solomon asked, "please tell us again what thy plans are and why they include Sunny."

"I have staked a claim on a homestead in western Wisconsin. Very near the Mississippi River." Noah's words were clipped. "Planting time is near. I need to return as soon as possible."

Sunny's emotions erupted—fear, worry and hope roiled inside her at Noah's words.

"That sounds as if thee is committed to leaving us for good." Solomon's voice was measured and without judgment.

Noah nodded.

"Why have thee chosen to ask Sunny to be thy bride and go with thee?" Eve asked.

Sunny nearly stopped breathing. Her throat muscles clenched with fear.

Noah propped his elbows on his knees and leaned forward as if thinking.

Many questions tumbled through her thoughts, but she could not make her mouth move. Was Noah asking out of pity? Was she in a position to say no to him even if it was? The memory of the man who had inappropriately touched her several days ago slithered through her again, as if he were here leering at her. *Dear God, no more.*

In spite of her inner upheaval, Sunny made herself sit very still as silence pressed in on all of them. She drew in a normal breath. Yes, she could refuse this proposal, but she had Dawn to think of. Would life with Noah be better for Dawn than life alone with her mother? Would he be a loving stepfather for Dawn?

"Noah?" Eve prompted.

"How does a man choose a wife?" Noah asked in return. "I need a wife and want one. I only know that Sunny has attracted my attention from the first time she came to meetings. I've watched her with her little girl. She seems sweet and kind."

It seemed to be a day for Sunny to be stunned. No one—no one—had ever praised her like this. A melting sensation went through her and she wished that the backless bench would give her more support. She tightened her posture.

"That is a very clear reply," Solomon said.

"Sunny, is thee ready to take a husband?" Eve asked.

Sunny swallowed, thinking of how he'd praised her. "I am." She paused, then honesty forced her to bring up the topic she did not want to discuss. "I have a past."

Noah gave a swift, stark laugh. "I have a past, too."

"It is good to be honest with one another," Solomon said, tempering the emotions with a glance.

"I have a daughter," Sunny said, each word costing her. She pleated her plain gray cotton skirt.

"I know, and I'm willing to take responsibility for her," Noah said, glancing toward her.

Sunny measured his tone. He sounded sincere. Nonetheless she had overheard a few words about his own family. And she must speak for her child. "Your father has been known to show temper."

"I'm nothing like my father," Noah said as if stung.

Sunny absorbed this reaction. The bad blood between the two had been plain to see even in her short time here. Maybe not getting along with his own father would make him a more considerate parent, could that be?

"I'm sorry I spoke in that tone to thee," Noah apologized. "I promise I will provide for your daughter, and I will protect her. I'll try to be a good father."

Noah had just promised Dawn more than Sunny's own unknown father had ever done for her. She nodded, still hesitant. "I… I believe you."

"I have watched thee all my life, Noah," Eve said. "And thee has not had an easy time. Losing thy mother so young, that was hard. And thy broken engagement when thee went off to war. But thee cannot change the past by merely moving to a new place."

Sunny wished Eve would explain more. Who had Noah loved and been rejected by?

Noah sat up straight again. "I know that. But I cannot feel easy here. My father doesn't need me. My five brothers are more than enough to help him." Though he tried to hide it, hurt oozed out with each word.

"Thy father loves thee," Solomon said. "But that does not mean that a father and son will not disagree."

Noah's expression hardened.

Sunny sensed his abrupt withdrawal. Noah Whitmore had been kind to her in public, protected her, something hardly anybody had ever done for her. He'd asked her to marry him and said she was sweet and kind. He offered her marriage and protection for Dawn. But could he love her?

How could she ask that? Did she even deserve a man's love?

She touched his sleeve. He turned toward her. When she looked into his eyes, she fell headlong into a bottomless well of pain, sadness and isolation. Shaken, she pulled back her hand and lowered her gaze, feeling his piercing emotions as her own. What had caused his deep suffering? She had met other veterans. Was this just the war or something more?

What had happened to Noah Whitmore?

"I want to start fresh—" Noah's words sounded wrenched from him "—and take Sunny and her little girl with me." Noah claimed her hand, the one she'd just withdrawn from him. "Sunny, will thee be my wife and go west with me?"

Noah's hand was large and rough but so gentle, and his touch warmed her. Then she did something she had barely learned to do—she prayed.

Dear Father, should I marry Noah Whitmore?

She waited, wondering if the Inner Light the Quakers believed in would come to her now, when she needed it so. She glanced up into Noah's eyes and his loneliness beckoned her, spoke to her own lonesome heart. "Yes," she whispered, shocking herself. Her words pushed goose bumps up along her arms.

Noah shook her hand as if sealing a contract. She wondered how this new beginning, complete reversal had all happened in less than one unbelievable day.

"We will make the preparations for the wedding to take place during this evening's meeting," Solomon said, helping his wife to her feet. "May God bless your union with a love as rich and long as Eve's and mine."

The elderly man's words were emphasized by the tender look he gave his spouse, who beamed at him in turn.

Oh, to be loved like that. Sunny turned to Noah and glimpsed stark anguish flickering in his dark, dark eyes.

Maybe Noah, born and raised among these gentle people, was capable of love like that. Am I?

But what could I possibly have to offer in the way of love?

I've never loved any man. The thought made her feel as bleak as a cold winter day. Would she fail Noah? Men had only ever wanted her for one thing. What if that was all she was able to give?

Chapter Two

The weekly Sunday evening meeting became Noah and Sunny's wedding. Two single straight-backed chairs had been set facing each other in the center of the stark meetinghouse. Noah sat in one with his back to the men.

Outwardly he'd prepared to do this. He had bathed, shaved and changed back into his Sunday suit—after Aunt Martha had come over to press it "proper" for his wedding. While she'd fluttered around, asking him questions about his homestead, Noah's brothers had been restrained and watchful. Only his eldest brother, Nathan, had asked about Wisconsin and had wished him congratulations on his wedding. His father grim, silent and disapproving. Nothing new there.

Now Noah—feeling as if he were in a dream— watched Constance Gabriel, who was carrying Dawn, lead Sunny to sit on the straight-backed chair set in front of the other women. His bride managed only one glance toward him before she lowered her eyes and folded her hands. Since he couldn't see her face, he looked at her small, delicate hands. Tried not to think about holding them, tenderly lifting them to his lips. Sunny brought out such feelings in him. He wanted to protect her and hold her close.

While away this year he'd thought of her over and over. He'd barely spoken over a dozen sentences to this woman yet he knew he couldn't leave her behind—here among the sanctimonious and unforgiving.

A strained, restless silence blanketed the simple, unadorned meetinghouse. Fatigued from tension, Noah quelled the urge to let out a long breath, loosen his collar and relax against the chair. Without turning his head, Noah knew his father sat in his usual place beside Noah's five brothers. He felt his father's disapproving stare burn into his back like sunlight through a magnifying glass.

Finally, when Noah thought he could stand the silence no longer, Solomon rose and came to stand beside him. Eve rose and came to stand near Sunny. Noah held his breath. There was still time for his father to cause a scene, to object to the wedding, to disown him again. Noah kept his eyes focused on Sunny.

"Sunny, Friends do not swear oaths," Solomon said, "but we do affirm." Then he quoted, ""For the right joining in marriage is the work of the Lord only, and not the priests' or the magistrates'; for it is God's ordinance and not man's; and therefore Friends cannot consent that they should join them together: for we marry none; it is the Lord's work, and we are but witnesses.'"

Noah's heart clenched at the words *the Lord's work*. Where had the Lord been when sizzling grapeshot had fallen around him like cursed manna? Cold perspiration wet Noah's forehead. He shoved away battlefield memories and tried to stay in the here and now, with Sunny.

Solomon continued, "When thee two are ready, my

wife and I will lead thee through the simple words that will affirm thy decision to marry."

Sunny looked up then.

Noah read her appeal as clearly as if she had spoken—*please let's finish this*. "I'm ready if Sunny is," Noah said, his voice sounding rusty, his pulse skipping.

Sunny nodded, her pale pink lips pressed so tight they'd turned white.

Noah gently took her small, work-worn hand in his, drawing her up to face him. He found there was much he wanted to tell her but couldn't speak of, not here or maybe ever. Some words had been trapped inside him for years now. Instead he found himself echoing Solomon's quiet but authoritative voice.

"In the fear of the Lord and in the presence of this assembly of Friends, I take thee my friend Sunny to be my wife." He found that she had lifted her eyes and was staring into his as if she didn't quite believe what was happening. "Promising," he continued, "with God's help, to be unto thee a loving and faithful husband, until it shall please the Lord by death to separate us." Noah fought to keep his voice from betraying his turbulent emotions.

Sunny leaned forward and whispered shyly into his ear. "Thank you."

Unexpectedly, his spirit lightened.

As Sunny repeated the Quaker wedding promise to Noah, her whole body shook visibly. When she had finished, he leaned forward and pressed a chaste kiss upon her lips. The act rocked him to the core. For her part, Sunny, his bride, appeared strained nearly to breaking. Was marrying him so awful? Did she think he'd be a demanding man? He would have to speak to her, let her know...

"Now, Sunny and Noah," Solomon continued, "thee will sign thy wedding certificate and I ask all those attending to sign it also as witnesses."

At Solomon's nod, Noah took his bride's arm and led her to a little table near the door. A pen, ink and a paper had been set there for them. At the top of the paper someone had written in large bold script, "The Wedding Certificate of Sunny Adams and Noah Whitmore, April 4, 1869 at the Harmony, Pennsylvania, Friends Meeting."

Noah motioned for her to go first, but she shook her head. "Please," she whispered.

He bent and wrote his name right under the heading. Then he handed her the pen. She took a deep breath and carefully penned her name to the right of his, her hand trembling.

Then Noah led her to the doorway. By couples and singles, Friends got up and went to the certificate and signed under the heading of "Witnesses." Then they came to her and Noah and shook their hands, wishing them well. All spoke in muted voices as if trying to keep this wedding secret in some way.

Adam and Constance Gabriel signed and both of them kissed Sunny's cheek. "Thee will spend thy wedding night at our house, Noah, if that meets with thy approval," Constance murmured, still cradling Sunny's baby.

"Thank thee," Noah replied. He'd known better than to consider subjecting his bride to a night in his father's house. He'd been planning on taking Sunny to a local inn but this would be better, easier on her, he considered, as a thought niggled at his conscience. Should he have confessed to Sunny his limitations before the wedding? That their marriage would not be the usual?

One of the last to come forward to sign the wedding certificate was his father. He stomped forward and signed briskly. Then he pinned both of them with one of his piercing, judging looks. "I hope thee know what thee are doing."

Sunny swayed as if struck. Noah caught her arm, supporting her. All the anger he'd pressed down for years threatened to bubble over, but to what purpose? *I will not make a scene.* "Thank thee, Father, for thy blessing."

His father scowled and walked past them. Then one by one his brothers signed, shook his hand and wished him the best. Finally his eldest brother, Nathan, signed and leaned forward. "God bless thee, Noah and Sunny. I'll miss thee. We all will. Please send us thy post office address. Though separated, we will still be a family."

Noah gripped his brother's hand and nodded, not trusting his voice.

"We will write," his bride said, offering her hand. "I will try to be a good wife to your brother."

Noah turned away and faced the final few well-wishers, suddenly unable to look at Sunny. *I promise I'll take care of thee, Sunny, and thy little one. Thee will never want and thee will never be scorned. But I have no love of any kind to give. Four long years of war burned it out of me. I am an empty well.*

It was done. Sunny had become a wife. And now in the deep twilight with Noah riding his horse nearby, she rode in the Gabriel's wagon on the way home to their house. The wedding night loomed over her. How did a wife behave in the marriage bed? Nausea threatened her.

Oh, Heavenly Father, help me not shame myself.

She wished her mind wouldn't dip back into the past, bringing up images from long sordid nights above the saloon. Why couldn't the Lord just wipe her mind clean, like he'd taken away her sins?

That's what she'd been told he'd done, but Sunny often felt like her sins were still very much with her, defining her every step of the way.

After arriving at the Gabriel home, she managed to walk upstairs to the bedroom she usually shared with the youngest Gabriel sister. She now noted that fresh white sheets had been put on the bed for tonight, her last night in this house. She stood in the room, unable to move.

Constance entered. "Thee will want to nurse Dawn before bed."

Sunny accepted her child, sat in the rocking chair and settled the child to her.

Constance sat on the edge of the bed and smiled. "We are very happy that thee has found a good husband."

Sunny didn't trust her voice. She smiled as much as she could and nodded.

"Each man and woman must learn how to be married on their own. It cannot be taught. I have known Noah from his birth. He was a sweet child and is an honest man. Adam and I had no hesitation in letting thee marry him."

Sunny heard the good words but couldn't hold on to them. She was quaking inside.

"The only advice I will give thee is what is given in

God's word. 'Submitting yourselves one to another in the fear of God.' And 'Let not the sun go down upon your wrath.'"

Sunny nodded, still unable to speak, unable to make sense of the words. Then the sweet woman carried Dawn away to spend the night in their room. Before Constance left she said, "When thee is ready, open the door for thy husband."

As Sunny went through the motions of dressing for bed, she experienced the same penned-in feeling that had overwhelmed her at fourteen when her mother had died. A week later, penniless and with no friends in the world other than her mother's, Sunny had taken her mother's place upstairs in the saloon. At this memory Sunny's stomach turned. That horrible first night poured through her mind and she fought the memories back with all her strength.

That was the past. Living away from the saloon, surrounded by the Gabriels' kindness, had begun softening her, stripping away the hard shell that had protected her from the pain, rejection and coarse treatment she'd endured.

It won't be like that. This is Noah, who called me sweet and kind and who has married me. Being with him will feel different. But how could he want her after she'd been with so many others?

From across the hall, Sunny heard Dawn whimper. She quieted, waiting to see if her child needed her.

Dawn made no further sound and Sunny took a deep breath. A new image appeared in her mind—her little girl in a spotless pinafore running toward a white schoolhouse, calling to her friends who were smiling and waving hello.

Marrying Noah Whitmore had given her daughter the chance to escape both the saloon and the stain of illegitimacy. And they would be moving to Wisconsin, far from anybody who knew of Sunny's past. Dawn would be free. Hope glimmered within her. *I've done right.*

She slipped on her flannel nightgown and then opened the door. Before Noah could enter, she slid between the sheets, to the far side of the bed. Waiting.

A long while later Noah entered and without a word undressed in the shadows beyond the flickering candlelight.

Sunny's heart thrummed in her temples. Harsh images from her past bombarded her mind but she tried to shut them out.

Noah blew out the candle in the wall sconce.

She closed her eyes, waiting for the rope bed to dip as Noah slid in beside her.

"Sunny, I don't feel right about sharing a bed with you tonight. We're nearly strangers."

I used to lie down with strangers all the time. She clamped her lips tight, holding back the words, afraid that he would realize he'd made a terrible mistake in marrying her.

"I'll bunk here on the floor. Just go to sleep. We've a long day tomorrow. Good night, Sunny." He lifted off the top quilt and rolled up in it on the floor.

"Wh-why did you marry me?" she asked as confusion overwhelmed her.

He turned to face her, scant moonlight etching his outline. "It was time to take a wife."

"You know what I was."

"Yes, I know. You lay with men who paid you. Did you ever kill anyone?"

The question shocked her. "*No.* Of course not."

"Well, I have. Which is worse—lying with a stranger for money, or shooting a man and leaving him to bleed to death?"

Stunned at his bleak tone, she fell silent for a long moment, not knowing what to say.

In the dark she moved to the edge of the bed and slipped to the floor. In the dim light she reached for his hand but stopped just short of taking it. "That was war. You were supposed to kill the enemy."

He made a gruff sound, and rolled away from her. "Good night, Sunny."

Her heart hurt for him. She longed to comfort him, but he'd turned his back to her.

Late into the night she stared at the ceiling, thinking about his question, about how he'd sounded when he'd spoken of war. Would they ever be truly close, or had too much happened to both of them? Was it her past that had made him sleep on the floor? Or was it…him? *Oh, Lord, can I be the wife he so clearly needs?*

"It's not much farther!" Noah called out, walking beside the Conestoga wagon, leading his horse.

Sunny, who was taking her turn at driving the wagon behind the oxen, waved to show him she had heard his first words to her in hours. Dawn crawled by her feet under the bench. Boards blocked the opening to the side and rear. She hoped her idea of "not much farther" matched his.

Beyond the line of trees with spring-green leaves the wide Mississippi River meandered along beside them, sunlight glinting on the rushing water, high with spring rain and snowmelt. Frogs croaked incessantly. After several weeks of traveling all she wanted was to stop living out of a wagon and arrive home, wherever that was.

The unusually warm April sun, now past noon, beat down on Sunny's bonnet. She'd unbuttoned her top two collar buttons to cool. The air along the river hung languid, humid, making perspiration trickle down her back. A large ungainly gray bird lifted from the water, squawking, raucous.

"I'm eager for you to see our homestead," Noah said, riding closer to her.

"I am, too." *And scared silly.*

Too late to draw back now.

Several weeks had passed since they'd wakened the morning after their wedding and set off by horseback to the Ohio River to travel west by riverboat. In Cairo, Illinois, Noah had purchased their wagon, oxen and supplies. Then they'd headed north, following the trail on the east side of the Mississippi. Noah pointed out that the trail was well-worn by many other travelers, and told her that French fur trappers had been the first, over two hundred years ago. She'd tried to appear interested in this since it seemed important to him. She'd known trappers herself. They weren't very special.

"It will take work to make our claim into a home," Noah said.

She gave him a heartening smile and ignored her misgivings. This was her husband, this was her fresh new start—she would have to make it work no matter her own failings. "I'll do my best."

He nodded. "I know that."

Sunny blotted her forehead with the back of her hand. Then she saw a town appear around the bend, a street of rough buildings perched on the river's edge.

"That's Pepin," Noah called out.

"Thank Heaven," Sunny responded, her spirit lifting.

Dawn tried to stand and fell, crying out. Sunny kept one hand on the reins and with the other helped Dawn crawl up onto her lap.

"Is she all right?" Noah asked.

"Fine. Just trying to stand up."

"She's a quick one."

Usually silent Noah was almost chatting with her. *He must be happy, too.*

Noah always slept in the wagon bed at the end near the opening, evidently protecting her but always away from her. But just last night he called out, "Help, help!" She'd nearly crawled to him. But he'd sat up and left the wagon and began pacing. She hadn't known what to do. Sunny was beginning to believe he slept away because of his nightmares. Because of the war perhaps?

She wondered if his lack of sleep made him silent. Whenever she spoke, he replied readily and courteously. Yet he rarely initiated conversation, so today must be a good day.

Soon she pulled up to a drinking trough along the huddle of rough log buildings facing the river—a general store, a blacksmith, a tiny government land office and a wharf area where a few barges were tethered.

And a saloon at the far end of the one street.

Buttoning her collar buttons, Sunny averted her face from the saloon, deeply grateful she would not be entering its swinging doors. Ever.

A man bustled out of the general store. "Welcome to Pepin!" he shouted. "I'm Ned Ashford, the storekeeper."

Noah approached the wagon and helped her put the brake on. Then he solicitously assisted her descent. Only then did he turn to the storekeeper. He shook the man's hand. "Noah Whitmore. This is my wife, Sunny, and our daughter, Dawn."

He was always careful to show her every courtesy, and every time Noah introduced her and her baby this way, gratitude swamped her. For this she forgave him his tendency to pass a whole day exchanging only a sentence or two with her.

Maybe it wasn't the sleepless nights. Some men just didn't talk much—she knew that.

But she could tell that he was keeping a distance between them. Their marriage had yet to be consummated.

She didn't blame him for not wanting her. Sudden shame over her past suddenly lit Sunny's face red-hot.

"You just stopping or staying?" the friendly storekeeper in the white apron asked.

"I have our homestead east of here claimed and staked." Noah sounded proud.

Our homestead—Sunny savored the words, her face cooling.

"I thought you looked familiar. You were here a few months ago. But alone."

"Right." Dismissing the man's curiosity, Noah turned to her. "Sunny, why don't you go inside and see if there's anything you need before we head to our homestead. It will be a while before we get to town again."

The farther they traveled, the more Noah dropped his use of "thee" in favor of "you." Noah appeared to be changing his identity. *I am, too.* And the sheer distance they'd come from more populated places heartened her. The farther north they went the fewer people there were. That meant the chances of her running into anyone who'd met her in a saloon were slimmer. A blessing, but now, Noah was saying they would be living far from this town?

Trying to quell her worries, she smiled and walked toward the store's shady entrance. The storekeeper beamed at her and opened wide the door.

A memory flashed through her of the storekeeper in Pennsylvania who had wanted her out of his establishment. She missed a beat and then proceeded inside, assuring herself that no one here would ever call her a harlot or touch her in a way that made her cringe.

Only Noah knew the truth about her past, about Dawn's illegitimacy. Wisconsin was far from Idaho Territory where Dawn had been born and she couldn't imagine meeting anyone from her old life.

Yes, only Noah could ruin her here.

But he'd never do that. Surely he would never betray her, now that she was his wife...would he?

She took a shaky breath. "I don't know if I need anything, Mr. Ashford. But it is good to get out of the sun and see what your fine establishment has to offer."

Mr. Ashford beamed at her. "Pepin County is growing every day, now that the war is over and men are looking for a place to settle their families. Of course in the 1600s the Pepin brothers first arrived—Frenchmen, you know. The river made it easy to get to."

As Sunny scanned the large store, Mr. Ashford's seemingly inexhaustible flow continued. "Now you go just a few miles east and you'll be in the forest and not much in the way of settlers. Your man was smart to homestead here in Wisconsin." The words *your man* warmed her to her toes. She'd always had *men,* not one who'd claimed her as his own.

"No soddy house for you. With all the trees here-abouts, he can build you a nice snug cabin and have firewood aplenty. 'Course that makes it harder to clear land for a crop. But…" The man shrugged.

Sunny suddenly sensed Noah and turned to see him just inside, leaning against the doorjamb, silently urging her to come away. This wasn't the first time that he'd let her know he wanted to keep his distance from others.

Today she could understand his urgency. It was time to go see their land. "Your store is very neat and well-stocked," she said as she reluctantly made her way toward Noah.

Mr. Ashford beamed at her again.

"Does thee…" Noah stopped and began again. "Do you see anything you need, Sunny? I want to get to our homestead with plenty of time left to set up camp for the night."

Still hesitant to leave this cool, shady place, Sunny considered once more. "No, thank you, Noah. I don't need anything."

Noah peeled himself from the doorjamb. "Store-keeper, I'll need a bag of peppermints."

Sunny turned to him, her lips parted in surprise.

"My wife has a sweet tooth." One corner of Noah's mouth almost lifted.

He'd noticed her buying peppermint drops in Cairo, and savoring one a day till she'd run out.

The storekeeper chuckled as he bagged peppermint drops and then accepted three pennies from Noah.

"Shall we go, wife?"

She smiled, stirred by Noah's thoughtfulness. "Yes. Good day, Mr. Ashford."

"Good day and again, welcome to Pepin!"

Noah helped her back onto the wagon bench and lifted Dawn up to her. Then he handed her the bag of candy, which she slipped into her pocket as she felt a blush creep over her cheeks.

Noah led them down the main street and then to a bare rocky track, heading east away from the river, away from town.

Just before turning onto the track, Sunny glanced back and saw a woman dressed in red satin come out of the saloon and lean wearily against the hitching rail. Sunny averted her eyes, her heart beating faster. But she couldn't afford to show any pity or sympathy with this woman.

I must remember which side of the line I belong on now.

She'd studied how decent women behaved and hoped her masquerade would hold up well. The happy image of Dawn in her white pinafore running toward school and friends bobbed up in her mind again.

She wouldn't fail Dawn, no matter what.

Because of the roughness of the track, they progressed slowly, cautiously, through the thick forest of maple, oak and fir. This forest had probably never felt the blade of an ax. Noah marveled at the huge trees and with each landmark, his excitement gained momentum. All those nights when he'd lain alone, sometimes in a tent, sometimes under the open sky, listening to the sounds of war playing in his mind. How long had he dreamed of having a place of his own? How long had he dreamed of having a wife to bring to it?

Longer than he could say.

Why did he continue to leave his wife alone at night? His lovely wife, with her soft voice and shy smiles. The truth was, he could not bring himself to touch her. What right did he have? The faces of men he'd killed continued to plague his nights, waking them both. His lungs tightened painfully. How could he touch her when he felt that he belonged with the damned?

This marriage was out of practical necessity for both of them, nothing more, he reminded himself.

Finally the big pine, nearly three feet in diameter, loomed ahead of him, the rag he'd tied to a low branch fluttering in the breeze. In the distance he heard the creek rushing with melted snow runoff. He turned to Sunny, feeling the closest thing to joy that he could remember in years. "Our land starts here."

Sunny reined in the oxen and looked around at the dense forest. "The storekeeper wasn't joking when he said there'd be a lot of trees."

He nodded with satisfaction. "Enough for all our needs. Let's head closer to the creek, to our homesite. We'll make camp there."

Sunny glanced at the sun, now hovering just above the horizon, pink-orange clouds shimmering in the tiny slits between the dark wide tree trunks. "We'll need to hurry to get ready before sundown."

He tried not to take her lack of enthusiasm personally. But he couldn't help noticing that she'd sounded much happier in town.

"I already cleared a place for our house. And I can

get started felling more trees for our cabin first thing in the morning."

She nodded. "I want to see it."

He led the oxen with his hand at their heads, enduring their slow progress as they shuffled their way through the undergrowth of the forest. Then the clearing opened before them. "Here it is."

Her watchful silence followed. He tried to see the clearing through her eyes but couldn't. "We want to be near the creek, but not so near that we get the mosquitoes that hang close there. And the house will be on the rise, so no spring flooding." He couldn't stop himself as he explained how he had chosen the site.

Sunny tied up the reins.

He hurried to help her down. She always seemed so frail, and he'd been surprised when she'd asked to learn how to drive the oxen, even though they were docile creatures. When she set her feet on their land, she gazed around assessing it. Then she looked to him. "You chose well."

He tried to stop his smile but couldn't, so he turned away. "I'll go draw us some fresh water and lead the oxen to the creek. They can drink their fill, and there's grass there for them to graze on. There's a spring here, too. We'll have a spring house—soon." The dam that held back his words had burst. He tried to stop before he revealed just how glad he was to finally be home.

"I'll gather some wood for a fire." She lifted Dawn, who was just beginning to fuss.

"You sit down and nurse her," he said as he unyoked the oxen. He saw her sitting on the step up to the wagon bench, settling Dawn to nurse, and he had to turn his head from the cozy picture they made.

Other men came back from the war and went on with their lives. What kept him from being a real husband to her? Why did he resist any attempt by her to get closer? There was a chasm between them he was responsible for and could not bridge. Was he truly protecting her from himself, from the horrible things that lived on inside him?

Or was he simply incapable of anything even resembling...love?

Chapter Three

In the morning Sunny awoke to Dawn's hungry whimpering. She stared up at the cloth covering of the Conestoga wagon, illuminated with sunlight, and stifled a sigh. She touched the rumpled blanket at her feet that Noah had slept upon—when he wasn't tossing with another awful nightmare. She heard him already outside, stirring up the cook fire. Lassitude gripped her.

Dawn began to cry and that moved Sunny. Noah had crafted a kind of hammock just inside the front opening of the canvas top. Sunny lifted her child down, changed her soaked diaper and then put her to nurse. The breeze blew warm and gentle.

Tears slipped down Sunny's cheeks. She clamped her eyes closed. Loneliness was stripping away her peace. Weeks had passed since she'd had a simple conversation with another woman. The faces of her mother's friends, her only friends in the world except for the Gabriels, came to mind. She'd left them all behind. How would she handle this loneliness, keep it from destroying her peace?

"Good morning, wife." Noah looked in from the rear opening.

Sunny blinked rapidly, hoping he wouldn't notice the tears. "Good morning," she replied, forcing a smile.

"I've got the coffee boiling." His words revealed little but the mundane. Didn't he ever long to sit with another man and talk of men things? Men came to saloons to do that, just to jaw and laugh. Not that she wanted Noah to go to the saloon in town.

But, Noah, why don't you want to talk with other men?

She patted Dawn, who wore the seraphic smile she always had when nursing. When Sunny looked up, she glimpsed a look on Noah's face that she hadn't seen before.

He looked away quickly.

She sensed such a deep loneliness and hidden pain in him. But she also keenly felt the wall he kept between them. "I'll be out soon."

"No rush. We have a good day. Perfect for felling trees."

Sunny tried to look happy at this news. He turned away and she heard him unloading tools from the storage area under the wagon.

This won't last forever. We'll go to town from time to time. I'll meet local women, become part of this community. Again she pictured Dawn dressed in a fresh white pinafore, running toward a little white schoolhouse, calling to her friends. And they were calling back to her, happy to see her.

I can do this. This is Dawn's future, not just mine.

After breakfast Noah picked up his ax and headed toward the edge of the clearing.

"Please be careful, Noah," his wife said.

Her concern made him feel…something. He couldn't put a name to it, but it wasn't bad, whatever it was. "I'm always careful with an ax in my hand."

She didn't look convinced, but in time she would be. He looked at her for a moment, at the way her lush blond hair flowed down her back as she brushed it, getting ready to pin it up for the day.

His wife was beautiful.

Turning away to shut this out, he studied the trees at the edge of the clearing and chose which one would be the first for their future cabin. He selected an elm thrice as tall and wide as he. He gauged where he wanted it to fall and took his position. He swung and felt the blade bite the bark and wood, the impact echoing through his whole body. He set his pace and kept a steady rhythm.

Finally at the right moment he swung and the tree creaked, trembled and fell with a swish of leaves. It bounced once, twice and shivered to a halt. Wiping his brow with a handkerchief, Noah grinned.

Sweat trickling down his back, he began to chop away the branches so he could roll the first fresh log aside and start on the next tree, a maple. Then he heard something unexpected. He stopped, checking to see if he'd actually heard it.

In the distance came the sound of another ax. And another.

Irritation prickled through him.

"Do you hear that?" Sunny asked from behind him. "Sounds like someone else is felling trees. Maybe they're building a cabin not too far away."

Hoping she was dead wrong, he glanced over his shoulder and glimpsed her smile as she listened intently.

She'd obviously just walked back from the creek, a dish-pan of washed breakfast dishes in her arms.

"Might be loggers. Or someone cutting wood for winter so it has time to cure before then." He turned back to the maple. "You need to keep back from me. When I take a swing, I don't want to hit you."

"I'll stay back. I'm setting up my outdoor kitchen and such," she said, moving away.

The sound of the other axes on the clean spring air echoed around his own swings, making it harder to concentrate and keep his own rhythm. He fumed. *I chose this site because it was miles from town and any other homestead. Whoever you are, go away.*

As if the logger had heard his thoughts, the distant chopping stopped.

He shook his arms and shoulders, loosening them. With renewed purpose, he swung his ax, eating into the corn-hued wood pulp, sending chips and bark flying.

In between swings he overheard Sunny singing to Dawn. He'd made the right decision. Sunny always kept cheerful, never complained and worked hard. They'd make do.

Noah was sizing up the third tree when something startled him.

"Hello, the wagon!" called a cheerful male voice.

Noah was puzzled for a second, then realized the greeting was a twist on the usual frontier salute of "Hello, the house," which people often said to let the inhabitants of a house know someone was approaching, giving them time to prepare to welcome rare visitors.

Just what Noah didn't need—clever company.

"Hello!" Sunny called in return. "Welcome!"

Her buoyant voice grated Noah's nerves. He lowered

his ax, trying to prepare himself to meet whoever had intruded. With one swift downward stroke he sunk the ax into a nearby stump.

Two men, both near his age, were advancing on him, smiles on their faces and their right hands outstretched. He didn't smile, but he did shake their hands in turn.

He wanted to be left alone, but he didn't want people talking behind his back, thinking him odd. He'd had enough of that in the army and in Pennsylvania. In the army his Quaker plain speech had marked him as odd and back home, he was a Quaker who'd gone to war. He hadn't fitted in either place. And he'd given up trying.

"We heard your ax," the taller of the two said. "I'm Charles Fitzhugh and this is Martin Steward. We're your closest neighbors."

"I'm Noah Whitmore." Then he introduced the men to Sunny and Dawn, his wife and child. "Your claims must not be very far away." He clenched his jaw. He'd checked every direction but one—northeast—since he'd been told that no claim lay in those rolling hills.

"Mine's a little over a mile away on the other side of a hill—" Charles pointed northeast "—and Martin's another half mile farther from mine." The man grinned affably. "I've a wife and two daughters, and Martin's building his cabin to bring his bride to."

Martin's cheeks reddened at this announcement. He had a round face and brown hair in a bowl cut. "She lives south near Galena, Illinois."

"What's her name?" Sunny asked, waving the men toward the fire. She soon was pouring them cups of coffee.

Noah ground his teeth. Maybe it was time he made things clear to Sunny about not being overly friendly.

He hadn't thought it necessary, based on her difficult past. He'd assumed she'd want to keep to herself as much as he did. Clearly he had much to learn about his wife.

Charles complimented Sunny on the coffee and then turned to Noah. "I'm helping Martin get his cabin up. Why don't we join forces and work together? Three men can get a cabin up in days. Since you've a wife and child, we'll come and help you first and then we can help Martin out. Get him married off sooner than later."

Martin face turned a darker red.

Noah nearly choked, his reluctance shooting up into his throat. "I—"

"Oh, how wonderful!" Sunny crowed. "So neighborly." And she wrung each man's hands in turn. "Isn't that wonderful, Noah?" She turned, beaming toward him.

Noah wanted to object, to tell them he didn't want their help. But the words wouldn't come. Quakers—not even his father—wouldn't rudely rebuff any offer of help.

He nodded and folded his arms over his chest.

"I already told my wife that we were coming down to stay the day and get a load of work done." Charles grinned, apparently oblivious to Noah's reluctance. He and Martin handed Sunny their empty cups.

"I'll have lunch enough for all of us," Sunny promised. She quickly glanced at Noah. "I'll warn you though, I'm not much of a cook."

Noah turned away and the men followed him, discussing which tree to cut down next. Martin said he was good at squaring off and produced his adze, stripping bark from the already-downed trees.

Soon Noah and Charles were chopping the maple as a team. With each stroke of the his ax, Noah swallowed down his annoyance. Why couldn't people leave him alone?

Sunny must be made to understand exactly how he wanted the two of them to live. He needed to make that clear. Once and for all.

By the cook fire Sunny and Noah sat on logs across from each other. Supper eaten, she eyed him in the lowering sunlight, her nerves tightening by the moment. The instant their neighbors had appeared, she'd noted her husband withdrawing. No one else had noticed. But it had been obvious to her. Now he was clenching and unclenching his hands around his last cup of coffee, frowning into the fire. Why didn't he like such kind neighbors coming to help?

Rattled, she didn't know what to do in the face of his displeasure—whether to speak or keep silent. She couldn't imagine Noah lifting a hand to her but in the past men had. One—in a drunk rage—had broken her hand.

Fighting the old fear, she nursed Dawn and then put her down for the night in the little hammock in the wagon. Then she stood in the lengthening shadows by the wagon, unable to stop chafing her poor thumb. As she watched her angry husband, she felt her nerves give way to aggravation. Nothing had happened that should make any man upset.

Finally she recalled one of Constance Gabriel's few words of advice: "Do not let the sun go down upon your wrath." These words from the Bible must be right. But

could she do it? Could she confront this man who'd only
been her husband for a period of weeks?

A memory slipped into her thoughts. Constance and
Adam Gabriel had been alone in the kitchen, talking
in undertones. She'd overheard Constance say, "Adam,
this must be decided."

So wives did confront husbands. Sunny took a deep
breath.

"Noah," she said, "what's wrong?"

"I don't want people hanging around," he muttered
darkly.

"Why not?" she insisted, leaning forward to hear
him.

He sat silent, his chest heaving and his face a mask
of troubled emotions.

"What is wrong, Noah? The men just came to help
us."

"I don't want their help. I want to be left alone. I don't
want us getting thick with people hereabout. I picked
this homesite far from town to steer clear of people.
I've had enough of people to last me a lifetime. In the
future, we will keep to ourselves."

His words were hammers. "Keep to ourselves?" she
gasped. The happy image of Dawn in her white pinafore
shifted to a shy, downcast Dawn hanging back from the
other children who looked at her, their expressions jeer-
ing as tears fell down her cheeks.

"No." Sunny said, firing up in defense. "No." She
came around to face him. "Why did you marry me if
you wanted to be alone?"

Noah rose. They were toe-to-toe. His eyes had
opened wide.

"Why don't you want to be neighborly?" she demanded, shaking.

He took a step backward. "I… I…"

"What if I get sick? Who will you call for help? If I get with child, will you deliver it alone? We have no family here. How can we manage without our neighbors?"

They stared at each other. Sunny shook with outrage at his unreasonable demand.

Noah breathed rapidly, too, as if he'd just finished a race. Finally he shook his head as if coming awake. "I don't want people here all the time," he said. "I just want peace and quiet."

"People have their own work to do." She clamped her hands together, feeling blood where she'd chafed her thumb. "Once the cabins are built, Charles and Martin will be busy with their own work."

He let out a rush of air and raked his hands through his hair. "All right. Just remember I don't want people here all the time."

She wanted to argue, but sensed much more was going on here than was being said. "I will keep your wish in mind," she said, scanning his face for clues as to what was happening inside him.

He stood, staring at her for a moment as if seeing her for the first time. "I'm going to clean up at the creek." He grabbed a towel from the clothesline she'd strung earlier in the day and stomped off.

Sunny slumped against the wagon, calming herself, consciously shedding the fear and anger. He didn't want people around him. Maybe he didn't want her around him? Maybe he'd only brought her here to cook and clean. That would explain why he showed no interest in getting closer to her.

The thought made her angry all over again.

Climbing into the wagon, she checked on Dawn who slept peacefully in her little hammock. She'd be safe here. Sunny climbed down, grabbed another towel from the line and headed toward the creek, too. The unusual high temperature and humidity combined with the argument had left her ruffled and heated. Earlier she'd noticed a bend in the creek that was shielded by bushes where she could discreetly cool off.

Noah already splashed in the wide part of the creek, deep with spring runoff. In the long shadows she skirted around, barely glancing toward him. Within the shelter of the bushes, she slipped off her shoes and tiptoed over the pebbles into the cool water. She shivered, but in a good way. Soon ankle-deep, she was bending and splashing water up onto her face and neck, washing away the grime and stickiness.

The cool water soothed her, the sound of its rippling over the rocks calmed her nerves like a balm. She sighed as the last of her indignation drifted away on the current. She waded out onto the mossy bank and dried off.

At the sound of her name she turned and found Noah walking toward her. Night had come; moonlight glimmered around them. She braced herself, waiting for him to reach her. Had he come to start the argument anew?

He paused a foot from her. "I'm sorry, Sunny." The soft words spoke volumes of anguish.

She gazed at him, uncertain. Their disagreement had been over nothing—or everything—and she sensed that Noah was struggling just like she was. She recalled his words on their wedding night, when he'd asked which was worse, lying with strangers or killing them.

Amid the incessant frogs croaking around them, he whispered, "Sunny, I just need space, peace."

His voice opened the lock to her heart and freed her. "Noah," she murmured.

"But I want you to be happy here, too," he added.

His tenderness touched her, but she didn't know how to respond. They were still strangers.

In the silent darkness he helped her gather her shawl around her shoulders and then they walked to the wagon. Sunny tried to figure out what had happened this evening, what bedeviled her husband, and how she could bring him peace. She had no answers.

At the wagon she hoped he would follow her inside so she could comfort him. But, as usual, he let her go in and then he wished her good-night from the foot of the cramped wagon bed.

Sunny lay very still, wondering if Noah would have another nightmare tonight, and if he'd ever reveal what the dreams were about. She had a feeling his nightmares and his reluctance to be around people were connected.

And she was determined to find out how. She just needed to be patient. But patience had never been one of her talents. Someday they would have to talk matters out. Maybe when Noah's nightmares ceased?

Chapter Four

The next morning Sunny had a hard time speaking to Noah. Or looking at him for that matter. She stooped over the flickering flames of the cook fire. A stiff breeze played with the hem of her skirt. To keep safe as she was frying salted pork with one hand, she held her skirt with the other. She didn't know what was causing the awkwardness she felt with Noah.

In the pan the pork sizzled and snapped like the words she'd spoken to him last night. Was it the fact that she'd spoken up to him for the first time? Or had the awkward feeling come because he'd shown such tenderness to her when he'd escorted her into the wagon? Tenderness from a man was not something she was used to.

Yet today Noah remained silent as usual. And this morning that grated on her more than it did normally. How was she supposed to act when the neighboring men came today to help?

She remembered her resolution to get to the bottom of Noah's reluctance and she decided to speak up again.

"I expect our neighbors will be coming to help soon," she murmured.

Noah nodded. "Probably." He took another sip of the coffee, steaming in the cool morning air.

Sunny glanced down. Lying on her back on a blanket, Dawn waved her arms and legs and cooed. As always, her daughter brought a smile to Sunny's face.

"She's having a good time," Noah commented.

Sudden joy flashed through Sunny, catching her by surprise. This was not the first time he'd taken notice of Dawn and said something positive, but it still caught her off guard. Taking this as a hopeful sign for the future, Sunny managed to nod. She finished the pork and quickly stirred in what was left of last night's grits. She deftly swirled the pan till the concoction firmed. "Breakfast is ready."

She lifted the frying pan off the trivet and served up their plates. Searching for more topics to discuss, she said, "I hope we can get some chickens. I will need eggs."

"We will. It won't be much longer that we'll be living like tramps," Noah said, sounding apologetic. "Before you know it, we'll be in our cabin."

"I know we will," she said quickly. "You're working so hard. I wish I could help more."

"You do enough," he said gruffly. "After the cabin's up, I'll make us a nice table and some sturdy benches."

"You know how to make furniture?" Sunny bit into the crisp pork, trying to ignore the way his dark hair framed his drawn face. She wished she could wipe away the sleepless smudges under his eyes.

"Yes, I had an uncle who was a cabinetmaker. He taught me one summer."

"You know so much. And I can barely cook."

"You do fine."

Her heart fluttered at the praise. She clung to their discussion to keep her feelings concealed. "Mrs. Gabriel taught me what I know. But I wish I'd had time to learn more."

"You do well," he said, looking at her, his dark eyes lingering on her face.

Impulsively she touched his arm. "Thanks."

His invisible shutters closed against her once more. Her action had pushed him deeper into reserve. She concentrated on eating her own breakfast and not showing that she felt his withdrawal, his rejection.

She passed the back of her hand over her forehead, sighing. *Be patient,* she reminded herself. *Maybe he just needs more time.*

"Hello, the wagon!" Their neighbor Charles Fitzhugh's cheerful voice hailed them.

"Good morning!" Sunny called, checking to see how her husband was taking the arrival of the two men. However, when she glanced toward the men, she froze. A petite, dark-haired woman and two little girls accompanied them. Her breath caught in her throat.

Noah rose and with his free hand gripped first Charles's and then Martin's hand. "Morning. Just about done with breakfast."

"Mrs. Whitmore, this is my wife, Caroline, and our daughters, Mary and Laura," Charles Fitzhugh said.

Sunny bobbed a polite curtsy, her heart sinking. Her hand went to her hair, which she hadn't dressed yet. Fear of saying something she shouldn't tightened her throat. What if she said something a decent woman wouldn't ever say? Would they know instantly what she was? What she'd been?

"Don't mind me," Caroline Fitzhugh said. "I just

came for a short visit and then I'll be going home. I knew it was early to be calling but I just felt like I needed a woman chat this morning."

Sunny nodded. She quickly smoothed back and twisted her hair into a knot at the base of her neck and shoved pins in to keep her bun secure. A woman chat, oh, yes—she'd longed for one, too. But after weeks of loneliness she must guard her overeager tongue, not let anything that might hint at her past slip out.

I can do this. I just need a touch of help, Lord.

Soon Sunny was washing dishes in the spring with Mrs. Fitzhugh down creek from her. Nearby, Caroline's little girls played in the shallows. Mrs. Fitzhugh held Dawn and dipped her toes into the water to Dawn's squeals of delight. Sunny's heart warmed toward this woman, obviously a good mother. But that sharpened the danger that she would let her guard down and give herself away.

Soon the two women were back at the campfire, sitting on a log and watching the children play with some blocks Mrs. Fitzhugh had brought in a cotton sack. Happy to gnaw on one block, Dawn watched the two toddlers pile the rest on the uneven ground. She squealed as she watched the blocks topple.

"You and Mr. Whitmore been married long?" the neighbor asked, accepting a fresh cup of coffee.

"Not too long," Sunny hedged vaguely. The sound of the men's voices and the chopping as they worked on yet another tree suddenly vanished as her heart pounded loudly.

Mrs. Fitzhugh smiled. "I just meant you look almost like newlyweds. It'll take a few more years to look like you've been married forever."

Sunny didn't know what to say to this. Was the woman suggesting that she and Noah hadn't been married long enough to already have a child?

"Where you from?" Mrs. Fitzhugh asked politely.

The woman's voice remained honest, not accusing or insinuating. Sunny managed to take a breath. "Pennsylvania. My husband came here earlier this year to find us a homestead while I stayed back with my family." That was true—the Gabriels had told her to consider them her family.

"I'm from eastern Wisconsin. Met Charles there."

Sunny knew that the woman wasn't asking her anything out of the way, but each question tightened a belt around her lungs. She looked toward the men and saw Noah send a momentary glance her way, his expression brooding.

"I'm…we're very grateful for your offer of help."

Mrs. Fitzhugh waved her hand, dismissing Sunny's thanks. "It's too early to plant and Charles isn't sure he will put in a crop this year. Kansas is calling him."

"Kansas?" Sunny gazed at the woman with genuine dismay. All the way to Kansas? Sunny thought of all the miles she'd traveled from Idaho to Pennsylvania and then here. "I'm not much of a traveler," she admitted.

Before Mrs. Fitzhugh could reply, another voice hailed, "Hello, the house!"

"Nancy! Is that you?" Mrs. Fitzhugh called out with obvious pleasure.

Soon another woman sauntered into the clearing—a big blonde woman obviously expecting a child, with a toddler beside her. While Caroline Fitzhugh dressed as neat as could be, this woman appeared disheveled but jolly.

"I was coming over to visit you, Caroline. And then I heard the axes and once in a while, on the breeze, a word that sounded feminine. I hope you don't mind me stoppin' in." She looked to Sunny.

"No. No. You're very welcome," Sunny rushed to assure the newcomer though she wasn't sure she meant it. "Please join us." She waved the woman to one of the large rocks around the campfire and quickly offered her coffee.

Two women to talk to—a blessing and a trial.

"I'm Nan Osbourne. My man and me live over yonder." She waved southward. "Glad to see another family come to settle."

"Mrs. Whitmore and her husband are nearly newlyweds," Mrs. Fitzhugh said.

"Well, none of us are much more than that." Mrs. Osbourne gave a broad wink. "You got any family hereabouts, Miz Whitmore?"

"No. No. I have no family…near," she corrected quickly. She'd just told Caroline that she had stayed with her family. "And Noah's family is all in Pennsylvania…too." Picking her words with such care quickened her pulse.

"That's hard, leaving family," Mrs. Osbourne said, looking mournful. "I cried and cried to leave my ma."

"My mother has already passed," Sunny said, her words prompting a sudden unexpected twinge of grief. Or was it recalling she was all alone in the world? Why would she mourn Mother's death now, almost seven years after it? Was it because so much was changing? *I'm not alone now. I've got Dawn and Noah.* Gratitude rushed through her. Could this be proof that God was forgiving her? There was so much she didn't understand about God and sin.

"I got news." Nan Osbourne grinned. "We got a preacher in town now."

"Really?" Caroline Fitzhugh brightened with excitement.

Sunny tried to keep her face from falling. A preacher? In the past more than one had shouted Bible verses at her, calling her a harlot and predicting her damnation. The fires of hell licked around her again. She touched Dawn, her treasure, smoothing back her baby fine hair, and the action calmed her.

"The preacher's goin' to preach this Sunday right in town. He says around ten o'clock," Nan announced.

"That's wonderful. I've been missing church." Caroline sighed.

Sunny tried to appear happy as her peace caved in.

"I think it's wonderful that he's goin' to preach out in the open like a camp meetin'. Then even them who don't want to hear the gospel will."

Sunny posed with a stiff, polite smile on her face. Was the woman talking about the people who'd be just waking upstairs at the saloon? Of course she was. Once more Sunny wished so much that she could help another woman get free of that life.

But I can't. I've got to make this new start work for Dawn.

"You'll be comin', won't you, Miz Whitmore? You and your man?" Nan asked.

Crosscurrents slashed through Sunny. *I want to go. I want You to know, God, how thankful I am for this second chance.* But would the preacher see right through her? Would Noah want to go? *Let* her go?

A thought came. Should she mention that Noah had been raised Quaker? He'd almost stopped using "thee."

Did that mean he didn't want to be considered a Quaker anymore?

Both women were gazing at her expectantly.

Sunny breathed in deeply. "I'll discuss it with him. I know I want to attend. Do you know what kind of preacher he is?"

"I didn't ask," Nan said. "Out here on the frontier, preachers are so rare we can't be choosy about them. He struck me as a good man."

Sunny nodded, hoping she hadn't asked the wrong thing. "I'll speak to Noah. But unless he forbids me, I'll be there."

Both women looked startled at this announcement.

Sunny cringed. She'd said the wrong thing, hinting that Noah might not be a Christian. And she couldn't let that simmer and turn into gossip. She leaned forward to give some explanation. "Noah was raised Quaker. I wasn't. So I don't know if he'll…" Words failed her.

Caroline patted her hand. "I understand."

"Quakers were against slavery," Nan said stoutly. "They did a lot of good with helpin' slaves get free."

Sunny gave a fleeting smile, tension bubbling inside.

"Nan and I will pray that you get to come to the meeting," Caroline said in a low voice. Nan nodded vigorously. And Sunny knew she'd made progress on making friends this morning. Her mood lifted—for a moment.

What would Noah say about going to the Sunday meeting? And her telling these friendly strangers that he'd been raised Quaker?

In the last rays of twilight Noah sat by the fire, his stomach comfortably full. Sunny didn't know how to cook many things but what she did cook tasted good.

Exhausted from felling trees all day, Noah realized he'd discovered a few muscles he hadn't known about—and they were not happy with him.

He held a narrow block of wood in his hand, whittling it into a new handle for a small ax. During this quiet time Sunny was acting funny—opening her mouth as if to speak, then closing it, and worrying her thumb by picking at it and hiding her hand behind her skirt. Why, he didn't know. Or want to ask. Last night had been enough honesty.

"How many more logs do we need for a cabin?" his wife asked.

She sat by the fire nursing Dawn who seemed fussier than usual. The firelight highlighted the gold in Sunny's hair. Once again, he realized he had married a pretty woman. Everything about her was so soft and this world was so hard. He wondered what it might be like to hold her.

"Noah?" she prompted.

"Sorry. My mind was wandering." He shut his mind to a surprising image of holding Sunny close, a daunting thought. He shaved some more from the wood. "Another day and we should have enough for a cabin. Then Charles and Martin will help me lift the logs into place."

"I'm so grateful to them."

His hands were beginning to tremble with fatigue as he whittled. "Who was that other woman who stopped by?"

"Nan Osbourne. She and her husband live nearby. She seems very nice. From her accent, I'd say she was from south of here."

Noah nodded. Sunny's continued pensiveness piqued

his curiosity. In spite of himself, he asked, "What did she have to say?"

Sunny startled as if caught doing something she shouldn't. "We just talked about recipes and they told me about the people who live hereabouts."

Noah examined the handle he was crafting, running his thumb over it. Sunny was definitely holding something back. But he was too tired to risk asking for more. He didn't have the energy to be irritated by hearing something he might not like. So he hesitated.Sunny also had a way of stirring him. She was now.But he couldn't act on this. He found it impossible to make a move.

The bottomless well of sorrow and dark things roiled up within. Sunny made him long to feel normal again. But he'd seen too much, done too much that was unforgivable. Repressing this, he rose while he still could stand. "I'm going to go to bed now. I'm worn out."

"I'll bank the fire. You go ahead, Noah. I should have seen how tired you were." She rose and briefly touched his arm. "Go on."

Her innocent touch made him ache with loneliness. He moved away, obeying her. Noah shucked off his boots and then hoisted himself onto the hard wagon bed and rolled into his blankets. His last thought as he fell asleep was that Sunny deserved better than him.

A few days later Sunny stepped inside their new cabin. She hadn't anticipated how it would make her feel. *This is my home, our home.* She'd never lived in a real house, never dreamed she would. She wanted to hug the walls and do a jig on the half-log floor that Noah had insisted on laying. A dirt floor might be all right in the summer but not in the winter, he'd said. Dawn whimpered in her arms and struggled to be put down. Sunny bent and set her on the floor.

"I'm glad this is done," Noah said from behind her.

She turned around and nearly hugged him, but his expression held her off. "Me, too. It's a wonderful home." During this bright moment the way Noah always held himself apart chafed her. Would it always be this way?

"Hello, the house!" Caroline Fitzhugh called out. "We came to see your new home."

Whisking Dawn up into her arms, Sunny stepped outside to see that Caroline and her family and the Osbournes had come to celebrate. Charles Fitzhugh carried a fiddle and the women each carried a covered dish.

"Oh, I have nothing prepared!" Sunny exclaimed.

"We're makin' this party!" Nan called out cheerfully. "We won't stay long, just wanted to see your fine new cabin and congratulate you."

Sunny said all that was proper but when she turned to Noah, it was as if he'd slammed all the shutters and locked the door against their company. She gave him an understanding smile but he stood like a tree, not responding by even a flicker of an eyelid. She went up on tiptoe and acted as though she were kissing his cheek in order to whisper, "They won't stay long. Don't spoil their happiness."

He glanced down at her, stony-eyed. Dawn began to cry and Sunny jiggled her in her arms.

Then he gave Sunny a tight-lipped nod. "Welcome to our new home." Sunny sighed silently with relief. "Come right in."

Nan had brought her husband, a tall lanky man with curly blond hair. He, along with the other guests, admired the large cabin with its roomy loft and lean-to for the animals.

Sunny was a bit embarrassed because Dawn continued to fuss. She tried to distract their company by talking about future plans. "Noah is going to dig me a root cellar. And build a spring house," Sunny said, caught up in the flush of showing her new home. She tried to check herself, knowing that Noah was scrutinizing, gauging each word.

"You're going to have a right nice place here all right," Nan said. "You must be plannin' to stay here."

"I plan to stay longer than five years to get title to the land," Noah said. "I traveled all over northern Illinois, eastern Iowa and southern Minnesota. I decided this land was the best I'd seen."

His loquaciousness shocked Sunny. Maybe Noah was feeling a bit of pride and happiness. Remaining cautious, she kept her mouth shut and let Noah do the talking.

"Well, you haven't tried to plow yet," Mr. Osbourne said wryly. "You'll find that Wisconsin's best crop is rocks."

"As long as they don't sprout and grow new ones, I'll do fine," Noah responded.

His voice was pleasant enough but Sunny sensed his disdain for a man put off by rocks. Dawn chewed on her hand and whimpered.

Mr. Fitzhugh drew his bow over his fiddle. "I'll play one song and then we all got to get back to our own work."

"And we'll help carry stuff from your wagon to your door," Nan said. "That'll lighten your load."

Before Sunny could speak, Mr. Fitzhugh began to

play a merry tune, the kind that beckoned clapping. Sunny hadn't heard music for so long. She had loved to dance in the saloon—it was the only fun she'd ever had there—and she was a good dancer. But Quakers didn't dance.

Dawn again wriggled to be put down. Sunny obliged and then tapped her toe to the cadence and couldn't stop her smile from widening.

Dawn stared at the violin, distracted from her fussing. Noah bent down and swung her up into his arms and Sunny's heart skipped a beat. Noah held Dawn by her waist and swung her gently back and forth to the tune. Dawn squealed with laughter. Then Sunny reached over and showed Dawn how to clap her hands. The three of them together, like a happy family. It was like a moment sent from Heaven.

But of course the song ended. Everyone clapped for Charles's fiddling, shook hands and the two couples started to leave. Just as Sunny was relaxing her guard, Nan turned and asked, "Have you and the mister decided whether you're comin' to meetin' this Sunday?"

Sunny's breath caught in her throat. "I've been meaning to discuss that with Noah," she managed to say.

"Meeting?" Noah looked askance.

"Yes, we got a preacher, a real nice old one who's come to live with his son's family in his declining years," Nan explained. "He's preachin' at ten o'clock in front of the general store."

"Can we pick you up in our wagon?" Mr. Fitzhugh invited. "We'll be passing right by your place. Even though I'm thinking we'll be heading to Kansas soon, I wouldn't want to miss preaching."

Sunny waited to see what her husband would say. She didn't meet his eye—she couldn't.

"I'll think on it," Noah said at last.

The other two couples tried to hide their surprise at Noah's less than enthusiastic response.

"I don't think he'll be preachin' anything that would go against you being a Quaker," Nan said.

Sunny's face burned. She knew she'd done the wrong thing by not telling Noah what she'd done.

"I'll keep that in mind," Noah said, his jaw hardening.

I'm in for it now. Sunny stood at her husband's side and felt waves of sick worry wash over her. Dawn began fussing again, chewing one of her little fists. Sunny knew Noah wouldn't raise a hand to her but he could freeze her with a glance. *Oh, Lord, help me reach him. Help me make him understand why I told them that he'd been raised Quaker. Lord, I want to do what is right. Help me explain this to him.*

Sunny couldn't get Dawn to hush. Night had fallen and she'd tried everything in vain—nursing her, bathing her, rocking her. Now she paced the rough new floor. What could she do to soothe her child?

As she paced, she scanned her new and very empty home. Earlier Noah had helped her arrange pegs in the wall to hang clothing and pots and pans. The only furniture was the rocking chair that the Gabriels had given them money to buy as a wedding present, a three-legged stool and a chest near the door which held their linens.

Her bedroll sat against the wall. Noah had put his up in the loft. Their continued nightly separation was a constant twinge in her side. Would he never forget that she was damaged goods?

Noah entered the cabin. Since the two couples had left, he had not said a complete sentence to her. Sunny wished Dawn would stop crying—the incessant sound had tightened her nerves like a spring. Sunny sat down and tried again to get Dawn to nurse so she would fall asleep as usual.

Noah stood watching Dawn fight Sunny.

"I'm sorry," Sunny apologized. "I think it's her mouth. She wants to nurse but I think it hurts her." As she tried to soothe the inconsolable baby, Sunny felt like crying herself.

Noah turned and went to a smaller chest he'd moved just inside the door. He lifted out a small bottle Sunny instantly recognized—whiskey. Dawn wept in pain, Sunny was frantic and Noah was going to get drunk? Sunny burst into tears.

Noah came and knelt in front of her. "Here. See." He opened the bottle and the all too familiar, unpleasant smell wafted to Sunny's nose. He tipped the almost full bottle and then stuck his little finger into the amber fluid. Then he slipped the little finger into Dawn's surprised mouth.

"What are you doing?" Sunny gasped.

"I saw a woman do this once when I was traveling. She said the whiskey numbs the gums. And the few drops of alcohol will soothe the baby. The woman said it was an old remedy for a teething child. See how red and swollen Dawn's gums are?"

Sunny felt like an idiot. Teething. Of course. Constance Gabriel had mentioned that the baby would teethe and it would hurt. Noah dipped his little finger in the bottle once more and then ran it around Dawn's swollen gums again. "That should be enough, just enough."

They both watched Dawn. In a few minutes she fell back exhausted, resting against Sunny.

"Thank you," Sunny said.

"Wish I'd thought of it earlier." He rose, capped the bottle and stowed it away. "This whiskey's just for medicinal purposes. I never cared for strong drink."

He turned and faced her. "I did get drunk a few times in the army," he confessed, "but never again. It doesn't help, just makes you sick and the next morning everything's as bad as it was before you got drunk. Only you've got a headache to boot."

Sunny nodded. She'd seen too many drunks in her life and the drink never did them any good. This was one of the rare times he offered something of his past, himself. She took it as his way of easing her worry over Dawn, over the bottle of whiskey. Sunny felt fatigue replacing anxiety.

Of her own accord Dawn began to nurse. Within a few minutes Dawn fell asleep, her lips still quivering as if she were nursing.

Noah lifted the baby and put her in the hammock he'd suspended from the high ceiling.

His tender care of her baby snapped Sunny's reserve. "I'm so sorry, Noah," she said impetuously. "I didn't mean to tell the women anything about you being a Quaker. I'm sorry." Embarrassing tears welled up in her eyes. She turned away and wiped them with the hem of her apron.

Noah just stood beside Dawn, making the hammock sway gently.

"You haven't told me," Sunny said, even as she tried

to stem the flow of words, "why you're not using *thee* anymore. And then they told me about the preaching this Sunday. And I didn't know what to say. They were looking at me, wondering why I wasn't saying right away that we'd be coming. So I said you'd been raised Quaker and I didn't know if you'd want to go to a different kind of meeting." She ran out of words and put her hands over her face. "I'm so tired," she whispered.

Noah pulled up the three-legged stool and sat beside her. His nearness made it possible for her to staunch her tears.

"Sorry," she whispered.

"When I enlisted in the army, I was put out of the meeting."

His tone sounded flat, unemotional. Yet Sunny sensed the words concealed a volcano of feelings. She waited, tense.

"When I came home, I just wanted to go back to my life, the way it was before the war. So I publicly repented of going to war and asked for forgiveness and was restored to the meeting. But of course, I couldn't go back to being who I was before the war. And at meeting, everybody still looked at me differently. Like I was…" He shrugged.

Like you were damaged goods. Stained. She knew how that felt. Awful.

"I've stopped using *thee* because I don't feel like a Quaker anymore."

She wanted to ask, *What do you feel like then? What do you have nightmares about?* But the words wouldn't come. Long silent moments passed as they sat together.

Noah rose and offered her his hand.

She let him help her from her chair, stunned by the

fact that he initiated the contact. "We'd better get some sleep."

He nodded. "Good night, Sunny."

He climbed a ladder to the loft and left her alone in the sparsely furnished room, still reeling from the feel of his hand in hers. She slipped off her dress and apron and hung them on pegs as she realized she still didn't have the answer to the question that had been weighing on her for days.

Were they going to the Sunday meeting—or not?

Steady showers came the next day, forcing the three of them to stay inside though Noah went out to fetch wood for the fire. He'd wisely left some in the wagon to keep it dry. The unusual April heat had fled, replaced with a chill and damp air.

Though Sunny thought they had cleared things up, Noah was brooding once more, which did not encourage her to ask what he'd decided about the Sunday meeting.

Dawn still fussed some, but Sunny had made a "sugar baby," a tightly knotted rag with sugar inside. Dawn gnawed on it and it seemed to give her some relief.

Noah had brought in a few slender logs about four feet in length, obviously not meant for the fire. He stripped away their bark.

"What are you making?" she ventured.

"Legs for our table."

"I see." *I see that you've gone back to your usual dour self.* She lifted the pan of breakfast dishes and carried it out. She set it on a convenient stump. She'd let the rainwater rinse the soap from the dishes she'd scrubbed.

Inside again, she sat in her rocker and lifted a shirt

from the mending basket, trying to ignore the unspoken question between them.

Noah methodically stripped the bark, making a neat pile of the shavings. Finally he rose from the three-legged stool. "I'll go see to the cattle."

He opened the door, letting in chilly moist air. "You can go to the meeting if you want. I won't be going." He shut the door behind him.

Sunny sat, staring at the needle in her hand. Dawn rolled on her back, watching her mother as if asking for Sunny's response to this. Should she go to the meeting without him or stay home, too? What did God want her to do as a good wife—stay home with her husband and wait till he wanted them to go? Or was she supposed to go because that was the right thing to do? What if Noah never wanted to go?

Chapter Five

Sunday dawned bright yet cool. Sunny wished her mood matched her name, but a heavy cloud weighed over her undecided heart.

She stood outside the door of their new cabin at the white enamel washbasin, set on a waist-high stump. She was washing her hands, preparing to go to meeting—without Noah. With closed eyes, she scrubbed her face and then bent over to rinse away the soap, shivering from the cold water and chill air.

She felt Noah push the linen towel into her wet hands. She accepted it and dried her face. Looking up, she met his dark eyes. She tried to read his expression, but couldn't. The shutters he'd put up once again concealed everything from her. The weight over her heart pressed down harder.

As he walked back into the cabin, Sunny realized this was just more evidence of Noah's constant courtesy. Distracted, she'd come out without a towel, so he'd brought her one. She held it in her hands, touched by his thoughtfulness.

Inside again, Sunny continued making breakfast. She

still wore her old everyday housedress. Did that make Noah think she wasn't going to the meeting in town?

Without thinking, she grabbed the handle of the cast-iron pot. Then yanked it back, scorched. She waved her hand and snapped her mouth shut so no ill words slipped out. She bowed her head. *God, please, I want to do what's right. Is going to the meeting the right thing?*

Of course no answer came. She used a quilted pot-holder and then stirred the oatmeal that had been sim-mering all night over the banked fire. After a sprinkle of fragrant cinnamon, she stirred in some sugar. "It's done."

As usual at meals, she sat in the rocker holding Dawn while Noah sat on the three-legged stool. Silence. She couldn't think of anything to discuss but the unan-swered question plaguing her. She ate and the oatmeal sat on the top of her uneasy stomach. The sun was gleaming around the shutters and she must get ready if she was going. It was time.

Noah finished his oatmeal and rose. "Going to let the oxen out to graze."

Then she was alone. Dawn squirmed and Sunny let her down so she could crawl around on the floor. Dawn's teething distress appeared to have abated. She cooed and gurgled. As Sunny watched her daughter, she suddenly knew what she had to do. This wasn't just about Noah.

She stood and opened the chest, and drew out the simple gray dress she had always worn to the Quaker meetinghouse. She also drew out a colorful paisley shawl she'd bought in Idaho. It would brighten up the drab dress. In the past, from a distance, she'd watched people go to church and they had all dressed up fine.

Within minutes she was ironing the dress and trying not to think too much about her decision so she wouldn't lose her breakfast to nerves. Before long she stood at the mirror, dressing her hair. The mirror was small so she couldn't see more than her head and neck. She smoothed her bodice and skirt, still warm from the iron. Then she lifted Dawn and quickly dressed her in a freshly pressed white dress.

Through the open door Sunny heard the jingling of a harness. Her ride to church was coming. Before she stepped outside, she tied her bonnet strings and collected a fresh handkerchief and a sugar baby in case Dawn fussed. Sweeping her shawl around her shoulders, she took a deep breath and carried Dawn outside.

Noah waited near the door, watching the Fitzhughs' wagon come nearer.

"You're sure you don't want to come?" Sunny murmured just for his ears. Her voice quavered.

Please, come.

He shook his head but wouldn't meet her eyes.

Her stomach roiling, she waited for the wagon to draw up to her. She exchanged greetings with the neighbors. The Fitzhughs were obviously trying not to stare at Noah, who was obviously not dressed for church. She approached the wagon and handed Dawn up into Caroline's arms.

"We can't persuade you to come with us?" Charles asked Noah with an encouraging smile.

"God doesn't want to see me," Noah said in a sour tone. However, with his usual courtesy, he had come to help Sunny climb up onto the bench.

She turned and leaned close to his ear and whispered, "I'm doing this for Dawn—and for us."

She sat beside Caroline and accepted her daughter back. She didn't dare look at Noah. The wagon started up, creaking and straining.

Though her heart beat like she'd run a race, Sunny knew in her soul that she was doing the right thing. She could feel it. She couldn't wait for Noah to come to terms with whatever troubled him. Life passed quickly day by day, and she must do what was needed.

Noah stood stock-still, watching his wife, perched stiffly on the wagon bench, disappear among the trees. Sunny's whispered words tightened around him like bonds. *Us.* She'd said *us.*

All at once the unseen chains holding back the past released. Cannon roared in his ears and men, horses, screamed. Noah staggered as if he'd taken a blow. He sat down hard on a nearby stump. A whirlwind swept through him, an inner storm of anguish. He bent his pounding head into his hands and swallowed down dry heaves. How could the simple words at parting stir up the past and swamp him so?

When he was able, he forced himself to his feet. "I have work to do," he said to the surrounding silence. His feeble words vanished in the air. He was alone— completely.

He headed to wide boards he'd split from an oak. "Dawn will want to sit on that three-legged stool soon. I better have a place for me to sit."

Why was he speaking out loud when no one could hear him? Was he losing his mind? Did he think he was chasing away the past? Determined to overcome the weakness, he stood one of the wide boards on end and ran his trembling hand over its rough surface. From the fine grain of the wood, he figured that the oak must have been over a hundred years old. He sucked in the cool breeze, trying to keep his inner hurricane at bay.

He'd constructed two sawhorses and now he lay the first board across them and began stripping the bark from the sides. Then he unearthed his plane from his tool chest and began planing the wood smooth for the tabletop. The slow rhythm steadied his nerves. But each time he guided the plane over the wood, sending up a ribbon, he heard his wife's whisper again. *I'm doing this for Dawn—and for us.*

He couldn't make sense of this. Did she mean that she wanted Dawn to be raised a Christian? Did she think that taking a baby to church would accomplish this? Did she want *him* to be a churchgoer? What did that mean to her? His father had attended meeting every Sunday, but had it changed, softened his hard heart? He slid the plane in a steady rhythm while images of Sunny's face slid through his memory.

The total lack of human presence crowded in on him. Though he fought it, he recalled that awful unspoken, crushing tension that had pressed down on him and all his company as another battle loomed before them. He felt a phantom sensation—a soldier pinning a paper lettered with Noah's name and his company on the back of his collar. This was the only way soldiers could be identified if something happened to them in the up-coming carnage. The sense of impending death blasted him once again.

The strength went out of Noah's legs. The plane fell from his hands and he slid to the ground. Leaning on an elbow, he gasped for breath. Why was this happening to him?

He looked upward, letting the sun warm his face. Then he shuddered violently once and let gravity take him down to the moist earth, to the wild grasses. Near his hand he noticed a tiny violet. He touched the petal and it made him think of Sunny—soft and delicate.

Why had she married him, a man so inadequate in every way?

As the wagon neared town, Sunny's heart was now racing at the prospect of being in a meeting with proper people who thought she was just like them. Could she pull this off?

"Just a perfect day for the meeting," Caroline murmured.

"Let's hope the preacher doesn't put us to sleep standing up," Charles said with a quirk to the side of his mouth.

Caroline tapped his arm, scolding in a low voice, "Charles, the children will hear you."

Little Mary and Laura rode in the back, holding on to the side of the buckboard. Dawn, half asleep, lay in Sunny's arms, lulled by the rocking of the wagon.

From the corner of her eye Sunny watched the interaction between the husband and wife beside her on the bench. She'd never really been around many married folk. These two were more lively than Constance and Adam Gabriel, but was that personality? Or was it that the Fitzhughs weren't Quakers?

This brought her back to the fact that she had no idea how she was to behave or what she was expected to do at this outdoor meeting. She'd only been to the Quaker meeting and the Gabriels had told her that it was different than a regular church service. She'd never told them she had never been inside a church and wouldn't have known the difference. Sunny's stomach rolled into a ball.

What if she did something no "Christian" would do at a meeting?

The wagon broke free of the shelter of the forest, rocking down the bluff to the flat ground beside the wide blue river. She had never given thought to how many people lived hereabouts. Now she saw around twenty or so men and women in family groups standing in front of the Ashford's General Store.

Charles helped Sunny down and then Caroline. In turn, the Fitzhughs each lifted out a daughter from the wagon bed. Holding Dawn still half asleep on her shoulder, Sunny stayed a bit behind using them as a shield. Nan and Gordy Osbourne waved and gravitated toward them. Sunny gratefully concealed herself within this group of neighbors.

A constant buzz of conversation made audible the buzz of excitement running through this wilderness gathering. Sunny's stomach tightened another turn.

An old man, very thin and with long white hair pulled back as it had been worn in the olden days, and in an old-fashioned black suit, sat on a straight chair on the store's porch. Before she could get more than a glance at him, he pulled an old watch from his vest, glanced at it and then stood. He raised both hands and everyone turned toward him, hushing children, expectant.

Sunny braced herself and heightened her awareness so she wouldn't miss a cue or fail in some way.

"My name is Old Saul and don't call me Mister or Pastor. I'm going to be seventy-one this year and Old Saul or Preacher is good enough for me." He held up a thick, well-worn black book. "And God's Holy Word is enough for me to base my life upon."

A man in the rear said quietly, "Amen."

Sunny stared at the Bible, wishing she were better with letters so she could read it and make more sense of its words.

"And I won't fly under false colors. I was not always a preacher, but was a sinner. I won't tell you about my sins. And I won't ask you about yours."

Sunny trembled with relief. But her taut nerves didn't relax. An eagle flew overhead, casting its shadow over them.

"We all have sinned and fallen short of the glory of God. But John tells us, 'if we confess our sins, He is faithful and just to forgive us our sins, and to cleanse us from all unrighteousness.'"

At these words a fire burned through Sunny—a good fire, a cleansing fire. She was able to draw breath more freely.

"My prayer is that this meeting will give all of you hope. That's what Christ is all about. If we don't have him, we have no hope."

"Amen," Sunny whispered reverently with many others the first time she'd spoken this aloud. She felt a pull toward this man and his good, plain words.

"I'm an old man and can't preach for long, so listen up!" Old Saul grinned at them. Something about him was working its way not only in Sunny but in those standing around her. Everyone was smiling and moving closer to catch every word.

"John goes on to say 'the darkness is past, and the true light now shineth. He that saith he is in the light, and hateth his brother, is in darkness even until now...

because that darkness hath blinded his eyes. I write unto you, little children, because your sins are forgiven you for His name's sake.'"

Forgiven, Sunny repeated to herself. *Oh, could that be so?*

Old Saul was true to his word and spoke only a few more minutes. Then he introduced his son and daughter-in-law, who led the gathering in a few hymns. They sang a line and the congregation echoed it.

Sunny kept quiet at first but soon was singing along. She had missed music. Saloons most always had a piano and someone to play it. Sunny caught herself, glad no one could read these thoughts. She shouldn't be thinking of saloon music here and now.

As the hymn ended, Old Saul stepped forward and asked for prayer requests. People spoke up where they stood. And the old preacher prayed for each. Then he led them in the Lord's Prayer, which Sunny had never heard before. It struck her as lovely.

When the meeting was over, Sunny followed everyone as they lined up to shake the old man's hand and greet his family. When it came her turn, she lowered her eyes and curtsied, mimicking softly what she'd heard others say. "Thank you for the preaching."

"Look up."

Sunny did, startled. Frightened.

"I like to see a pretty woman's face," Old Saul said, grinning. A few around them chuckled.

Sunny blushed warmly.

"Now don't take that wrong. I'm not flirting with you."

More people chuckled. Sunny wished she could slip back into the shelter of the crowd.

"Your husband didn't come with you?" Old Saul lifted a bushy white eyebrow.

Sunny was mortified, and couldn't think of a word of reply.

"No, sir, he didn't," Charles spoke up behind her. "He's a good man, though."

"I have no doubt," Old Saul said. "I'll come visit him if I'm able, Mrs. Whitmore."

Sunny inhaled sharply. Noah would think she'd set him up, which surely would cause trouble.

"Don't worry, ma'am. I'll let him know it was my idea, not yours," the preacher assured her as if he'd read her caution.

Sunny tried to smile as she stepped aside to let Charles and Caroline take their turn greeting the old man. She stood back and watched, wondering what Old Saul would have said if she—or another woman—had come out of the saloon in a red satin dress to listen to him. Did he mean what he said about all having sinned? Or did he believe that some sins—like living upstairs at a saloon—couldn't be forgiven or forgotten?

On the next day, midmorning, axes echoed in the forest clearing. Sunny walked toward the sound, her baby in her arms. Dawn squirmed, wanting down. "No, honey, we're going to see where Martin will bring his bride. We're almost there."

To distract Dawn she began to sing a silly song about a girl named Susannah. Dawn stared at her, an endearing look in her wide blue eyes.

"Yes, your mama can sing silly songs if she wants to."

Dawn crowed.

Sunny wished she felt as cheery as she was acting. When she'd arrived home, Noah had not asked about the Sunday meeting, but had merely talked a bit to Charles who'd given him a gentle scold. Noah had just half smiled and shaken his head.

She had been feeling such a bleak sense of separation from Noah, even though she was glad she'd gone to church. How could she reconnect with him? How could she make him understand why she'd done it?

Weighed down with this heavy burden, she followed the narrow track made by wagon wheels that had crushed the wild grass. Four men labored in the clearing. Nan's husband, Gordy, had joined the effort to build Martin's cabin.

Under the blue sky, she paused to watch the four of them working together. Noah was chopping in rhythm with Charles Fitzhugh while Gordy and Martin worked on another tree across the clearing from them.

Sunny waited at the edge of the green woods. She didn't want to startle the men during such dangerous work. In fact, she didn't really want to be here. But she'd been drawn to seek out Noah, to bring something warm for the men to drink as a kind of peace offering. The distance she felt between her and Noah made her feel lost and scared. Maybe she shouldn't have gone to the preaching in town after all.

She shook the thought from her head—she was glad she'd gone. It had been…important.

When she'd arrived home yesterday she'd wanted to share about the white-haired and kind-eyed preacher who called himself Old Saul. She'd come home aching to let it all out but Noah had silently warned her away. He'd barely spoken six words to her all afternoon and evening. Her husband had gone deep within himself, even more than usual. At first she thought it was anger at her, but that didn't feel quite right. It was more like Noah was angry at himself.

Or perhaps... God?

"Timber!" Charles shouted. Their tree fell. Sunny stepped back farther into the shelter of trees, breathlessly watching the felled tree bounce and bounce, branches whipping back and forth. The ground under her feet shook. Finally it lay on the ground, shuddering still. Her husband and Charles moved to it and began stripping the branches off with hatchets.

How did they have the courage to do this terrifying work? Shaking her head, she ventured into the clearing. "I brought fresh hot coffee!" she called, holding up a jug wrapped in old cloth.

Her voice was drowned out by another voice.

"Timber!" Gordy yelled.

Sunny stepped back within the forest again. The second tree creaked, cracked, plummeting to the earth. It bounced, once, twice—and headed straight toward Noah and Charles.

Sunny shrieked, threw the jug down and ran forward heedlessly. "Noah!"

The huge log bounced high and sailed over Charles. Then it began dropping. In a rush of branches and leaves, it clipped her husband.

He fell.

"Noah!" she shrieked again. Sunny's heart pounded as she pelted toward her husband, now lying on the ground. Dawn began to cry as Sunny clutched her tightly.

The logged tree careened on till it slammed into the trees ringing the clearing. It dropped then—hard.

Sunny fell to her knees beside her husband. He lay, gasping, on the still dewy grass. He clutched his left shoulder as a moan was wrenched from him. "Is it broken?" she asked.

"Can you move your shoulder and arm, Noah?" Charles asked, standing at her side, leaning over.

Noah looked up at him as if dazed. Then with teeth clenched in a grimace, he slowly rotated his left shoulder and flexed his elbow and wrist. "It didn't…break anything."

Still shuddering with fright, Sunny hugged Dawn to her.

"Man, if you hadn't ducked, it would have taken your head clean off," Charles said, sounding amused.

"Good… I ducked then," Noah breathed rapidly, catches in his voice signifying pain.

Men. Joking at such a time.

Sunny set Dawn down and reached out for Noah's hand. She examined him and saw that the log branches had whipped the side of her husband's face, leaving streaks of gouged skin and blood. His sleeve had been nearly torn off at the shoulder. She pulled the cuff, ripping off the sleeve to expose the lacerated arm. Fortunately none of the cuts looked deep but blood oozed up.

"Martin? You have a spring, don't you? Would you bring me fresh water and a clean cloth for bandages?" Sunny asked.

"Right away. I got a big bottle of iodine, too." The younger man hurried away to his tent.

"My woman sent along a jar of arnica ointment to share when we're done for the day." Gordy turned and ran to a bag, which hung from a tree branch nearby. He returned with it and handed it to Sunny with a roll of cloth bandages. "Her grannie makes it with that herb. It's real good for bringing down swelling and bruises."

Soon Sunny was washing away blood from Noah's face and arm. Then, from a scared-looking Martin, she took the bottle of iodine. She steadied herself to cause her husband pain. She noted Noah bracing himself to withstand it.

Dr. Mercy in Idaho had taught her that infection could kill and that iodine fought infection. So she tipped the bottle at the top of Noah's shoulder and trickled the brown liquid down over his lacerated face and bleeding upper arm.

Noah gasped and gritted his teeth. Sunny knew it burned like fire. The men stood by solemnly, enduring the pain with him. When she'd anointed every cut, gouge and scrape, she began to rub the arnica ointment into the bruised skin around his shoulder joint.

"Rub it in good," Gordy urged. "That might help keep the shoulder from swelling so much he can't move it."

Sunny obeyed and then wrapped the cloth bandages around Noah's arm. When Martin handed her a large square of muslin, she fashioned a sling. And when all the doctoring was done, she bent her head down, feeling waves of weakness. And sheer terror. *He could have been killed. I could have been widowed today.* But she had done what a wife was expected to do. She'd taken care of Noah. That steadied her.

"I think we should back it down to just two of us felling and the other two stripping," Charles said. "Logging is unpredictable. Don't want anybody else hurt today."

"I could use a drink of something," Noah said.

Ignoring her light-headedness, Sunny found the jug she'd dropped in the grass. The jug's lid had held. She unscrewed it and poured out a cup of coffee for Noah. "I have enough for all. Martin, do you have mugs?"

Soon the four men sipped the still-hot coffee. Then Charles helped Noah to his feet, holding on to him, steadying him.

"My right hand and arm are okay," Noah said, still breathing in gasps. "I can help with the stripping. It'll keep my mind—"

Sunny supplied silently, *off the pain.*

"—busy," Noah finished.

Sunny wanted to object. Noah needed to lie down and rest, help his body heal, not stress it with work. But she knew better than to voice this. Men didn't show weakness. And Noah wouldn't appreciate her coddling him in front of other men.

She hardened herself and kept quiet. "I'll be back with lunch later."

"No need, Miz Whitmore," Gordy said. "My Nan is bringing stew and biscuits over at midday."

Sunny merely nodded, tight-lipped. "That's nice of her. I'll drop by to see her then, too." The desire to show her husband some affection nearly swept her from her feet, but they didn't show affection to each other. "You men, be careful. I think you cost me a few years of life just now," she said, sounding as calm as she possibly could.

The men chuckled but she glimpsed in their eyes that the accident had shaken them, too. Well, good, maybe they'd be more careful. She lifted Dawn and told her to wave goodbye to the men.

Still shaking inside, Sunny headed for home. Stark, cold fear coursed through her but she set a steady pace toward home. One thought echoed in her head the whole way: *I could have lost him today.*

Noah sat on his stool in the cool faint light, his arm and shoulder still aching from his accident several days ago. He'd slept like the dead from fatigue though the pain awakened him occasionally. As they ate breakfast, Sunny sat in the rocker nearby.

"When Martin's cabin is done and he goes south to claim his bride, I'll finish our table and benches," Noah announced.

"You're helping Charles and Gordy finish work on Martin's cabin today?" she asked.

He tested his arm. "Yes, and I think I can leave off the sling soon."

Sunny glanced at him. "I'm glad you're feeling better. And there has been no infection."

"That iodine nearly burned me to death," Noah said, making an attempt at humor. He could tell Sunny was trying to hide her concern.

"Dr. Mercy Gabriel, Constance's daughter, taught me about cleaning wounds."

He nodded. "You did good."

His words of praise clearly made her happy. A beautiful smile lit up her face and Noah had to look away. He sipped his coffee, focusing on how glad he was that he would be able to work a full day again without showing weakness.

Sunny had been right about being neighborly. He wanted to go to Martin's today. It was a good feeling to want to be with other men. The time spent laboring at Martin's place had restored something in Noah. He hadn't thought it possible, but he'd liked working together as he and his brothers had labored together on their dad's farm. He didn't want to lose it.

"I can't understand why Charles plans to take his family to Kansas. Everything a man needs is here," he said.

Sunny sighed deeply. "I don't understand it, either. But it's a free country."

"I like to be where there are trees."

"Me, too. I lived on the plains and didn't like the… emptiness. They made me feel—"

Noah stopped her. "Look."

Dawn had been crawling on the floor. But now near him, she was trying to get on her feet. Noah watched, fascinated as the baby tried to pull herself up on the rim of his stool.

"Should be walking before long," Sunny said, sounding proud.

"We'll have to watch her then. You heard them last night."

Sunny tilted her head. "Last night?"

"The wolves were howling at the moon. I spoke to you. You let me know you heard them, too."

"I don't remember. I must have been talking in my sleep."

When he saw the fear in Sunny's eyes, he regretted telling her. "I don't want you to be upset. Just keep an eye on Dawn when she starts walking. We need to remember we aren't living in town. And I've seen bear scat, too."

Sunny nodded solemnly. "I'll remember." She looked

at him. "I've been walking over to Martin's place by myself."

"That's okay. Bear will steer clear of humans. Wolves usually don't bother an adult but I think a child alone might be different."

Sunny nodded. Then Dawn's knees weakened. She plopped down and squawked her displeasure.

Noah smiled. The baby added life to their quiet cabin. Watching Dawn made him think of the coming Sunday. When he'd seen the tree heading for him, in the face of death he'd realized how glad he was to be alive. And then watching Sunny hurry to care for him… Whether he lived or died hadn't mattered to anybody for so long. He must care for her, too.

I'm doing this for Dawn—and for us. Sunny's words suddenly began to make sense to him. His wife was wise, much wiser than he. He inhaled deeply and felt himself calming. Now he knew what he should do, but could he actually do it?

Chapter Six

Outside, Noah stood before the mirror hanging on a peg by the door. With his almost-healed arm free of the sling, he carefully shaved his face with his honed razor. He'd moved the mirror out here so he could see himself clearly in the crisp morning light. He needed to shave…because he was going to attend Sunday meeting this morning.

Fear that he might not be able to make it through the meeting clutched his stomach with cold hands.

He was aware that his wife was eyeing him and holding back the obvious question. He wanted to tell her but somehow he couldn't say the words, *I'm going to meeting.* Once he'd come to understand Sunny's reason for attending, he'd faced the truth. *I have to do this for Dawn, and for Sunny—and for myself.*

He rinsed away the soap and then wiped his damp face with a towel, inhaling the bracing air. "Sunny?" He cleared his clogged throat. "Will you press my dress shirt and suit?"

"Right away, Noah." She scurried into the cabin.

He heard her open the chest, which kept their better clothing clean and safe. He should have told her yesterday so she wouldn't have had to iron on Sunday. The old ways still clung to him—no work on First day, what Quakers called Sunday. He gazed into the limitless blue above the tall treetops, drawing strength from the serenity around him.

Finally he went inside and stood watching Sunny finish ironing his trousers. Her hands were deft and watching her was a pleasure, carrying his mind away from what he must do today.

Dawn crawled to him, grabbed his pant leg and tried to haul herself up to stand. Glad of the distraction, he reached down and swung her up into his arms. She crowed, exultant. He jiggled her and she crowed again. Such innocence. A fierce protectiveness surged within him. This child depended on him. He murmured silently, *I won't fail you, child.* Not like his father had failed him. His heart clenched into stone.

Dawn patted his chest with her soft tiny hand, easing in some indefinable way the tightness there. He picked up the child's little pink palm and kissed it. Then he lifted her high overhead, again causing her to squeal with joy.

"Thank you," Sunny said, "for keeping her busy."

When he glanced at his wife, she had looked away. Her soft hands moved over the dark cloth. Steam rose from the dampened fabric. The heavy iron slid along the cloth, pressing the wrinkles and creases flat and fresh. If only humans could lie on an ironing board and have their imperfections ironed out.

He lowered Dawn to his chest, clasping her close,

and stepped outside with her. He walked to a nearby
pine tree and took her hand and stroked her palm across
one needled bough. The little girl's face showed intense
concentration and awe. "Those are pine needles," he
murmured. "Pine needles."

All of a sudden the child collapsed against him. He
realized she was hugging him, an unexpected boon.
And for what? The only gift he'd given her was lifting
her to touch a pine tree.

Sunny stepped outside. "Your clothes are pressed."
She looked at her daughter hugging him still.

Their gazes linked, connecting them in some powerful way. "She's so bright. Everything's a wonder to
her," he managed to say.

Sunny nodded, then walked to him. She held out her
hands for the child so he could go dress.

He didn't want to relinquish the little one—he didn't
want to go inside and dress to face this thing he must do.

Dawn made the decision for him. She turned and
launched herself at her mother, who caught her. "If you
dress now, Noah, I'll have time to do my hair and finish—"

He nodded mechanically, cutting off her appeal. He'd
made his decision, but every step toward the goal jolted
him. "Right away."

Soon they were both attired in their First day best,
standing at the end of their track, waiting for the
Fitzhughs to arrive. Noah's heart beat like train wheels
racing over iron tracks.

The jingling harness announced the wagon and then
their friends came into view amidst the trees. Charles

beamed at him. Noah merely nodded, holding in his
inclination to turn back home.

"We're so happy to see you, Noah," Caroline said.

Noah ducked his head politely. He led Sunny to the
rear and helped her and Dawn up. Then he hoisted himself onto the wagon bed beside her. Charles chirruped
to the team and they took off with a lurch and bump.

In front of the store, Noah lifted Dawn into his arms
and accepted and returned greetings. He glanced at the
chattering people gathered around. Sunny stood beside
him. He wished he'd said something to her, but her
presence was both a comfort and an accusation. Why
couldn't he explain things to her?

Why couldn't he explain *himself* to her?

A brisk breeze blew off the river. He shielded Dawn
as best he could. The little girl squirmed to be let down
and he knew the same urge—to get down and go about
his business, not stand here waiting, dreading.

An old man arrived in a wagon with a couple and
two teenage boys. With what looked to be his son's help,
the old man got down from the wagon bench. From the
crowd's reaction, Noah knew this must be the preacher.
At once the man's frailty and strength touched Noah.

The preacher was thin with age but his hands told
the tale of years of labor. People around him called out
greetings. The old man lifted a gnarled hand in reply
and then took the seat that Ashford the storekeeper
brought out for him.

Noah felt the crowd move forward, carrying him
and Sunny closer than he wanted to go. Then the old
man smiled broadly—and it was like he drew them all
to him. Feeling the strain of being with others, Noah

gathered the invisible bonds that held him together. He didn't belong here, but he'd come so no one would single out his family as strange or different.

He'd thought that was what Sunny's words had meant. However, now that he'd arrived, it was clear that wasn't what she'd meant at all. The past which he'd bottled inside him strained to be released. He tightened his control, clenched his teeth against it. *I faced cannon and sabers and cavalry horses. I can stand down this man.*

Sunny watched her husband, had watched him all morning. What had made him decide to come to this gathering? His presence caused her to be even more nervous than she had been last Sunday. Would he remain her silent Noah or had he come to say something? All around her, everyone was smiling. Though nervous, Sunny forced herself to do the same.

Dawn squirmed in Noah's arms. Sunny reached over and gently took the child and set her down. Noah didn't object—in fact, he didn't look toward her at all. He looked to be in pain. Sunny touched his arm.

He glanced down.

She smiled up at him, trying to let him know that everything was all right.

He gazed at her and gave the slightest nod. Then, he drew her hand into the crook of his arm.

At first, Sunny was shocked. Then she felt herself beaming with pride at this show of oneness. This man, the handsomest here to her mind, was not ashamed to claim her here in front of everyone. No other man had ever done so. When Dawn pulled herself up using Sunny's skirts, Sunny felt for the first time that the three of them stood together, a family.

The son and daughter-in-law of the preacher began to lead the gathering in a hymn. Though aware that Noah remained silent beside her, Sunny sang along as best she could. Then the son and his wife moved to the side, sitting down on the bench outside the store.

Suddenly Sunny was shocked to see that during the hymn singing, Dawn had somehow left her side and crawled up to the porch, and was now in the process of hauling herself up—using the trouser leg of the preacher!

Sunny's hand flew to her mouth as she gasped. "Dawn!"

The old preacher reached down, grasped the little hands and helped the baby stand up.

Sunny rushed forward through the couples. "I'm so sorry—"

Old Saul held up a hand. "No need to be sorry. Jesus said, 'Suffer the little children to come unto me, and forbid them not: for of such is the kingdom of God.' What a sweet little girl." He patted Dawn's back and the little girl crowed.

Sunny paused, unsure what to do.

"Just let her be," the old preacher reassured her. "She's doing no harm." He closed his eyes and began to pray for Dawn, for her family, for this town.

Sunny calmed and drifted back to Noah. Dawn remained at the preacher's feet, alternately crawling, cooing and dragging herself up to stand. Old Saul watched her with evident pleasure. "Jesus loved little children. He loved them, no doubt, because the world had not yet twisted them, harmed them." He touched Dawn's bright curls lightly.

"How many of us," he continued, "wish we could shed the sorrows and worries of this life and be like children, playing until we are exhausted and then falling into deep sleep without nightmares or cares to wake us?"

Noah stiffened beside her. Sunny moved a few inches closer to him. He still had the nightmares, and he still had not told her about them. She wanted to slip her hand back onto his arm, but he was very far away—she could see that in his eyes. The preacher went on speaking about repentance, forgiveness and becoming as innocent as children again. Then they sang another hymn, which Sunny thought beautiful. *Amazing grace, how sweet the sound that saved a wretch like me. I once was lost but now I'm found, was blind but now I see.*

Then they lined up to shake Old Saul's hand but more to hear his words, different for each of them as if he knew just what to say. Sunny wished this didn't make her nervous. But surely the man would have little to say to her now that her husband had come. They were a couple just like all the others.

When her turn came, she shook his hand and smiled. Old Saul beamed at her and mentioned how he'd enjoyed her little girl's part this morning.

Then Noah accepted the older man's gnarled hand, shook it and with a murmured phrase, tried to step back. Old Saul gripped his hand, keeping it. He didn't say anything, just looked up into Noah's eyes a long time. Then he said, "I served under Old Hickory, Andrew Jackson, at the Battle of New Orleans."

Noah didn't move or speak for a few moments. Finally when he nodded curtly, Old Saul released his hand.

And with relief Sunny stepped aside for the Osbournes to take their turn, Noah by her side. Sunny wished she could make sense of the older man's words. She knew that there had been a president named Andrew Jackson, but what about the Battle of New Orleans? She regretted once again her lack of schooling.

But more worrying was the edginess she sensed from Noah. She realized that the time might be nearing for her to confront Noah as she had after Charles and Martin had come and logged that first time.

Going to meeting had stirred him up again, just like that day. She didn't want to make him face what was bothering him, but she needed to know why he'd come to the meeting this morning. She needed to understand him.

And perhaps there were some things he needed to understand about her, as well.

A few days later Noah cleared his throat at the end of supper. "We should go over to the Fitzhughs now."

"Oh?" Sunny looked up. The weather had been cool and gloomy all day so the door was shut. Only faint light filtered in around the closed shutters. They would put glass windows in before fall, Noah had promised.

Today's weather matched Noah's mood. She hadn't gotten up the courage to ask Noah why he'd gone to worship. But maybe it wasn't the right time. Noah had had the worst nightmare of all last night, and she could see he didn't feel like talking.

"The Fitzhughs are leaving in the morning for Kansas."

Noah's words crushed her spirit. For a moment she couldn't speak. Caroline had been her first friend here. Was losing Charles's cheerful presence one cause of Noah's renewed edginess? The Fitzhughs had been the ones to bring Noah and her into the community. Was losing them hitting Noah hard, as well?

"Oh, Noah, I thought they might wait till Martin's bride came. Or change their minds about leaving."

"Charles is itching to head west in time to find a place and plant a crop." Noah's tone was dark.

Heavyhearted, Sunny rose, shed her apron, donned her bonnet. Then she thought of something and knelt by the door to open the chest. After she tucked the small gift into her pocket, she picked up Dawn and stepped outside. Noah shut the door behind them, pulling out the latch string.

"I'll carry Dawn," Noah said.

Three deer leaped across the path ahead of them. How graceful they were.

"Plenty of game hereabouts." Noah followed the game with his gaze. "We'll eat well."

His commonplace observation sat at odds with the turmoil she sensed in him. Last night he'd had such a nightmare that he'd wakened Dawn. He climbed down from the loft and paced outside till, exhausted, Sunny had fallen asleep. She'd hoped the Sunday service would have helped. What would help Noah?

The two of them walked the trail in silence. The trees cast long shadows and from the nearby creek, peepers—little frogs—peeped all around them. And then they were at the Fitzhughs' place.

The Osbournes had come as well as Martin. They all gathered outside the entrance to the small one-room cabin.

"I wish you'd stay long enough to meet my girl Ophelia," Martin said. "I wrote her about our neighbors."

"When you tie the knot, you write us, Martin," Caroline Fitzhugh said, looking down.

Sunny recognized the tremor in Caroline's voice. She recalled that Caroline had family in Wisconsin. What was Charles thinking taking his family all the way to Kansas? Why, there still were Indians and buffalo out there.

Martin nodded glumly. "You've been such good neighbors."

"Well, Martin, you tell Ophelia," Nan Osbourne said stoutly, "she'll still have me and Miz Whitmore nearby."

"That's right," Sunny agreed quickly.

The men moved apart, talking. The women gravitated to each other. Sunny set Dawn down to play with the other children. She didn't know what to say so she let the other women do the talking. Finally the sun lowered enough for Noah to say they needed to head home.

Sunny shook Charles's hand and then hugged Caroline farewell. She pushed the length of the blue ribbon she'd brought into Caroline's hand. "For your girls. To remember us by."

"That's real nice," Nan said, standing at Sunny's elbow. Nan's voice trembled as if tears threatened.

The visitors all walked together to the wagon trail. There, Martin turned the other direction and parted with a wave. Together, the Whitmores and the Osbournes walked westward down the track in the waning light, subdued and quiet. Nan leaned close just before she and her husband turned off toward their place. "My time is getting near. Can my husband come and get you when I need help?"

Shock shot through Sunny. "Of course I'll come. But I've only been to my own birthing."

"Gordy will head into town to bring out the storekeeper's wife," Nan explained further. "She's had ten herself and said she'd be glad to come help me. But while Gordy's gone, I'll need somebody to sit with me just in case."

"Gordy," Noah spoke up, "you come and fetch Sunny. Then *I'll* go to town for you. You should stay with your wife."

Noah's quick offer of help encouraged Sunny. He wasn't as withdrawn today as she had first thought. Then recalling the nightmare he'd suffered last night cast a veil over her hope. The dreams seemed to be getting worse, not better.

"Thanks, Noah. Thanks." Gordy shook his hand and the Osbournes waved and headed toward their place.

With Dawn already heavily asleep on Sunny's shoulder, they reached the cabin just as the last rays of sunshine flickered through the trees and disappeared. Noah shut the door behind them. Sunny laid Dawn in her hammock.

Noah turned to climb up the ladder to the loft to leave her to dress for bed alone as usual. The Fitzhughs moving on still lowered her mood. But Noah's offer of help to the Osbournes kept repeating in her mind.

Noah had not wanted to get "thick" with their neighbors but he obviously couldn't go against his own good nature. Hope bobbed within her and she decided to speak.

"Noah." she paused, then went on, feeling as if she were venturing out onto new ice, "I'm concerned about your nightmares." There, she'd said the word neither of them had ever spoken.

"I didn't mean to wake Dawn last night." His voice was gruff.

"That isn't my concern." She found she didn't have the words she needed. Exactly what was she trying to say? "You're my concern." The words startled her. But should they? This was her husband. And he needed something. But was it something she could offer?

"I can't help having them." He started up the ladder to the loft.

She went after him. "Don't leave me. Let's talk. Maybe if we talk—"

"Talking is just words," he barked.

"Words can be important. We spoke words and we became husband and wife. God spoke words and the world was created. Can't we talk about your nightmares? Maybe it would help." The last sentence wobbled from her lips.

"'Maybe it would help,'" he mocked. "Words can't change what happened." He hurried up the last rungs.

"Noah—"

"Let it be, Sunny," he growled.

"Noah, I can't let it be. We need to talk this out. It can't hurt and it might help." She wasn't really sure about the first part.

He came down the ladder, carrying his blanket and pillow with him. He headed for the door.

Panic shot through her. Was he leaving her? "Where are you going?"

"I'll sleep in the wagon." He stalked to the door.

She hurried after him. "No, Noah—"

He shut the door in her face.

Leaving her caught between fear and frustration, she wanted to go after him, but fear held her back. What if he left her and Dawn? She'd only tried to be a good wife, but she'd failed. She slumped into the rocker, shaking inside. Those moments standing together as a family at Sunday worship, had they just been an act? Had they made no progress toward becoming a real family? Had she done more harm than good tonight? Pushed him further from her?

Weary from lack of sleep, Noah inhaled the morning air, scented with pine. The chill each morning was lessening. Spring was drifting toward summer. He'd need to break ground soon to plant in time to harvest. Sunny and Dawn had gone over to Nan's early this morning. They were sewing some dishcloths and potholders for Martin's bride.

Noah remained behind alone, working on his table and thinking of the argument he and Sunny had had last night. She had made him so angry, and yet he could tell it was because she was worried. Still, he didn't like being pushed.

He'd felt something else last night, too. He'd wanted to reach for her, to grab her and pull her into his arms. He thought about taking her arm Sunday morning in town, showing possession. Something was changing between them. No matter how much he tried to convince himself that theirs was a marriage of practicality, he couldn't deny that there was something else happening. Was that why he'd spent the sleepless night, tossing and turning in the wagon?

The sound of an approaching harness jingling wafted to him on the breeze. Crosscurrents sawed through his mind. He wanted to be left in peace; he wanted whoever it was to stop.

The wagon came jouncing over the track through the trees toward his cabin. Noah froze in place. The preacher had come to call.

And Sunny wasn't here to handle the social niceties and keep the preacher busy, away from him. Noah stiffened himself. He had done all right in town on Sunday, not letting his real feelings show. He could handle this. He had to. He didn't want to be the local oddity—again.

He bent his reluctant mouth into a smile of greeting. "Preacher!" he called out in false welcome. He put down his tools and walked over to the wagon.

The preacher stopped well into the clearing. He laid his reins down, turned and scooted to the edge toward Noah. "Will you help an old man down?"

Noah offered both hands and let the preacher take hold and ease down rope steps that had been hung on the side of wagon. "I thank you," the older man said on solid ground.

Noah felt his jaw tightening. He smiled broader to loosen it.

"I won't stay long. I can see you're working. Show me your place."

The simple request had an odd effect on Noah. This was the first time he'd ever been able to show anybody what he and Sunny had accomplished already and in only a little over two and a half weeks. As Noah led him to the cabin, the older man leaned on Noah's arm.

"Charles Fitzhugh and Martin Steward helped me get my cabin up."

The older man stepped inside and tapped the log floor with the toe of his boot. "I do like a good foundation."

"Martin and Charles helped me lay the rock foundation underneath the whole. We stirred a slurry of rock, sand and water and poured it all over the stones as mortar. This cabin will stand, not shift or sink."

The older man nodded. "You built yourselves a nice big cabin. It will do for the large family I hope you and your pretty wife will be blessed with."

Noah felt the strain return, wrap around him. Would he and Sunny ever have a family? Not as things stood between them now, they wouldn't. He hated to be reminded of his failing. When would he be able to reach for her? How could he break through to where he wanted to be? His stiff smile slipped. Sleeping outside hadn't helped.

"You've already been blessed with that pretty little girl. Do you know how lucky you are?"

Lucky wasn't a word he'd use to describe himself. And he'd argued with Sunny. And wakened Dawn with that nightmare. Noah felt the preacher studying him. "Dawn is a joy," he said at last.

The older man went to the stone fireplace. "This is

fine stonework. Who taught you how to build a fireplace without mortar?"

"I had a grandfather who was a stonemason. He taught me to lay a hearth."

"You could make this a trade. There're a lot of people around here who would pay good money to have a hearth like this."

Noah shrugged. He had no interest in working for others.

"Keep that in mind, son. There might come a time when you need some cash money."

With a mere nod, Noah led the preacher outside and showed him the lean-to and the oxen grazing along with his horse. The preacher's easy words were calming to Noah. He worked hard to keep alert for any word-trap the man might set for him.

"Now I see that you also work with wood. You are a man of many talents," Old Saul said as he noticed the table Noah was building.

Noah shrugged again, not offering any response. When would this man leave him in peace?

"Well, you let me stretch my legs. If you give me a glass of your spring water, I'll get back up on the wagon and go on to my next stop. I'm glad you showed me your place."

The older man was as good as his word. He drank his cup of water. Noah helped him to get back up onto his wagon bench and he turned the team and jingled away.

Noah had expected a homily, or stiff sermon, or some kind of prosy pap. Why had Old Saul come? Noah couldn't figure it out. Then he recalled the only comment the old preacher had said that didn't address the cabin and its furnishings had been about Dawn. *Do you know how lucky you are?* He imagined Dawn's hug and had trouble drawing a deep breath. *I don't feel lucky, but I am. I'm not alone anymore.*

The next morning Sunny stared across at Noah, sitting on the three-legged stool. Somehow, when she saw Noah's long, lean form stretched over the low stool, her heart ached for him. He looked vulnerable, haggard from lack of sleep. She supposed she looked the same way—they hadn't spoken much since their argument.

Once again she had to stifle words of comfort. Noah, like most men, didn't want to admit to any weakness. At least he'd slept in the loft last night, not out in the wagon. Her stomach rumbled with anxiety and she caught herself worrying her thumb. It was already red and nearly bleeding again. Should she apologize for pushing him so hard to tell her about his nightmare? Should she explain why she wanted to know? That her curiosity was because she cared so deeply?

"Hello, the house!" interrupted her thoughts.

Glancing to each other, she and Noah both went to the door and he opened it.

Martin sat on his wagon bench. "I'm off this morning to get married." If the man could have smiled wider, his face would have split in two.

Sunny spontaneously clapped her hands. "Oh, wonderful!" She hurried forward, drawn to the man's palpable joy.

Noah scooped up Dawn and followed her. "How long will you be away?"

"About ten days or so. Ophelia has everything ready for our wedding and is already packed to come north."

Sunny chuckled. "We will make your bride welcome."

"I know you will. I wrote her already that we have good neighbors." The groom blushed.

"You travel careful." Noah stroked the neck of one of Martin's horses, a chestnut.

"I will. I've got the preacher's blessings—he stopped to see me yesterday."

"He must be making the rounds. He stopped here, too," Noah said.

Sunny swung around to look into Noah's eyes. He hadn't said anything about the visit. Why had the preacher come? Her nerves jittered.

"Seems like a good man," Martin replied. "Ophelia was happy to learn we got a preacher. She'd miss going to worship."

Sunny tried to look as if she felt the same way as Martin's bride. But she couldn't stop worrying about what the preacher had said when he'd visited. Had he come to ask questions about her? Did her past show in some way she didn't understand?

"Well, I'm off." Martin slapped the reins and turned his wagon. He responded to their enthusiastic goodbyes with a wave over his head. The creaking wagon retreated down the track.

Sunny did not want to start another argument, but she had to know. She clenched the hand she had worked raw. "You didn't say that the preacher had come."

Noah turned to her slowly. "He just stopped to look over our place. That's all."

"And he stopped at Martin's, too," Sunny mused.

"Seems so."

Noah didn't seem angry, so she pushed on. "What did the preacher mean about Andrew Jackson and the Battle of New Orleans? That couldn't have been in the War Between the States."

Noah offered her the child. "No, that battle took place in 1815 in the second war with England. I've got work to start now. We may have a table to eat off tonight."

Sunny accepted Dawn. She could tell Noah did not want to pursue the topic any further. Yet why had the preacher said those words to Noah? What did late President Jackson and a battle over fifty years ago have to do with Noah?

Sunny trailed Noah, no longer able to keep her curiosity in check. She hovered nearby as he unearthed his woodworking tools from the chest, trying to come up with the right words. She followed Noah to the area where his two sawhorses stood ready. He laid a board down and began planing it, making a rhythmic scratching sound, and sending up curls of wood shavings. Dawn squealed, reaching toward the curls.

Noah looked up. "Do you need something, Sunny?"

She chewed her lower lip. "I do, Noah. Tell me— why did you go to meeting?" Her voice quavered just above a whisper.

Noah paused in his work.

Sunny waited, Dawn straining to get down from her arms.

"Isn't it enough that I went?" he asked gruffly, beginning to plane again.

"Noah," she murmured coaxingly, "I just need to know you. Know why you changed your mind. Before when I asked you to go, you said…you sounded…" She couldn't think what more to say. She gave up and turned.

"I thought over what you said."

His words stopped her. She swung back around. "Something *I* said?"

"About doing it for Dawn, and for us. You were right. We don't want to stick out, be different. In the army I was the private that used *thee* and then back home, I was the Friend who had gone to war. I, *we*, will not stand out as the strange ones here. It just causes talk. We don't need that."

She paused, stunned at the amount of words that had just flowed from Noah's mouth all at once. And then his meaning burst over her. He'd gone to meeting for Dawn and for her, not just himself.

Sunny rushed forward and with Dawn between them, pressed herself against him. He didn't hug back. He still held his plane, but he bent his head forward, his chin grazing the top of her head.

They silently shared a moment of the most tender connection. Sunny blinked back one tear. And then stepped away. "I need to get busy baking some bread or we'll have none for supper."

"Sounds good."

Sunny hurried into the cabin. Part of her wanted to stay with Noah and talk. So many questions she wanted to ask him. Why had he gone to war? Why had his father been so angry with him? What did he dream in his nightmares?

The moment of being close to Noah, not only physically but also as partners, two people pulling together for their family, had nearly lifted Sunny off her feet. But she couldn't press her luck. She'd felt dreadful, fearful, when she'd confronted Noah. She didn't want to spoil this feeling, this special first.

Soon Dawn played with some jar rings, clacking them on the wood floor. Humming, Sunny kneaded the soft, cream-colored bread dough, covered it with a clean cloth and then set it on the mantel to rise.

She still felt like a pot simmering and realized she needed to calm down. Noah was a complicated man. She didn't want to do anything that might disturb the progress they'd just made. An idea of how she might please him occurred to her. She smiled and set about her baking, still humming and now grating fresh cinnamon.

Chapter Seven

Noah concentrated on planing the table and two benches, but he couldn't banish the feeling of Sunny pressed against him. Her softness threatened to weaken him. He had to remain strong, keep himself in check. Her questions were getting more and more pointed, closer to things he himself didn't understand—it made it hard for him to talk to her.

The wood flowed under his plane. He paused to stroke the tabletop—time to start sanding it smooth and then he'd oil it. The thought of sitting at a table tonight, a real table, pleased him. It would please her, too. If he couldn't answer her questions, at least he could give her a table on which to serve her meals.

Later in the afternoon Noah first carried in the broad tabletop, standing it against the wall. Then he brought in the trestle and two substantial squared and footed table legs. While he put the base together, Sunny held Dawn. He felt her intense gaze on him. He then lay on his back on the hard floor under the table and fastened down the top, pounding in the wood bolts he'd whittled.

Dawn was making urgent sounds and straining to

get down to come to him. He got up and pinched her cheek. As he bent over his work, he hid a smile at her preference for him. The preacher's words about how lucky he was rang in his ears.

He stood back for just a moment, admired his handiwork and then ducked outside to bring in the benches.

"We have a table, Mrs. Whitmore." He couldn't keep the pride of workmanship out of his tone. But he stepped out of reach so she wouldn't hug him again.

"Oh, Noah, it's lovely." Sunny set Dawn down and stroked the tabletop. "The wood grain is beautiful and the table just fits our room."

"Should sit up to ten easy." More of the preacher's words came back to him about Sunny and he having a family large enough to fit their cabin. Hot shame at his inadequacy as a husband sent him swiftly out the door. "Got to water the stock," he said, excusing himself.

"I'm making cinnamon buns for supper!" Sunny called after him.

He caught the worry in her tone. She sounded afraid he was irritated with her. How could he tell her that wasn't true? The irritation, frustration, aggravation he felt—it was all directed at himself.

In the small sunlit meadow Sunny bent over the green leaves, moving them to reveal the tiny red berries hiding underneath. Only a few feet away Nan bent in the same posture. They were picking wild strawberries, and Sunny's mind was racing with ideas about what she could make with them. The cinnamon buns hadn't had the desired effect on Noah, but perhaps fresh strawberries would draw him closer.

"I'm so happy you let me know," Sunny said. "I love strawberries."

"Well, my auntie had a nice berry patch at home and hers were bigger, but these will do with some sugar on 'em."

Dawn and Nan's little boy, Guthrie, crawled among the plants and wild grasses, entertaining themselves. Careful not to bruise or crush the soft velvety berries, Sunny gathered and dropped them into a wood bucket she'd brought. Nan appeared to have such an easygoing life compared to Sunny's. And, of course, their pasts obviously separated them. This difference constantly niggled at Sunny.

Sunny had become accustomed to Nan's ways and that in itself made her especially wary. She continued to fear that she might, by some chance remark, reveal her past. She couldn't let herself get too comfortable with anybody or she might lose everything she'd worked for since leaving Idaho. She and Noah couldn't move on to make another fresh start. They had their cabin finished and they were becoming part of the community.

"Well, I can't bend over another second. I'll just have to sit and scoot," Nan declared with a bit of humor and a deep sigh. The woman's pregnancy was obviously drawing to a close. She eased herself down to sit among the wild vines and began picking in this new position.

"How are you doing?" Sunny asked with sympathy.

"I'm getting to that stage where I just want it over!"

Sunny recalled how she'd felt the last few weeks before Dawn had been born. The breeze through the high leaves overhead sounded something like laughter, a cheery, soothing sound. "I understand."

Nan sighed loudly again. "You only been pregnant once?"

"Yes." Sunny stilled within. Why had Nan asked that?

"This is my third time. I lost my first."

Sunny snapped upright. "Oh, Nan, I'm so sorry."

"I'm just tellin' you because it's got Gordy worried. My first delivery just…" The young woman fell silent. "It was bad. And the baby didn't survive. It was a little girl."

Sympathy swamped Sunny as she tried to imagine what that had been like. She chastised herself for thinking that Nan's life had been easy.

"Will you ask your man to stay with Gordy during my birthing? He'll need somebody to talk with. Even though Guthrie came out right, my husband's worried I'll have a bad time again."

Sunny moved swiftly to Nan, bent and hugged her shoulders. "Yes, of course. And you're going to be fine. Mrs. Ashford will know how to help. And I'll be there, too."

Nan squeezed Sunny in return. "I know and I'm praying every night for another safe delivery. My mom birthed thirteen and she only had trouble the first time. That's what I keep telling Gordy, but…" The young woman shrugged.

Sunny straightened up and moved back to where she'd been picking, thinking of how everyone seemed to have secrets, or private pain. Suddenly, she caught movement from the corner of her right eye. She glanced over and nearly screamed. "Nan," she whispered, shaking, "there's a bear at the edge of the clearing."

"Which way?"

"Over your right shoulder." What had Noah told her to do if she met a bear? *Had* he told her what to do?

"Don't act riled," Nan said soberly. "I'm going to stand up slowly and start talking so it'll know we're humans. They don't see very good."

"Okay." Sunny's knees weakened but she kept on her feet. She located Dawn nearby, crawling on the ground, pursuing a butterfly.

"Well, good afternoon, bear," Nan said conversationally. "I know you like berries, but we got here first. We'll leave you some—don't you worry. Sunny, I'm going to start singing now. Only humans do that. You sing along. 'You are my sunshine, my only sunshine.'"

Sunny tried to sing along but couldn't get her voice to work.

"Sunny," Nan said after a moment, "it's a mama bear with a cub. Are you good at climbing trees?"

Sunny didn't think she could budge, much less climb. "No."

"Okay, we'll just sing some more and back away real slowlike. Let her know we're not going to mess with her baby."

How could Nan sound so calm?

Sunny stared at the bear, trying to join the song, and took a few halting steps backward.

The bear paused as if listening and then rose a bit, sniffing the air.

"Oh, good, she's smelling us."

Sunny didn't know how this could possibly be good. But then the bear herded her cub away and ambled off into the woods.

Giving way, Sunny sank to the warm earth.

"Are you all right?" Nan walked awkwardly to her side.

Sunny stared up at the woman. "Weren't you scared?"

"Yes, but I've seen bear before. She's just naturally going to protect her young. We can understand that. We're mamas with cubs, too."

This simple statement of fact sent Sunny into a storm of laughter. Then Nan began laughing, too. The two children wandered over to watch their mothers collapse on the ground and laugh themselves silly. Yet, Sunny also experienced a new strength. She'd faced a bear and hadn't panicked or done anything foolish. And she could laugh about it.

"You what?" Noah demanded, stopping his coffee mug halfway to his mouth.

Sunny turned from the hearth where she was stirring tonight's stew. "I said Nan and me saw a mama bear and her cub when we were berry-picking this afternoon."

"Didn't I tell you to be careful of bears?" He realized he was gripping the handle on his mug so tight that if it had been china, he'd have snapped it.

"I was careful." Sunny looked puzzled. "Nan told me what to do and then the bear herded her cub away from us. It was really funny."

Funny? A mother bear with a cub—was there anything more terrifying than that? He imagined Sunny and Dawn ravaged and left for dead. He set his mug down with a clunk.

"You look upset with me," she said, her voice tentative.

He clasped his hands together, holding in the anger and terror that flashed through him. He wanted to rage at her, *You could have been killed. Dawn could have died.* He chewed the insides of his mouth, trying to release his rage, keep from upsetting Sunny. "I'm not angry with you. Just be careful, all right?"

"I did just what Nan told me to do. I'll be careful, Noah."

He nodded woodenly, still roiling inside. "Good. Good."

Sunny bustled around the kitchen, then halted.

"Noah," his wife said with audible hesitation, "Nan asked me to ask you a favor."

"Nan wanted a favor from me?" He couldn't think of what another man's wife would want from him.

Sunny didn't look up while scooping stew into bowls and getting them on the table. "Nan's first baby didn't survive the birthing." She glanced up and then down quickly. "She didn't have any trouble when she had Guthrie. But Gordy's still worried about this baby coming."

What can I do about that? He forced himself to calmly sip his coffee.

"Nan hopes you'll stay with Gordy while he's…while she's in labor. She thinks it will help him get through it easier." Sunny looked him full in the face then, and then bent to pick Dawn up.

Of course he'd rather refuse this request. Nonetheless he couldn't say no. Gordy had become a friend. He wanted to make one thing clear, however. "I don't know anything about birthing."

"You just need to keep Gordy company outside till the baby's born," Sunny assured him.

"I said when Nan's time came, I'd go to town for him," Noah recalled.

"And then when you return with Mrs. Ashford, you can sit outside with him, keep him company. Will you?"

Noah nodded. "I can do that." Suddenly he wondered, *How would I feel if Sunny lost a baby? Our baby?* He forced down a sudden lack of breath. "I will."

Sunny exhaled. "Good. It will make it easier on Nan."

Dawn squirmed and Sunny let her down. The little girl crawled straight to Noah and pulled herself up at the end of the bench next to him, grinning.

"I'm almost jealous," Sunny teased. "She prefers your company to mine."

He grinned at the baby and ran his fingers through her red-gold curls. "Hey there, Dawnie."

The little girl crowed with delight.

Noah picked her up and swung her high above his head. Dawn's innocent happiness lifted him. He shouldn't scold Sunny about the bear. They lived in a forest and nothing had happened. He was glad he hadn't sparked another argument.

"Children are a joy," he said without meaning to. His gaze connected with Sunny's and he couldn't look away. If only the war hadn't come and swept away the joy of living, he and Sunny wouldn't be separated by the past, his past. He set Dawn down on her feet again.

The baby flapped her palms against the bench, scolding him.

He touched her nose. "I've got to feed the cattle quick, little lady. We will meet again."

He left without meeting Sunny's eye. "I won't be long."

The next morning, Gordy, his curly blond hair wild from the wind, came running into the clearing. "Noah!"

Noah had been busy laying a rock foundation for

the spring house, a place where they could keep food like milk cool. He intended to buy a cow before winter. Now he climbed out of the trench he'd dug around the spring. "What is it?" But even before the words left his mouth, Noah knew what had brought Gordy hurrying to their door.

"It's Nan's time. Will you—"

"I'll just wash my hands and be off to town," Noah replied. Hiding the jolt Gordy's words brought, he turned and called, "Sunny!"

"I heard, Noah." Sunny stood in the open door. "Just let me get a few things together, Gordy, and I'll come with you."

Noah washed his muddy hands in the basin by the door. He could hear Sunny opening the chest inside. Gordy stood in the midst of their clearing, plainly jumpy with nerves.

Noah didn't bother to saddle his horse. He just threw a blanket over his mount and climbed on. He waved to Gordy and took off. "See you at the Osbournes!" he called to Sunny.

Careful to keep his mount on the faint wagon track, Noah let his horse go at a brisk run, which the animal appeared to enjoy. Soon he arrived at Ashford's store, hitched his horse and swung down. The bell jingled as he opened the door. "Mr. Ashford!"

After the bright sunlight Noah paused just inside the store door to let his eyes adjust to the fainter light inside.

"What can I do for you?" the storekeeper's familiar voice came from the shadows.

"I need Mrs. Ashford. Mrs. Osbourne's time has come and your wife said she'd help."

"I'll get her right away." Ashford turned and hurried up the steps to their living quarters over the store.

Then Noah noticed that a rough-looking stranger stood near the old preacher who was also in the store with his daughter-in-law, a tall, spare woman with silver in her hair. Belatedly removing his hat, Noah nodded politely, hoping the older man wouldn't start a conversation.

"You tell Mrs. Osbourne that I'll continue praying she has a safe delivery," Old Saul said.

"I will, sir."

The stranger lounged against the counter, eyeing Noah. The man's expression made Noah uncomfortable. He hoped Ashford kept an eye on him. The storekeeper hurried down the stairs. "Mrs. Ashford says she'll come right after her bread is out of the oven."

Noah didn't welcome this delay. He propped his hands on his hips. "Does she know the way to the Osbournes?"

"Give me the directions," the storekeeper said, "and I'll explain them to her."

Noah told him and then stood there anyway, wanting to move the man's wife along quicker.

Ashford chuckled and winked. "Don't worry, young man. Babies aren't usually in a rush to be born. There's time."

The preacher's daughter-in-law spoke up. "I'll come, Mr. Whitmore. We haven't spoken, but I'm Lavina Caruthers. I've helped deliver babies, too."

Wanting to avoid more contact with the preacher, Noah hedged. "That's nice of you, ma'am, but I don't want to put you out."

"It's no problem. Old Saul can drive home by himself and I'll come with you. We brought our extra horse into town to be shod, so I'll ride over. Sometimes an extra pair of hands are good to have."

Noah said his thanks and walked outside. He threw a leg over his horse and headed toward the Osbournes. He didn't like returning without help—what if Ashford was wrong? What if the baby came before the midwife?

When Noah arrived at the Osbournes, he found Gordy outside sitting hunched on a log. Since the day was fine, both Dawn and Guthrie played at his feet. The man glanced up, looking strained but hopeful.

With a tight throat Noah delivered the news. "Mrs. Ashford has to finish baking her bread before she comes."

Sunny was standing in the doorway. "Did Mrs. Ashford say how soon that would be?"

"Not long. The preacher's daughter-in-law was at the store and said she'll be coming soon, too." He tried to gauge how things were progressing with Nan but could read nothing but concern in his wife's stance. Sunny nodded and then went back inside.

Noah hobbled his horse to graze at the edge of the clearing and then went to sit on the log beside Gordy. He forced himself to ask, "How are things going?"

"Nan says not to worry. Everything's going as it should." Gordy's voice sounded on edge.

Noah had no idea what this meant but found he didn't want to know. What could they talk about to get their minds on something else? "You heard about the bear?"

Gordy chuckled and shook his head. "Takes a lot to ruffle my wife."

Noah couldn't think of anything to say to that, and the men sat in more silence. Noah knew he wasn't helping. "I'm thinking of clearing more land. I need to put in a garden and plant some corn," he finally said.

Gordy glanced around at his heavily wooded land. "Same here. We'll have to get busy with that soon."

Even more silence descended. Noah knew he was failing, and when he heard a horse approaching, he jumped up, grateful someone had come.

The preacher's daughter-in-law arrived, then Mrs. Ashford, a plump woman who had a determined cast to her face, drove up in a wagon. The women disappeared inside, and the long hours went on and on. In the shade, the two toddlers napped on a blanket. Noah could tell Gordy was worried and gave up trying to make him talk. Gordy's eyes strayed toward the cabin constantly. Noah suddenly couldn't stand the tension. He rose abruptly. "You know, why don't we split some wood for kindling?" A man could always use more wood.

Gordy stood also. "Sounds like a good idea."

The two men headed toward the stump and the stack of logs nearby. "I'll watch the kids first while you split."

Gordy nodded. The two worked hard as if they could help the birth by chopping wood. Noah watched Gordy's strained face, wondering how he would feel if their roles were reversed. Nan could die. The baby could, too. The thoughts made Noah's mouth go dry. He wished he had some comfort to give Gordy.

Through the open door Sunny heard the sound of the ax hitting wood. "Sounds like the men are keeping busy." The sound of their normal chore helped calm Sunny. And she needed to be calm for Nan's sake. The preacher's kin Lavina sat by the open window and sewed as if the day were just like any other.

Nan and Sunny were pacing slowly back and forth in the cabin, Nan leaning on Sunny's arm. Mrs. Ashford said walking would hurry the birth along. So they paced the dirt floor, packed down hard.

That floor bothered Sunny. Gordy hadn't taken the extra effort to make a half-log floor. This cabin wouldn't be as snug as hers and Noah's would be this winter. Was it because the Osbournes were from farther south and didn't know how the cold would come up from the frozen earth?

Mrs. Ashford stood over the fire. Comfrey leaves steeped in a pot of boiled water gave off a dreadful smell. "My grandma taught me how to brew this. We'll soak cloths in it and then, when your time is near, we'll poultice you and the baby will have an easier time making his appearance."

As a labor pain wrenched her, Nan paused, turning to grasp Sunny's elbows. Sunny braced herself to withstand Nan's fierce grip.

"They're getting closer together," Lavina commented, looking up from her sewing.

Slumping with evident relief after the contraction, Nan leaned her head on Sunny's shoulder, gasping for air. "That was a hard one."

Sunny felt helpless. She could do nothing to ease her friend's pain. But Lavina was right—the pains were much closer together now and seemed more powerful. That was good news, hard but good. *God, protect my friend Nan in this time. Please.*

"It's near past supper time. I'm going to make sand-

wiches and take them out to the men and children."
Lavina rose and began preparations.

"Let's see how you're doing, Nan." Mrs. Ashford
motioned toward a makeshift pallet near the fire, prepared for the birthing. Nan had refused to use her bed
for the messy business of childbearing.

Sunny helped her friend lie down and endure the in-
trusive examination. Averting her eyes, she wondered
what Noah was thinking.

Noah had been so angry about her and Nan encoun-
tering the bear. Did that mean he cared? She remembered giving birth to Dawn. No man had waited like
Gordy was. But Noah would care; he already had taken
to Dawn, hadn't he?

Noah and Gordy had finished chopping enough kindling to last the family for a month or two. Now back
on the log, the fathers each held a child. Staying calm
for Gordy's sake, Noah swallowed the question that
had plagued him repeatedly since he arrived: How are
things going?

A pained moan—very loud, very long—came from
inside.

Gordy jerked up as if to go inside, but remained in
place.

Noah's heart thudded dully.

A long low bellow issued from the cabin, louder and
filled with pain and hurt.

Goose bumps rose on Noah's arms.

Gordy moaned and then uttered a fervent prayer,
"Oh, God, oh, God, take care of my Nan. What would
I do without her?"

Noah felt the words as his own. *Oh, God, oh, God, what would I do without Sunny and Dawn?*

Almost two hours later, with the spent sun nearly setting, Sunny came outside, beaming. "Gordy, your daughter's been born. You can come in now."

The weight lifted in an instant. Noah rose up and clapped Gordy on the back. "A girl! You've got a daughter!"

Gordy looked punch-drunk. "How's my wife?"

"Very tired but well," Mrs. Ashford said as she came out, pulling on her shawl. "Mr. Whitmore, would you hitch up my team?"

Gordy wrung the woman's hand. "Thank you, ma'am. Thank you." Then he swung his son up into his arms. "Let's go see your baby sister!"

Mrs. Ashford smiled and bustled toward Noah who had hurried to do the hitching. After he waved the storekeeper's wife off, he turned to find Sunny, who waited outside for him.

When he came abreast of Sunny, he murmured, "Is everything all right?"

"Yes, not a bad delivery according to Mrs. Ashford. She is a very competent midwife. That's good to know."

Then his throat closed up. Sunny's words about the midwife repeated in his mind. The import of what she said hit him. She meant if she ever got pregnant, a competent midwife lived nearby. Would he ever feel able to give Sunny children?

"Here she is," Gordy said, coming to the door and holding up a tiny red-faced baby wrapped in a small white blanket.

Noah tried to look appreciative but he'd never seen

a newborn. No doubt the baby would look better as she got older.

"Beautiful," Sunny said from his side.

Lavina joined the knot at the door. "Nan will be lying in for a few days. I'll stay to help tonight."

"I'll come tomorrow," Sunny said. "I can come some every day." She looked to Noah as if asking approval.

"Of course," he said, unable to look away.

Dawn tugged on his pant leg and he swung her up in his arms.

"Sunny!"

Much later that night the sound of her name woke Sunny from a deep, exhausted sleep. Had she imagined it?

"Sunny!" The cry split the silence.

She sat bolt upright on her bedding. Her eyes adjusted to the dim light from the banked fire. Up in the loft Noah began moaning. Another nightmare.

She looked to Dawn. Noah's distress had not woken her yet.

"Sunny, Sunny," he moaned as if beseeching her to save him.

Sunny couldn't bear it. Throwing back her quilt, she hurried to the ladder and climbed up into the loft.

Noah thrashed, fighting his blankets. "Noah," she said in a firm, loud voice. She reached over and shook his shoulder. "Noah, you're having a nightmare." She repeated this several times, still shaking his shoulder more and more insistently.

Then he jerked and sat up. "What…what?"

"Noah, you were having a nightmare," she said in

an even tone without any scold in it. "You were calling my name."

He stared at her.

Was he fully awake? "Noah?" she whispered.

"Sorry." His voice was rough and dry.

"No need to apologize. I was just concerned." She patted his arm. "I'll sit with you till you fall asleep again."

"No need," he replied gruffly. "Sorry I bothered you."

Men didn't show weakness, she reminded herself. Nevertheless she had to choke down the urge to offer comfort again. "Good night then." She went to the ladder and then climbed down.

On the main floor she checked on Dawn, sleeping peacefully in her hammock, and then slipped between her quilts again. Would the nightmares ever end? She'd asked him, thinking she could help Noah by talking them out. He'd shut her out. Everything within her yearned toward this man, her husband. Oh, to have the privilege of holding him and comforting him. But the truth chilled her. *He doesn't want me. And maybe I'm not what he needs.*

Chapter Eight

Sunny felt shy with Noah at breakfast. Perhaps because she'd never before gone up into the loft when he had been there. She'd never tried to help him in the midst of his nightmares. Had she done right or wrong?

Right, she told herself. *He is my husband.*

She dragged her mind back to the present. She and Noah sat on opposite benches at the new table, eating a silent breakfast of cinnamon buns and salt pork. Dawn had crawled down from her lap and was trying to climb up onto the bench beside Noah. Sunny put down her cup. "I'll get her."

"No." Noah set down his fork. He lifted the little girl to sit on his lap. Dawn cooed happily and patted the edge of the table with both her palms. "She's always so happy." Wonderment resonated in Noah's voice.

Sunny had a hard time swallowing. Dawn somehow was able to pierce Noah's shell in a way that she couldn't. "She is a blessing," Sunny murmured.

"I'm so glad that Nan and the baby came through well." Relief radiated from each of Noah's words. He looked closely at her, as if watching for her reaction.

Impulsively, she reached over and barely touched his hand lying on the table. "Me, too." Why was he still looking at her like that? Like there was something he wanted to say?

Careful not to overstep this fragile link between them, she removed her hand and went back to eating the last of her breakfast. As they ate, Dawn's cooing and the birdsong from outside were the only sounds.

"Noah, I'm going to clean up after breakfast and do my morning chores. Then I'm going over to help with Nan and the baby. Is that all right?"

"Of course," Noah said as he helped Dawn stand up on his lap and then held her under her arms while she bobbed up and down. Dawn leaned against his chest, hugging him and talking baby talk to him.

She could tell Noah was taking pleasure in Dawn's innocent glee. And she was happy that Dawn could take him away from his cares, even if she couldn't.

"Sorry...about last night," Noah said as if he'd been struggling with what to say all morning.

"It was nothing, Noah," she assured him. "I'll leave your lunch keeping warm in the back of the hearth." In spite of his dark mood, Noah had eaten four of her cinnamon rolls, and that made her feel she wasn't completely a failure at being a good wife.

"Fine. I'm going to start clearing more land for our garden. Gordy and I are going to help each other get everything planted as soon as the frost danger is past, near the end of this month."

"I've never tended a garden," she admitted, rising to clear the table. No gardens behind saloons. For her whole life until she'd lived with the Gabriels, all her food had come from cafés. What did Noah think of a wife who'd never tended a garden?

"It's not hard to learn," Noah said, wiping his lips with his colorful pocket handkerchief. "I'll teach you what weeds look like and then it's just a matter of watering and weeding." He rose, still holding Dawn.

Something Old Saul had said in a recent sermon came into her mind, about their lives being like gardens and prayers being the key to weeding out the bad. *I need to pray for my husband more.*

Noah handed her Dawn, who complained loudly. He touched Dawn's nose and promised to play with her later.

Constance Gabriel had taught Sunny that she could pray anytime and anywhere and in any way. Sunny had always felt that she had no right to claim God's ear. *But this is for Noah, not me,* she thought.

Sunny felt an almost physical movement around her heart and, with awe, wondered if this was what Constance had meant by the Inner Light.

"Anything wrong?" Noah asked, pausing just outside the door.

Sunny felt herself beaming as the prayer formed in her mind. "No, nothing."

Dear God, heal my Noah's heart.

Noah stood outside, the morning sun warming his head and shoulders. He watched Sunny, carrying Dawn on her hip, on their way to Nan's house. Though glad she was going to help, he found he wished she was staying home.

The wish caught him by surprise.

Sunny always lived up to her name, and Dawn did,

too. He clamped down on the good feeling trying to rise in him. One brief recollection of the humiliation of Sunny climbing up into the loft because he'd wakened her again did the trick. His heart turned to brick.

But he had blessed work to do. He turned to tackle choosing the best place for the garden. He loved string beans and ruby-red beets and their tender greens with scarlet veins that tasted like sugar. His mouth watered just thinking of the produce he'd harvest this summer, God willing. He heard the last two words repeat in his mind, *God willing.* Why had he thought that now?

He gazed up at the green trees, singing with the breeze. But got no answer. He loved this forest. However it did make finding a full-sun area difficult. And a garden needed water, too. He started walking toward the creek, trying to block out Sunny's concerned expression over breakfast. *I've got her walking on eggs again and I don't want her to feel that way.*

No matter how he tried to keep her out, Sunny kept finding her way back into his thoughts.

The sound of cheery whistling announced that Gordy had come as promised. "Mornin', Noah!"

Noah turned to greet the man, noticing how different his neighbor looked today. The tension of the birthing had melted away and now a proud, happy father marched into the clearing. Gordy carried his ax over his shoulder and a smile covered his face.

"Morning. How's your wife and babe?"

"Fine. When he was a baby, Guthrie was some colicky, but this one—we named her after my ma and Nan's, Pearl Louise—just whimpers a little when she's hungry."

Noah let the man's good humor and joy flow over

him. Gordy had a right to feel good. Noah refused to let his mind drift back to Sunny.

"Well, where do you think you want your garden?" Gordy asked.

"I'm thinking near the creek. More sun there and water will be near if the rain is sparse."

"Good thinking. Let's see the lay of the land." They walked together to the nearby creek.

Noah decided then that he'd try to work himself to exhaustion today and then perhaps he'd sleep so sound he wouldn't dream and disturb Sunny.

He hadn't made it more than five seconds without thinking of her again.

"Have you ever sent a letter?" Gordy asked out of the blue.

With a pang Noah recalled all the letters he'd written while encamped in the army, letters to his brothers who always wrote back. But never to his father. Those dark days gripped him momentarily. "Yes…yes."

"I've never done it. Never had to. But I need to write and tell my family and Nan's that we have a daughter and that we're doing well. I feel bad we haven't written home before now."

Noah heard in his mind his elder brother's words at his wedding about keeping in touch. "I haven't written my…brothers, either."

"Who do you think handles the post hereabouts?"

"Probably Ashford. Usually if there isn't a post office, the post comes to the general store. Sunny and I are going to town for seeds—we can pick up paper and ink, if you need it."

Gordy nodded and hefted his ax handle in his hand. "Let's get your garden plot cleared today. And we'll tackle mine tomorrow." He looked up at the cloudless sky. "If this weather holds. We'll almost be farmers then."

The two walked up and down the creek and chose a spot on an upper slope of one the gentle hills. The slight elevation would keep a heavy rain from flooding the garden. They chose the trees that needed to be thinned to let full sun fall on the plot for most of the daylight hours. Then the sound of their axes echoed in the clearing. For a brief time, Noah's mind quieted and he was able to work in peace.

Six days later Sunny let Noah help her up onto the bench of their wagon. Then he swung Dawn up to her arms. Soon he sat on her other side and slapped the reins. Sunny had pocketed a list of items for them and for the Osbournes.

The warmth of the sun eased her tension and she relaxed against the back of the bench. She was going to town with her husband and daughter to bring home supplies just like any other family. She glanced at Noah from the corner of her eye. They even looked like every family hereabout.

She'd taken extra care with her appearance and Dawn's, and planned to be very careful in town to look the part of a contented wife and do nothing to call attention to herself. Her concern over saying or doing something that would reveal her past was becoming a burden. Would it lift in time?

Dawn had learned to patty-cake and was showing off, trying to get Noah to pay attention to her. And it was working. The grim mood he'd awakened with appeared to be lightening.

Soon they pulled into town and halted in front of the general store. Sunny's easy happiness vanished in a blink.

Mr. Ashford was chasing a woman from his store and swatting her back with his broom, hard. A little boy was hitting Ashford's leg, yelling for him to stop.

Without thinking, Sunny jumped down, throwing herself between the storekeeper and woman. The broom came down upon her back with force, nearly knocking the wind from her. She cried out.

No second blow fell. Instead Mr. Ashford cried out in shock.

Sunny whirled around to see Noah jerk the broom from the storekeeper's hands. He threw the man backward against his store, pinning Ashford to the window with the broom across his neck. Murder blazed in his expression.

Everything had happened so fast, leaving Sunny shaken by her own behavior as much as anyone else's. "I'm all right, Noah," she said, hurrying to pick up Dawn where Noah had set her on the wooden sidewalk.

Mr. Ashford made a gurgling sound, his face turning red.

"Noah," Sunny implored, hurrying to him. "You can let Mr. Ashford go."

"I didn't mean to hit your wife," the storekeeper croaked with difficulty. "Just that thieving woman."

Noah stepped back, releasing the man. He still held the broom like a sparring stick.

The storekeeper rubbed his neck and gasped. "She was stealing from me…behind my back…that Indian."

Indian? Sunny turned to see the woman racing north along the river with a little child by the hand.

A horrific scene from Sunny's childhood streaked through her and she started off, calling after the woman. She caught up, panting. "Please, please!" she called. "Stop!"

The woman ran on and Sunny pursued her.

Then Sunny got a hitch in her side and had to stop. She leaned over, gasping and rubbing her side.

"Are you all right?" a hesitant voice asked.

Sunny looked up into the woman's pinched face and, between gasps, asked the same question, "Are you all right?"

"I am sorry the storekeeper hit you."

Sunny nearly repeated the same words, but stopped herself. Instead she let the woman help her to stand upright again. "I just got a stitch in my side."

The woman was wearing clothes much like Sunny's, not the buckskin dress of Indian women out West. Sunny offered the woman her hand. "I'm Sunny Whitmore. This is my daughter, Dawn."

The woman looked surprised but shook Sunny's hand. "Then her name is like mine. I am Bid'a ban. It means It Begins to Dawn. This is my son, Miigwans, Little Feather."

Sunny listened but paid more attention to how shabby their clothing was and how thin they looked. The woman would have been pretty if her face hadn't been so drawn and her eyes so desperate. "You need help," Sunny said simply.

Bid'a ban pressed her lips together.

"I'm sorry. Sometimes I speak out of turn." But Sunny didn't leave. This woman obviously needed aid urgently. Sunny knew how the edge of desperation could cut deeply. The little boy looked to be about ten years old. He clung to his mother's hand as if ready to defend her yet uncertain if he could.

"I do need help," the woman admitted. "Since my man was killed in the war, I have…trouble."

"The war? You mean the War Between the States?"

"Yes, my man fought for the Union. Many Ojibwa, or white call us Chippewa and Winnebago, went to war," the woman continued.

"My husband did, too."

The two women gazed at each other, linked by this connection. Sunny couldn't ignore the need she saw. And there was more to the story than the woman would admit—Sunny could see it in her eyes.

She heard Noah coming up behind her. She cringed, wondering how he was taking this.

At first she couldn't make herself look into his face. Nonetheless she felt the waves of tension flowing from him. A stolen glance upward told her that he was clearly angry.

"Bid'a ban, where do you live?" she asked.

"Along the river, the Chippewa." The woman motioned northward. "About three miles north from town."

Sunny nodded. "I'll come visit you. Soon."

The woman took one look at Noah's face and then turned and began walking briskly away, her son in hand.

"We got shopping to do," Noah said curtly.

Sunny merely nodded. Now wasn't the time to contradict him. She knew why he'd become upset with her. She'd made a scene, which was exactly what Noah wanted to avoid at all costs.

She hurried alongside him to the store. Inside, the atmosphere was strained, wrapping around her, nearly smothering her.

"I'm sorry, Mrs. Whitmore. I didn't mean to strike you," Mr. Ashford said stiffly.

"I know you didn't, Mr. Ashford. I just acted...without thinking. I put myself in the way of hurt." Sunny smiled though she felt like telling the man what she thought of his actions.

Noah fumed silently at her side.

"I'm very sorry," she apologized again, though the words nearly stuck in her throat.

"No problem, ma'am. What can I do for you today?"

One glance told Sunny that Noah remained too upset to speak. "We need seed for our garden, writing materials and a few other items. We're also picking up things for the Osbournes." She removed the list from her pocket. She and the storekeeper went through the list with Noah a brooding presence.

Finally Noah carried out the newspaper-wrapped packages. Mr. Ashford hovered near Sunny at the door. "I'm really sorry. We don't have any law hereabouts and what's a man to do to protect his property?"

Sunny checked her own feelings, making sure she concealed them. "Mr. Ashford, I understand completely." Sunny didn't like prevarication, but she knew better than to say that she understood thievery couldn't be tolerated but that this was a case of unmistakable need. "Please give Mrs. Ashford my kind regards."

He smiled and nodded, finally looking relieved.

Noah helped Sunny up onto the wagon. Dawn was fussing, wanting to nurse. Sunny soothed her till they drove into the cover of the trees. Then she put the child to nurse and prayed for the right words.

"I'm sorry, Noah. I didn't mean to make a scene."

He did not reply.

Sunny held herself together. Noah might be angry but he wasn't going to strike her or leave her. He just needed time to cool off. Then she could discuss the widow's plight. Sunny silently rolled the unusual names around in her mouth, Bid'a ban and Miigwans. Sunny had never realized that Indians might have fought in the same war as Noah. Sunny knew what having no one to turn to felt like. She'd faced life alone—after her mother died. She recalled the day a man had attacked her mother and her, just like Bid'a ban. Would she be able to make Noah understand why she must do something to help this woman and child? Or would she have to do it against his disapproval?

At home Noah helped her down. Dawn slept in her arms so she went inside to lay the child into the hammock. Noah and she carried in the packages from the store, then he left the cabin without a word. She heard through the open door Noah unhitch the oxen and then put the cattle to graze among the trees. They had intended to stop at the Osbournes and leave their supplies, but obviously Noah was in no mood to visit neighbors.

Burdened with a heaviness, Sunny washed her hands outside, then refilled the pitcher with water. Inside she lifted off her bonnet and donned her apron. With a pot-holder she lifted the kettle she'd left simmering at the back away from the fire. The grouse stew with beans and wild mushrooms would be ready when Noah came in.

She bowed her head. Unbidden the parable of the Good Samaritan came to mind.

The Gabriels had explained the story to her. A man who had been beaten up by thieves and left for dead. Two holy people had walked by without helping him, till the Samaritan—a person considered to be unholy—had stopped and cared for the man. Everyone in Pepin—if they knew the truth about her—probably would class her as a Samaritan. So she'd do what the Good Samaritan had done. Somehow, someway, she'd help this woman. Whether Noah agreed or not.

"Noah! Come eat!" she called later, stepping outside. She waited.

He didn't come.

She picked up Dawn and listened, shushing the child's prattle. She heard Noah working on the spring house foundation. She took a deep breath and headed toward him. He'd had a couple of hours to calm down, but regardless, they needed to eat. "Noah, dinner's ready."

Noah stood hip deep in the shallow pit he'd dug around the natural spring that he'd found on their land. He paused in his work, leaning on his shovel.

"I know you're upset with me," she said conversationally but with determination. "But we need to talk about what's bothering you and then eat our dinner without upset stomachs."

Noah did not look up, which wasn't like him.

She'd spent hours pondering how to get him to talk about what had upset him, to get it out into the daylight. "I know you don't want us to stand out different than others. I didn't mean to make a scene in town. But I didn't do it on purpose. I couldn't help myself."

Noah still wouldn't look at her.

She jiggled Dawn, who was trying to get down to go to Noah. Sunny felt the same urge. Perhaps she should just tell him here and now.

"Noah, when I was a little girl, one preacher in a

town we lived in for a short while would stand out in front of the saloon and shout at the women inside."

She had tried to forget this incident. "One day my mother and I were walking home from eating at the café and he came out of a store and started shouting at my mother, calling her a harlot and worse. Then he snatched up a walking stick and began hitting my mother. She picked me up and ran for the saloon."

A lonely mourning dove cooed in a nearby tree. Even Dawn had stilled. Sunny's voice had gotten away from her and had come out with stronger emotion than she wanted to show. The memory still had the power to make her tremble.

"No one helped us. They just watched him beat her as we ran. When we got safely through the saloon doors, he stopped. But he kept shouting till the bartender brought out his shotgun and threatened the man." She looked at Noah for any sign of understanding.

"No one helped us," she repeated in a whisper. She refused to cry. All that had happened so long ago. She hugged Dawn to her, thanking God no one would ever do that to her little girl.

Finally Noah climbed out of the spring house foundation. He looked like he didn't know what to say. "You said dinner was ready?"

She nodded, looking away.

"Then let's go eat."

Sunny wanted more than this, knew Noah needed to talk this out to let it go. But evidently he wasn't ready. She pressed her lips together. She would wait and pray.

But she would also go tomorrow and find Bid'a ban and help her. And there was nothing anyone could do to stop her. Not even Noah Whitmore.

* * *

The next morning, Noah rubbed his gritty eyes. He hadn't had any nightmares last night because he hadn't slept. He kept seeing Ashford hitting his wife. Then he imagined Sunny as a little girl running from a preacher who was beating her mother.

Sunny poured his coffee and he wrapped his hands around its warmth. He had rarely given much thought about Sunny's life before they'd met. But now he knew she'd been born into the saloon. And that moved him.

Sunny sat down with her coffee across from him. Their plates of breakfast sitting untouched. Dawn sat on the floor, knocking over blocks and prattling. He sipped the steaming coffee in a strained silence at the table. He wanted to speak, to comfort Sunny, to make things right. But how?

She cleared her throat. "Noah, I want to take the horse north along the shore to the river and find that woman. If I can. She's hungry and it's not right to leave her and the boy that way."

Shocked at this unexpected request, Noah put down his cup. "You want to what?"

She repeated her intentions. What caught him was that she sounded like she expected him to argue with her. Was that what she thought of him? "I would never let any woman go hungry," he said fiercely.

Sunny rested her hand beside his. "I know you wouldn't but after yesterday, I didn't know if you'd want me to go after her. People don't think much of Indians—"

He cut her off with a sweep of his hand. "That doesn't weigh with me." The words he'd held back rolled forth.

"Yesterday upset me because Ashford struck you. I'm supposed to protect you."

Silence. Then Sunny wrapped a hand over his. "Thank you, Noah, you did protect me. And today I don't think anybody will bother me, but I have to help this woman. She doesn't have anyone else to turn to."

He recalled the times when he'd tried to help others. "Some people don't like taking charity. I haven't met many Indians, but they're proud people."

"Maybe she doesn't need charity," Sunny replied. "She told me her husband served in the Union Army and was killed. Shouldn't she be getting a widow's pension?"

"Her husband was a soldier?" He sat up straighter. Indignation burned in his stomach.

"I want to find her, help her get what's coming to her," Sunny said.

"She should be getting her husband's pension," Noah stated firmly. "The government promised that." He turned the problem over in his mind. "She may not have told you the truth about where she's living. I've heard the government is trying to move all the Indians hereabout out of Wisconsin."

Sunny frowned. "I don't think she lied to me. She said her place was north on the Chippewa River."

"The Chippewa does run north of town. It flows into the Mississippi." He began to calculate how to get there, how long it would take.

"Would you let me take the horse? And some food?" Sunny sounded determined but uncertain. "I don't want to leave her in need."

"No."

Her face fell.

"I'll take you myself. I can't let you go alone. Why would you think I'd let you do this alone?"

"Noah, I'm sorry." She reached for his hand, smiling tremulously. "I didn't understand. You didn't tell me."

He offered her a shrug in apology and then picked up his fork. His stomach burned and he had no appetite, but he needed strength to do this. "We better eat and then get ready to go."

"Yes, Noah." She looked at him as if he'd just done something special. That kind of hurt. *I should be kinder to my wife. I'm not doing a very good job of being a good husband.*

Chapter Nine

Noah stood beside the table, figuring out how to do this thing, how to go to help this widow in need. They couldn't take the wagon since there probably wasn't a road or even a trail where they would be going.

As usual, Dawn had gravitated to his side. Her constant preference for him managed to lighten his heavy heart. As he looked down into Dawn's eager face, he had an idea. "Sunny, I need a large dishcloth or a baby blanket."

Sunny looked surprised.

"I need to make something so we can carry Dawn with us on horseback."

Sunny nodded, though obviously mystified, and got him one of Dawn's smaller blankets.

"While I get this rigged up, you gather some food and necessities for the woman and her boy." While he sounded as if this were an everyday occurrence, he carried this new responsibility as a palpable burden.

Sunny gathered some essentials, such as food and pans, and stowed them in a couple of flour sacks while Noah folded the blanket corner to corner and tied it over one shoulder. As he did so, he considered the possibility that he was planning, once again, to go against the community he lived within. The thought didn't please him.

"Oh, you're making a little hammock for her," Sunny said.

He nodded. "I saw women working in the fields in the South carry their babies like this. See? My hands are free."

"I'll put a fresh diaper on her and two extra soakers."

He smiled at her thoughtfulness. And her kind nature. Of course Sunny wouldn't let this widow and fatherless child suffer.

Soon they were outside. Dawn didn't mind Noah settling her against him. In fact, she looked happy to be so close to him. He tried not to let this hearten him and failed. Dawn had captured him all right.

He climbed on the saddle and then helped Sunny up behind him. The sacks of provisions and necessities had been hung on the saddle or tucked into the saddlebags. Through the towering trees Noah set off westward toward the river. He wondered what she'd do if they couldn't find the woman and her boy.

Even worse, they would have to ride through town. He hadn't wanted to go there again so soon. He'd wanted to give people a chance to exhaust all the gossip about Sunny and Ashford. But it couldn't be avoided. A soldier's widow needed help. And they had to go where he could follow the river.

When they rode through town, Noah tried to keep his mind blank. The emotions and images from the day before kept trying to rise up and bring back the anger he'd burned with when he saw Ashford hit Sunny. The magnitude of his rage had scared him—still scared him.

For those few moments he'd lost control, consumed by fury. Finally Sunny's voice, her gentle voice, urgent but soothing, had penetrated his fiery haze. That had saved him. *She* had saved him.

"Sunny," he said, "I was upset at Ashford for striking you. But if we stood out as different than everybody else, it was my anger, not your…charity."

Sunny pressed against his back and tightened her arms linked around him under Dawn's sling. "Maybe we can't help being a bit different," she said in a hesitant voice for his ears only. "I mean, you and me have lived different lives than most around here…" Her voice trailed off.

He pressed a hand over hers for a moment to show he understood. His tongue tied again, he couldn't speak more. They rode unflinchingly through town, mostly deserted today. As if nothing was wrong, he doffed his hat at a woman coming out of the store and Sunny called out a friendly greeting.

When they put town behind them, Noah breathed easier but the thought of trying to find the Indian woman tightened his nerves—for many reasons.

They covered the remaining miles northward along the Mississippi till they reached the mouth of the Chippewa, flowing into the wide blue. Then they turned their backs to the big river and started eastward. Noah thought of the hungry woman. He'd never known hunger till serving in the army. It gnawed and weakened a person, sharpening every bad feeling.

Much to Noah's relief they'd only ridden a few miles upriver when he saw a thin trail of smoke above the trees. "See," he said to Sunny, pointing to it. "That might be her fire." He urged his mount through the trees toward the smoke, hoping their quest had come to an end. They came out of the forest to a tiny rough clearing with the ruin of an old cabin, only half its roof intact.

The little boy stood in the gap where there should have been a door. Upon sight of them he ducked farther inside.

"Don't be afraid!" Sunny called out. "I'm the lady who helped you in town yesterday. My husband and I have come like I promised. Where's your mother?"

The little boy stepped outside. "Please. Come. She has a fever."

Noah slid down and helped Sunny dismount. "Go on."

Sunny hurried inside with Noah bringing up the rear. A low fire burned in the old fireplace and Bid'a ban lay by it, wrapped in a tattered blanket. "I've…we've come to help," Sunny said simply, and knelt down by the woman.

With a soft exclamation Bid'a ban turned to her, looking starved and wan.

Sunny felt her forehead and then looked up at Noah. "She is feverish. I'll need to make her some willow tea and something to eat." She patted the woman's arm. "Don't worry now. I'll do my best for you."

Bid'a ban gripped her hand weakly and tried to speak but couldn't.

Hurriedly, Noah brought in the saddlebags and lay them on the hard earth floor by his wife. The woman's sickly pallor drained his relief at finding her. "I'm going to keep Dawn away from the contagion."

"Good." Sunny didn't even glance at him. "But please. I need water."

"I'll get some," the little boy said. He grabbed a water skin hanging by the fire and hurried outside.

Noah followed and watched the boy fill the skin with river water. Dawn had fallen snugly asleep against him. The dilapidated wreck of a cabin, probably built by a fur trapper years and years ago, depressed him. He brooded about Bid'a ban's husband, no doubt buried somewhere far from home.

The boy's father hadn't wanted this for his wife and son. Resolve hardened inside Noah. He couldn't help the thousands of war widows and orphans, but he could help this family—or what remained of it.

The boy hurried past Noah.

"After you take that inside, we're going to gather wood and then fish," Noah said.

"You got a hook and line?" The boy glanced up at him then, his eyes shadowed with fear.

"Always." He remembered to smile as he followed toward the door. "Don't you worry. My wife is good at nursing people to health." He didn't know where this assurance had come from, but Sunny had shown herself to be wise in many ways.

The boy came outside. Noah offered his hand. "I'm Noah Whitmore."

"I'm Miigwans." He put out his small hand, trusting Noah's larger one.

Noah gripped it, letting the boy feel his support. Standing just outside the doorway, Noah watched Sunny quickly fill the trivet pot they'd brought. She set it in the fire to heat.

The woman seemed even weaker than yesterday. She barely made a sound or said a word. Sunny bathed her face with water.

Noah hoped the woman wasn't as close to death as she appeared from her sunken eyes. But he could do nothing for her just standing here.

He forced himself to speak without betraying worry. "Miigwans, let's find us a willow branch for a fishing pole." The two headed for the riverbank, thick with black willow trees. "Your mother is in good hands."

The boy reluctantly walked beside Noah, looking back at the cabin. Noah gripped the boy's shoulder, encouraging him. "We're here. Don't worry." He knew he was saying it as much for himself as the boy.

The long chilly night had ended. Sunny's knees ached from kneeling on the cold hard earth beside Bid'a ban. Had her help come soon enough for this woman? Would she recover fully from this fever?

In the thin light of morning falling on them from the open roof, Sunny gazed at Noah. Sound asleep, he rested back against the wall, his long legs stretched out in front of him. Dawn slept on his chest in the sling that he still wore. And opposite Dawn, Miigwans rested his head on Noah's belly, one arm thrown over him.

This sight told her everything about her husband. Once again she suppressed the physical pull toward him. *Lord, You gave me a good man.*

"Sunny?" Bid'a ban said, her voice a thread.

Sunny glanced down. "Good morning." With an encouraging smile, she rested her wrist on the woman's forehead. "Your fever broke early this morning."

"I feel so weak."

Sunny forced the worry from her voice. "That's the fever's work. But we'll get you back to health soon." Sunny knew that fevers that might not kill could still weaken a heart, a life. She prayed that wouldn't be the case with this brave woman.

"Her fever broke?" Noah asked softly.

Sunny had a hard time holding in her gratitude toward him. Pressing down the words she wanted to say, she merely nodded.

"Let's have some of that oatmeal then and head home."

Oh, no, she couldn't leave yet. "Noah, I can't—"

"We'll *all* go home. We can't leave them here like this." Noah addressed Bid'a ban. "Ma'am, you and your boy will come home with us. You need to get your strength back and we need to write the government about your widow's pension."

Bid'a ban began to weep.

Sunny understood. They were tears of relief. She patted the woman's shoulder. "Don't worry any more. My Noah will see that you get what's coming to you."

"I will," Noah promised.

Suddenly Sunny realized a plain, simple, lovely truth: she had fallen in love with her husband.

If only he loved her back.

Dread pooled in Sunny's middle. Just ahead lay town. And they must ride through it. The dense forest away from the flats of the Mississippi shore made travel too difficult. She and Bid'a ban rode on the horse. Noah had strapped the weak woman to Sunny so she wouldn't fall off. Miigwans walked beside Noah, who still carried Dawn in the sling. Her sweet daughter prattled happily, occasionally playing patty-cake to make Noah smile.

Sleeping nearly outside and not being able to shake out their clothing or even comb their hair—what a sight they would be. And with Bid'a ban and her son with them. Sunny knew the deep prejudice that most whites felt toward Indians.

She braced herself and lifted her chin higher.

They entered town. And only then did Sunny remember that it was Sunday. Her stomach sank to her knees. Nearly the whole community had gathered in front of Ashford's store. And nearly the whole community turned to gawk at them. Sunny refused to bow her head. Stolidly she gazed at the faces turned toward her as if she weren't doing anything unusual.

"Morning, Mr. and Mrs. Whitmore!" Old Saul called out from Ashford's porch.

Noah doffed his hat but kept moving. Sunny nodded, acknowledging the older man's greeting. But they didn't pause. No one else said a word. Not even Gordy, there without Nan who was still lying in. That cut deep.

Well, they'd done it now. Nothing could have made them stand out more than what they'd just done. But Sunny couldn't feel any dismay. And Noah looked determined in spite of it all. They might be outcasts from now on, but she couldn't have stayed home and done nothing.

She—*they*—had done the right thing.

The next afternoon Noah heard the sound of a wagon coming close. Miigwans was helping him finish the spring house. After their parade through town during Sunday meeting, Noah couldn't guess who was coming or what to expect. Then he saw Old Saul driving into the clearing.

"That old man was in town yesterday," Miigwans said.

Who had Miigwans thought was coming? "Yes, he's

the preacher hereabouts. Come on." Noah's strained voice grated his throat. "We need to wash our hands and be polite."

The two of them cleaned up and then Noah grimly strode to the wagon, dreading this visit. *I don't care what he says or what people think.*

Noah took a deep breath and rested a hand on Miigwans's shoulder. "Good day, Preacher."

"Call me Old Saul," the old man said.

After a polite nod, Noah helped him down as he had the last visit.

"Who is this young fellow?"

Noah introduced Miigwans, who was too shy to speak.

"I'm stiff," Old Saul said. "It would be good for me to walk a bit. Show me how you're doing on that spring house."

"Miigwans has been helping me," Noah replied, letting the man lean on his arm. Surely the preacher had heard about the ruckus in town between him and Ashford and he must have come to put his two cents in. Irritation bit and chewed on Noah's mood.

The older man stood by the spring house, nodding with approval. "You've done well. I think I could use a cup of that good spring water of yours. I hear from Lavina you finished that table I saw you making on my last visit."

After fetching the water, Noah led Saul to the house. The moment had come to introduce him to Bid'a ban. "Sunny, the preacher's here."

"I heard," she replied. "Come in. I have the kettle on and am making fresh coffee."

"Noah's got spring water for me, but after that, a cup

of coffee would be welcome, ma'am. And who is this?" he asked, after he crossed the threshold.

Standing beside Bid'a ban, who was lying in bedding near the fire, Sunny performed the introductions. Bid'a ban looked fearful and Noah wondered if she feared white people in general or some in particular.

Old Saul surprised Noah by kneeling beside the woman and taking her hand. "I'm so glad you found the help you needed, ma'am." Then the old preacher said a prayer over her. "Miigwans," he said. "I can get down by myself but I need a hand up."

The little boy hurried to help him to his feet. Noah came, too, in case he was needed. He wanted to thank the old preacher for his prayer and kindness, but words couldn't fit through Noah's tight throat.

Old Saul patted the boy's shoulder. "Thank you, son. Noah, I'll take that cold water now."

Miigwans stayed beside his mother while Noah and Old Saul sat at the table. The older man ran his hand over the tabletop appreciatively. "I heard all about Ashford hitting your wife and then saw you ride through town with Bid'a ban and I figured out what had happened. I came to see if I could help."

This struck Noah completely speechless.

Sunny spoke up. "Noah is going to write to Washington, D.C., for Bid'a ban so she can get her widow's pension. Her husband served with the Union Army."

Old Saul shook his head with evident sorrow. "We lost so many good men. War brings such suffering that words fail me."

Then a familiar voice from outside hailed them, "Hello, the house!"

"It's Martin!" Sunny exclaimed and got up, hurrying toward the door.

Noah and Old Saul trailed after her. Noah glanced at Martin's round, honest face and grinned in spite of himself. The man sat beside a pretty woman and looked about to burst with pride. "Who is this lady with you, Martin?" Noah teased.

"This is my bride, Ophelia Steward. We won't get down. I just wanted Ophelia to see where our closest neighbors live." Then Martin carried out the introductions.

Ophelia was a pretty little thing with curly brown hair and big brown eyes. But if she had aged a day over seventeen Noah would eat his old hat.

Martin waved toward the back of his wagon where a cow was tied and a noisy crate of chickens sat. "I brought extra chickens to give you and the Osbournes so you'll have eggs. And now we'll have a milk cow, too."

Noah congratulated him and thanked him for his generosity.

"I'll come over and visit as soon as I can," Sunny was saying. "We're so glad you are here. Martin has worked so hard to make a home for you."

Old Saul stepped forward. "We hope to see you this Sunday, weather permitting."

"Yes, sir," Ophelia said, "we'll be there."

"You'll find you have another new neighbor," Noah said.

Martin glanced at him. "Somebody else staked a homestead claim?"

"No, Nan and Gordy have a little girl now."

"Well, that's fine," Martin said, beaming. "We'll go

now and meet our newest neighbor." Then the young man's face changed. "Who's that standing in the door?"

Noah braced himself, hoping Martin wouldn't turn against them as Gordy seemed to have done. "Miigwans, come here and meet our neighbors."

The little boy reluctantly came to stand beside Noah.

"He and his mother are staying with us till she feels better." Noah read the shock on both Martin's and Ophelia's faces as they took in that Miigwans wasn't white.

The newlyweds left soon after this realization. Noah stiffened inside.

"They're young," Old Saul said. "They haven't lived among strangers like you have, Noah."

Noah looked into the wrinkled face. How did this old man sense things, sense Noah's feelings? Then he noticed Saul's fatigue. "Why don't we go inside so you can finish your coffee?"

Old Saul took Noah's arm and the two walked slowly into the cabin. Noah settled him into the rocker and brought his coffee to him.

Sunny looked worried and quickly sliced some corn bread and sprinkled it with sugar for Saul and then gave some to everyone.

"I thank you for that," Old Saul said. "I was feeling down." After he'd finished the snack, he looked at Noah. "Will you help me to my wagon?"

Noah moved to help Saul up, walked him out to the wagon and then boosted him up onto the bench.

Old Saul thanked him. "I can remember being a young sprout like that boy inside. I couldn't sit still and now I'm as creaky as a rusted gate." He shook his head ruefully. "You and Sunny have done right to help this woman and child."

"Most won't like it."

"God loves everyone regardless of their color. Don't let what others think keep you away on Sunday."

Noah didn't think highly of this suggestion. "I'll talk to Sunny."

"Then I know I'll see you on Sunday. You married a strong woman. Pretty, too." He grinned and slapped the reins and soon the old wagon rocked away down the uneven track.

Sunny met Noah outside. "Don't take it so hard. Martin and his bride will come around. And the Osbournes, too. They're good people."

Noah shrugged. "It doesn't matter. We did right. Did what we needed to do."

Sunny leaned forward and rested her head on his chest. "That's right." Then she turned and hurried inside.

Awash in a flow of emotion and sensation, Noah watched her go and watched Miigwans come to him.

"Are we going to work some more?" the boy asked.

Noah ruffled his dark chocolate-colored hair. "Yes. Come on." As he walked toward the spring house, he recalled what Sunny had said to him before about their being different because their lives had been so different. They had that in common, all right. And he went over what Saul had said. He had married a strong woman. And that was right and made him proud.

Noah knew too well how it felt to be rejected for being out of the ordinary. If his neighbors didn't like them taking in these two—so be it.

Sunday morning had come and Noah climbed down the ladder from the loft, hearing the preacher's words repeat in his mind. His nerves churned. But he knew that they had to go to worship.

Sunny had dressed earlier and was fixing breakfast. Now strong enough to sit at the table, Bid'a ban still looked much too thin and frail. Miigwans had become Noah's shadow, trailing him outside where both of them washed their hands and faces.

Back inside Noah sat down. Dawn crawled to him and pulled herself up beside him, baby talking all the while. He tousled her golden curls, marveling at their softness. Then he announced what he'd decided. "Sunny, we'll be going to Sunday meeting today."

Sunny nearly dropped the ladle of oatmeal she held over Bid'a ban's bowl. "We're going?" Her voice quavered.

"Yes, we are. Old Saul asked us specifically to come." Noah didn't know where his forceful spirit had returned from but he was ready and willing to take on the whole town today.

Sunny sat down and gazed at him intently. Then she nodded. "I'm with you."

Bid'a ban looked back and forth between them as if trying to read the veiled tension. She opened her mouth to say something to Sunny, but seemed to change her mind. Again Noah thought she looked afraid.

"What's the Sunday meeting?" Miigwans asked.

"You remember that older man with the white hair that came to visit?"

Miigwans nodded.

"He is a preacher and on Sundays he tells us about God and how we should live."

"Oh," Miigwans said. "Can I go?"

Sunny was trying to hide her worry, but Noah read

it clearly. "I think you should stay home and take care of your mother today."

"I will." But the boy had caught the unspoken worry and it showed on his face.

Noah patted his arm. "Everything will be fine." He hoped that would be true.

As they left for the meeting, Noah drove over the uneven track and thought about the unfriendly reception they were likely to receive.

On Thursday he'd walked over to Gordy's to give him his seed and such, and had immediately felt an unusual coolness. Maybe not coolness, but more a wariness. He'd helped Gordy log out his garden but he hadn't been invited inside. And Gordy had said that they would be driving into town on Sunday with Martin and his bride, offering no invitation to join them. Even though he'd expected rejection when he'd decided to keep Bid'a ban, he hadn't expected it from Gordy. He drew in a sharp breath. The memory of the ride through town last Sunday rippled through him. But he'd stood up to his own meeting all those years ago. He couldn't back down now.

Finally they drove out of the trees to the flats at the river and joined the gathering in front of Ashford's store. A few people waved to them but most just stared.

Maybe he shouldn't put Sunny through this.

"Do you want to go home?" he whispered to her.

She looked at him and her eyes blazed, reminding him of how she'd looked when she'd put herself between Ashford and Bid'a ban. "No, we have done nothing wrong. We need to face this head on."

Proud of her, he climbed off the bench and went around to help her down. When he lowered her, he took her by the hand and led her to the outskirts of the gathering. Sunny looked at him in surprise, then squeezed his hand. No one welcomed them, though Gordy looked worried and shuffled closer to them. Was he coming to back them or cross them?

Old Saul's son drove up and helped the older man down and to the porch. Lavina waved to Sunny and Sunny returned the gesture. Soon the hymn singing had started. Sunny didn't sing as usual and Noah felt a surge of protectiveness for his obviously uncomfortable yet brave wife. Nobody better say anything rude to her.

Old Saul rose, opened the worn Bible and read, "'Pure religion and undefiled before God and the Father is this, To visit the fatherless and widows in their affliction, and to keep himself unspotted from the world.' St. James tells us this in the first chapter of his book. Last Sunday we witnessed a living example of this when the Whitmores passed through town."

The older man's words seemed to galvanize his hearers. They all stiffened, yet no one turned to look at Noah and Sunny. Dawn's baby talk was the only sound for a few seconds. Noah increased his grip on Sunny's hand. He had a hard time drawing a full breath. Out of the corner of his eye, he noticed someone familiar. It took him a moment to place the man: the stranger who had been lurking at the general store. He stood far back from the crowd, uneasy and edgy. Noah turned his attention back to Saul.

"I visited the Whitmores on Monday and met the Ojibwa widow and her son. The woman is a widow because her husband served in the Union Army and gave his last full measure of devotion for our country. Noah and many of you also served and witnessed the terrible loss of husbands, fathers, brothers and sons."

A few of the men shifted on their feet and then turned and nodded at Noah who returned the same to them. The tight band around his lungs loosened a notch.

"Mr. Whitmore," Old Saul continued, "is going to write to the government—"

"I have already written to the War Department," Noah declared. He drew the letter from his pocket. "Need to leave this with Mr. Ashford to go out on the next mail boat. The widow and her boy should be getting a pension. They will be staying with us till we get papers from Washington, D.C. Then she wants to go to her people in the lakes area farther north and east." *Let anybody try to fight me about this.*

"We'd appreciate prayer," Sunny requested then. "We'd like her to be able to go north before winter and you know how slow government is about matters."

Rueful laughter agreed to this. Leave it to Sunny to sweeten up people. He smiled down at her in appreciation.

Old Saul grinned, too. "Now I hope you will all pray for the Ojibwa woman and her son and for all the widows and orphans left by the war. Lavina, I need to sit down. Will you start the next hymn?"

At the end of worship some people came to Noah and Sunny, but many kept their distance. Men who'd also served in the army gathered around the Whitmores, offering their help. Noah forced himself to accept their hands and words, but the looks they'd sent to him and Sunny last week still rankled.

Prejudice against Indians was not going away anytime soon.

Finally Martin and Ophelia came to them with Gordy. "We'll help, too," Gordy said. "We just didn't know what you were doing."

"Well, now you know." Noah tried to keep the twist of hurt from his voice, but failed.

Gordy flushed red and looked down.

"Misunderstandings can happen," Ophelia said tactfully. "I'd like to invite you and Nan over for a sewing circle this week, Sunny. Nan's lying in will be over then. From what I've seen of the little boy, he could use some new clothes."

"Thank you," Sunny said. "That would be a help."

As Sunny and Noah made their way to their wagon, Noah remembered the stranger, and took a look over his shoulder. The man stood apart, watching Noah and Sunny carefully. Noah's instincts told him the man was up to no good. After he helped Sunny into the wagon, he looked back again. But the man was nowhere to be seen.

Noah kept his observations to himself.

On Monday in midafternoon Sunny walked toward Martin's house. She carried Dawn on her right hip and her sewing basket on her left elbow. Today would be the first day she'd faced people without Noah beside her since the scene in town. Once again Noah had shown everyone his regard for her and he'd stood up to everyone. She let pride in him flow through her.

The month of May had proved to be changeable just like the people in Wisconsin. Today was overcast and a cool wind blew in from the west. Sunny wondered when summer would arrive and what a Wisconsin summer would be like—more like Idaho or Pennsylvania?

Ahead through the trees Sunny glimpsed the smoke

from Martin's cabin. Would Ophelia prove to be a friend? Sunny had grown up with real friends. To the women who lived their lives above a saloon, friendship meant a lot. They depended on each other because they had no one else. Did friendship mean as much to women who had husbands and families?

Before she'd reached the cabin, she heard Nan call her name. Sunny paused, letting Nan catch up, her heart beating fast.

"Gordy and I are right sorry he didn't come straight over and see what was going on at your place," Nan said. "In town he heard *such talk*—about Noah beating up Mr. Ashford and Indians coming back hereabouts. We should have known Noah and you would only do what's right."

Sunny didn't know how to respond to this.

"Didn't you bring the Indian woman with you today?" Nan asked in her unabashed way.

"She is still too weak to walk far and is very shy," Sunny said while beginning to walk toward the door.

Nan grasped her arm, stopping her. "Please say you forgive us, Sunny. And I'll never doubt you and yours again. I promise."

Sunny gazed up into Nan's plump, honest face. From the Sunday before last, the humiliation of the ride through town—unkempt and with Bid'a ban tied to her—snared her. What it would have meant to her that first Sunday if Gordy had stepped out from the crowd and asked if they needed anything.

Nan bowed her head, her little one in her arms whimpering.

Who am I to stand in judgment of anyone? "Of course, Nan. Forgiven. Forgotten."

"You were so good to me when Pearl Louise was coming," Nan said with a sad smile.

Sunny put one arm around her friend. "I'm glad to see you're up and around. Now we best get to the door. If Ophelia is peeking out the window, she'll think we're gossiping about her."

Nan nodded, but momentarily pressed a cheek against Sunny's. Then the two walked toward the cabin.

"Hello, the house!" Nan called out in her normally cheery voice.

Ophelia opened the door and burst into tears.

Sunny and Nan exchanged glances and hurried forward.

Chapter Ten

Several minutes passed before Sunny and Nan could calm Ophelia enough to make sense of what she was saying in the midst of her sobs. Nan laid her baby girl on the bed in the corner to nap and they set the two toddlers on the floor to play. Finally they all sat on a bench at the table—Sunny on one side of the bride and Nan on the other. Then they were able to staunch the tears.

"Now you can tell me and Sunny anythin'," Nan said. "We don't gossip and we want the best for you and Martin."

"Yes, that's right," Sunny agreed, patting Ophelia's arm.

"I just didn't know…" Ophelia inhaled deeply and wiped her eyes with a frilly hankie. "I didn't know I'd miss my family so much."

"Ah, homesickness," Nan said knowingly. "It is hard leaving home for the first time."

Ophelia nodded forlornly.

"But it will pass," Nan said. "Won't it, Sunny?"

The question rattled Sunny. She could not remember ever being homesick. One had to have a home in the first place and she'd never had one. Until now. But homesickness might be something like the mourning she'd felt after her mother had died. Maybe someone homesick missed the people, not the home. "Everything in this life passes," Sunny said truthfully.

Over the bride's head Nan lifted an eyebrow at her, but went on soothing the girl. "Now the secret to getting through homesickness is keeping busy. How about we start sewing?"

Ophelia nodded glumly. The women opened their sewing baskets.

"I brought fabric," Sunny said. "Miigwans needs a new pair of pants. His are about worn through. I chalked a rough pattern from his old pair onto this cloth." She rose and smoothed the heavy brown broadcloth out on the tabletop. "Does this look right, Nan? Ophelia? I've never made boy's pants before."

"I have two little brothers." And then the bride burst into tears again.

Sunny and Nan exchanged looks. Not much sewing would be accomplished today, it seemed.

"I'm sorry," Ophelia sniffled.

"Why don't you tell us about it?" Sunny asked, sitting down again. Perhaps the girl just needed to talk it out.

"It's just that everything is so different here." Ophelia waved her hands. "I've never lived out of town before."

"You're a town girl?" Nan commented, sounding intrigued.

"Yes, I lived in Galena. It's much smaller now that the mining has gone down, but I'm not used to being where there are no streetlamps at night or paved streets."

"I've never lived in a big town," Sunny said, and then

stopped herself before revealing more. The old fear of exposure tugged at her as she noted how much more stylish Ophelia's dress was than either hers or Nan's.

"Me, neither," Nan said.

"Will this awful emptiness really go away?" the bride asked.

The girl's forlorn tone prompted Sunny to press her hand over hers. "Yes, you will find that Martin becomes your home. I mean, if he's with you then you are home."

The truth of this flooded Sunny. Wherever Noah and Dawn were, that meant home for her. "I felt a bit lonely here at first till I met Caroline and Nan. But now I don't feel so lonely." Sunny decided she better stop talking. Her sympathy might lead her to indiscreet words.

"Mama warned me that it would be hard to live on the frontier," Nan said.

"I know I should be stronger, but…" Ophelia looked lost.

"You're young," Sunny said.

"But you'll get older!" Nan added in her usual sassy way.

This forced a trace of a smile from Ophelia. "I said I wanted to help make clothes for that little Indian boy. So let's do that. Now, I have sewn clothing for my brothers, and we should make a really deep hem because they grow so fast."

Sunny silently sighed with relief. "That makes good sense." Sunny drew out her white tailor chalk and drew the pant legs several inches longer.

"Is it funny having an Indian living with you?" Nan asked. "I mean, how do you understand her?"

Sunny stiffened. "Bid'a ban speaks English and so does her son."

"Really? And she doesn't wear deerskin like I thought Indians wore." Nan folded the fabric in two.

"I haven't asked her about that." That had struck Sunny as unusual, too. Western tribes wore buckskin. She began cutting the fabric along the chalk lines. "Maybe it's because the French lived around here almost two hundred years ago."

Nan looked surprised. "Two hundred years ago?"

"Yes, Noah told me." Sunny felt a touch of pride in Noah's knowledge.

After the pant pieces were cut, the women arranged them together.

"I'll sew one pant leg and you can sit across and sew the other," Ophelia offered.

Finally the time to go home arrived. With Ophelia's help, Sunny nearly had the pants sewn. She'd just need to do some finishing work to them. Nan and the bride had been helpful and Sunny felt almost natural with them again.

"I need a favor," Ophelia said, her eyes downcast.

Caution jabbed Sunny.

"What do you need? We'll help," Nan offered genially as she changed the baby's diaper on the bench.

"I learned to cook and clean, but my mother never let me help with the laundry. She always sent it out to be done." The bride lifted both hands. "But I can't do that here."

Sunny and Nan both stared at the girl momentarily.

"Where did your ma send the laundry to be done?" Nan said as if she didn't quite believe this had happened.

"An Irish woman in town took in laundry," Ophelia replied.

Sunny had sent her laundry to the Chinese in Idaho,

but most everyone in town had. "Ophelia," Sunny said, "I'm doing laundry toward the end of the week. You can bring your laundry over and we'll do it together."

Nan and Sunny left with waves and pleasantries. As they were about to part ways, Nan paused. "I'm glad we're not brides. We've learned about being married and know our husbands and are settled."

Pinched by this thought, Sunny tried to look as if she agreed. She knew now that she'd come to love Noah, but did she know him? Were they settled? Not really.

As Sunny walked home, an idea occurred to her, a wild idea that frightened her almost immediately.

What if I told him? What would Noah Whitmore do if I told him I loved him?

Laundry day dawned bright and balmy. Sunny usually enjoyed the act of cleaning their clothing, making everything fresh and sweet smelling. Would Martin's bride show up? Or decide she didn't really want to come to a house where Indians lived?

Just then Ophelia appeared, trudging up the trail through the trees. Sunny mustered a welcoming smile. The girl must be desperate to learn. *Or perhaps I'm judging her. And wrongly.* "Good morning!"

Ophelia waved. She was half carrying, half dragging a full cloth sack.

Sunny sensed Bid'a ban standing in the doorway. She turned. "Come out, Bid'a ban. Sunshine will be good for you."

The thin woman slipped outside and came near Sunny. "You have a friend come?"

"Yes, she needs to learn how to do laundry."

Bid'a ban looked surprised at this. "I'll go inside."

"No, stay," Sunny murmured. She wasn't going to let her guest be ignored.

Ophelia came close and then halted shyly.

"Ophelia, this is Bid'a ban." She introduced the two as if it were a normal meeting. "Now, Ophelia, have you separated your laundry?"

"What does that mean?" Ophelia asked.

"Spill out your sack and we'll make two piles—one for colored clothing and one for whites. If we mix the two, you will no longer have any whites," Sunny teased.

Ophelia grinned and proceeded to dump the contents of her bag onto the dewy grass. Sunny helped her divide the clothing while Bid'a ban observed. Ophelia kept stealing glances at Bid'a ban as if uncertain of her.

Overlooking this, Sunny showed Ophelia how to shave soap into the deep pot set up outside over a fire. Soon the whites were simmering and Sunny set Ophelia to stir the clothing with a broom handle. The acrid odor of lye hung in the air.

"This is how white women do laundry?" Bid'a ban asked curiously.

"How do Indian women do laundry?" Ophelia asked, sounding interested in spite of herself.

"We take our clothing to the river and lay it on broad river rock and beat it with a stick."

Sunny recalled that she had seen men doing this in a mining camp.

"Why do you heat the water?" Bid'a ban asked, peering into the simmering pot.

"I think it gets the dirt out better. We don't beat it but we do rub places where the dirt is ground in on this." She lifted the washboard that had been leaning against the cabin.

Bid'a ban stroked the rough washboard. "I see." Ophelia glanced over and looked intrigued, too.

Sunny had become used to doing the laundry. The curiosity of the two other women made her reconsider this weekly chore. "Keeping clean is important. It's healthier."

"Mother always said, 'Cleanliness is next to godliness,'" Ophelia added piously.

Bid'a ban stroked the washboard once more with a dubious expression.

Just then Noah came into the clearing from the creek with Dawn in his arms and Miigwans beside him. "We're going to take the oxen over to Gordy's to pull out stumps today."

"Noah says I can go with him, Mother," Miigwans said.

Bid'a ban sent a look of concern toward Noah.

Noah gripped the boy's shoulder. "He'll be fine, Bid'a ban. I want him to learn how to handle a team."

"Please, Mother," Miigwans begged.

Bid'a ban nodded. Noah deposited the sleeping Dawn in her hammock inside and then he hitched the oxen and they were off down the track.

"You have a good man," Bid'a ban murmured.

Sunny nodded, touched by Noah's kindness to the fatherless child. She thought of her idea yesterday, her idea to tell Noah that she loved him. She wasn't sure she was supposed to—was the man supposed to say such things? What if he said he didn't feel that way—what then? Would he leave her?

The sound of a horse coming broke into Sunny's thoughts. A stranger appeared through the trees, riding slowly up the trail to their house. Strangers were such a rarity, a shot of fear jolted through Sunny. "Ophelia, Bid'a ban—come stand behind me. Now." Sunny's voice sharpened. Better safe than sorry.

The two women looked startled. Ophelia scurried to stand behind Sunny, who positioned herself in front of the doorway. Bid'a ban seemed frozen in place for a moment, then she moved behind Sunny as well, hidden from view.

"They told me there was an Indian here," the man said. "Indians aren't allowed here anymore. The government moved them all away to Nebraska." The man's tone was menacing.

Sunny edged backward, nudging the other two women through the door. Her heart thudded, but this was her fight. She must take charge. She studied the man's face so she could identify him. He had dirty blond hair that hung around his shoulders. He sported a mustache, flecked with gray, and his eyes were hooded. He'd tied what looked like a woman's scarf around his neck.

When the other women had taken shelter in the cabin, she reached inside the door. She drew out the loaded rifle that Noah always left there for protection. "You are on my husband's property," Sunny said evenly, quelling her spiking fear. "I think you'd better leave."

The man spit sideways. "I lost my family in Minnesota to Indians in '62."

"You had better leave," Sunny repeated and raised her rifle so it would be easy to take aim and fire. She forced her arms not to show how she shook inside.

"Can you shoot that, woman?" the man sneered.

"Yes." She raised the rifle higher and took aim. Her heart leaped against her breastbone.

Ophelia squealed and ducked lower behind Sunny.

The man stared hard at her. "This isn't over." He spat again as if in contempt.

"Come back when my husband is here," Sunny said, "and it will be over."

"Your husband a tough man?" The stranger turned his horse as if the rifle in her hand didn't bother him.

"He's a Union Army veteran and has the scars to prove it," Sunny said, careful not to let her voice reveal how close to panic she'd come.

"This isn't over," he repeated and then rode away at an insolently slow pace.

Once he disappeared from sight, Sunny backed inside and shut and barred the door. Then she sank onto the rocking chair, trembling all over.

Ophelia sat hunched on the bench by the table as white as paper. "You were so brave."

Sunny could barely nod; she was still shaking.

On the floor, Bid'a ban wept silently, leaning against the wall. "I bring trouble on you."

"No," Sunny said. "He's a man looking for trouble. There are men like him all over." She'd seen his ilk before. Men who rode into a town, aching for a fistfight or gunfight. "They don't need a reason. They just want to shed blood."

"Do you think he'll come back?" Ophelia asked.

"Yes," Sunny said with certainty. She pressed a hand over her heart as if that could calm it. "But my Noah will settle matters with him." And she was positive of that. Noah knew how to fight. He'd survived four years of a bloody war. This stranger didn't know who he'd come up against.

At Gordy's, Noah had set Miigwans on the neck and shoulders of one of the oxen for his safety. The big creatures were docile but their very size caused them to be a danger to a small child. The men had roped the team to a stump and Noah was encouraging them to wrest the stump from the sandy soil.

As soon as Gordy and Martin had seen he'd brought the boy, they'd gotten quiet. Yet they had greeted Miigwans politely. For his part, Miigwans had also become silent and watchful. But Noah had decided since Miigwans had no father, it was best for the boy to be with the men and learn men's work. And Noah thought if these were his friends, they would take the boy in stride—*if* they were his friends.

The stump creaked and groaned as the roots fought to stay in the earth. Then came a cracking sound as when ropes in a high wind snapped. With a groan, the stump sprang free. "Ho!" Noah halted the team.

"Well, that's one down and a many more to go," Gordy said wryly.

"But it has to be done," Martin commented. "I look forward to the day when we'll all have our fields cleared."

Gordy agreed, releasing the ropes from the stump. "We might have to work logging or something to make ends meet."

"I think logging might be a poor choice," Noah said, his arm tingling with remembered pain. "Old Saul said I could work as a stonemason building hearths for people."

"You also know how to make furniture," Martin said, helping Gordy tie the ropes around the next stump. "You're a knowing man. I spent a lot of time reading law."

"You're an edjicated man?" Gordy asked.

Martin nodded, flushing with embarrassment. "Ophelia comes from a prosperous family. Her father is a judge. They didn't like her marrying me and coming to the frontier. But that's what her father did when he was young. Went West and established himself."

From the corner of his eye Noah suddenly caught the sign of movement. He stilled. The likelihood of any wild animal attacking in daylight was scant. He focused and realized it was a dog, crawling on its belly toward them.

"A dog," Miigwans piped up.

The animal crooned pitifully and halted. It had long brown ears, a sleek head of the same brown and a white and speckled body. It looked starved.

"Everyone be quiet. Here, boy," Noah called and held out his hand. "It's okay. We like dogs."

The animal very plainly looked at him, assessing, and then it crawled forward. The clearing had gone absolutely quiet except for the dog's whining and the huffing of the winded oxen. A flash of memory carried Noah back to a battlefield after the cannon had fallen silent—wounded men crawling and begging for help. He stopped his mind there, shaken.

The dog stopped a few feet from Noah, who then knelt on one knee. "Come here, boy." He patted his leg and offered a hand, keeping the past at bay.

The dog crawled slowly, slowly toward the men, still whining piteously, till it reached Noah. It put one paw on Noah's knee. The bloody paw had something embedded in it.

"What happened, boy? Did you run into a porcupine?"

"Be careful, Noah," Gordy cautioned. "He doesn't know you."

"But he is asking for my help." Noah petted the dog's head warily and spoke soothing words to him. When the dog relaxed, Noah drew out his knife. "I'm going to get that out of you now."

With the dog watching his every move, Noah stripped from the quill the barbs that had prevented the dog from working the quill out himself. Then Noah pulled out his handkerchief and grasped the end. "This is going to hurt, boy," he said to the dog.

Gordy took a sharp breath.

The dog stared into Noah's eyes and Noah read the trust and appeal there. He tightened his grip and yanked. The quill came out as the dog yowled with pain and snapped just over Noah's hand. Then the dog immediately began licking the wound.

"You helped him," Miigwans said, rich with feeling. "He's a good dog, isn't he? He didn't bite you."

Noah stroked the dog's head and long ears, his own nerves easing. "Yes, he's a smart dog, too. He knew he needed help. He must have lost his family. Are you lonely, boy?"

Gordy and Martin approached quietly, slowly. "Looks like a hunting dog. They can be worth their weight in gold to a man."

The dog rested its head on Noah's knee for a few seconds as if in thanks.

"Well, he's adopted you, Noah," Martin said. "You're his new master."

Noah knew it was foolish, but a rush of warmth coursed through him. "He'll be a fine dog after I get him cleaned up a bit. Martin, bring me my sack. I'll give him my lunch. He looks starved."

Soon Noah was feeding the dog. It stood and Noah

ran his hands over him. "Well, I guess I should be calling you 'girl.'" He felt her bulging abdomen. "And you're full of pups."

"Whoa, that's good. Put me down for one," Gordy said. "Please."

The last word sounded uncertain as if Gordy didn't know if he could ask this of Noah. This told Noah more than anything else could that Gordy felt their estrangement maybe as much as Noah did. "Sure. How about you, Martin?"

"Excellent. I've always had a dog," the younger man replied, sounding touched.

"Can I have one?" Miigwans asked.

"We'll ask your mother. And we don't know how many she'll have or if they'll all be healthy." Noah watched both Gordy and Martin lean forward to pet the stray. Then Miigwans ventured to touch the dog's head. The dog licked the boy's hand.

"She likes me." Miigwans smiled.

"Means she's a good judge of character, son," Gordy said.

Noah's heart warmed toward this man—his friend.

"*Ninga wegimind!* My mother!" Miigwans shouted as he ran ahead of the oxen into Noah's clearing where the clotheslines sagged with clothing. "We have a dog!"

Noah and Martin walked beside the oxen and exchanged grins at the boy's exuberance.

Sunny raced out of the cabin and straight to Noah. She flung her arms around his chest. "Oh, I'm so glad you're home." Her voice vibrated with fear.

Noah dropped the oxen leads and wrapped his arms

around her as she shivered against him. "What's happened?" he said, his voice sharp.

"A man came and threatened us," Ophelia said, running to Martin. "I've been so frightened. I couldn't walk home without an escort. Oh, Martin, he threatened us and Sunny aimed a rifle at him."

Shock shot through Noah in barbed waves, followed by hot rage. "A man? Threatened you?"

Sunny drew in a deep breath and looked up at him. "I'm glad you always leave a loaded rifle inside the door. I think that's the only reason he backed off."

"But why did he threaten you?" Noah asked, gripping Sunny's elbows. Anger leaped inside him like flames.

"Because of me," Bid'a ban said from the doorway. "He came to get me."

"Why?" Martin asked.

Bid'a ban's eyes filled with tears and she seemed unable to answer.

"He said that Indians aren't supposed to be here," Ophelia said, then lowered her eyes and voice. "He said that he'd lost his family in the trouble in '62."

"What trouble?" Noah asked, trying to control his white-hot anger. He'd been too busy in 1862 just trying to stay alive to catch much news.

"The Dakota tried to push the whites out of Minnesota. Many whites and Dakota died," Bid'a ban said. "I'm not Dakota. My people have lived in peace with the whites for a long time. I should have stayed in Lac du Flambeau with my people, not come south. All I have gotten is trouble here."

Noah tried to absorb all this information. But the main point was that a stranger had come and threatened his wife. He held Sunny close, feeling her softness against him, feeling her fear. "Describe him to me." *I will find him and teach him to leave my family alone.*

As Sunny told Noah what the man looked like, Noah immediately thought of the stranger he'd seen lingering in town, staring at them.

He looked at Bid'a ban, who would not meet anyone's eyes.

There was something more to this story than he and Sunny knew.

Chapter Eleven

Distracted with worry, Sunny somehow got herself busy preparing supper. Since Martin had taken Ophelia home, Bid'a ban had remained silent, sitting against the wall near the hearth, looking crushed. Sunny tried not to look at the rifle, propped again by the door. Perversely her eyes insisted on drifting toward it, prompting her heart to race—just as it had when she'd confronted the stranger. What would happen now? Would the stranger return?

Noah sat in the rocking chair, brooding. The dog he'd brought home lay in front of the door, tracking Noah with its soulful brown eyes. Sunny had bathed the dog's paw with salt water to help it heal and then fed her some leftover corn bread. Even Dawn appeared to have absorbed everyone's pensive mood. As usual, she'd pulled herself up at Noah's knee. But instead of filling the cabin with her baby talk, she merely gazed up at him.

Sunny wished she could break the heavy silence. But she could think of nothing to say that wouldn't make Noah feel worse—no doubt he was upset that he'd been away when trouble came to their door. But as soon as Noah had come home, she'd felt instantly safe. Should she tell him that?

Stopping herself from adding salt to the pot a second time, she sighed. "Let's eat, even if we don't have much of an appetite." The four of them gathered at the table. Noah said grace and they began eating, still in melancholy silence.

Finally Noah looked across the table to Bid'a ban. "What did bring you so far south from home?"

Sunny wondered at his question.

The woman looked distressed. "My husband was Ho-Chunk. The whites call them Winnebago. His people lived near here. He came north to work logging. We married. After he died, I thought I should visit his mother. But I arrived at the wrong time." She put an arm around her son. "The soldiers came and made the Ho-Chunk leave, go to Nebraska."

"Nebraska?" Sunny echoed. "Why so far?"

"When the Western tribes cause trouble, we all suffer." Bid'a ban looked down. "I could not persuade the soldiers I was Ojibwa and should go north, go home. When we went south through Iowa, my husband's mother died. I buried her. Then we slipped away. You see I dress like a white woman. With my bonnet, no one could see I wasn't white. I put a hat on Miigwans and we slipped away."

Sunny read between the lines—the injustice, the outrage, the helplessness of being swept up in something like this, something like an avalanche she had witnessed in Idaho. Sunny knew how being overpowered by life felt. She reached across and patted Bid'a ban's hand.

"Have you ever seen that stranger before, Bid'a ban?" Noah asked.

At first Bid'a ban didn't answer Noah, and Sunny was upset with him for asking such a question. But the silence was heavy as they waited to hear what she'd say, and Sunny began to wonder if Noah was right to ask her such a thing. Finally Bid'a ban looked Noah in the eye and said, "I know him."

Sunny was stunned. "How, Bid'a ban?"

"When I reached Wisconsin, my bonnet did not fool him. He knew what I was. He knew I couldn't ask others for help. I had to...live with him."

Sunny felt sick to her stomach. She understood exactly what Bid'a ban wasn't saying. They were more alike than Bid'a ban would ever know.

"Was he lying when he said his family had been killed by Indians?" Noah asked.

"All I can say is that he is a man who hates Indians. All Indians," Bid'a ban said, her voice barely more than a whisper.

Sunny read more than the words. The man had abused Bid'a ban and terrified her. This woman had fled just as Sunny had when she went to the Gabriels. Sunny swallowed down her own memories. "You will stay here with us, Bid'a ban. You will stay here until we know you and Miigwans are safe."

Noah looked sharply at Sunny, causing her face to burn. Had she said something wrong? Surely Noah agreed with her—didn't he?

Bid'a ban glanced at Noah, looking both afraid and resentful.

Sunny didn't blame her. She fought the fear that

whispered up her spine. *I'm not alone and neither are you, Bid'a ban.*

After supper Bid'a ban sat by the fire, sewing the final details on Miigwans's new pants. Sunny tried to do some mending but her needle kept poking her. Noah and the boy led the dog to the creek to take a bath with them. When the three returned, the dog hesitated at the door. Noah beckoned her in by the fire.

Noah's adopting the stray didn't surprise Sunny. She watched him stroke the dog and speak to it softly. She felt her love for him rise up inside her again.

"We should name her," Miigwans said.

Bid'a ban scolded him in their language.

"I mean *you* should name her," the chastened boy amended.

Noah ruffled Miigwans's hair. "What do you think we should name her?"

"She's awful pretty," the boy said, petting the dog.

"It is time to sleep," Bid'a ban said abruptly. "Can the dog get a name tomorrow?"

"Fine," Noah assented and led the dog to lie in front of the door. "I think it would be best if we all remained dressed tonight."

Sunny paused in putting Dawn in her hammock, anxiety bringing up gooseflesh on her arms. Noah meant trouble might come in the night. She looked at Noah. But he was busy barring the door and securing the shutters from inside.

Bid'a ban came close to her and whispered, "I am better now. You should go back to your man." She motioned toward the loft. "You belong there."

The suggestion hit Sunny, completely unexpected. She couldn't think of a word to say, a word she *could* say. She looked to Noah, knowing that if she hesitated to do what Bid'a ban suggested, Noah would be cast in a strange light.

"Thank you, Bid'a ban," Noah said. Then he motioned for Sunny to precede him up the ladder while he received her blankets from Bid'a ban.

Sunny felt as if she were on stage and a host of onlookers ogled her as she climbed the ladder to the loft, the loft where she had only ventured once before when Noah was in the cabin. Being up here alone with Noah would only sharpen her shame over his rejection of her. She swallowed hard, keeping her emotions in check.

Noah came up the ladder and offered her the blankets.

She busied herself arranging them several feet from his bedding. "I'm sorry," she whispered lamely.

"Sunny," Noah said in a low voice, "Bid'a ban cannot stay here long."

"But, Noah—"

"That is final. We will help her as best we can, but she cannot stay here indefinitely."

"But she needs our help, Noah!" She spoke in a heated whisper.

"It is not safe for you, or for Dawn or for the other women and children who live nearby. We don't know what he might do to force us to give her up."

"You don't understand what Bid'a ban's been through. You cannot put her out. She's in danger. He'll find her and hurt her."

Noah gazed into her eyes. "I know that."

Sunny waited for him to go on. In vain.

"Good night, Sunny." Noah wrapped himself in his blankets and turned his back to her.

Tears moistened her eyes as she loosened her clothing and settled herself in her bedding. The soft wool blanket muffled her weeping. She hadn't felt this lonely since the night her mother had died.

The next morning Noah had planned to meet up with the other men at Gordy's, but he didn't think he should leave the women and children alone. He lifted his coffee cup and gazed at Sunny. He noticed that she was looking everywhere but at him. Was she upset by their conversation last night? Or by having to sleep in the loft with him?

He'd awakened several times as if aware—even in sleep—of her presence. He'd found listening to her breathing a soothing sound. But having her so close merely sharpened to a razor-edge his failure to perform as a husband. Well, there was one way in which he could not fail her: keeping her safe from harm.

But how could he do that if Bid'a ban still lived with them?

He considered how many weeks a letter could take to arrive in Washington, D.C. He concluded if they were lucky, the War Department would reply by snowfall. Conceivably, Bid'a ban and her son might need somewhere to stay till next spring. Two more mouths to feed and a long winter ahead. "Bid'a ban," he began.

Sunny lifted her eyes to Noah as if suspicious of anything he said to Bid'a ban.

Before he could go on, the dog by the door interrupted, barking.

"Hello, the house!" Gordy's voice rang out.

"Quiet, girl. It's a friend." Maybe Gordy had come to help. Noah rose quickly and opened the door. Growling low, the dog came to his side as if ready to defend against the intruder.

"I thought I was supposed to come to your place today," Noah said.

Stepping inside, Gordy looked pained. And for the first time he carried a rifle to their door. "Martin brought his wife over early this morning and told me what happened here yesterday. We think the women should all come with you to our place today. Shouldn't be left alone."

Noah faced Gordy. The younger man looked uncharacteristically stern. Noah felt his own face harden into harsh lines. "I think that makes good sense."

"Any man who will threaten decent women on their own land is trouble. Can't be trusted to act normal."

Noah frowned at Gordy and gave the tiniest shake of his head. He didn't want Gordy frightening the women any further.

Gordy nodded a fraction, letting Noah know he understood.

"Sunny," Noah said, "I'll do the outside chores while you and Bid'a ban get ready to spend the day at the Osbournes'." This solved the problem of how to protect the women today, but this crisis demanded a permanent solution. Just how *permanent* a solution this stranger would make necessary remained to be seen.

Sunny came close to Noah. He walked outside and waited for her. Gordy politely remained inside. Beside Noah, Sunny stood on tiptoe. "Thank you for not putting Bid'a ban out today."

Noah looked shocked. "I never meant to. How could you think that?"

Sunny felt helpless to explain. "You wouldn't answer me last night. What are we going to do?"

"I don't know. But something will occur to us. I can't believe you thought I'd knowingly let any man take advantage of a woman."

She recalled how he'd confronted that awful man on the main street that day he returned to Pennsylvania. She tried to form words to let him know how much his helping Bid'a ban meant to her. But she merely touched his cheek and then hurried back inside to prepare for the day away from home.

A little over an hour later, Noah, Gordy and Martin stood in a tight circle, contemplating Gordy's garden of stumps. Noah had set Miigwans to stay in front of Gordy's cabin with the dog to sound the alarm if the stranger came back. The little boy had looked determined to protect his mother.

Now Noah's real intent was to discuss privately with his two neighbors what he planned to do. And the last of his doubts as to whether they were friends or not had vanished with one look at their faces when he'd explained exactly what had happened, and who the man was. Their expressions had said clearly that the threat to Noah and his family was deemed a threat to them all.

"So what's the plan?" Gordy asked, his rifle on a strap slung over his back.

"I'm going into town to see if I can find the stranger. Sunny described him in detail to me. I'm going to *persuade* him to leave us alone," Noah said.

"How're you going to do that?" Martin asked, gripping his rifle with white knuckles.

"I'll start with words," Noah replied, his lungs constricting. He breathed deeply, trying to loosen the tension.

Gordy nodded. "I'm comin' with you."

"Me, too," Martin said. A heron squawked from the creek over the hill.

"No." Noah stepped back from them. "I don't want to leave the women alone."

"I see," Gordy said, folding his arms. "Well, then one of us should stay here with the women and the other two should go into town and see if the stranger has cleared out. Or not."

Noah held up a forestalling hand. "I can handle this—"

"No," Martin said, edging forward. "You're not doing this alone."

Noah stared at them and realized they were dead serious. "All right. Martin, will you stay behind and guard the women and children?"

"I will." Martin looked determined.

"So we'll just ride to town to mail a few letters Nan and me wrote to family," Gordy said with false nonchalance, the tacit understanding in his stance that this is what they'd tell the women so as not to worry them.

Like a bow string at the ready, anxiety tautened within Noah. He'd been called to arms again.

Noah and Gordy rode through the forest, approaching town. He couldn't get out of his mind the look on Sunny's face as they'd left. He'd seen fear in her eyes. But something else was there, too. Admiration. Gratitude. It warmed him. She'd merely whispered in his ear, "Be safe." But he would do what it took to protect his family.

Would that mean adding another killing to his soul? A weight settled over his heart.

"I been in something like this before," Gordy spoke up from behind Noah.

"Oh?"

"A gang of thieves set up in our county. We didn't have no law nearby, either. Finally they…hurt a woman… bad."

Noah understood the implication and his own resolve to settle this intensified.

"So the decent men got together and one night ambushed them. I was just sixteen and scared stiff."

"Did you get the job done?" Two crows landed in a tree overhead, complaining stridently about something.

"Yes."

Lord, help me run the man out of town, nothing more.

When they rode into town, the dirt street along the river appeared as usual, nearly empty.

"Where do you think we can find him?" Gordy asked.

"We'll ask Ashford. He doesn't miss much."

"Doesn't miss anything," Gordy added with a hint of amusement.

The two dismounted, hitched their horses and entered the store. Ashford looked up warily. "Hello, what can I do for you gents?"

"We're looking for a stranger," Noah said, focused, intent. "He's got longish dark blond hair, a mustache and wears a woman's scarf around his neck."

"I've seen him all right." The storekeeper's tone announced his low opinion of the stranger loud and clear. "He rode into town a few days ago and spends most of his time at the saloon. Came in here once to buy tobacco. Didn't have much to say about himself." Ashford paused. "But he asked me about that Indian woman you have at your place. He'd heard about her, I guess."

Noah stilled. He refused to ask Ashford what he'd told the man.

"That stranger came out to Noah's place and threatened his wife," Gordy said.

Ashford's face expanded with shock. "That's not called for. A man threatening a decent woman? We can't have that."

"That's why we're here," Gordy said.

Noah turned, heading for the door. "Thanks, Ashford. We'll see if he's at the saloon." As he and Gordy marched down the street, he heard Ashford's door slam again. Behind them Ashford had taken off running to another store.

Noah's gut constricted as it always did before a fight. But he wouldn't stop till he'd settled this threat. Sunny wasn't going to live in fear. He couldn't do everything a husband should do for a wife, but he would protect her and Dawn.

Noah pushed through the doors into the nearly empty saloon. He spotted the man sitting alone at a table in the back, shuffling cards. Sunny's description fit him perfectly. "Let me handle this," Noah muttered to Gordy who nodded but stayed by his side.

The two of them went straight to the man. "You trespassed on my land yesterday," Noah said, staring hard into the man's eyes. "I've come to tell you not to come near my place or mine again."

The man's face sneered. "I came for the Indian—"

So much for words. Noah upended the table toward the man with a crash.

The bartender shouted. The stranger leaped up, face fiery red. He reached for a gun on his side.

Striking his hand away, Noah grabbed the man's collar and yanked him around the table. He flung him back against the bar, grabbed the man's gun and tossed it to the barkeep, who caught it.

As Noah fended off the man's every attempt to get past his guard, he said, punctuating each movement with a word, "You-are-going-to-leave-town. Now."

"I'm going to get my Indian!" the man roared.

"No, you're not." A voice from the door startled Noah but he didn't need to look around. It was Ashford. The stranger's face drained of color. Now Noah stepped back and glanced over his shoulder.

Ashford and a few other men he recognized stood in the doorway. Each one carried a rifle or a club.

"We don't want your kind in our town," Ashford ordered, slapping his club in one palm. "Not a man who threatens a decent woman on her husband's land. Now clear out. All of us know what you look like and we can describe you to the county sheriff. Clear out."

The man looked cowed. He reached for his gun only to remember he didn't have it. The barkeep emptied the chambers and then handed it to him. The man let loose some choice words and bumped into Noah on purpose but kept on moving. All the men followed him outside and watched him get on his horse and ride north, away from town.

Noah tried to take in what had just happened. He couldn't find his voice. He'd put himself in the line of fire again and hadn't flinched. Sudden relief loosed through him.

"Well, thanks a lot," Gordy said to the men. "I think Noah was quite able to run the troublemaker out—"

"I got the other men in town to come, too," Ashford spoke up. "We wanted to make it clear that it wasn't just you and Whitmore that wanted him gone. We got a peaceable town here and we don't need his sort."

Noah nodded. A powerful reaction he couldn't describe flowed through him. "Thanks" was all he could say.

That night Sunny settled Dawn in her hammock and looked up into the loft, her stomach tying and retying itself into knots.

"Good night," Bid'a ban said, tucking Miigwans in beside her on the floor.

Sunny returned the same wish. Her relief over the stranger leaving town had been tempered by the worry that he might not have gone for good. That question just wouldn't leave her alone.

The still-nameless dog lay against the barred door. Sunny walked over and stroked the dog's head. She appreciated having her. If anybody approached by stealth in the night, she would sound the alarm.

Noah had preceded Sunny up into the loft. When she climbed up near him, she found him lying on his side. He didn't look away.

She must voice her concern even though he might not like it. Kneeling beside him and bending close, she whispered, "Do you think that stranger really left for good?"

Noah leaned up on one elbow. "I don't know. But the fact that more than just Gordy and me came against him might make him realize it's not worth the trouble.

Starting a fight with one man is different than taking on a whole town."

"None of them would have stood up for Bid'a ban if you hadn't first," she said, her voice low yet strong.

"I'm no hero, Sunny. You've heard me. I have nightmares like a scared kid."

His tone so filled with anger at himself hurt her and made her brave. "You dream about the war, don't you?"

He didn't answer.

She wouldn't give up this time. "It's the war, isn't it?"

"Yes." The one word sounded dragged from deep inside him.

Longing to touch him, show him comfort, strangled her. "I don't know how you did it, how you faced death over and over." *Noah, please talk to me, let it out.*

"I couldn't talk about it—when I came home. I was just supposed to forget it. But some things a man can't forget."

Sunny inched closer to him, encouraging him to trust her.

"The first battle, I just froze. I should have died, but an older man shoved me behind a tree and told me to get myself under control."

"I'm glad you didn't die," she said simply.

And then something wonderful happened.

Noah opened his arms and drew her close. "Don't worry about that stranger," he whispered close to her ear. "I won't ever let anyone hurt you or Dawn. You know that, right?" He rubbed her back tentatively.

She nodded against his chest, nearly afraid to inhale, not wanting to break this connection as delicate as a breath. For several moments he held her and then he kissed her forehead. "Now go to sleep. You're safe."

She moved away from him with reluctance. As she lay on her back, looking at the darkness, she savored the fact that Noah had held her for the first time, and kissed her and spoken of his nightmares. She could find hope for their future based on these small acts. Maybe there would come a day when they truly would be as normal as their friends believed them to be.

The next day was even warmer than the day before. With Miigwans and the dog at his side Noah stood at the edge of his clearing, looking things over, dismissing yesterday's drama from his mind. Still his rifle rested against the nearest tree, close at hand.

His cabin and spring house stood against the clear sky and leafy trees, well built to last. But he needed a barn before winter. When he'd visited this area in March, the snow had been deep and the wind bitter. His oxen and his horse would need more shelter—the lean-to just kept the rain off them. And he wanted to get more chickens and a cow of his own, or a goat. Dawn would need milk when she stopped nursing.

"I've been thinking of names for your dog," Miigwans said.

"What have you come up with?"

Noah considered whether he'd have to clear more trees before building a barn. He'd want a big sturdy one, so it would do them for years.

"We could call her friend. In our language, that's *Neechee*."

Noah looked down at the boy and tried to read his expression. This wasn't just about a dog.

"If we named the dog a word from my language,

when you say her name, you would remember me." The boy looked down.

Touched, Noah stooped to be at eye level with him. "*Neechee?* That will be a good name for her. And, Miigwans, I will remember you. I am your *Neechee.*"

Miigwans looked up and grinned shyly.

The dog barked an alert, looking behind them toward the track. Noah petted the dog and silenced her. He reached for his rifle.

The jingle of a harness and the creaking of a wagon sounded amid the birdsong. He guessed who was coming and wasn't disappointed when he finally glimpsed the old preacher through the trees. He couldn't figure out what kept bringing Old Saul here. What did he want from them—from Noah?

Nonetheless, soon he was helping the older man down from the wagon. Breathing quickly, Old Saul stopped and looked around. "You've a fine start here. But you need a barn before winter."

Noah chuckled. It sounded rusty, but felt good, too. "I was just thinking the same thing. What can we do for you, sir?"

The older man sent him a reproving look.

"I mean, what can we do for you, *Old Saul?*"

The preacher rested a hand on Miigwans's shoulder. "Is that your dog, son?"

"No, it belongs to Noah. Her name is Neechee. That means friend."

The older man nodded several times. "A good name. Is your mother inside?"

"Yes, *Nimishómiss,* my Grandfather."

"Take me to her." Beaming at the compliment, Old Saul took Miigwans's hand.

The three of them walked to the cabin. Inside, Sunny was kneading dough on the table and Bid'a ban was sewing a shirt for her son.

"Good day, ladies." The old preacher removed his hat and Noah hung it on a peg by the door.

Sunny curtsied but nodded toward her hands, deep in the bread dough. "I have to keep at this, sir."

"Please do. I came because I needed to discuss something with your guest."

"With me?" Bid'a ban looked startled and a little afraid. Her glance darted to Noah and Sunny, and back to the preacher.

"Yes." Old Saul accepted Noah's polite gesture and sat in the rocking chair while Miigwans sat near the door with Neechee.

Noah stood, his back against the wall, curious in spite of himself.

"I heard all about that stranger." The older man looked strained as he spoke to Bid'a ban. "And even though he has evidently left the area, I think it wise that we take further action to protect this woman and her child."

When Bid'a ban could not respond, Noah stepped in.

"What do you propose?" Noah asked.

"At fifteen, my grandson is old enough to offer adequate protection for a woman. I propose that he take our horse and accompany this woman and her child north to her people."

Bid'a ban looked startled. "Take me home?" she managed to say.

"We haven't heard back from Washington yet," Noah pointed out, straightening up.

"That's so. But when you do, my grandson will ride

up there and give the letter to Bid'a ban. If I'm right, there will be an Indian agent up north, I think in Bayfield on Lake Superior. Her pension might be conveyed through him."

"There's something you're not telling me," Noah said, the worry from yesterday perched on top of his midsection.

Old Saul nodded. "I've been thinking on this. That stranger can still cause trouble for this woman and child. The Indians in this part of Wisconsin have been sent to Nebraska. If he tells someone in the army that she's here, they could come and take her away. And he wouldn't have to go too far. Fort Snelling in Minnesota is about sixty miles away across the Mississippi."

Bid'a ban gasped.

Noah felt the same lurch inside.

And Miigwans protectively hurried to her side. "No."

"I didn't think of that." Noah chewed his lower lip. "What do you say, Bid'a ban? Would you go north with Old Saul's grandson?"

"Yes! I want to be with my family again." Bid'a ban stood and bowed with gratitude to Old Saul. "Would your grandson do this?"

"He's old enough to test his wings," Old Saul said. "His parents are some worried about him going so far alone, but he's got to start being a man sometime, no longer a boy. It will do you good and him good. In a few years he might have a wife and child to care for like you, Noah. Better start practicing. People nowadays coddle their young." Old Saul shook his head, frowning.

"Migwetch." Bid'a ban wrung Old Saul's hand. "Thank you." She repeated the words several times, bowing.

"I'm glad you will be reunited with your family." Old Saul patted her shoulder. "Tomorrow my grandson will come to get you."

"We'll have food ready for him to take along," Sunny said.

Noah's gut loosened some. This was for the best. This woman and her son would be much safer among her own people than here.

Old Saul rose with some effort. "I'll be going home then and getting the young man ready for the journey."

With the boy and dog trailing behind, Noah walked Old Saul outside and helped him back onto the wagon. When the older man sat on the bench again, Noah looked up at him. "I hadn't thought about that stranger stirring up more trouble. I'm glad you did."

"I'm glad you helped her." The old man lifted his reins. "She could have died and left that boy an orphan. You're a fine man, Noah Whitmore."

Noah reacted with a sound of derision. "I just want to live my life in peace."

"Peace. Yes, we old soldiers all crave that." Old Saul started his team turning around to go home. "War leaves a mark on a man."

"You mean like Cain?" Noah said, charged with sudden anger at himself, at what he had done. "Marked for killing his brother? I saw that happen—brothers coming face-to-face, one in gray, one in blue." He couldn't go on. The anger left him as quickly as it had come.

The older man paused and stared at him for several moments. "Someday we'll talk about that. But not today. I've got to go home and soothe my daughter-in-law's worries about her 'baby boy' going all the way to Lake Superior on his own."

Still digesting the comment about old soldiers, Noah just raised his hand in farewell. The wagon rocked and creaked its way down the track to the rough road.

Beside him, Miigwans's head hung low.

"Don't you want to go home?" Noah asked.

The boy looked up. "I won't get to see the pups born. I wanted to see Neechee's babies."

Noah pulled the boy into a one-armed hug. "Don't worry. If the pups are strong and there are at least three, I'll send one to you—a girl if I can, so she can have pups, too. Then you can have dogs that remind you of Neechee and me."

Noah let the boy lean into him for a moment. His father had always pushed him away. He vowed he would never do that to a child.

From the doorway Dawn called to Noah in her baby talk, cheering him up as always. He scooped up Miigwans and tossed him into the air and caught him. The boy squealed with laughter. And a grin won over Noah's face. Then Noah ran to Dawn, set down Miigwans and lifted her with both hands, jiggling her and making her laugh, too.

Sunny watched him from just inside. The tenderness in her gaze was directed to him, not Dawn. A frisson of awareness vibrated between them, wonderful yet terrifying.

Chapter Twelve

"I don't know why that old man is showing us kindness," Bid'a ban murmured to Sunny that evening. They were washing the dishes from supper alone in front of the cabin.

Sunny had wondered why Bid'a ban had remained so silent ever since Old Saul had left. "He's a good man."

Bid'a ban nodded, drying a bowl and then setting it on a shelf that Noah had crafted and hung. "Why? What makes one man bad, and another, like your husband, so kind?"

Sunny thought over what she'd learned when her life changed, when she'd gone to live with the Gabriels. She'd asked them why they were willing to help her in spite of the stigma attached to her. They had quoted the Bible, saying they were showing her God's love. How would an Ojibwa woman take that for an answer?

"I think it has to do with God," Sunny ventured.

"You mean *Gitchie Manitou,* the Great Spirit?"

"Do you know about God, Bid'a ban?" Sunny paused in scrubbing the stew pot.

"Who can know Him? His name also means the Great Mystery and he is to us, his children."

God remained a great mystery to her, too. "I don't know much about God. But I have learned that those who love Him, *truly* love Him, show that love to others. That's why Old Saul can be kind."

Sunny recalled that awful day so long ago when the other preacher had chased and beaten her mother. Why hadn't he shown any of God's love that day? Being a preacher evidently didn't prove one knew much of God.

Bid'a ban nodded, looking thoughtful. "At my home a *Zhaagnaash,* a white man, comes to speak to us about the white man's God."

"Does he show love?" Sunny asked.

"Yes, he is kind and helps us."

Sunny's tension eased. "Then listen to him." They finished washing and drying and went inside to put away the clean pot and dishes.

"I will listen to that *Zhaagnaash,*" Bid'a ban said.

Sunny wanted to say more, but couldn't find the words. Instead she pressed her cheek to Bid'a ban's and the woman returned the gesture. Sunny realized that she felt differently with Bid'a ban than with her other friends. She didn't have to guard every word from this woman. This woman understood how life could be cruel in the same way that Sunny herself did.

Noah, Miigwans and Dawn came inside and the moment with Bid'a ban ended. Noah sat down on the bench. Neechee lay down across the threshold. Miigwans sat beside her, petting the dog.

Sunny praised God for this sturdy cabin, and for the man who'd built it and who now held her daughter on his knee, playing pony. Bid'a ban sat by the fire and began finishing Miigwans's new shirt. And Sunny began packing food for Bid'a ban's trip, trying not to think of their parting.

The next morning found them outside the cabin early, while dew still wet the grass. Caught between laughter and sorrow, Sunny picked up Dawn and hid behind her daughter. How could she bear to bid her friend goodbye?

Standing opposite her by the wagon, Old Saul, his son and daughter-in-law Lavina waited with Saul's gawky grandsons. The one named Isaiah, who was going with Bid'a ban, held the reins of the packhorse. Noah was securing two sacks of provisions onto the horse's back along with those Isaiah had already packed on.

Finished, Noah crossed to Miigwans who stood with a hand on Neechee's head. When Noah reached Miigwans, the boy swung an arm around Noah's waist. Nearby, his mother hesitated beside Sunny.

Bid'a ban appeared to be experiencing the same crosscurrents of emotions as Sunny. Nevertheless, she held out a hand toward Noah. "I can never thank you enough for what you did for me, *Nin awema,* my brother."

"We were glad to help," Noah said, squeezing and releasing her hand, a trace of a smile flickering on his somber face.

Sunny couldn't stop herself. With Dawn on one hip, she wrapped one arm around Bid'a ban. "I'll miss you," she murmured.

"I will miss you, *Nimissè,* my sister." Bid'a ban pressed her lips together as if holding back tears and stroked Dawn's curls lovingly.

Sunny rubbed the woman's arm. "I know you will be safe with Isaiah." The young man barely sported peach fuzz on his chin but he looked sturdy and sensible. She recalled Ophelia's homesickness. No doubt he'd feel the same distress. But he looked like the kind who would stick to this journey and see it through.

"I think we should be going," Isaiah said, blushing when his voice cracked. "I want to put as many miles behind us as we can before sundown." They would follow the Chippewa River northeast to the Flambeau River, which would lead them onto the Ojibwa land. About a week or so and they would reach Bid'a ban's family.

Bid'a ban motioned, wordlessly prompting Miigwans to come away with her.

The boy buried his face into Noah's shirt.

Sunny ached for the boy who'd found a father for a short time—and was now leaving him.

With an arm around the boy's shoulders, Noah pressed the child close. "You'll be fine. And Isaiah will bring you news of us and maybe a pup sometime before snow. I will miss you, Miigwans." Noah's voice halted, as if he, too, were choking back the sadness of parting.

Sunny moved closer to Noah and hugged Miigwans, who then bent to hug Neechee around the neck. The dog barked once and licked Miigwans's face. The boy rose and went to his mother. Waving a pudgy little hand, Dawn babbled baby talk as if also saying farewell.

"We'll pray once more." Old Saul removed his hat and bowed his head. "God, we know that we are in Your hands. Keep our Isaiah and this lady and her son safe as they travel north. Bring help if they need it and good weather. We thank You, Lord. Amen."

"I will say *Gigawabamin Menawah*. That means we will meet again," Bid'a ban said, lifting her hand in farewell. Miigwans echoed her greeting, hanging his head.

Sunny sucked in air, not wanting to cry.

As Isaiah's mother wiped away tears, the threesome—Isaiah leading the packhorse, Bid'a ban with Miigwans nearby—turned and walked down the trail.

"I'm sure they'll be fine," Sunny murmured to Lavina.

The older woman sighed long. "He's in God's hands, as he always has been. We'll see you Sunday then?"

"We'll be there," Noah replied. Sunny went and took her place beside him as the other family settled themselves on the wagon and headed down the track for home. Noah laid his arm upon her shoulder and she drew closer to him.

Noah and Sunny didn't move until the wagon disappeared around the bend thick with trees, until they were alone again.

Dawn began squirming and holding out both hands toward Noah and he lifted her from Sunny's arms. "I'll play with her for a moment. Then I have to go to Martin's to work on pulling out stumps."

Missing his touch, Sunny didn't relish being left alone. "Do you think the stranger is gone for good then?"

"I should have said *we'll* be going to Martin's."

Sunny nodded. The heaviness of fear had lifted some but she agreed with Noah. They couldn't let down their guard. "You don't think he'll be able to find out that Isaiah has taken Bid'a ban north and go after them, do you?"

Noah considered this as he swung Dawn up and

down like a swing. "No, but I think he might tell the military at Fort Snelling. Though that won't make any trouble for us. And if they come for her, she'll already be far away. Are you ready to leave?" he asked.

"I'll get my sewing basket." Sunny wondered how long she'd have to spend every day with one of her neighbors. Inside, she checked on the slowly simmering pot of salt pork and beans that she had hung over the banked fire. She inhaled deeply, pushing away the grave sorrow of parting. And then gathered what she needed for her day's visit with Ophelia.

Within an hour she and Noah arrived at the young couple's cabin. Martin met them at the door, looking strained. "I'm glad you've come, Mrs. Whitmore." Before she could respond, he began talking to Noah.

Noah was carrying Dawn on his shoulders and he lifted her down to give her to Sunny. The baby squawked and struggled to stay with Noah.

"She sure loves her papa," Martin said, grinning.

The comment stung some hidden place deep inside Sunny. Of course no one here would ever know that Noah was not Dawn's father. So she smiled as expected. Noah headed toward the nearly cleared garden with Neechee and Martin.

With difficulty, Sunny carried the squirming and complaining child into the cabin.

Where she found Ophelia bent over the chamber pot, retching.

"Oh, dear!" Setting down Dawn, Sunny dropped to her knees. "Are you ill?"

Ophelia, pale and clammy looking, gazed at her in obvious misery. "I don't have a fever, but I was sick like this the last two mornings and now again today. Yet I'm fine by lunchtime. What's wrong with me, Sunny?"

At this unexpected news, Sunny sighed and hurried to dampen a cloth to wipe the young woman's face. After several more minutes bent over the chamber pot, Ophelia found the strength to rise and sit on a chair at the table.

Suddenly Sunny noticed that Dawn was not making a sound. She looked around the neat cabin, dropped to her knees to look under the bed—no Dawn. And then she realized the door stood ajar. She rushed outside and cast frantic glances around, looking for the child and calling, "Dawn? Dawn!"

Then just as she recalled Dawn's insistence on wanting to go with Noah, she heard Neechee's frantic barking. She raced toward the sound. "Noah!" she shrieked. "Dawn's outside! Watch for her!" Sunny ran the short distance toward the garden by the spring.

In one dreadful moment she spotted Dawn crawling fast only a yard or so from the men. Neechee was barking the alarm, and Noah—at the head of the team of oxen—turned.

His face blanched. "Ho!" he ordered the team to stop and swooped down to intercept the baby nearly concealed by the high grass.

"What were you thinking?" he thundered at Sunny.

She couldn't speak. The image of her baby under the feet of the huge oxen left her feeling light-headed.

"She could have been crushed!" Noah roared, holding Dawn close.

His loud voice frightened the baby and she began wailing.

Still light-headed and with her heart throbbing painfully, Sunny walked toward him slowly, as if walking through thick mud.

"Why did you let her get away from you?" Noah asked.

"Ophelia isn't feeling well and I was distracted. I'm sorry. Dawn has never before tried to go outside without me." Sunny heard her voice as if from a distance. She realized she was about to faint. She dropped onto the nearest broad stump and lowered her head.

"Are you all right?" Noah asked, his voice now soft with concern.

"I feel faint, that's all," she said, her voice still sounding as if it were coming from somewhere else.

Noah hovered over her, comforting Dawn and speaking gently to Sunny. "I didn't mean to yell at you. I was just so scared for her."

Sunny nodded, the earth beneath her still swaying.

"Sunny?" Ophelia came to her side. "Mr. Whitmore, let me have the baby. I'll walk your wife back to the cabin and give her a stiff cup of coffee."

Noah helped Sunny up. "I'll come, too."

Sunny held up a hand. "No, I'll be fine. You go on with your work."

Ophelia carried Dawn and walked Sunny back to her cabin. There, Ophelia settled them in a chair at the table and poured Sunny coffee. "This will buck you up."

Sunny didn't want coffee, but lifted the cup anyway.

A sudden fit of dry heaves came over Ophelia. The young woman bent away from Sunny. Finally she regained command of herself. "I apologize. I just don't know what's happening to me."

Sunny did.

"How long have you and Martin been married now?"

"Almost six weeks." Ophelia looked at her.

Sunny sighed. "Have you ever heard of morning sickness?"

Ophelia shook her head no.

"Not all women get it but some do. It means you may be expecting a child."

Ophelia's mouth dropped open and stayed open.

"Didn't your mother explain the signs of pregnancy to you?"

Ophelia again shook her head.

This disgusted Sunny. Not teaching Ophelia how to do laundry was one thing. But how could a mother send her daughter away without sharing these very necessary facts with her? So Sunny explained to the young bride how it felt to some women to be pregnant. And how a woman knew she was with child.

Though Ophelia appeared dumbfounded and slightly afraid, she asked, "Is there anything I should be doing? I mean for the baby, so it will be healthy?"

"Just eat well and loosen your stays. We'll need to sew you a Mother Hubbard dress for when your regular dresses don't fit—though with the first baby women don't show as early as with the following pregnancies."

Ophelia nodded solemnly.

Then they heard Nan's voice call from outside and she opened the door. One look at them prompted her to ask, "What's wrong?"

"I'm expecting," Ophelia said, and promptly burst into tears.

"Well, that happened fast." Grinning, Nan shut the door firmly and settled Guthrie to play with Dawn on the floor. Sunny then lifted Pearl Louise from her mother's arms and cuddled her.

Smiling her thanks, Nan soothed Ophelia and went about brewing her a cup of chamomile tea. "Now, you'll be just fine. It's common to be emotional—I mean extra emotional—all the way through and even after the baby's born. But this morning sickness usually only lasts for a few months. Then you'll be fine, right, Sunny?"

Sunny didn't reveal that since she'd worked every night in the saloon, she'd experienced her morning sickness in the afternoon. She merely nodded in agreement.

"Let's see," Nan said, looking thoughtful. "You'll be having a baby about the end of winter then. Late February, maybe March."

"I didn't plan on having a baby so soon."

Nan laughed heartily at this. "Babies have a way of coming when they will."

Sunny was not about to reveal that she knew how to prevent pregnancy but she'd gotten pregnant anyway. Nan was right—babies did come.

"I'm so glad I have the two of you nearby." Impulsively, Ophelia claimed one hand from each of them and held on. "There's so much about being a married woman I don't know."

Sunny echoed the same thought silently. Neither of these women lived the complex, hidden life she did. But this large, good-natured blonde and this innocent, pretty brunette had become her friends. She smiled and squeezed Ophelia's hand, encouraging her. And kissed little Pearl Louise's forehead.

Sunny paused a moment to recall her daughter demanding to be in Noah's arms. That they had been a family for only near to two months was hard to believe. Dawn certainly didn't remember a time when Noah wasn't there to play with her.

The fact that Sunny had not yet become this good man's wife completely twinged sharply within. *I must be grateful for what I have. Dawn will have a good life and I have a sheltered one.* The memory of Noah's light kiss and brief embrace eased the twinge. *I must be grateful for what I have,* she repeated to herself. But she couldn't help but wonder now that Bid'a ban had gone, would she return to sleeping by the fire tonight?

Over a week later in the early balmy afternoon, Sunny drove into town with Nan and Ophelia, who rode behind in the wagon bed with the children. At the end of Sunday's gathering Mrs. Ashford had issued an invitation to come to town to join a quilting circle.

Noah, along with the other two husbands, had decided that the threat from the stranger had ended and the three women could go to town without any male escort. So Sunny had of course accepted along with Nan and Ophelia. But Sunny didn't really relish visiting Mrs. Ashford, a woman who seemed to take herself very seriously.

Now each of them got down and carried a child and a sewing basket, Ophelia carrying Nan's Guthrie. Mrs. Ashford, with gray threads in her dark hair and wearing a crisp dress of navy blue bombazine, stood outside her husband's store. She was chatting with Lavina. Both women waved in welcome.

Then for the first time, Sunny followed Mrs. Ashford through the store past a beaming Mr. Ashford and up the stairs into the beautiful living quarters above. Why had Mrs. Ashford—who behaved as if she were the leader of Pepin "society"—invited them?

Surely Sunny and Noah had branded themselves as renegades?

"I'm so glad that you were able to come," Mrs. Ashford said, motioning them to take seats around a long dining table near the large lace-curtained windows that overlooked the street.

"You have a lovely view of the Mississippi," Ophelia commented. Across the street sunlight glinted on the wide blue river, dazzling.

"I do enjoy it. I don't like living in a forest. I can't see what's coming."

"I find the forest cozy," Sunny said, surprising herself. "The trees are like arms around me."

All the women looked at her.

"Sometimes I have funny thoughts," she apologized, her cheeks warm.

"That was kind of like poetry," Nan said.

Sunny looked at Nan. Poetry from her?

Mrs. Ashford lifted one eyebrow.

"Well, I like both, forest and town," Ophelia said. "I saw that three more families have staked homesteads hereabouts. Have you met them, Mrs. Ashford?"

"Yes, but only one brought a family with him." Mrs. Ashford's tone disapproved of the two bachelors. "I think having a family steadies a man."

Lavina nodded. They all sat around the table, which looked to be polished walnut with very ornately carved legs. Mrs. Ashford's parlor and dining room combined was larger than Nan's whole cabin. The room contrasted with Sunny's simple cabin. To her, this room felt crowded with too much furniture and bric-a-brac. Sunny found herself unimpressed by the finery. She began to relax.

Mrs. Ashford's youngest daughter, a thin thirteen-year-old, volunteered to take the children out back to play. But neither toddler would leave their mother. So the girl, holding Nan's baby, lured the children to the sitting area by the cold fireplace and spread out blocks and two rag dolls on the floor. Dawn began chewing a block and Guthrie flapped one of the rag dolls on the floor like a hammer.

"I've started a quilt," Mrs. Ashford said, standing at the head of the table and unrolling a partially sewn quilt top. "And I thought it would be nice to have a community quilting circle. We probably won't meet very often during the summer months—we'll have gardens to tend and preserving and canning to do. But the long winter will be much easier on us if we have a monthly circle to look forward to. Don't you think?"

Even though Sunny's nerves had at first been tightened into little hard knots, the plan for a regular social get-together did appeal to her. So no more at ease, she smiled with the other ladies and murmured something polite.

The fact that she had never quilted before in her life set her teeth on edge. But she listened and watched. From a bag, Mrs. Ashford plucked out colorful scraps of cloth and distributed some to each woman to create a quilt square. Sunny watched Nan play with the scraps she had been given and was intrigued when Nan began to set them into a pattern.

Sunny mimicked Nan and began to enjoy herself. Soon she was sewing the pieces together and listening to the women discuss babies and husbands.

"I hear your father is a judge in Illinois?" Mrs. Ashford quizzed Ophelia.

"Yes, he is a circuit court judge. My Martin has read law, too."

"How interesting." Mrs. Ashford turned to Sunny. "Your husband is certainly becoming a leader in our community."

Sunny's needle poked her finger and she slipped it in her mouth so she didn't bleed on the fabric. "Noah?"

"Yes, indeed," Lavina agreed.

"Gordy really respects Noah," Nan added.

"And Martin does, too," Ophelia said, nodding decidedly. "He says Noah can do so many things, knows so much."

"And isn't afraid to take a stand and see it through." Lavina stopped sewing. "Maybe people didn't like that Indian woman and her boy coming here, but they respect that Noah stood up for them."

"And was able to put that stranger in his place without violence," Mrs. Ashford said. "And everybody can tell Noah Whitmore's educated. And a Union Army veteran, too. Your husband has a future in this community."

Dawn suddenly demanded loudly to be nursed, which set off Nan's baby, too. This saved Sunny from having to reply. Sunny and Nan went to sit in comfortable rockers near the cold hearth. Sunny hummed to Dawn as she nursed, pondering all the storekeeper's wife had just said. Sunny was proud of Noah but hadn't realized others noticed how special he was.

The other women continued quilting and discussing the latest fashion. Skirts were becoming more and more narrow and the hoop had definitely gone out. Sunny could barely listen—all she could think about was what the women had said about her husband.

Noah was the kind of man who garnered respect.

She just hoped nobody would say this to him—after all, only a month and a half ago they'd had their first argument over whether or not to even associate with their neighbors. But it turned out Noah wasn't the kind of man who ignored the needs of others. Which was exactly why she had fallen in love with him. When would she have the courage to tell him that?

The image of Dawn in her spotless white pinafore standing in the schoolyard came to mind. And Sunny knew for certain that in the future Dawn would be proud of her father.

Sunny's face felt hot as she thought about the night after Bid'a ban left, when Noah had not suggested by word or look that Sunny should leave the loft to him alone at night. They still slept far apart but they were at least on the same level now.

"What are you smilin' about?" Nan asked in an undertone.

Sunny blushed. "Noah."

Nan chuckled and murmured for her ears only, "Yes, we both got handsome husbands."

Sunny smiled but didn't reply.

"Katharine!" Mr. Ashford called up the stairs.

Mrs. Ashford hurried to the open rear door. "Yes, Ned?"

"Tell Mrs. Whitmore that a mail boat just came in and I have a letter for her husband from Pennsylvania. That's quick all right. Only took about two weeks. The new railroads are making mail faster all right."

A letter for Noah? Sunny wondered if it brought good news or bad news. Remembering Noah's conflict with his disapproving father, she hoped Noah's brother had written instead.

* * *

Noah and Neechee met Sunny at the head of their track. "I heard you ladies coming."

From the wagon bed Sunny smiled at him. The quilting circle had been fun, but mainly because of her two friends and Lavina. Mrs. Ashford obviously was forming her "social" circle with the women she thought prominent.

From subtle clues Sunny had realized that Nan would not have been included except for her obvious friendship with both Sunny and Ophelia. Katharine Ashford did not deceive Sunny. Her friendship was paper-thin while Nan's ran to the bone. And Ophelia's affection shone as honest, too.

Even after such a short separation Sunny experienced a rush of affection for Noah. But of course she couldn't show it. It wouldn't be appropriate in front of the other women.

Soon Nan drove away toward Ophelia's. Dawn insisted that Noah hold her, so Sunny only carried her sewing basket as they walked toward their cabin. Neechee barked playfully at Dawn. Now that they were alone, Sunny reached into her pocket. "Noah, I have something for you."

He looked up.

She held out the letter that she'd tucked into her pocket with care.

Noah stared at it as if he didn't know what it was.

She extended her hand farther, insisting he receive it. Why did he hesitate?

"It looks like it's from your brothers. Or your father."

He finally took the letter and stared at it as though he could read it through the envelope.

She waited till Dawn's struggling to get Noah's attention became impossible to ignore. She retrieved the child and set her down. Determined, Dawn crawled straight back to Noah and pulled herself up, using his pant leg. Noah ignored Dawn, an unusual occurrence. Neechee barked once as if trying to shake Noah's preoccupation.

Maybe it's me. "I'll let you read your letter in privacy." She moved toward the cabin.

"No." He slipped the letter into his breast pocket. "I've got some work to do." He picked Dawn up and then handed the child back to Sunny. He walked away, Neechee trailing after him.

Sunny was dumbfounded. There was something in that letter that Noah did not want to face. What was Noah hiding from her?

That evening the letter sat on the mantel unopened. Noah watched as Sunny got ready to serve supper. On the floor Dawn crawled after a ball of leather he'd fashioned for her. Neechee lay across the threshold as usual, but her gaze fixed on her master. Noah sat on the bench by the table and stared at the letter. He knew he must open it. He wouldn't sleep, knowing it sat there. Noah had just sent a note about arriving safely. He struggled with the fact that he feared reading it. His brother wouldn't have responded so quickly unless he had important news. To him that boded ill.

Delay in opening the letter had ruined the afternoon, making it more miserable than any in recent memory. Though Sunny had not asked why he didn't just open the letter, she acted as if she were stepping on eggs again. She kept glancing up at the letter and then away.

He hated upsetting her. He must read it now.

He stood. Retrieved the letter. And sat down. Sunny paused and then went back to stirring the pot. Dawn crawled over and watched him slit open the letter with his pocket knife.

He spread it out on the table, smoothing the creases. He read the brief, poignant letter and tried to decide what he was feeling. He couldn't.

Still Sunny didn't ask. She kept her back to him.

He took a deep breath, trying to shift the solid block of grief within. "Nathan, my eldest brother, wrote to tell me that my father has had a stroke and is now bedridden."

Sunny turned quickly. "I'm so sorry to hear that."

"He also tells me that our father can't speak."

"That is bad." She looked to him as if asking what he meant to do about this.

"My brother says they have hired a nurse to care for him. So I'm not to worry."

"These things happen," she replied, pouring stew into bowls on the table.

These things happen. Noah realized that he was once again frozen inside. He folded the letter and returned it to the envelope.

Sunny sat across from him with Dawn on her lap. "Your father didn't seem to approve of you going to war."

Her timid words touched a sore spot. He snorted. "It wasn't just that. Nothing I ever did pleased my father. We could never understand why everything I did irritated him."

"I'm sorry."

He shrugged.

"Will you say grace, Noah?"

He nodded and bowed his head. A few words and they began to eat.

Why was it that no matter how far he went, ties of blood still held? Why did a father love some sons and not others?

Dawn babbled. Then quite clearly she said, "No-No." He glanced over at her. "No-No."

Sunny looked thunderstruck.

"No-No," Dawn repeated, patting the table and staring at Noah. "No-No."

"I think she's trying to say *Noah*," Sunny said with wonder in her voice.

Strong emotion brought tears just behind Noah's eyes. Reaching across the table, he gripped one of Dawn's plump little hands. "Hey, Dawn."

"No-No!" she squealed triumphantly.

He rose and lifted the baby into his arms, his spirit rising. "I'm Papa, Dawn. I'm your papa."

"No-No." Dawn flung herself against Noah's chest, giving him one of her unabashed hugs.

He smiled, his joy overflowing. "Okay, for now you can call me No-No. Sunny, you'll have to start calling me her pa. We'll scandalize the neighborhood if we let her call me Noah."

Sunny rose and came to stand beside him. She leaned her cheek against his arm as she spoke to their daughter. "This is your papa. Pa-pa."

Yes, Dawn, you're my little girl. And then one tear slipped down his cheek. His father lay ill far away, but he'd always been far away from Noah. His daughter was here, now.

What had he ever done to deserve this little girl and her mother?

Chapter Thirteen

Near his garden, Noah, Gordy and Martin stood, exhausted but satisfied. Fleetingly, the image of Miigwans's face came to mind. Neechee lay in the shade nearby, another reminder of the little boy. Was he safe now?

Turning from these thoughts, Noah leaned against one of his oxen and stroked the animal's back. "Couldn't have done it without you," he murmured to the animal.

"You were smart to invest in oxen, Noah," Martin said. "They can outwork our draft horses."

Noah patted his ox's rump once more. "My father always used oxen. We had horses for driving, but oxen for the heavy work." He thought of his stiff-necked father now reduced only in his fifties to an invalid and at such a young age. Life took many strange twists and turns.

Matters here hadn't turned out just the way Noah had imagined. He'd married Sunny in part so he wouldn't be totally alone here. But events had caused him to make friends, real friends. These men had stood with him against that stranger. And they seemed to now look to him as the one who knew what had to be done. He'd never quite thought of himself as a leader before, but it wasn't necessarily a bad thing.

"We all need barns before winter," he suddenly announced.

The other two men looked at him in dismay.

"Noah Whitmore, you beat all," Gordy said, shoving back his hat to wipe the sweat on his forehead with his sleeve. "We just got the final garden cleared and still need to plow and plant. And you're talkin' about winter."

Martin groaned and moved as if his back were aching. "This starting from scratch is more work than I anticipated."

Noah looked at the younger man. "You thinking of going back to Illinois?"

"No," Martin said firmly. "I've read law but I was raised on a farm and I can do the work. It's just that my dad did the hard work of settling and getting a farm started. He warned me how it'd be."

"Well, I could have stayed home and worked with my pa and brothers," Gordy offered. "But I wanted better, more for my Nan and kids, a place of our own."

"Then we better talk about raising our barns before snow flies," Noah said laconically. "The preacher said something to me about holding barn raisings this summer. Maybe we should ask who else needs a barn. If everybody works at logging out what they need, we could gather and get a barn up in a day or two. Maybe do one a month. How's that sound?"

"Sounds like you have that all figured out right well," Gordy said. Then he paused. "I hate to ask but my cabin was not tight and warm for winter last year. Nan and me nearly froze to death. I see, Noah, how you built a foundation for your cabin and a log floor..." Gordy's voice trailed off.

Noah folded his arms and nodded. "I'll help you add on a larger room and you can use the old cabin as a cold room this winter. I might ask to store some provisions there, too."

"You'd be welcome to." Gordy looked and sounded relieved.

"I'll help, too," Martin volunteered.

"And if I run short of money, I'll let it be known that I can work in stone," Noah continued.

"I figure I can cut more firewood than I'll need," Gordy said, "and sell some for hard cash or barter at the store."

"I'm thinking of holding school a couple of days a week come fall. But until then we'll be raising barns and another cabin. Whew," Martin breathed out. "We're all going to be trim and with muscles like rock."

This hit Noah funny. He broke out into a laugh.

"Well," Gordy said, smiling broadly, "I guess Noah Whitmore can laugh."

Noah hadn't realized they'd notice his lack of humor. This made him think of how Dawn was the one who'd brought back his laughter. Noah thought of Dawn's latest feat. "A few days ago Dawn said her first word—my name. She called me No-No." Noah had never understood the expression puffed-up before but he felt it now.

"Wow," Gordy said, looking impressed. "That's early to be talking. And now that you got one child up a bit—" Gordy winked "—I guess you'll be the next family expectin' another young-un."

Noah's good mood evaporated.

Oblivious, Gordy settled his hat back on his head.

"I'll head home now. I think there'll be enough light I can get my plowing started today."

Martin made his farewell also. The two younger men headed off together. Noah didn't turn to watch them go. Gordy's words lay heavy, souring his stomach. If matters went on the way they had, Dawn would be his only child.

He hadn't realized that he would like being a father. Noah leaned against the ox. He recalled every time Sunny had touched him. How pretty she was and he glimpsed then that he desired her. But that was all. He didn't seem to be able to move forward. What would it take to make him whole again?

Sunday turned out gloomy. Sunny tried not to let it further dull her mood. She had begun to worry about Isaiah and Bid'a ban and Miigwans. Since they'd left, three Sundays had come and gone; the gardens had all been planted. Had the threesome reached Lac du Flambeau?

Sunday meetings in town had become a looked-for event. People smiled and waved at them as they arrived in Gordy's wagon. It was a far cry from the chilly reception they'd once received.

Martin had an arm around Ophelia who was struggling still with morning sickness. The tender care that Martin showed his bride had increased and it nipped Sunny in a tender spot. The young couple's love for each other gleamed so apparent. How must it feel to be loved like that?

Very pale, Ophelia had her handkerchief pressed to her mouth and Sunny hoped she wouldn't be sick in town—every gossip would know that she was expecting. Both Sunny and Nan had counseled her to wait till the crucial third month had passed before letting the news be known. Better to wait till the worry of early miscarriage passed.

Gordy parked the wagon under a spreading oak. Noah helped Sunny down and swung Dawn to sit up on his shoulders. The little girl squealed with delight.

Old Saul and his family already waited on Ashford's porch. Sunny moved forward, greeting people who greeted her back and smiling generally, always mindful that these were the people Dawn would grow up amongst.

When closer, Sunny noticed that Lavina looked strained. So Isaiah had not yet returned. Sunny hoped sincerely that no harm had come to him. And she hoped Bid'a ban and Miigwans were even now safe in the arms of their family.

Sunny determined to say a few encouraging phrases to Lavina. Surely God was protecting the young man who had volunteered to help a widow and orphan. Isn't that the kind of thing God did?

Lavina and her husband started the service with hymn singing. Sunny hummed along and smiled, watching Dawn on her high perch listen intently to the music. After a few rousing hymns, Old Saul stood from his chair and raised both hands. "Another Lord's Day, what a blessing to see you all and know that he is here with us."

He opened his Bible but did not look down as he recited, "'My little children, these things write I unto you, that ye sin not. And if any man sin, we have an advocate with the Father, Jesus Christ, the righteous: And he is the propitiation for our sins: and not for ours only, but also for the sins of the whole world.'"

Suddenly Sunny noticed that everyone was glancing behind to the west and she heard the sound of a boat's horn. A riverboat must be docking.

Old Saul chuckled. "Let's sing some more. I know everybody wants to see if anybody or anything's getting off the boat."

Lavina stepped forward and began a hymn. People sang along but, in truth, the boat docking had distracted everyone. Sunny felt the pull of curiosity, too. So little happened outside the daily routine of chores. The boat would bring newspapers from downriver and maybe mail.

Then Sunny heard Ophelia gasp. The bride turned completely toward the river. Sunny swung around to face the same way.

From the boat ramp, an older, very expensively dressed lady with a younger woman was advancing toward the Sunday gathering. The hymn trailed off.

The older woman waved a lace handkerchief and hurried forward. "Ophelia!" she exclaimed.

"Mother?" Ophelia said, her eyes wide.

"Yes, Ophelia, I'm here." The woman said the words as if Ophelia lay on her death bed.

Just before Ophelia's mother reached her, the bride pressed the handkerchief over her mouth and wailed softly, wordlessly.

Quickly, Sunny moved to Ophelia's side. "Are you indisposed?"

"Yes." The young woman looked about to faint.

Sunny took charge. "Mrs. Ashford! Mrs. Steward

is indisposed! May we take her upstairs to your quarters, please?"

Mrs. Ashford swooped down and helped Sunny assist Ophelia inside. Martin hurried behind them and Ophelia's mother began calling out instructions in rapid fire from the rear.

Soon the five of them arrived in the Ashfords' parlor. Martin had carried Ophelia up the steps at Sunny's suggestion. He lay his wife on the sofa and stood beside her. "Do you need anything?"

Sunny noted that Ophelia was trying to swallow down nausea. "Mrs. Ashford, a basin please."

"Is my child ill?" the newcomer demanded in a voice that went up Sunny's spine like a coarse brush.

Mrs. Ashford handed Sunny the basin just in time. Ophelia lost the scant breakfast she must have eaten.

"Is there a doctor in town?" Ophelia's mother demanded.

Sunny wished the woman would show some sensitivity. She offered her free hand. "No, we don't have a doctor yet. I'm Mrs. Noah Whitmore, ma'am, Ophelia's neighbor."

"I'm Mrs. Buford Cantrell, Ophelia's mother." With lifted nose, the woman shook hands as if she were the lady and they were the lowly and then turned to her daughter. "I can see I didn't come a moment too soon." She began chafing Ophelia's wrist trying to increase circulation.

Martin retreated, but stayed near his wife.

"Mother, please," Ophelia begged faintly, "don't fuss. I'm fine."

Mrs. Cantrell managed to snort in a very refined way. "I told you that you were too delicate to venture onto the frontier. I had this terrible premonition that something awful—"

"I don't think expecting her first child is something awful." Nan's matter-of-fact voice startled all of them. They glanced toward the top of the stairs where Nan stood near Martin. Nan came forward, smiling with outstretched hand. "I'm Nan Osbourne, another friend of Ophelia's."

Mrs. Cantrell's mouth gathered up like a drawstring purse and instead of taking Nan's hand, she nodded curtly. "Mrs. Buford Cantrell. Charmed, I'm sure."

Sunny bristled.

"Oh, a baby—this is good news," Mrs. Ashford said, obviously trying to help keep everything polite. "I'm so happy for you, Mrs. Steward."

Mrs. Cantrell ignored this and went on. "I had a premonition that my Ophelia needed me. I can see she must come home where I can care for her."

"Mother!" Ophelia protested. "I'm not going home with anybody but Martin."

"But there's no doctor here," Mrs. Cantrell protested. "And anyone can see you're in need of one."

Sunny wanted to shake the melodramatic woman.

"She's having a baby, that's all," Nan said. "She'll be fine. Mrs. Ashford helped birth my little Pearl Louise not too long ago."

Mrs. Cantrell looked as if she wanted to say more—much more—but evidently realized that she couldn't disparage Mrs. Ashford in her own home. So she turned on Nan. "You obviously are the kind of hefty woman who has no trouble with childbearing, but my Ophelia is so delicate."

Sunny caught the insult and gasped.

Ophelia sat up on the sofa. "Mother! Why have you come?"

"Because I thought by now you'd realize that you don't belong here."

"I belong wherever my husband is."

Sunny realized why Ophelia had married so young and had been willing to leave for the frontier. Mrs. Cantrell struck her as a bad dream.

Finally, when Ophelia burst into tears over her mother's unkind words, the younger woman who had arrived with Mrs. Cantrell stepped into the room and cleared her throat. "I think, Auntie, it would be best if we returned to the riverboat now. Your daughter needs peace and some rest. And our noon meal will be served soon."

This precise and very cool speech caught Mrs. Cantrell in midstream. She blinked.

The young woman, who was also dressed stylishly, looked to Martin. "Martin, why don't you convey Ophelia home and then return to town and take us out to see your place? I know I'm eager to meet your friends and see how much you've accomplished. That's why we came." The young woman emphasized ever so slightly the last sentence.

Sunny waited for a backlash—in vain. Mrs. Cantrell swallowed several times and then pinned a painfully artificial smile on her face. "An excellent idea, Ellen. I'm afraid finding Ophelia in such straits discomposed me."

Her head resting on the back of the sofa, Ophelia spoke up. "Everyone, this is my cousin, Miss Ellen Thurston. I'm happy to see you, Ellen."

Ellen inclined her head to all politely and gestured for the older woman to precede her down the stairs. Ellen then turned to Mrs. Ashford. "Thank you so much

for opening your charming home to strangers like us.
So kind."

Beaming at the compliment, Mrs. Ashford accepted the younger woman's thanks and showed the ladies down the staircase. Ophelia looked to Martin and burst into fresh tears of frustration as soon as her mother was gone.

Nan sat down and put her arms around her. "There, there," she murmured, "this is just commotion, that's all. We'll all smile about it in the future."

Sunny thought that would be much, much further in the future. Maybe when they were grandmothers.

Martin looked chagrined, but said gently, "Are you able to go downstairs?"

Ophelia held out both her hands. "Oh, Martin, I'm so sorry. I hate the way she talks to you."

He took her hands and helped her up. "Now, Mrs. Osbourne is exactly right. This is all sound and fury, nothing to concern you. Your mother is just being herself—I'm only grateful I'm married to you, not her." He shepherded his wife to the stairs and over her protests, carried her down.

"What next?" Nan asked, shaking her head. "I got an aunt just like Ophelia's mother—loves an audience. Shoulda gone on the stage."

Sunny laughed out loud and then put her hand over her mouth. And the two of them followed the young couple downstairs and outside. What next indeed?

Sunny recalled her mother's pretty face and sweet smile. Warmed, she knew her mother would have loved Noah, loved seeing Sunny and Dawn with him. *I still haven't been able to tell him I love him.* A sad thought, one that prodded her.

* * *

Later that day Noah remained dressed in his Sunday best, as did Sunny. They sat on a bench just outside their door, enjoying the spring day. The gloomy layer of clouds had blown away and now the sun shone down and a breeze fluttered the leaves overhead. Sunny was beside him, Dawn asleep on his lap, Neechee lying at his feet. He recognized it as a moment of contentment, something he'd not felt for a long time.

Martin had made a plan for the afternoon with the Osbournes, and with Noah and Sunny. He would drive his mother-in-law and Ellen Thurston to his homestead and then on their way back to the river, stop to visit Noah and Sunny. Gordy had been invited to come also. Strength in numbers, Noah thought.

Martin had muttered to Noah and Gordy that his mother-in-law was the main reason he had headed for Wisconsin. The woman considered herself among the leading lights in Galena society and deemed Ophelia to have married beneath her. Martin had Noah's sincere sympathy.

Neechee stood up and barked once. "Well, Neechee's right. I hear a wagon coming."

Nodding, Noah stroked Dawn's fine hair. The little one had fallen asleep in his lap after lunch. She didn't stir now.

Sunny smiled at the babe. Noah's fingers brushed Sunny's cheek. He tried to ignore the urge to lean forward and follow the touch with a kiss. These feelings startled him.

"I feel sorry for Martin," Noah muttered.

Sunny had stayed very still after he brushed her soft

cheek. Now she sighed as if releasing some pent-up emotion. Looking as if she agreed.

Then they heard an unexpected sound—horse hooves, not a wagon creaking. Up the track rode Isaiah.

Elated, Noah rose, lifting Dawn to his shoulder. "Isaiah!"

Sunny bounced up, too. "Oh, you're home. I'm so glad!"

The lanky teen slipped off his horse. "Got home in time for Sunday dinner. But wanted to bring you news and gifts from Bid'a ban right away."

Sunny pressed her hands together as if trying to contain her obvious happiness. "They're well then?"

"The trip north took a bit longer than I'd guessed. But we got there and her family celebrated her homecoming for three days." Isaiah beamed at them. "Relatives from her clan came from miles around. They thought they had lost her for sure."

Neechee barked again. Noah looked past Isaiah, expecting to see Martin. But instead Old Saul and his family were arriving.

"I'm glad I baked a double layer cake yesterday," Sunny whispered to Noah. They went forward to welcome their guests. Then Noah and Isaiah carried out the table and the other bench for their company.

"What a beautiful day," Lavina said, looking happier than she had in many weeks.

Noah brought out the rocker for Old Saul and the older man lowered himself into it. Before he got settled, Martin's wagon drove into the yard with Ophelia and her family on the bench and the Osbourne family riding in the back.

For a moment Noah was taken aback by the prospect of entertaining so many—and all at once.

"This should prove interesting," Sunny murmured and then went forward in welcome.

For a few minutes Sunny bustled around, making coffee and bringing out the cake. Mrs. Buford Cantrell sat in stony silence at the table. On the other hand Miss Ellen Thurston spoke cordially to everyone as if she were accustomed to sitting outside a cabin in the woods.

As soon as everyone was settled and began eating cake and sipping strong coffee, Old Saul nodded to Isaiah. "Our guests don't know that my grandson just returned from a trip north to Chippewa land. Why don't you tell us all about it, son?"

"Why would he go to Indian land?" Mrs. Cantrell snapped.

Complete silence.

"Mother, you don't have much time before your boat leaves in the morning," Ophelia said. "Maybe we should just finish our cake and take you back to town."

Mrs. Cantrell sniffed.

"We're very happy to have your daughter and her husband in our town," Old Saul said.

"This is not the life I wanted for my daughter." The older woman seemed to have reached her limit. She sounded like an over-tired child who wasn't getting her way. "And now my first grandchild will be born in a cabin," she complained.

Again, silence.

Sunny almost felt sorry for the woman. She must be very used to getting her way.

Lavina cleared her throat. "I understand how you feel, ma'am, but our children only belong to us till they grow up and leave home. Still, it's hard not to want to continue protecting them, guiding them. I'm afraid in spite of my praying for Isaiah, I worried every day till he returned home. I know I should have more trust in God to take care of him, but he's my baby."

"Mother," Isaiah objected.

"But of course he's a young man now," Lavina said with an apologetic smile. "And this trip has helped him see his path forward."

"Yes, I learned so much and saw so much," Isaiah put in eagerly. "There is such need there, especially for teaching."

His enthusiasm impressed Sunny.

"I don't know what any of this is about," Mrs. Cantrell said. "Or why my daughter would want to live here in the wilderness." She stood abruptly. "Martin, it doesn't seem as if I can make my daughter see sense. Take us back to the riverboat."

Ophelia looked mortified but Martin looked relieved. "If that's what you wish, Mother Cantrell."

The woman marched to the wagon and Martin hurried after her. Miss Thurston wiped her lips and rose. "Mrs. Whitmore, the cake was delicious. Thank you so much for the refreshments. The setting of your home is lovely and I know from my cousin Ophelia how supportive her neighbors have been. I must, however, bid you farewell. For now."

Everyone bid the nice young woman a warm good-bye and Martin drove off. Ophelia rode in the back, looking forlorn.

A moment of strained silence followed their departure.

"Ophelia's mother told me that Miss Thurston's uncle

is a state senator in the Illinois legislature," Nan informed them, "and she comes from a wealthy family, too." Nan's tone informed them that Mrs. Cantrell had sought and failed to impress Nan.

"Well, she's a much happier woman than Ophelia's mother," Old Saul said mildly. "Meddling is a sin, too."

"And I think all she has accomplished is that she's alienated her daughter," Lavina said.

Sunny agreed silently. And determined never to behave so foolishly with Dawn.

"So, Isaiah, how's Miigwans?" Noah asked.

Isaiah grinned. "He is fine. Missing you, but fine. He is hoping for a pup real bad."

Noah shook his head, smiling. "Scamp."

"Isaiah, what was it like up that way?" Sunny asked.

"Beautiful. Lakes everywhere. I mean, everywhere. So blue and crystal clear water." His face darkened. "But such poverty. It nearly broke my heart. There's a lay preacher there and an old priest. They do their best to help bridge the gap between the Ojibwa and the whites. But it's hard to see some of their men who ought to provide for their families drunk on our liquor."

"Well, that could be said of any town in our country," Old Saul commented.

"The lay preacher is named Sam White. I plan on going back this fall to work with him through the winter."

Lavina and her husband looked shocked. Old Saul nodded, unperturbed.

Isaiah plunged ahead. "Sam says he needs someone to help him. He's over seventy and is suffering with arthritis bad. He holds classes for people who want to learn how to read and write English and he teaches a

Bible Study weekly. He supports himself as a trapper and will teach me that, too."

Sunny watched Lavina absorb this. She glanced at Dawn, lying drowsily on Noah's shoulder, and wondered what it would be like when her daughter brought a young man in and said she was marrying and leaving home. An icy needle pierced Sunny's heart. Slight understanding of Ophelia's mother flickered.

"Oh!" Isaiah stood and lifted down one of his saddlebags. "Bid'a ban sent gifts from her family to you and Mrs. Osbourne." He pulled out four small pairs of moccasins, each beaded with skill and lined with rabbit fur. "For the children." He handed two pairs to Nan—and two to Sunny. "To keep their feet warm this winter."

Noah took one of the small moccasins, smiling at Dawn. Sunny put her hand on his arm, sharing the moment, their little girl's first pair of shoes. Bid'a ban had made them.

"Oh, how sweet," Nan cooed.

At first, Sunny was confused. Then she blushed, thinking of Bid'a ban telling Sunny that she was better, and Sunny should return to the loft to be with Noah. She stroked the soft deerskin leather and silken fur lining. "How thoughtful. Thank you for bringing them." She looked at Noah, who had a strange smile on his face as he took in the two pairs of tiny shoes. That smile made her heart skip a beat.

As their guests prepared to leave a bit later, Noah helped Old Saul back onto the wagon.

"Well, we'll be seeing you for the first barn raising then. Two weeks from last Friday," the older man said.

"Are you sure you want to build mine first?" Noah asked.

"Yes, because you'll show everyone how a stone foundation should be done. Most don't know how and a good foundation is important. For barns as well as people."

The preacher's family rode away as Nan helped carry dishes to the outside basin. "This has been quite a day," Nan said with a sigh as she dried the final dish. "I'm ready to go home." Gordy took her hand and the couple and their children waved goodbye.

Sunny watched them leave. "Well, company is fine, but that's enough for a while," Sunny said.

Noah put an arm around her shoulder. "You did us proud with that cake."

At his unexpected praise and touch, Sunny had to swallow sudden tears. "My pleasure."

"But I like it when it's quiet here. Just the three of us." Neechee barked as if agreeing or arguing with Noah. "I mean the four of us."

Sunny bent to pet the faithful dog. As she stood back up, Noah shocked her.

He pulled her around and into his arms.

Chapter Fourteen

Drawing Sunny into his arms had felt as natural as a sunrise to Noah. The top of her head brushed the underside of his chin. Her hair smelled of the lavender water that she combed through it each morning. He liked her feminine ways, how she always looked trim and neat.

He savored the softness of her within his arms. *Sunny, I'm glad you're my wife.* He wished he could say the words to her—she deserved to hear them. But he couldn't make his throat and mouth work. Sunny had captured him and made him mute.

Then with an irresistible sigh she rested against him, trusting him to hold her.

He buried his face into her pale golden hair and tightened his arms around her. For once he didn't think of his life before Sunny. Like honey poured on a cut, her presence soothed and healed. He hoped she was as content as she always seemed. But he vowed to make her happy—truly happy—or die trying.

He would figure out how to be her husband—he owed her that.

He felt the familiar sensation of Dawn grabbing his

pant leg and pulling herself up to stand. He chuckled deep in his chest. His little Dawn.

"No-No," the baby said, patting his knee. "No-No."

Sunny stepped back. "Dawn wants her *pa-pa,*" Sunny said, emphasizing the two syllables. "Pa-pa," she repeated.

Dawn crowed, arching her back and squealing.

Noah swung her up into his arms. He kissed her cheek, and then bent and kissed Sunny's cheek for good measure.

"Maybe I'll invite Mrs. Buford Cantrell to stop by again sometime." Sunny's smile sparkled as she teased. "She seems to have had quite an effect on you."

The three of them sat again in a row on the bench outside their cabin. Dawn clamored to get down and roll in the grass with Neechee. Squirrels scampered from tree to tree, shaking branches and chasing each other, chirruping. Noah relaxed as the golden sun lowered behind the trees. He let his arm go around her waist and rest on the bench behind her. For the first time in recent memory contentment flowed through him, something he would never have again thought possible. And for now, he let himself enjoy it.

Sunny had rarely been this keyed up in her whole life. Eight families, including the old preacher's, were coming for the first barn raising at their place. She had put a haunch of pork wrapped with wild onions to slow roast in the large oven Noah had expertly crafted in their stone hearth. The scent tantalized her as she finished her grooming.

She ran her hands down over her crisp white apron. *Oh, Lord, please keep everyone safe today.* She remembered the day the tree had bounced into Noah and could have killed him. So many men working together could invite disaster.

Noah stepped into the doorway, their little girl hugging his neck. "Mmm. That pork sure makes my mouth water."

She managed a tight smile.

"Wonder what the other women will bring?" He offered her Dawn. "You'll have to keep her. They'll be arriving soon—"

Neechee's barking interrupted him. Sunny accepted the baby who complained loudly at being separated from Noah.

"Make sure the women keep watch over the children," Noah warned. "I don't want any children near us as we work with the stone."

Sunny nodded. "I'll make sure."

Then the families began arriving. Most left their wagons on the trail and walked up the track to the Whitmore clearing. Every face was smiling. The men shouldered spades, axes and shovels. The women, all in fresh white aprons, carried covered dishes and sewing or knitting baskets. The Osbournes arrived, bringing more benches for the women to sit on while they sewed in front of the cabin. And the Stewards brought chairs. The weather couldn't have been better for a day of working outside. The sun shone bright and the breeze was warm without heat.

Soon the men were at the far side of the clearing. Noah had piled a hill of stone from plowing the garden and stacks of logs he, Gordy and Martin had felled in the past two weeks. With shovels in hand, the men began digging the foundation trench.

Sunny supervised the donated food. Some had been stowed in the spring house to keep cool and some set on the hearth to keep warm. When the breeze was just right, delectable fragrances wafted over the women.

After the initial greetings the ladies began telling about their families back home and how they'd come to settle in Pepin. Frantically, Sunny tried to remember what she'd told Caroline when they'd first met.

"Well, that's how Gordy and I picked Pepin—it was as far as our fare on the riverboat took us." Nan laughed at this. "We took it as God's providence and so it has been." Nan sent Sunny and Ophelia a special smile.

Sunny tried to hold on to that, but she had to concentrate on her words. Because it was her turn now. "I lived out West. After my mother died, a friend sent me back East to her family." That was true.

"Where was your pa?" one woman whom Sunny barely knew asked.

Sunny's mind spun. "We'd lost him years before."

"Losing both parents young is hard," Ophelia said solemnly. Murmurs of sympathy caused Sunny to writhe inwardly.

"How did you meet Noah?" Nan asked.

Sunny drew a deep breath. "He attended the same church as the family I lived with."

The women made cheery, knowing sounds, and Nan nudged her. "Flirting at church, hmm?"

Sunny knew she must smile and she curved her mouth, hiding how her lips threatened to tremble.

"How did you and Noah choose Pepin?" Lavina asked, looking up from the shirt she was mending. She cast a concerned glance toward the men. Her father-in-law, Old Saul, was insisting on helping with the stone foundation, obviously worrying her.

"Noah decided he wanted to homestead and early this year, he traveled to Illinois, Iowa, Minnesota and then Wisconsin. He liked Pepin best. He came home in April."

She caught herself just before she said "and we married." Horror over almost saying these indiscreet words nearly made her gasp. Instead she finished with, "We came here." *Please don't ask me any more. Please.*

"Now, Ophelia, you're the new bride," Nan said with a teasing voice. "How did you fall in love with your Martin?"

Ophelia began speaking about meeting Martin at a political rally for President Grant when he visited his home in Galena. The bride blushed sweetly.

Sunny sighed silently. She had made it through. She began to relax. The caution was all on her part; these women saw her as one of them, something she had doubted possible once.

The men had worked till early afternoon before stopping to eat lunch. After eating and then resting for a while, the men rose to troop back to the barn site.

Lavina walked beside Old Saul, trying to persuade him to lie down inside for a while. "You've been on your feet or sitting on a log for most of the day. You need to rest now."

Old Saul waved away her caution. "The sun is doing me good. I'll just sit and watch, Lavina. No harm in that."

Sunny watched the woman shake her head, obviously concerned.

Noah must have heard because he requested that the lady in the rocking chair give up her seat, and he carried it to a shady spot where Old Saul could watch the work in comfort.

"Your husband is such a thoughtful man," Lavina said softly to Sunny as Old Saul lowered himself into the chair.

Sunny nodded. "He is." She gazed at the barn, which was amazingly taking shape in one day. The stone foundation was almost done and men were notching the logs to fit together at the corners.

Then she heard Noah's shout. She swung her gaze to him. He was kneeling beside Old Saul who had slumped onto his shoulder.

Lavina ran toward their wagon. She retrieved a small bag and raced toward her father-in-law.

All work stopped. Everyone rushed forward to help.

Noah called out, "Everyone, please keep back! He needs air!"

Lavina knelt beside Noah and drew out a packet of pills. "Here's your digitalis." She slipped one into her father-in-law's mouth and called for water.

Sunny ran to get the pitcher of spring water and dipper. Noah accepted it from her and poured the dipper full. She stepped back, leaving Lavina and her husband to care for the older man.

His face etched with pain, Old Saul gasped for breath and pressed a hand over his heart.

Noah carefully held the dipper to his mouth and trickled water in.

Nan and Ophelia came and put their arms around Sunny. "Oh, I hope he'll be all right," Ophelia whispered.

Sunny echoed this silently. She was wringing her hands and realized then that this older man had become dear to her. He had shown love to Bid'a ban and Miigwans. Even Neechee voiced a long worried moan in the troubled silence in the clearing.

Oh, God, please help Old Saul.

The next day Noah sat on the bench at his table with his coffee cup, staring into space. In his mind's eye he saw the old preacher clutching his chest. Old Saul's face had gone sheet-white. Fear thrummed through Noah. He didn't want to lose the old preacher. He realized how much he'd come to like the older man's unexpected visits, and how helpful he'd been in so very many ways.

"No-No," Dawn called to him from the floor.

"Say pa-pa," Sunny corrected. "Noah is your pa-pa."

"No-No!" Dawn insisted.

Noah set down his cold coffee and lifted the child into his arms. How could he have known what a comfort holding this little child could be?

"No-No," she said, patting him happily. Oh, to be innocent of grief and pain like this little one.

He recalled how Old Saul had said a few words about being a soldier. It wasn't much, but it said everything. Maybe that was another reason he felt connected to Old Saul. They'd both faced war.

Sunny came up behind him and rested a hand on his shoulder. "I've been praying for Old Saul," she murmured.

He lifted a hand and pressed hers, nodding. Neechee growled and got to her feet.

"Hello, the house!" a familiar voice soon called out.

Noah rose and carried Dawn to the door. He looked out. "Isaiah?" His heart sank.

"My grandfather's alive!" the young man called out and slid from his horse. "He sent me to get you, Noah. He says he wants to talk to you."

Noah blanched. Not a deathbed visit—he'd done too many of those, kneeling beside comrades, watching the light flicker from their eyes. No.

"Don't worry," Isaiah said. "He says he's much better. He just wants to talk over some things with you. Says he's been meaning to talk to you for some time but keeps getting interrupted. Will you come?"

What could he say? This young man had taken Miigwans home. And Old Saul had proved himself a true friend to them. "Of course I'll come." He turned to Sunny. "Did you want to come along?"

Sunny looked to Isaiah. "Yes, I'll come, too. I'd like to visit Lavina today."

The preacher's family lived a couple of miles northeast of town along another creek that flowed into the Chippewa. As they traveled, Noah barely spoke a word to Isaiah. He felt wooden inside.

When they arrived, Lavina came out and greeted them in a subdued tone. "Saul will be glad to see you." She looked to Sunny.

"Shall we sit outside? It's such a nice day."

Lavina nodded and then said to Noah, "Go in."

Noah dismounted, handed Isaiah his reins and helped Sunny and Dawn down. Then he doffed his hat to enter the shadowy cabin. The dam inside him began to break up, unruly currents swirling. Noah tightened his self-control.

Old Saul lay on a narrow rope bed on the far side of the fireplace. "Noah." He lifted a hand momentarily and then, as if tired by the effort, let it fall.

Reluctantly Noah went and sat in a chair beside the bed. "Good morning, sir."

The older man shook a finger at him.

The reminder prodded Noah into a half chuckle. "I mean, Old Saul."

"I'm not planning on dying just yet," the preacher said in a gravelly voice. "But I've been wanting to talk to you about war."

Noah wanted to get up and leave, but he owed this man. Irritation ground inside him. "I don't like to talk about it."

"Then just listen to me as I talk." Old Saul inhaled a rattling breath and closed his eyes. "I was barely fourteen when war broke out with England a second time. I had been raised on stories of the Revolution and was afraid I'd miss this war, my generation's war." The old man paused as if drawing up strength.

These words stirred up memories in Noah, wretched ones. Those awful weeks when he'd planned on enlisting and wondered how to tell his family, his fiancée. He fidgeted in the chair.

"I hear you were raised Quaker. I know they don't believe in going to war. I bet that made it harder for you to enlist."

Noah barked one unpleasant dry laugh. "I was put out of meeting. They had worked in the Underground Railroad, helping escaped slaves. When abolition helped trigger a war, they wanted none of it. But I couldn't turn a blind eye to the war that could bring freedom to so many."

Old Saul nodded. "My family was proud of me, but they were as ignorant as I was. At fourteen, I marched off with the other young men from my Kentucky town to fight under Andrew Jackson."

He fell silent, but his hands on top of the blanket moved restlessly. "I don't have to tell you what a shock the first battle was. I'd never killed a man before. I didn't know how that would tear at me afterward."

Noah tried to block images from his mind, but he was bombarded. Startled, agonized faces amid the black powder cloud— He bent his head into his hands. "Please, no more."

"I nearly died of a wound, and it weakened my heart," Old Saul continued. "But after my body healed, the worst was the nightmares. And the sudden fear that someone was aiming a gun at me. Or about to run me through."

Noah lifted his head and his gaze connected with the old man's. *So I'm not the only one.*

"I see the dark circles under your eyes. And the way you hold back from people. You must be suffering nightmares."

Finally the question that had plagued Noah could be asked. "Did you get over it? Get back to normal?"

"Yes, God healed me finally. I was wild after the war, wild to drink and carouse and incurred more damage to my body. It took nearly getting killed one night in a fracas to get my attention. I sobered up. Somehow I found a sweet wife who prayed for me and gifted me with children. Their love worked on me."

Noah felt Dawn's phantom touch, her little chubby hand patting his cheek.

The older man looked as if he were peering into the

past. "I took long walks in the solitary woods talking to God. I was never the same—I was better. Any trial stretches a man, a person. I think that was the beginning of my wanting to preach."

Noah sat bent with his elbows on his knees, his hands clasped together. "I have a sweet wife. And a child."

"I know. I see a true, a humble, heart in Sunny. But she carries some burden, too. I just wanted you to know you can be restored. You need to let God in more and let his Holy Spirit do the healing."

Noah tried not to reject these words outright—Old Saul had earned a hearing. Yet healing just didn't seem possible. How could one wipe away all the blood he'd shed?

"I'm tired now, son."

Noah accepted the dismissal and rose. "Yes, rest. We still have more barns to raise this summer."

A smile tugged at the older man's mouth. "God be with you, Noah Whitmore."

"And with you," Noah said automatically.

Soon he mounted his horse with Sunny and Dawn, bid everyone farewell and headed home, turning over in his mind all that had been said. As usual, Sunny didn't speak when she realized he didn't want to. So he could just think.

He wanted to believe the old man but did his experience really match Noah's? Noah didn't know about opening himself to God. It sounded dangerous.

He'd worked so hard to keep everything in—could he let go without flying apart?

Two weeks later on Sunday, Sunny was surprised and pleased to see Old Saul had returned to meeting.

He wasn't sitting on the porch as usual, but in his wagon bed in a rocking chair tied down tight. Would Old Saul's presence be good for Noah or not?

Noah had come home from Old Saul's and had been quiet for days. This had disturbed her but she merely tried to behave as if she didn't notice.

She would pray this morning silently for her husband during Old Saul's prayer when he asked for special requests. Surely if the old preacher asked God to bless Noah, he would.

On the porch Lavina and her husband lifted their hands and began the first hymn. Then Lavina's husband spoke the opening prayer. Sunny began to worry that Old Saul had come merely to observe, not to preach. But then, in the wagon, Old Saul lifted his hands in his usual signal that he was going to speak. Appreciation whispered through the gathering.

He cleared his throat. "Even if you didn't attend the first barn raising at the Whitmores, you must know by now that my heart let me know that it's older than my seventy-one years. I'm afraid I've put my heart through a lot."

Sunny thought that the older man looked straight at Noah then.

"It's had to beat longer, many more times than any of yours. I have a medicine that helps but it's just a matter of time till my heart will give out and I will no longer be among you."

A sad silence greeted this. Nothing but a seagull squawking over the Mississippi sounded nearby, and gentle waves slapping a boat moored at the wharf. Sunny edged closer to Noah.

"I don't say this lightly, but for a purpose. Preachers are hard to come by on the frontier. After I pass, it might be some time before a new one will come to town. And not all preachers know God, know his love and forgiveness. Some preach so they will get the prime seats and free apple pies."

A few chuckled at this.

"There is a Bible passage that tells how the apostles chose someone to replace Judas Iscariot, the one who betrayed Christ with a kiss. They chose two worthy men and then cast lots to let God tell them who should be chosen."

A feeling of uncertainty slithered up Sunny's spine.

"Yesterday I asked my son to write down the name of every man who attends our meeting on a piece of paper. I want God to choose the right man to lead you when I'm gone."

Old Saul fell silent, gazing out to them, in turn catching the eye of each one.

Sunny didn't like where this was going. She edged closer still to Noah.

"What if you choose my name," Gordy spoke loud enough to be heard, "and I don't know enough about the Bible to do a good job?"

Old Saul nodded approvingly. "I'm doing this now while I still have time and energy to instruct the one chosen. I must tell you that the Lord laid this on my heart. Over and over He has directed me to study over the choosing of prophets and kings and apostles. I feel certain that He has someone here in mind."

Everyone looked solemn and the men watchful. Only the children prattled and the gulls on a nearby sand-bar fought over carrion. Sunny wanted to touch Noah's arm but didn't want to make any move that would call attention to them. She wondered if this was why Old Saul had summoned Noah.

Oh, Lord, not Noah. He didn't even want to attend meeting here.

"'And a little child shall lead them,'" Old Saul quoted Isaiah. "Gordy, bring your boy up. He can choose."

Gordy carried the boy up and set him in the wagon. Old Saul spoke quietly to the child and then asked him to pull out a paper from a cloth bag he opened.

Guthrie looked to Gordy who nodded and urged him to do as asked. The little boy stuck his hand in and drew out several slips.

"Choose just one," Saul said, holding up his index finger.

Guthrie looked at the slips in one hand and pulled one free. Old Saul received it with thanks.

Gordy lifted Guthrie and carried him back to Nan.

Everyone gazed at the slip of paper in Old Saul's hand. The older man opened it and then seemed to pray. Then he looked up. "God's choice is Noah Whitmore."

Sunny sucked in breath so fast she nearly choked.

Noah let out a gasp.

Still reeling, Sunny couldn't put everything together. People crowded around, saying words, smiling, patting her on the back. But nothing penetrated. She tried to smile and nod but could not quell her shock.

No, this can't be happening.

The ride home had been quiet, solemn and had stretched on like an endless journey. Sunny had barely been able to respond to the few comments their friends had made as they made their way in the wagon. Noah had been stone-cold silent. What would happen now?

Gordy drove into their clearing. Neechee barked in welcome and frolicked forward.

Noah helped Sunny down from the wagon bed. Sunny tried to smile for her friends but her mouth had frozen.

Gordy cleared his throat. "I know this has been a shock, Noah."

"A shock," Martin repeated.

"But an honor, too, Noah," Gordy said.

"We're behind you," Martin added. "We know it won't be easy to take on."

"If you need anything, you just ask, okay?" Gordy said with an earnestness that touched Sunny.

"We'll be prayin' for you," Nan said.

Ophelia whispered, "Yes, we'll all pray."

Noah nodded and raised a hand, bidding their friends a silent farewell. He and Sunny stood together, watching the wagon drive away. Somehow their friends' understanding of how hard this was proved once more their friendship.

Inside she had to remember to take off her bonnet. Then she stood in her kitchen, trying to think what she'd planned to have for dinner. A pot hung toward the back of the hearth. She went about the preparations but wondered if she'd be able to eat.

Noah came in, still holding Dawn. He sat down at the table and Dawn squirmed and prattled, letting him know she wanted to get down. Finally he set the child on the floor. Then looked at Sunny. "I can't do it."

She sank on the same bench. What if Noah refused?

The image of Dawn in the schoolyard shifted, and now her friends didn't welcome her, they stood apart and whispered about her. Dawn looked miserable.

Sunny burst into tears.

"I can't do it," Noah said, his voice becoming stronger. "I can't teach people about God. Or lead them. I killed men. I'm a murderer."

And I was a prostitute, Sunny added silently, unable to say the words aloud. Tears rolled down her cheeks.

"I can't do it," he repeated.

"What will happen if you refuse?" she murmured.

"I don't care." Noah shot up from the bench and burst out the door.

Dawn shrieked his name, expressing Sunny's own feelings, but he didn't turn back.

How could this have happened? How could God have let this happen?

Chapter Fifteen

Sunny watched as a downhearted Neechee returned, whimpering in distress. Noah must have ordered the dog back. Sunny could do nothing but stand still, staring at the open door. Where had Noah gone? What would happen now?

The past bombarded Sunny with days and nights she longed to scrub from her memory. The repulsive sensation of being manhandled by a stranger swept through her as sharp edged as if it were happening today. She gagged and hurried outside to retch. She fell to her knees, enduring the spasms.

What am I going to do, God?

With her head bent, she wept bitter tears. Everything had been going so well. Hope, flaming within, had been blown out like a candle in the wind. All the horrible names she'd ever been called, all the scathing glances she'd ever endured slammed into her once again.

The tall trees stood high above her, their tops gently moving with the breeze as hot tears flowed down her face onto the grass.

Noah didn't come back.

Sunny dragged herself up. She went inside and changed Dawn's diaper and settled her into the hammock for a nap. Then Sunny stood in the middle of the empty cabin—bereft, alone.

I can't just let this happen. Just let that little slip of paper destroy everything.

Minutes passed. She kept listening, hoping to hear Noah returning. Neechee lay across the threshold, whimpering on and off, giving sound to Sunny's own longing and fear. What if Noah didn't come back? What if he just left her here?

Old Saul's lined, drawn face came to mind. He had started this—and she must go to him for help. But how could she? How could she explain why Noah wouldn't be a preacher and she—of all women—couldn't be a preacher's wife?

She shoved these questions to the back of her mind. Old Saul was the only one with the power to change this thing that had come upon them.

After saddling the horse, Sunny retrieved Dawn from her hammock and settled her into the sling that Noah always used. She managed to mount from a stump. She'd never ridden the horse alone here, but she knew how to ride and she knew where the preacher lived. She headed up the track.

Fortunately the town was deserted on Sunday afternoon. When she left it behind, she breathed easier, riding north along the Mississippi to the preacher's house.

Within an hour she walked the horse into the clearing of Old Saul's son's house. Lavina sat outside in a curved chair with her sewing basket open at her feet. The woman rose in greeting. "Sunny, what brings you here?"

"I need to talk to Old Saul." Sunny tasted her own sour breath as she spoke for the first time in many hours. She slid from the horse's back, now feeling presumptuous.

Lavina hurried forward. "You look distressed."

"I am," Sunny admitted. Why lie? "Can I see him?"

Lavina lifted a waking Dawn from the sling. "Of course. He's lying down, but he'll see you."

Sunny followed Lavina to the door.

"Saul, Sunny Whitmore has come to see you," the woman announced. Lavina waved Sunny inside. "I'll play with the baby and leave you two alone." She shut the door.

Sunny stood in the midst of the neat cabin, smelling the remnants of the noon meal, feeling very out of place.

On the other side of the hearth Old Saul lay on the bed, gazing at her steadily. He gestured toward a chair by his bed. "Come and tell me what's troubling you, Mrs. Whitmore."

Sunny perched on the chair. How could she make this man see what the casting of lots had triggered? She fingered her skirt, trying to think what words to say.

You must tell him everything.

Sunny did not know where the thought had come from and she most certainly did not want to do what it said. But would anything less work? This was not a time for half measures. She must make this man understand and help her to work matters out so she wouldn't lose Noah or this place that had become their home.

How could she again face strife as she had when they'd helped Bid'a ban? Turning down Old Saul would garner even more censure.

I love Noah. This has wounded him. And I can't let

him suffer without doing everything to keep him, make him whole.

"You wish to speak to me in confidence?" Old Saul suggested.

She nodded woodenly. Her heart thumped, making her feel sick again. If she told him the truth about herself, there would be no going back. She would be exposed and in this man's power.

Saul reached out and grasped her hand. "Trust me."

"I was a prostitute." The four simple words burst through her, shaking her so that she shuddered. She gasped for air.

Saul patted her hand. "Why are you telling me this?"

"So you'll see why I can't be a preacher's wife. It isn't fitting." The shaking continued. She clung to him, expecting him to shove her away, but Saul kept her hand in his, gripping it firmly.

"I find it hard to believe that you were in that trade. You don't have a hard look about you."

Sunny understood what he meant. The hard veneer of many of the women she had worked with had hidden deep wells of sorrow. But she'd had a mother who'd loved and protected her as much as she could. Maybe that had made the difference, kept her from becoming hard.

The guilt she'd carried for years overwhelmed her, wanting at last to be spoken. "My mother was a prostitute, too."

Each word cost her. "I've always felt guilty about that. You see, when she realized she was pregnant with me, she told the father…"

"And he abandoned her."

Sunny nodded, sick at heart. "And her own father shut her out of the family."

Old Saul exhaled long and slow. "I'm so sorry." He paused. "So you were born into that life?"

Holding back tears required all her strength. "Yes. My mother died when I was fourteen and I had no other way."

"Just a child." Saul kept her hand and patted it with his other. "You poor child."

His sympathetic tone helped her breathe, helped her go on. "So you see, I can't be a preacher's wife. Not after what I've done." She forced herself to look him in the eye. Would he keep her confidence? Or was her new life now ruined?

"No one will ever hear this from me," he said solemnly as if reading her thoughts.

She drew in a ragged breath, still shaking. "Thank you," she whispered.

"Does Noah know this?" he asked.

"Yes."

"But he wanted you for his wife?"

"Yes." *And I don't know why.*

Old Saul nodded. "Have you ever heard the story of David and Bathsheba?"

His abrupt change of topic caught her off guard. "No, I've never heard of them. Are they in the Bible?"

Old Saul squeezed her hand and shifted his position in bed. "Yes. And a sad story it is. David was a young shepherd boy who grew to be a man of God and God set him as king over all of Israel. David was handsome and he took many wives." Old Saul looked at her. "That was when a man could have as many wives as he could afford. And David had become rich."

Sunny tried to keep her focus on what the man was saying, but so far it didn't mean anything to her.

The old man paused, sighing. "To give you the main part of the sad story, David forgot God and took another man's wife in secret. That was Bathsheba. Then she found herself pregnant while her rightful husband was off to war and unable to father the child. So David had her husband killed in battle."

"This is in the Bible?" Sunny had a hard time believing this. "A man like that?"

Old Saul looked directly into her eyes. "Yes, a man like that. God called David 'a man after his own heart.' And he was an ancestor of Christ. But even though David knew God, he committed both adultery and murder."

"What did God do to him?" She couldn't have guessed that there were sinners in the Bible.

"God confronted David with his sin. And the child conceived in adultery died."

Sunny sucked in a sharp breath and glanced toward the door, cold with fear. *Would God take Dawn?*

"Do you know what God did then?" Old Saul prompted.

Sunny was afraid to even shake her head no.

"After David confessed his sin, God forgave David and Bathsheba, and blessed them with another son, who became a king known as Solomon, the wisest man who ever lived."

Sunny tried to absorb this but couldn't. "I don't understand."

"Psalm 103 tells us, 'as far as the east is from the west, so far hath He removed our transgressions from us.' Have you confessed your sins to God?"

"He knows them." Sunny felt defeated. None of this made sense.

"Ah, you speak wisely. God knows our sins. Did you repent of your sins—not just adultery but everything else?"

Sunny gave this some thought. "I did."

"Then He forgave you and wiped your sins away."

Trusting this man who had not been shocked by her past, she asked the question that had plagued her since meeting the Gabriel family. "I don't understand. How can He just wipe them away?"

"God can do things we can't. Let me show you a bit of how He thinks of us. Dawn is your child. Is there anything she could do that would cause you to stop loving her? Would you put her out of your house?"

"No. Never." Had her grandfather loved her mother at all? He couldn't have, not if he sent her into a life of prostitution.

"God is our father. Your mother's father may have put his daughter out but God never did."

"Then why didn't God help her stay out of the saloon?" *Why did I end up there?*

"I don't know. We are told that God always provides a way of escape. Maybe your mother didn't know to look for that other way. I don't know her heart. But I do know your heart, Sunny Whitmore."

This confused her more. She tilted her head as if questioning him.

"You have a loving, willing, humble heart. And you want to please God."

"Yes," she whispered. "But I never know how I'm supposed to feel. How does it *feel* when we are forgiven?"

He gripped her hand again. "It isn't about how you feel. It's about God being the one who can and does forgive. Sometimes a person will feel something when they come to God with a repentant heart, but not always. Yet that doesn't mean the person isn't forgiven."

Sunny held the older man's large hand in hers. She turned over all he had said in her mind. "I just have to believe I'm forgiven? Like having faith in God?"

"Exactly."

"Noah doesn't know that," she said haltingly. "He thinks he's guilty of murder because he fought in the war."

"Your husband is a man capable of deep feelings and unwavering conviction. He sacrificed much to fight for the end of slavery, was willing to give his life to accomplish that. Nevertheless, it's time he put that war to rest."

"How?" She listened intently, hoping.

"He must do what you have done. Have faith in God. Have faith in God's power to forgive and to heal."

Sunny had heard some of this from the Gabriels but not how it worked, how it demanded faith. "It sounds too simple."

"It is. The world likes to make God and faith hard but what's real, what matters, is very simple."

She shook her head. "But having faith is hard to do."

"Yes, it's giving up control. Letting God do it for us goes against our nature. We want to have to do some made-up penance. We humans are strange beings."

The two sat, their hands still clasped. And Sunny did feel something, a lightening of her spirit. *I am forgiven,* she repeated, trying to believe it, etch it into her heart.

"I don't know what Noah is going to do. He just up

and left. He said he couldn't be the preacher," Sunny told Old Saul.

"I know. I saw it in his eyes. I feared it when I read his name on the slip of paper. But I trust that God knows what He's doing. He has plans for Noah. For all of us."

"What if Noah doesn't want to follow God's plans?"

"When God laid choosing a successor on my heart, I prayed long and hard. And I've been praying ever since I read Noah's name aloud. I think that Noah is listening to God, has always been listening to him. A man who is sensitive to God would take killing men harder than a heedless man. Do you see?"

Sunny pressed the man's hand. "Yes, Noah takes everything seriously." And then Dawn came to mind, pulling herself up using Noah's pant leg. Sunny grinned. "Except when Dawn makes him happy."

"The blessing of children. A child's love is so genuine and without reservation. And we don't have to do anything to reap it. A true boon."

"So my past...doesn't mean I can't be a preacher's wife."

"No, I think it will make you a kind and understanding preacher's wife."

The way he said the words, she thought he really meant them. She glimpsed herself as forgiving and being able to show forgiveness to others.

The older man patted her hand. "God's at work in Noah. Just love him and respect him as I know you do." The older man's eyelids drifted down. "I'm sorry, but I need to rest now," he murmured.

Sunny rose. "Thank you, Old Saul." She bent and kissed his cheek. "You've given me peace about my past."

She turned to fetch her daughter and head home. She would pray the whole way and let God handle this—this was certainly more than she could work out. She had found some answers, but the answers just seemed to raise more questions, one of which plagued her most of all.

Would Noah be there when she got home?

Noah finally glimpsed the thin smoke of his fire above the surrounding trees. From ahead he heard his dog bark in welcome and run forward through the brush. Exhausted, Noah waited for Neechee to reach him. When she did, he stooped down to receive her joyful wiggling and wagging. She licked his hands and his chin and barked, almost appearing to smile. "You're my girl, Neechee. Yes, you are."

The dog's affection helped him steady a bit more. *How long have I been gone?* He gazed at the sun that now had sunk well past its peak.

He still carried a solid chunk of iron in his gut. His head ached. His mind felt like newspaper soaked in water, limp and easily torn. How far he had walked before he'd turned back, he didn't know. But he'd been walking for hours now. Hunger had finally turned him toward home, feeling used up.

All he wanted was to sit down at his own table and lift Dawn onto his knee. Sunny might want to talk but if he didn't, she would let him be. It was one of the things he most appreciated about her—she could be quiet with him.

He rubbed his temple with the flat of his hand and tried not to think about that little slip of paper that had turned his life upside down. He trudged the last half mile toward home, forming a simple apology to Sunny for leaving so abruptly. He couldn't think past that, how to confront this thing that had broken and shattered him.

He forded the stream, stepping on rocks one by one while Neechee splashed beside him. Then he passed his fenced garden, noting the green shoots had grown at least another inch this week. How could he even think of leaving this place? He'd done too much to make this place home. But what would people say when he refused Old Saul? The chunk of iron in his stomach weighed heavier.

He stepped into his clearing. The oxen grazed, tethered to their stakes. But his horse was gone.

"Sunny!"

He hurried to the cabin and pulled open the latchstring. The faint scent of salt pork and beans hung in the air. The pot still hung high over the banked fire. But no Sunny. No Dawn. Neechee whined at his feet.

"Where did they go, girl?"

Noah stood in the middle of his cabin. For that moment he stood alone, bereft, exposed to God.

Help. I need her. I need them. Help me.

He sank onto the bench and held his head in his hands. The old scenes of battle raged through him—cannon roaring and shaking the earth, bugles, drums blaring, black powder fog choking and twisting, angry faces screaming and cursing. The tumult overwhelmed him.

Neechee barked and ran out the door. The soft sound of horse hooves came. Noah wrenched himself from the past and hurried outside. He ran to help Sunny down and lead the horse to the lean-to. Dawn slept in the sling peacefully. With an arm around her he walked Sunny into the house and then lifted the baby into his arms.

The love he felt for the child and her mother swept away everything like a spring flood. "I love you, Sunny. And I love this child." He couldn't have held back the words if he'd tried.

Sunny threw her arms around him. "I love you, too. Oh, Noah, I've wanted to tell you for so long."

He turned from her and gently stowed the child in her hammock.

Then he turned back to his wife, his dear wife.

For a moment shyness caused him to hesitate. Then that, too, was swept away. He must be near her, hold her. He felt his love for her flow through him, forceful, demanding. "Sunny," he said, his voice becoming husky.

She buried her face against his shirt. "I was so worried," she said.

He lifted her chin and bent his lips to hers. "My sweet Sunny, my sweet wife." He thought to kiss her gently but yearning swept him up in its current.

She clung to him and kissed him back.

He breathed in her lavender scent and fresh strength flowed through him. What he had been powerless to change had come right. He lifted her into his arms and carried her toward the ladder to the loft. "Sunny, my sweet, please…"

She smothered his entreaty with a kiss, a kiss that breathed into him her love and gave him life.

Sunny, my sweet wife.

Chapter Sixteen

In the loft of the quiet cabin Sunny lay in Noah's strong arms—her husband's loving arms—replete. She didn't want to move or speak, fearful of disturbing their perfect peace. Nothing separated them in this moment, one she would treasure all the rest of her life.

"I'm sorry, Sunny," he murmured.

She couldn't think of what he was apologizing about. "For what?"

"For just leaving like I did. You didn't deserve that."

With the back of her hand she stroked his rough cheek. She loved the stubbly feel of it. "I was worried. I didn't know what to do." Then fear swirled cold in her stomach. Better to confess what she'd done right away. "I went to see Old Saul."

"All by yourself?"

She loved the concern she heard in his voice. "Yes, he was the only one who could help. He was the only one who could change things."

Noah kissed her temple. "My brave Sunny." Then he stilled. "Did he have a way to let me out of this?" The thought of what had been asked of him still defeated him, but here, now, with Sunny in his arms, he could face it.

"He said he'd pray about it." Sunny paused. She must tell him all. "I told him about my past."

"Why?" Noah increased his hold on her.

"I didn't think I could be a preacher's wife after what I'd done." Shame warmed her cheeks.

Not for the first time Noah wished he could make up for the life she'd been forced to live. The idea that men were free to sow their wild oats with impunity but a woman must stay pure or be ostracized had never made sense to him. The double standard was cruel, heartless and the woman always paid the price.

"Sunny, I don't think like that." He kissed her soft ear.

"I know." Her gratitude prompted her to snuggle even closer. "Old Saul told me about David and… I can't remember her name…it's in the Bible."

"Bathsheba. About their adultery?"

"I can't believe that something like that is in the Bible."

Noah laughed harshly. "There's worse than that in the Bible. God doesn't pretty up how people do to each other and to themselves."

Sunny ran her fingers through his hair. She sensed the hurt in his tone had more to do with him than David. "Old Saul said that God forgets our sins and wipes them away. 'As far as—'"

"'—the east is from the west, so far hath He removed our transgressions from us.'" He'd heard it since he was a child. Why didn't he believe it?

Again Sunny heard the pain and regret under the words. "I don't understand it, either. But I'm going to have faith that God has forgiven me. Noah, we can't hold on to all the bad things that have happened to us. You're a good man—"

He tried to interrupt.

She pressed her fingers against his lips. "You are a good man, not a perfect man."

He tried to interrupt her again.

She kissed away his words. "Look at me, Noah," she demanded.

He obeyed her, amazed a little at her fierceness.

"Most men looked at me and saw a cheap harlot. But you looked at me and saw a wife, a woman you wanted to have with you, by your side. When I look at you, I see the most honorable, most kind, man. You're hard on yourself, Noah. Do you know more than God?"

That stopped him. "What do you mean?"

"If God says He forgives us, do we know more than He does?" She held her breath, hoping this would connect in his mind, too.

Noah rested his head against hers. "I wish I could feel that."

She still had trouble believing in forgiveness herself. "It's trusting God. Maybe it just takes time."

"What did Old Saul say about this... I mean, me being chosen?" Noah's heart thudded with dread.

"He says he's praying about it and wants to talk to you." She gently stroked his face.

Then Dawn called out from her hammock below, "No-No!"

Noah chuckled low in his throat. "Somebody's awake."

Sunny loved how Dawn's waking up amused him. She stirred, feeling languid, loved, complete.

"Take your time, Sunny. I'll get her up."

She listened to him, rustling down the ladder and over the half-log floor. She stretched and sighed with satisfaction. *Oh, Lord, please let this continue, this new harmony.*

She rose and got herself together. She hoped she'd added enough water and salt to keep the stew from drying out completely. Noah must be hungry. She, however, was filled to the brim.

The next afternoon Noah rode into the clearing at Old Saul's place to face this thing. This thing that had shaken him to his core yesterday. He and Sunny had agreed they would not leave Pepin. They'd put too much into their home and their community. So Noah must find a way to do this thing—or bow out gracefully.

Contrasting with his despair just twenty-four hours ago, Noah could not recall feeling as good as he did today. The final barrier between his wife and him had been breached and he couldn't stop the joy inside him. And last night with Sunny snuggled against him, he'd slept without one nightmare. With this thought he called out, "Hello, the house!"

Lavina opened the door and stepped outside. She smiled. "My father-in-law said he thought you'd stop by today. Come right in."

Noah dismounted, hitching his horse to a low branch. Inside the door he doffed his hat and let his eyes adjust to the dim interior, preparing himself.

"I'll leave you two alone to talk. I have a garden that needs weeding." Lavina left them, shutting the door after her.

Noah gazed at the old preacher as if seeing him for the first time.

"I'm glad you're here. Come sit beside me, son."

In that startling moment Noah felt as if he'd come home from the war—at last. This proved to be the welcome he'd been longing for, the one his own father had not been able to give him.

Noah swallowed down the emotion this sparked and went to sit beside the narrow bed. "Old Saul, I'm grateful you treated Sunny so kindly."

"You have been blessed with a special, very sweet woman. Hearing what she went through hurt me for her."

"It's not right, the way she was treated before." Noah's voice sounded low in his throat.

Old Saul reached out.

Noah accepted his hand.

"Have you come to start learning from me?" Old Saul asked, searching his eyes.

Noah had come to try to get out of this new responsibility. But with these words his heart leaped.

His name had been the one chosen. Did God know what he was doing? Noah's uncertainty didn't disappear, but he could approach this now. "Yes, I've come to start learning, but…"

Old Saul raised his eyebrows in question.

"I think there should have been two of us. More like the apostles—they picked two."

"In a way. But you're right. We will hold a second drawing. Better to have a deacon to help you. Did you bring your Bible, son?"

"It's in my saddlebag." Noah realized that this revealed that on some level he must have decided to accept his new responsibility even though he hadn't thought that true. This added to the strength growing inside him.

"Bring it in. We'll pray and read some passages about pastors."

So began Noah's education to become the next pastor. *God, You chose me. Now get me ready.*

A triumphant shout rose in Noah's throat and joined those around him. The last piece had been set in place on the roof of his barn. Though panting and perspiring, the men around him beamed. Old Saul sat on his rocking chair in the shade, his feet propped high on a footstool Noah had crafted for him.

The old preacher clapped his hands momentarily and then let them fall. This show of the older man's weakness saddened Noah. Not long ago Noah had unloaded much of his feelings about the war to Old Saul. Just getting them said aloud to a man who understood had been healing.

Gordy clapped Noah on the back. "Well, one barn down and seven to go!"

Noah grinned. "You're always such a cheerful cuss."

Much to his surprise Gordy had been chosen by lot as the first deacon for the Sunday meeting. Now Gordy and Noah met weekly with Old Saul, learning about the Bible and how to pastor. Noah looked forward to these sessions.

The women came forward to admire the new barn. The structure only needed a door and bar to latch it, both of which Noah would craft himself. He looked around for his wife, but didn't see her. "Where's Sunny?"

"She's with Neechee," Nan said with a smile as big as the sky. "Neechee's already birthed one pup."

"Why didn't somebody tell me?" Noah squawked. He turned and pelted toward his cabin. Hoots of laughter followed him.

He stopped at the open cabin door and doffed his hat and wiped away his sweat with his pocket handkerchief. "Sunny," he asked as he entered, "how's our Neechee doing?"

"Just fine." Sunny held up a chubby brown-and-white pup. "This is number one." She nodded toward another pup, which the mama was grooming. "And I think there may be a number three." Sunny had laid an old ragged shirt of his before the fire and that's where Neechee lay.

Noah knelt by Sunny's side and stroked Neechee's head. The dog whined her pleasure at seeing him, then went back to licking clean the second pup.

Before long a third pup slid forth, and Neechee was done.

"I guess this means that the little Ojibwa boy will get his pup," Gordy said from just outside the open door.

"And that means," Noah said, as he turned, proudly holding one pup high, "that you and Martin will each get one, too."

"This is a big day," Gordy pronounced. "The first barn done and three pups born."

From behind Gordy came the sound of cheerful congratulations from others who were resting from their labor on the benches and chairs outside.

Dawn woke where she'd fallen asleep on her blanket on the floor near Sunny. The baby knuckled her sleepy eyes.

"Look, Dawnie," Noah said tenderly. "Puppies."

The little girl looked astounded and crawled quickly over to Neechee.

Still kneeling, Noah laid the pup back by the mother and then drew Dawn to stand beside him. "These are our puppies. Pup-pies," he repeated.

Dawn looked puzzled but then bounced up and down, bending her knees. She clapped her hands.

"That's right," Sunny said. "Today is a day for clapping hands." She clapped her hands, too.

Noah chuckled and clapped his, his heart lifted high and singing. He would never forget today, ever. God had been good to him. He knew that now. And he was immeasurably grateful.

Epilogue

With her shawl wrapped around her, Sunny stood in the chill autumn afternoon. Isaiah had come to say goodbye and to claim Miigwans's puppy. Tomorrow at dawn, the young man would be heading north to help Sam White and see how Bid'a ban was faring. Sunny felt joyful and sad at the same time.

Noah stood beside her with Dawn in his arms. "I wish I could go with you."

Sunny knew what he meant. She wished she could see her friend again. How could she and Bid'a ban have bonded so deeply in such a short time? "Maybe someday we'll go visit them."

Recognizing the longing in her tone, Noah brushed her cheek with his lips. Then he handed her Dawn and lifted the leather bag of gifts they and their friends had gathered for Bid'a ban—fabric and buttons and needles and thread and other little items that would travel light but be of use to her.

Onto the young man's shoulders Noah positioned the sling he'd fashioned for Isaiah to carry the pup. Then he went to Neechee and bent to pet her. "It's time for your last pup to go to his owner, Neechee. You remember Miigwans. He'll take good care of your little one." He lifted the pup and stowed it in the sling. "You be a good traveler, okay, little pup?"

Neechee rose to her feet and barked as if in farewell.

Isaiah patted the pup in the sling and murmured to it. "He'll be good company for me. Well, I best be off. Mom cooked a big dinner at noon and is baking me a cake for my last supper at home."

Sunny hugged Isaiah and petted the pup. "Be good, both of you," she teased, lightening the mood.

Noah shook hands with the young man and bid farewell to the pup. Then he stood with his arm around Sunny and watched the lad ride down the track and disappear around the bend of trees. From Sunny's arms, Dawn waved bye-bye. Neechee barked but remained at her master's side.

"I'll miss having the last pup here," he said at last.

Sunny turned to him and gave him a smile. Leaning close, she whispered, "I think we'll have another little one around here come next summer."

At first he didn't understand her. But when she placed his hand on her abdomen, he grasped the news. His heart skipped a beat.

"You mean it?" This was too good to be true. A child?

She nodded and then leaned her head on his chest. "Are you happy?"

"There aren't words," he murmured as his heart exploded with joy. He kissed her fragrant hair and tucked her closer.

Dawn objected loudly to being pressed against him so tightly. "Pa-pa!"

He lifted the child from her mother's arms. "Papa, is it? Now you know who I am?"

Arms wide, Dawn threw herself against him in one of her impulsive hugs. "Pa-pa!"

Noah drew Sunny under his arm and he stood with his family, bursting with love and gratitude. Never had he imagined such blessings.

Thank You, God, a thousand times, thank You.

* * * * *

THE BABY BEQUEST

I am come that they might have life,
and that they might have it more abundantly.
—*John* 10:10

And be ye kind one to another, tenderhearted,
forgiving one another, even as God for Christ's sake
hath forgiven you.
—*Ephesians* 4:32

To Carol, Nan and Chris, my knitting pals!

And in fond memory of Ellen Hornshuh,
a special lady

Chapter One

Pepin, Wisconsin
August, 1870

Clutching the railing of the riverboat, Miss Ellen Thurston ached as if she'd been beaten. Now she truly understood the word *heartbroken*. Images of her sister in her pale blue wedding dress insistently flashed through her mind. As if she could wipe them away, she passed a hand over her eyes. The trip north had been both brief and endless.

She forced herself back to the present. She was here to start her new life.

The sunlight glittering on the Mississippi River nearly blinded her. The brim of her stylish hat fell short and she shaded her eyes, scanning the jumble of dusty, rustic buildings, seeking her cousin, Ophelia, and Ophelia's husband. But only a few strangers had gathered to watch the boat dock. Loneliness nearly choked her. *Ophelia, please be here. I need you.*

The riverboat men called to each other as the captain guided the boat to the wharf. With a bump, the boat docked and the men began to wrestle thick ropes to harness the boat to the pier.

As she watched the rough ropes being rasped back and forth, she felt the same sensation as she relived her recent struggle. Leaving home had been more difficult than she could have anticipated. But staying had been impossible. Why had she gone against her better judgment and let her heart take a chance?

The black porter who had assisted her during her trip appeared beside her. "Miss, I will see to your trunk and boxes, never fear."

She smiled at him and offered her hand. "You've been so kind. Thank you."

Looking surprised, he shook her hand. "It's been my pleasure to serve you, miss. Yes, indeed it has."

His courtesy helped her take a deep breath. She merely had to hold herself together till she was safely at Ophelia's. There, with her cousin—who was closer than her sister—she could mourn her loss privately, inwardly.

Soon she was standing on dry land with her luggage piled around her. She handed the porter a generous tip and he bowed his thanks and left her. Ellen glanced around, looking for her cousin in vain. Could something have happened to her? Even as this fear struck, she pushed it from her mind. Ophelia was probably just a bit late. Still, standing here alone made her painfully conspicuous.

A furtive movement across the way caught her attention. A thin, blond lad who looked to be in his midteens was sneaking—yes, definitely sneaking—around the back of a store. She wondered what he was up to. But she didn't know much about this town, and she shouldn't poke her nose into someone else's business. Besides, what wrong could a lad that age be doing?

She turned her mind back to her own dilemma. Who could she go to for assistance? Who would know the possible reason why Ophelia wasn't here to meet her? Searching her mind, she recalled someone she'd met on her one visit here a year ago. She picked up her skirts and walked to Ashford's General Store.

The bell jingled as she entered, and two men turned to see who had come in. One she recognized as the proprietor, Mr. Ashford, and one was a stranger—a very handsome stranger—with wavy blond hair.

Holton had the same kind of hair. The likeness stabbed her.

Then she noticed a young girl about fourteen slipping down the stairs at the rear of the store. She eased the back door open and through the gap, Ellen glimpsed the young lad. Ah, calf love.

Ellen held her polite mask in place, turning her attention to the older of the two men. "Good day, Mr. Ashford. I don't know if you remember me—"

"Miss Thurston!" the storekeeper exclaimed and hurried around the counter. "We didn't expect you for another few days."

This brought her up sharply. "I wrote my cousin almost two weeks ago that I'd be arriving today."

The storekeeper frowned. "I thought Mrs. Steward said you'd be arriving later this week."

"Oh, dear." Ellen voiced her sinking dismay as she turned toward the windows facing the street. Her mound of boxes and valises sat forlornly on her trunk at the head of the dock. How was she going to get to Ophelia? Her grip on her polite facade was slipping. "I could walk to the Steward's but my things…"

"We'll get some boys to bring them here—"

The stranger in the store interrupted, clearing his throat, and bowed. "Mr. Ashford, please to introduce me. I may help, perhaps?" The man spoke with a thick German accent.

The man also unfortunately had blue eyes. Again, his likeness to Holton, who had misled her, churned within. She wanted to turn her back to him.

Mr. Ashford hesitated, then nodded. "A good idea." He turned to Ellen. "Miss Ellen Thurston, may I introduce you to another newcomer in our little town, Mr. Kurt Lang, a Dutchman?"

Ellen recognized that Mr. Ashford was using the ethnic slur, "Dutch," a corruption of *Deutsche,* the correct term for German immigrants. Hiding her acute discomfort with the insult, Ellen extended her gloved hand and curtsied as politeness demanded.

Mr. Lang approached swiftly and bowed over her hand, murmuring something that sounded more like French than German.

Ellen withdrew her hand and tried not to look the man full in the face, but she failed. She found that not only did he have blond hair with a natural wave and blue eyes that reminded her of Holton, but his face was altogether too handsome. And the worst was that his smile was too kind. Her facade began slipping even more as tears hovered just behind her eyes.

"I live near the Stewards, Miss Thurston," the stranger said, sounding polite but stiff. "I drive you."

Ellen looked to Mr. Ashford a bit desperately. Young ladies of quality observed a strict code of conduct, especially those who became schoolteachers. Should she ride alone with this man?

Mr. Ashford also seemed a bit uncomfortable. "Mr. Lang has been living here for over six months and is a respectable person. Very respectable." The man lowered his voice and added, "Even if he is a foreigner."

Ellen stiffened at this second slur from Mr. Ashford.

Mr. Lang himself looked mortified but said nothing in return.

With effort, Ellen swallowed her discomfort. The man couldn't help reminding her of someone she didn't want to be reminded of. More important, she would not let him think that she embraced the popular prejudice against anyone not born in America.

"We are a nation of immigrants, Mr. Ashford," she said with a smile to lighten the scold. She turned to Mr. Lang. "Thank you, Mr. Lang, I am ready whenever you are."

Mr. Lang's gaze met hers in sudden connection. He bowed again. "I finish and take you."

She heard in these words a hidden thank-you for her comment.

A few moments later, she stood on the shady porch of the store, watching the man load her trunk, two boxes of books and her valises onto the back of his wagon along with his goods. She noticed it was easy for him— he was quite strong. She also noticed he made no effort to gain her attention or show off. He just did what he'd said he'd do. That definitely differed from Holton, the consummate actor.

This man's neat appearance reminded her that she must look somewhat disheveled from her trip, increasing her feelings of awkwardness at being alone with the stranger. She'd often felt that same way with Holton, too. His Eastern polish should have warned her away— if her own instincts hadn't.

At his curt nod, she met Mr. Lang at the wagon side and he helped her up the steps. His touch warmed her skin, catching her off guard. Rattled, she sat rigidly straight on the high bench, warning him away.

Just then, the storekeeper's wife hurried out the door. "Miss Thurston! Ned just called upstairs that you'd arrived." The flustered woman hurried over and reached up to shake hands with Ellen. "We didn't expect you so soon."

"Yes, Mr. Ashford said as much. I'd told my cousin when I was arriving, but perhaps she didn't receive my letter."

"The school isn't quite ready, you know." Mrs. Ashford looked down and obviously realized that she'd rushed outside without taking off her smeared kitchen apron. She snatched it off.

"That's fine. My cousin wanted me to come for a visit, anyway." Ophelia's invitation to visit before the teaching job began had come months before. Ellen suffered a twinge, hoping this was all just a minor misunderstanding. Then she thought of Ophelia's little boy. Little ones were so at risk for illness. Perhaps something had happened?

She scolded herself for jumping to conclusions. After a few more parting remarks were exchanged, Mr. Lang slapped the reins, and the team started down the dusty road toward the track that Ellen recognized from her earlier visit to Pepin.

The two of them sat in a polite silence. As they left the town behind them, Ellen tried to accustom herself to the forest that crowded in on them like a brooding presence. The atmosphere did not raise her spirits. And it was taking every ounce of composure she had left to sit beside this stranger.

Then, when the silence had become unbearable, Mr. Lang asked gruffly, "You come far?"

"Just from Galena." Then she realized a newcomer might not know where Galena was. "It's south of here in Illinois, about a five-day trip. You may have heard of it. President Grant's home is there."

"Your president, he comes from your town?"

She nodded and didn't add that her hometown had a bad case of self-importance over this. They'd all forgotten how many of them had previously scorned Ulysses S. Grant. "Before the war, he and his father owned a leather shop." She hadn't meant to say this, but speaking her mind to someone at last on the topic presented an opportunity too attractive to be missed. She found President Grant's story extraordinary, though not everyone did.

"A leather shop?" The man sounded disbelieving.

"Yes." She stopped herself from saying more in case Mr. Lang thought that she was disparaging their president. The wagon rocked over a ridge in the road. Why couldn't it move more quickly?

"This land is different. In Germany, no tradesman would be general or president."

Ellen couldn't miss the deep emotion with which Mr. Lang spoke these few words. She tilted her face so she could see him around the brim of her hat, then regretted it. The man had expressive eyebrows and thick brown lashes, another resemblance to Holton. Unhappy thoughts of home bombarded her.

As another conversational lull blossomed, crows filled the silence, squawking as if irritated by the human intrusion. She felt the same discontent. She wanted only to be with dear Ophelia, and she wasn't sure she could stand much more time alone with this disturbing stranger.

She sought another way to put distance between them. "I am going to be the schoolteacher here. Do you have children?" Ellen hoped he'd say that he and his wife had none, and hence she would not come in contact with this man much in the future.

"I am not married. But I have two…students."

"I'm sorry, I don't understand," Ellen said, clutching the side of the wagon as they drove over another rough patch, her stomach lurching.

"My brother, Gunther, and my nephew, Johann. They will come to school."

This man had responsibilities she hadn't guessed. Yet his tone had been grim, as if his charges were a sore subject.

"How old are they?" *Do they speak English?* she wanted to ask. She sincerely hoped so.

"Gunther is sixteen and Johann is seven." Then he answered her unspoken question. "We speak English some at home. But is hard for them."

She nodded out of politeness but she couldn't help voicing an immediate concern. "Isn't your brother a bit old to attend school? Most students only go to the eighth grade—I mean, until about thirteen years old."

"Gunther needs to learn much about this country. He will go to school."

The man's tone brooked no dispute. So she offered

none, straightening her back and wishing the horse would go faster.

Yes, your brother will attend, but will he try to learn? And in consequence, will he make my job harder?

The oppressive silence surged back again and Ellen began to imagine all sorts of dreadful reasons for her cousin not meeting her on the appointed day. Ellen searched her mind for some topic of conversation. She did not want to dwell on her own worry and misery. "Are you homesteading?"

"*Ja.* Yes. I claim land." His voice changed then, his harsh tone disappearing. "Only in America is land free. Land just…free."

In spite of herself, the wonder in his voice made her proud to be an American. "Well, we have a lot of land and not many people," she said after a pause. If she felt more comfortable at being alone with him, she would have asked him to tell her about Europe, a place she wished to see but probably never would.

"Still, government could make money from selling land, yes?"

She took a deep, steadying breath. "It's better not to look a gift horse in the mouth."

More unwelcome silence. She stole another glance at him. The man appeared in deep thought.

"Oh," he said, his face lifting. "Not look gift horse… to see if healthy."

"Exactly," she said. She hadn't thought about the phrase as being an idiom. How difficult it must be to live away from home, where you don't even know the everyday expressions. Homesickness stabbed her suddenly. Her heart clenched. Perhaps they did have something in common. "It must have been hard to leave home and travel so far."

He seemed to close in on himself. Then he shrugged slightly. "War will come soon to Germany. I need to keep safe, to raise Johann."

"You might have been drafted?" she asked more sharply than she'd planned. During the Civil War, many men had bought their way out of the draft. Not something she approved of.

"*Ja*—yes—but war in Germany is to win land for princes, not for people. No democracy in Germany."

"That's unfortunate." No doubt not having any say in what the government did would make being drafted feel different. Ellen fell silent, exhausted from the effort of making conversation with this man who reminded her so much of Holton. She knotted her hands together in her lap, as if that would contain her composure. Would this ride never end?

"We—the men—we build the school…more on Saturday," he said haltingly.

This pleased her. She wanted to get her life here started, get busy so she could put the past in the past. "How much longer do you think it will take?"

"Depends. Some men harvest corn. If rain comes…" He shrugged again, seeming unable to express the uncertainty.

"I see. Well, I'll just have faith that it will all come together in the next few weeks. Besides, the delay gives me more time to prepare lessons."

At that moment, Mr. Lang turned the wagon down a track and ahead lay the Steward cabin. Ellen's heart leaped when she saw her cousin, carrying her baby, hurry out to greet her.

"Ophelia!" she called.

Mr. Lang drew up his team. "Wait," he insisted. "Please, I help." He secured the brake.

But Ellen couldn't wait. She jumped down and ran to Ophelia, the emotions she'd been working so hard to keep at bay finally overtaking her. She buried her face in Ophelia's shoulder and burst into tears. Her feelings strangled her voice.

Chapter Two

"**W**hy weren't you at the river to meet me?"

Ellen grasped her cousin's hand desperately as Mr. Lang drove down the track away from them. She had managed to pull herself together enough to bid Mr. Lang goodbye and thank him for the ride, but she was glad to see him leave—his presence had pushed her over the edge emotionally. The man had only been kind to her, but being alone with him had nearly been more than she could bear.

"Why weren't you at the river to meet me?" Ellen repeated.

Ophelia pulled a well-worn letter from her pocket. "You said your boat would dock tomorrow. 'I will arrive on the sixteenth of August,'" she read.

"But that's today."

"No, dear, that's tomorrow. It's easy to lose track of days when traveling. I know I did."

Ellen thought her own mental state must be the explanation. As Ophelia guided her to a chair just outside the log cabin and disappeared inside, Ellen tried to appear merely homesick and travel-weary, not heartsick.

She must master herself or this thing would defeat her. She stiffened her spine.

Soon Ophelia bustled into the daylight again and offered her a cup of tea. "This will help. I know when I arrived I…" Her cousin paused, frowning. "I cried a lot. It's a shock leaving family, leaving home." She sat down beside Ellen and began nursing her little boy.

Ophelia had thoughtfully offered her an excuse for her tears and she would not contradict her. Yet the invisible band around her heart squeezed tighter. Ellen took a sip of the tea, which tasted like peppermint. "I'll adjust."

"Of course you will. You've done right coming here. Pepin has the nicest people, and those with children are so happy to have a teacher. They can't wait to meet you."

A weight like a stone pressed down on Ellen's lungs. She'd never taught before. Would she be good at it? "I'm glad to hear that."

"The schoolhouse with your quarters isn't finished yet, but Martin and I will love having you spend a few weeks with us."

That long? How could she keep her misery hidden that long, and from Ophelia, who knew her so well? "I'm sorry for arriving early and putting you out—"

"You're not putting me out," Ophelia said emphatically. "Having family here—" the young mother paused as if fighting tears "—means a great deal to me."

Touched, Ellen reached out and pressed her hand to Ophelia's shoulder. "I'm glad to have family here, too." *Family that loves me,* she thought.

Her cousin rested her cheek on Ellen's hand for a moment. "I'm sorry I missed Cissy's wedding."

The image of Holton kissing her sister, Cissy, in their parlor, sealing their life vows, was a knife piercing Ellen's heart. What had happened had not been her naive younger sister's fault, she reminded herself. "Cissy was a beautiful bride," she said bravely.

"Oh, I wish I could have been there, but we couldn't justify the expense of the riverboat fare and the time away from our crops. It seems every varmint in Wisconsin wants to eat our garden and corn." Ophelia sounded indignant. "You'd think our farm was surrounded by a desolate desert without a green shoot, the way everything tries to gobble up our food."

Ellen couldn't help herself; a chuckle escaped her. Oh, it felt good to laugh again.

"It's not funny."

"I know, but *you* are. Oh, Ophelia, I've missed you."

And it was the truth. Ophelia had been a friend from childhood, slipping through the back fence to Ellen's house, escaping her own overbearing, scene-making mother.

"I miss your parents. They were always so good to me," Ophelia said in a voice rich with emotion, rich with love and sympathy.

The cousins linked hands in a silent moment of remembrance.

"They were good to me, too," Ellen murmured. Strengthened, she released Ophelia's hand. "But they are with God and I am here with you. To start a new life, just like you have."

"Ellen, about Holton." Her cousin paused, biting her lower lip.

Ellen froze, her cup in midair. What about Holton? What could Ophelia possibly know? And *how?*

"I wondered… My mother wrote me that when he first came to town, he was making up to you…"

Ellen suffered the words as a blow. She should have foreseen this. Ophelia's mother, Prudence, completely misnamed, was also one of the worst gossips in Galena. Of course Aunt Prudence would have told Ophelia how, when he first came to town, Holton had buzzed around Ellen, only to switch his attentions when her prettier, younger and easier-to-manage sister came home from boarding school in Chicago.

Ellen tried to keep breathing through the pain of remembering.

At that moment, Ophelia's husband, Martin, walked out of the woods, a hoe over his shoulder and a dog at his side, saving her from having to speak about Holton and his deception of her. She had gotten through mention of the awful day of Cissy's wedding without revealing anything. No doubt it would come up again, but perhaps every day that passed would distance the pain.

This move would work out. It had to.

As she thought of her future in Pepin, the handsome but troubled face of Kurt Lang popped into her mind. What was wrong with her? Did she have no defense at all against a handsome face? A handsome face belonging to a man that might mislead and lie just as Holton did?

She vowed she would never again make the mistake she'd made with Holton. Never.

Kurt found Gunther sitting beside the creek, fishing. The lanky boy was too thin and his blond hair needed cutting. A pang of sympathy swept through Kurt. His brother was so young to carry their family shame.

Gunther looked up, already spoiling for an argument. "I did my chores and Johann did his."

And just like that, Kurt's sympathy turned to frustration. He knew why Gunther simmered all the time, ready to boil over. But the lad was old enough to learn to carry what had happened to them like a man.

Upstream, Johann, who had been wading in the cooling water, looked up at the sound of Gunther's voice. He waved. "Hello, *Onkel* Kurt!" The barefoot boy splashed over the rocks and ran up the grassy bank to Kurt.

Kurt pulled down the brim of the boy's hat, teasing. Johann favored his late father's coloring with black hair and brown eyes. "You keep cool in the water?" Kurt asked in careful English.

Johann pushed up the brim, grinning. "Yes, I did." Then the boy looked uncomfortable and glanced toward Gunther.

In return, Gunther sent their nephew a pointed, forbidding look.

Kurt's instincts went on alert. What were these two hiding?

His guess was that Gunther had done something he knew Kurt wouldn't like and had sworn Johann to secrecy. Kurt let out a breath. Another argument wouldn't help. He'd just wait. Everything came out in the wash, his grandmother used to say and was said here, too.

"You bring me candy? Please?" Johann asked, eyeing Kurt's pockets.

"Candy? Why should I bring you candy?" If he wasn't careful, he'd spoil this one.

"I did my chores this week."

After feigning deep thought for a few moments, Kurt drew out a small brown bag. "You did do your chores well, Johann." Kurt lapsed into German as he tossed the boy a chunk of peppermint. Then he offered another chunk to his brother.

Gunther glared at him. "I'm almost a man."

Irritation sparked in Kurt's stomach. "Then act like one."

Gunther turned his back to Kurt, hunching up one shoulder.

Kurt regretted his brusque tone, but he couldn't baby Gunther. Everyone said that had been the root cause of their father's downfall. Their father had been a very spoiled only child who had never grown up. Kurt would not let Gunther follow in their father's disastrous footsteps.

"Your schoolteacher arrived today."

Kurt stopped there, realizing that the unexpected meeting had upset him. Miss Ellen Thurston was a striking woman with a great deal of countenance, but so emotional. He'd heard all the gossip in town about her. She was a well-educated woman and a wealthy man's daughter, and her family was even in government in Illinois. Far above his touch. His brow furrowed; he recalled the scene at the Stewards', her brown eyes overflowing with tears. Why had she burst into tears like that? He shook his head again. Women were so emotional, not like men.

But wondering about the new schoolteacher was just wasting time. His life now was raising Johann and guiding Gunther. Brigitte's betrayal tried to intrude on his thoughts, but he shook it off—he did not want to spare one more thought for his former fiancée.

"I'm not going to school," Gunther insisted.

Kurt stiffened.

"Nicht wahr?" Johann asked and went on in German.

"I think it will be fun. At least we will get to meet some others here. I want to make friends. Don't you want to make friends, Gunther?"

A fish took Gunther's bait, saving them from another angry retort.

The deep pool of Kurt's own sorrow and shame bubbled up. He inhaled deeply, forcing it down. Would the weight he carried never lift? Kurt watched his brother deftly play and then pull in a nice bass. Kurt tried encouragement. "A fine fish for supper. Well done."

Gunther refused the compliment with a toss of his head.

Kurt's patience began slipping. Better to leave before he traded more barbed words with the lad. He relaxed and spoke in German, "Catch a few more if you can. Johann, help me put away what I bought at the store. Then we will look over the garden to see what needs picking."

Johann fell into step with him. Kurt rested a hand on the boy's shoulder. Again he thought of the schoolteacher, so stylish and with soft brown curls around her aristocratic face. He'd anticipated a plain woman, much older, with hair sprouting from her chin. What was Miss Ellen Thurston doing here, teaching school? It was a mystery.

Then, in spite of the sorrow that never quite eased, Kurt began teasing Johann about how much peppermint he thought he could eat at one time.

Things would get better. They had to.

Riding on the wagon bench, Ellen dreaded being put on display for all of Pepin today, nearly a week after arriving. But the men had decided to hold a community-wide workday on the school and attached living quarters, and she must attend and show a cheerful face to all. In light of the wound she carried and concealed day by day, it would be one long, precarious ordeal. She had to portray confidence above all.

When the Stewards' wagon broke free of the forest into the open river flat, she welcomed the broad view of the blue, rippling Mississippi ahead. She took a deep breath. The normally empty town now appeared crowded and her heart sank another notch—until an impertinent question popped up: Would Mr. Lang come today? Ellen willed this thought away.

Ophelia touched her hand. "Don't worry. You'll get to know everyone in no time and then this will feel more like home."

Ellen fashioned a smile for Ophelia. If only shyness were her worry. "I'm sure you're right."

"You met my friends Sunny and Nan last year. They are eager to make you welcome."

Ellen tried to take comfort from her cousin's words.

Ellen and Ophelia joined the ladies who were storing the cold lunch in the spring house behind the store. Then they gathered in the shade of the trees with a good view of the unfinished log schoolhouse and claimed places on a rectangle of benches. Small children rolled or crawled in the grass in the midst of the benches, while older children played tag nearby.

Though scolding herself silently, Ellen scanned the men, seeking Kurt Lang. He had made an impression on her and she couldn't deny it. She also couldn't deny that she resented it.

"Miss Thurston," Mrs. Ashford called. "This is my daughter Amanda." Mrs. Ashford motioned for a girl in a navy blue plaid dress, who appeared to be around fourteen, to come to her. "Make your curtsy to the schoolteacher, Amanda."

The thin, dark-haired girl obeyed, blushing. With a start, Ellen recognized her as the girl she'd seen slipping downstairs to meet a boy on the day Ellen had arrived.

Ellen took pity on the girl, obviously enduring that awkward stage between girlhood and womanhood, and offered her hand. "I'm pleased to meet you, Amanda. Your dress is very pretty."

Mrs. Ashford preened. "Amanda cut and sewed it all by herself. She is the age where she should be finishing up her learning of the household arts. But Ned and I decided that we'd let her go to school one more year, though she's had enough schooling for a girl."

Ellen swallowed her response to this common sentiment, quelling the irritation it sparked. *Enough schooling for a girl.* Her older brother's wife, Alice, had the gall to tell her once that the reason Ellen had never "snared" a man was she had had too much schooling for a woman. *I couldn't stand my sister-in-law's sly rudeness and innuendo a day longer.* What would this storekeeper's wife say if she announced that she intended to earn a bachelor's degree and perhaps teach at a preparatory school someday?

Ellen limited herself to saying, "I will be happy to have Amanda in my class."

The men began shouting words of instruction and encouragement, drawing the women's attention to the schoolhouse. They were coordinating the positioning of four ladders against the log walls, two on each side. With a start, Ellen spotted Kurt Lang as he nimbly mounted a ladder and climbed toward the peak of the joists.

Ellen felt a little dizzy as she watched Mr. Lang so high up in the air, leaning perilously away from the ladder. An imposing figure, he appeared intent on what he was doing, evidently not the kind to shy away from hard work.

As she watched, a barefoot boy with black hair and a tanned face ran up, startling her. "You are teacher?" he asked with an accent. "The girls say you are teacher."

"Yes, I am going to be the teacher. Will you be one of my students?" Was this Mr. Lang's nephew?

He nodded vigorously. "I want school. I like to read."

"Good. What's your name?"

"Johann Mueller." He pointed toward the school. "My *onkel* Kurt." Then he pointed to a teenager standing by the ladders. "My *onkel* Gunther." The boy said the name so it sounded like "Goon-ter."

Ellen noted that Gunther, working with the men on the ground, wasn't paying attention to the work going on around him. He was staring across at Amanda. She then recognized him as the young man Amanda had slipped out to see that first day she'd come to town.

Over the hammering, she heard Mr. Lang's voice rise, speaking in German, sounding as if he were scolding someone. She caught the name, "Gunther."

She saw Gunther glare up at Mr. Lang, then grudgingly begin to work again.

Ellen felt sympathy for the younger brother. Why was Mr. Lang so hard on him? He was just a boy, really.

Johann bowed. "I go. Goodbye!" He pulled on his cap, gave her a grin and ran toward the children.

Mrs. Ashford pursed her lips, looking peevish. "I hope you don't have trouble with those Dutch boys."

She nodded toward the unhappy Gunther. "That one's too old for school and Mr. Ashford told Mr. Lang so."

Ellen agreed. A sixteen-year-old could stir up all kinds of trouble at school, not only for the other students, but for her. Mr. Lang, of course, probably hadn't thought of this. She drew in a breath. "I'm sure he thinks it best for his brother."

"Well." Mrs. Ashford sniffed. "I think the homesteading law should have specified that land was only for Americans, not for foreigners."

Ellen bit her tongue. The homesteading law had been designed specifically to attract people from other countries to populate the vast open area east of the Rocky Mountains. There simply weren't enough American-born families to fill up those vacant acres.

Ellen recalled Mr. Ashford's whisper that Kurt was respectable even if a foreigner. It must be difficult for Mr. Lang to face this prejudice against immigrants day after day. Even though she didn't agree with Mr. Lang's treatment of his brother, she felt a keen sympathy for him—he and his charges had a difficult path ahead of them in so many ways.

This very feeling of sympathy led Ellen to resolve to keep her distance from Mr. Lang as best she could.

Hours later, the lunch bell rang. The men washed their hands at the school pump and gathered around the tables. While the women served the meal, the older children were permitted to sit by their fathers and listen to the men discuss the progress of the school building.

Despite her decision to keep her distance, Ellen tracked Mr. Lang's whereabouts and listened to catch his words.

For distraction, she insisted on donning an apron and whisking away empty bowls to replenish them. As she approached Mr. Lang's table, she heard him laugh—his laughter was deep and rich. Just as she reached him with a heaping bowl of green salad, he turned and nearly swept the bowl from her arms.

"*Tut mir leid!* I'm sorry!" he exclaimed, reaching out and steadying her hold on the bowl with his hands over hers.

The unexpected contact made her smother a gasp.

"No harm done." She set the bowl on the table and stepped back, slightly breathless. Perspiration dotted his hairline and his thick, tawny hair had curled in the humidity. She nearly brushed back a curl that had strayed onto his forehead. The very thought of it made her turn away as quickly as possible to get back to work.

As she made her way to the next table, she noticed Mrs. Ashford's daughter pause before slipping into the trees. The girl looked over her shoulder in a furtive move that announced she was up to no good.

Ellen recalled how Gunther had earlier been staring at this girl. A kind of inevitable presentiment draped over Ellen's mind. She glanced around. Gunther was nowhere to be seen.

What to do? After listening to Mrs. Ashford's opinion of foreigners, Ellen didn't want to think of the repercussions in this small town if someone found the two young people together. And she didn't want people gossiping about Amanda—she knew how that stung.

She excused herself and followed Amanda into the cover of the trees, threading her way through the thick pines and oaks. She hoped the young couple hadn't gone too far.

She also hoped she wouldn't find them kissing.

When she glimpsed Amanda's navy blue plaid dress through the trees, the young girl was testing the flexed muscle of Gunther's upper arm. A timeless scene—a young man showing off his strength to a young, admiring girl. Innocent and somewhat sweet. However, that wouldn't be how the Ashfords would view it.

At that moment, she heard footsteps behind her. She swung around to find Kurt Lang facing her. She jerked backward in surprise.

Before she could say anything, Mr. Lang glimpsed the couple over her shoulder. His face darkened. He opened his mouth.

Impetuously, without thinking about her actions, Ellen shocked herself by reaching up and gently pressing a hand to Mr. Kurt Lang's lips.

The lady's featherlike touch threw Kurt off balance. He grappled with the cascade of sensations sparked by her fingers against his lips.

"Please, you'll embarrass them," she whispered, quickly removing her hand as her face flushed.

She was so close, her light fragrance filled his head, making him think of spring. He fought free of it. "They need to be embarrassed," he replied emphatically. "I see you follow the girl Gunther likes. Then I see Gunther is not at table. He is not to flirt with this girl. He is too young."

"But do you want everyone to hear, to know?" she cautioned.

Kurt thought about the wagging tongues, and realized she was right. "No. But I must discipline him. He must do what he is supposed to."

The lady bit her lower lip as if she wanted to say more but then she fell back.

"Gunther." He snapped his brother's name as a reprimand.

In an instant, Amanda dropped her hand, blushing. Gunther jerked back and glared.

"We're not doing anything wrong," Amanda said in a rush.

The schoolteacher preceded him toward the couple. "No, you aren't," she said evenly, "but slipping away like this would not please your parents, Amanda. Why don't you go back before you're missed?"

Kurt admired her aplomb. She was definitely a lady of unusual quality.

"Yes, ma'am." Amanda snuck a last look at Gunther and then hurried away.

The lady schoolteacher sent him an apologetic look filled with an appeal for the young couple. Why did women want to coddle children?

When the two females had moved out of earshot, Kurt told his brother what he thought of such a meeting. The boy flushed bright red and began to answer back.

Kurt cut him off. "You embarrass me in front of your teacher."

Instead of apologizing, his brother made a rude sound and stalked away. Kurt proceeded back to the tables.

The other men were finished eating. With the hot sun blazing down, they lingered at the shaded tables, talking and teasing one another about minor mishaps during the morning's work. Kurt envied their easygoing good humor, wishing he could participate, but inside, he churned like the Atlantic he'd crossed only months before.

He could not afford to lose his brother as he'd lost his father.

An older man sitting in the shade away from the tables in a rough-hewn wheelchair with his feet propped up motioned for Kurt to come to him.

Kurt obeyed the summons. "Sir?"

The older man reached out his hand. "You are Mr. Kurt Lang from Germany. I've seen you come to worship and I've been wanting to meet you, but my days of calling on folk are over. I'm Old Saul."

"I hear you were pastor before Noah Whitmore." Kurt shook the man's hand and sat on a stool beside his chair. "I'm pleased to meet you, sir."

"Just call me Old Saul."

Kurt digested this. People here thought differently about social status. Few wanted titles of respect beyond Mr. and Mrs. or Miss. It puzzled him. But he was never left in doubt of their low opinion of him, an immigrant.

Old Saul nodded toward the lady schoolteacher. "I didn't think I'd still be here to greet Miss Thurston, but God hasn't decided to call me home just yet." Then he looked directly into Kurt's eyes. "You carry a heavy load. I see it. You're strong but some burdens need God's strength."

The old man looked frail but his voice sounded surprisingly strong. Kurt didn't know what to make of what he'd said, yet for the first time in many days, Kurt relaxed, feeling the man's acceptance deep within his spirit.

"It's hard starting out in a new place," Old Saul continued, "but you'll do fine. Just ask God to help you when you need it. God's strength is stronger than any human's and God is a very present help in times of trouble, Mr. Kurt Lang. Yes, He is." Then the older man's gaze followed the lady teacher.

Kurt could think of nothing to say so he watched the schoolteacher, too. Even though she was dressed simply, she had that flair that lent her a more fashionable look. He thought of her following the Ashford girl and his brother, trying to protect them from gossip. She must have a caring heart.

Miss Ellen Thurston, the lady schoolteacher.

Kurt drew in a breath and before anyone caught him staring at her, he turned his attention back to Old Saul. *She is far above me, a poor farmer who speaks bad English.*

Chapter Three

Ellen's heart beat fast as she prepared to ring the hand-bell on the first day of school. Children, obviously scrubbed and combed and wearing freshly ironed clean clothing, had begun gathering over the past half hour and milled around the school entrance.

Then she glimpsed trouble. Mr. Lang marched into the clearing, his face a thundercloud. He grasped his brother Gunther's arm and headed straight for her. Little Johann ran behind the two, trying to keep up.

Oh, no, she moaned silently. Didn't the man have enough sense not to make a public scene?

As she rang the bell, the children ran toward her, looking excited. But when they reached her, they turned to see what she was looking at with such consternation, and watched the threesome heading straight for her.

Ellen racked her brain, trying to come up with some way to avert Gunther's public humiliation. In the moment, she only managed to draw up a welcoming smile.

"Good morning, Mr. Lang!" she called out in a friendly tone, hoping to turn him up sweet.

She watched him master the thundercloud and nod

toward her curtly but politely. She turned to the children, hoping to move them inside. "Children, please line up by age, the youngest students in the front."

Some jostling and pushing happened as the line shifted.

Mr. Lang halted at the rear. Gunther tried to pull away from him, but couldn't break free. Looking worried, Johann hurried past them to the front of the line as instructed.

"Eyes forward," she ordered when children turned to look back at Gunther. She set the school bell down on the bench inside the door and then asked the children their ages and did some re-sorting in the line. She sent the children in row by row, keeping Gunther and Mr. Lang at the rear.

Finally, the older children went inside. Mr. Lang released Gunther to go with them with a sharp command in German.

Ellen stepped forward, intercepting Mr. Lang before he could turn away. She lowered her voice. "I wish you hadn't called so much attention to Gunther. He already stands out as it is."

"Gunther disobeyed. He is my brother, Miss Thurston. I must do what I think is best."

Helpless to better the situation, Ellen struggled in silence. Obviously Gunther had balked at coming to school. Mr. Lang had excellent intentions, but this public humiliation would only bring more adverse attention from the other children. Was there ever a schoolyard without hurtful taunting?

"Perhaps you should take a moment to remember your school days, recall how children treat newcomers," she said in an undertone.

He looked up, showing surprise.

Hoping she'd given him something to think about, Ellen turned to go inside to take charge of her classroom.

Gunther slouched on the bench by the back door as if separating himself from the rest. She didn't say a word, hoping to let the whole situation simmer down. How was she going to gain Gunther's cooperation and reach him?

From her place with the other older children, Amanda Ashford peered at him until Ellen gently reminded her to face forward.

At the front of the class, Ellen led the students in a prayer, asking God to bless them as they began the first year together in this new school, smiling as brightly as she could. With a heavy heart, Ellen sighed. This promised to be a challenging year of teaching. However, uppermost in her mind was the image of Mr. Lang. His square jaw had been clamped tight and his eyes had been angry, but underneath she'd seen the worry.

What drove the man to push his brother so? And how could she help Gunther—and Mr. Lang?

By the end of the day, Ellen had the beginnings of a headache. The children for the most part were well behaved but most of them had little or no experience in a classroom with other students. Concentrating on their own lesson while she taught a different lesson to another age group taxed their powers of self-control.

Ellen had kept order by stopping often to sing a song with the children. This had occurred to her out of the blue and worked well, bringing a release of tension for her as well as the students. Grateful that the school year started in warm weather, she also had granted them a morning and afternoon recess in addition to the lunch recess.

Now their first day together was nearly done. From the head of the classroom, she gazed at her students, fatigue rolling over her. "Students, I am very pleased with your performance on this, our first day together. I think that I have been fortunate in starting my teaching career with a very bright class. However, we must work on concentrating on our studies. I haven't punished anyone today for not listening and not sticking to their own work, but I may have to tomorrow. Do you take my point?"

"Yes, Miss Thurston," they chorused.

"I will do better," Johann announced in the front row.

Some of the students tittered.

Ellen frowned at them, letting them know this mocking would not be tolerated. And she didn't reprimand Johann for speaking out of turn, since she liked his eager reply and most other students nodded in agreement. "I am sure each of you will. You are fortunate to have parents who care about you enough to build a school. Now pick up your things and line up as we did to go out for recess. I will meet you at the door."

Ellen hadn't planned to do this, but she recalled that her favorite teacher had always waited at the back of the schoolroom and had spoken to each of them on their way out. She had looked forward every schoolday to those few precious words meant just for her.

She took each student's hand in turn and thought of something pleasant to say, showing that she had noticed them specifically. Each student beamed at the praise, and she promised herself to end each school-day this way.

Finally, she faced Gunther and offered her hand. "Gunther, I hope you'll find school more pleasant tomorrow."

He accepted her hand as if her gesture in itself insulted him and he wouldn't meet her gaze. Then he stalked off with Johann running to keep up with him, talking in a stream of rapid German.

She slipped inside and immediately sank onto the bench at the back of the room as if she could finally lay down the load she'd carried all day. If Mr. Lang had been there, she would have gladly given him a good shake.

During afternoon recess two days later, Ellen watched the younger children playing tag. Then she noticed that the older children had disappeared. Where? And why?

Then she heard the shouting from the other side of the schoolhouse, "Fight! Fight!"

She ran toward the voices and unfortunately the younger children followed her.

There they were—Gunther and Clayton sparring, surrounded by the older boys and girls. As she watched, horrified, Clayton socked Gunther's eye. Gunther landed a blow on Clayton's jaw, making his head jerk backward.

She shouted, "Stop!"

At the sound of her voice, the older children surrounding the two combatants fled from her.

She halted near the two fighting. The fists were flying and she didn't want to get in the way of one. "Clayton Riggs, stop this instant! Gunther Lang, stop!"

Neither boy paid the slightest attention to her. She couldn't physically make them obey. Or could she? She ran to the pump. Soon she ran back. The two were now rolling around on the ground, punching and kicking each other.

She doused them with the bucket of cold water.

The two rolled apart, yelping with surprise and sputtering.

"Stand up!" she ordered. "Now!"

Gunther rose first, keeping his distance from the other boy. Clayton, though younger than Gunther, matched him nearly in height and weight, rolled to his feet, too.

"Both of you, go to the pump and wash your face and hands. Now." She gestured toward the pump and marched them there, hiding her own trembling. She was unaccustomed to physical fighting and it had shaken her.

She stood over them as if they were two-year-olds while they washed away the dirt and blood from the fight. The cold water had evidently washed away their forgetfulness of where they were. Both looked embarrassed, chastened. Possibly wondering what their elders would say?

She then waved them into the schoolhouse and told them to face the opposite walls near the front. She called the rest of the children inside then.

No child spoke but as they filed in, all of them looked at the backs of the two miscreants. A question hung over them all. What would the teacher do to Gunther and Clayton?

She was asking herself the same question. She knew that Clayton had been taunting Gunther for two days—subtly in class and blatantly on the school ground. She had tried to keep them busy and apart, hoping to prevent fisticuffs. She'd failed.

Now she went to the front of the classroom and faced her students. "I didn't think I needed to tell any of you that fighting on school grounds will not be tolerated."

"Are you going to paddle them?" a first grader asked in breathless alarm.

"The idea that I would have to *paddle* any one of my students is repugnant. I expect my students to show self-control in every situation. No matter what the provocation, fighting is no way to settle an argument. Gunther and Clayton will stand the rest of the day, facing the wall in shame."

The same first grader gasped. Some of the children gaped at her.

"If any more fights take place, I will have to inform the school board and they will mete out corporal punishment. I am a lady."

She added the last as her justification and she saw that her instincts had proven true. The other children nodded in total agreement. Miss Thurston was a lady, and ladies didn't paddle students.

Dear Lord, please don't make it necessary for me to talk to anybody about this.

Later, Ellen rose from the table at the end of another evening meal at the Ashfords, who had finally agreed to let her pay them for providing her meals. Ellen could cook over a woodstove but could only make tea or coffee on the hearth in her quarters.

Though the meal had been delicious, the pleasure had done little to raise her spirits. The lady of the house gazed at her questioningly and then glanced toward Amanda, who was clearing the table. Mrs. Ashford had apparently picked up on Ellen's preoccupation and Amanda's forlorn mood during the meal.

"I hope everything is all right at school," the lady of house said with a question in her voice.

Ellen decided that everyone would soon know what had happened so she might as well be frank. "I'm afraid that two boys came to blows during recess this afternoon." The fight had ended in a nosebleed for Clayton and a black eye for Gunther.

"It wasn't Gunther's fault," Amanda declared from the doorway to the kitchen. "That Clayton boy was making fun of how he talks and calling him names all day. Gunther ignored it till the Clayton boy started saying nasty things about Gunther's uncle and little Johann."

Both Mrs. Ashford and Ellen turned to the girl, stunned. Amanda had never shown such spirit before. Yet Ellen wished Amanda had kept her peace.

"I'm afraid I can't allow fighting between students," Ellen said patiently. "Even if there is provocation. I must maintain order."

"Quite right," Mrs. Ashford agreed. Unfortunately, she added, "I knew that Dutch boy would make trouble."

"It wasn't Gunther's fault!" Amanda stomped her foot.

"That will be enough sauce from you, miss." Mrs. Ashford's face reddened. "Now get busy washing the dishes before I wash your impertinent mouth out with soap."

On this unhappy note, Ellen said her thanks and descended the steps into the deep honey of twilight. Since she'd moved into her quarters, a large room behind the schoolroom, she'd dreaded the lonely evenings, which gave her too much time to fret, which she began as soon as she touched ground.

What should she do about Gunther Lang? Why didn't his older brother realize the situation he'd put Gunther in? Her mind drifted back to home and brought up her sister exchanging vows with Holton. How long did heartbreak linger?

When she walked through the trees into the schoolyard, she was surprised to glimpse Kurt Lang, sitting dejectedly on the school step, clearly waiting for her as his horse grazed nearby. Of all people, he was the one she felt least ready to face—she had no doubt he'd come to discuss the fight.

"Mr. Lang," she said.

He jumped up and swept off his hat. "Miss Thurston, I am sorry I am come so late. But I know Gunther had a fight. Please, I ask—do not put him out of school."

Ellen walked toward him, trying to gather her scattered thoughts. This disturbing man put her at a disadvantage. He was handsome like Holton, but he never tried to charm her like Holton. Mr. Lang reminded her more of a determined bull.

Nothing she'd said so far concerning Gunther had made the least impression on him. She knew in her heart that there was nothing she could do to help Gunther fit in—too much separated him from the other students. But how could she make this man believe her? See he was doing harm to his brother?

Glum about her prospects at persuading him, she sat

down on the school step, facing the river. He sat down a polite distance from her. For a few minutes neither of them talked. Finally, she cleared her throat. She would try once more.

"I realize that you want Gunther to learn more English so he is better prepared for life here."

His powerful shoulders strained against his cotton shirt. "Yes, that is so."

Her heart went out to him, a man trying to raise a teenage brother and a little boy by himself. Nonetheless, why did he have to be so stubborn? "But Gunther is too much older and too sensitive about being different from the others. Making him sit with little children won't work."

"Gunther must learn to obey." Mr. Lang's words rang with deep feeling.

She tried to imagine what was driving this man to continue to put his younger brother in such a difficult situation. Maybe if she talked about her family, he might reveal something about himself.

"I have a younger sister." She didn't mention that her elder brother was full of himself or that she'd had a baby brother, too. It cost her enough to speak of her sister Cissy and what her sister had unwittingly put her through. She paused a moment, grappling with her own rampant emotions. "My parents made the mistake of always saying to her, 'Why can't you be more like your sister?'"

Where am I going with this? How is this being help-ful?

She shook herself and then drew in a breath. "Nothing you do or say is going to change Gunther's mind or behavior. The struggle is not between you and him. It's really between Gunther and this new set of people, this new place." She sighed.

Several moments passed before he spoke. "You speak truth. But Gunther is too young to know what is good for him."

"Human nature will not be denied." Each word increased her confidence that making the lad attend school would not end well. "Gunther is a young man and we've put him in a situation that wouldn't be normal for any lad his age. You see that."

"Yes." Mr. Lang didn't sound happy or convinced. He rose. "I will keep Gunther home tomorrow. I must go, and think." He bowed his head politely, his unfailing courtesy impressing her once again.

"I think that's best." Ellen watched him don his hat and ride away. She stood motionless long after he'd vanished through the trees. Even after he had disappeared from view, his image stayed with her. A handsome, brave but troubled man. She wondered if his broad shoulders ever tired of the responsibilities he carried. The deep sadness she sensed in him drew her sympathy.

She shook herself and went inside, her own heart heavy. Never far from her mind were the charming words Holton had spoken to her. She reminded herself that she must stop noticing Kurt Lang so keenly. After everything she'd been through with Holton, the last thing she needed was to be the focus of whispers about the foolish old-maid schoolmarm.

Of course it was one thing to stop noticing him. It was another thing to stop thinking of him completely.

Chapter Four

Standing outside the Stewards' cabin after Saturday supper, Kurt tried to figure out exactly what he was doing there. He'd been surprised when the Stewards had invited him and his family to eat with them and Miss Thurston. The meal had been tasty, and he'd enjoyed talking about farming and the fall hunting with Martin, who was about his age. Unfortunately, Gunther had eaten in sullen silence, in contrast to Johann's lively chatter.

As the sun had disappeared behind the trees, a sudden awkwardness Kurt couldn't understand sprang up.

"Mr. Lang," Mrs. Steward said in a voice that didn't sound quite genuine, "I wonder if you would save Martin a trip and drive my cousin back to the schoolhouse?"

The question startled him. And it also startled Miss Thurston. He saw her glance at her cousin.

In Germany, this request would have caused Kurt to suspect matchmaking. Here, however, he could not think that he'd been invited for this reason. So why?

Miss Thurston's face turned pink, revealing her embarrassment.

"Yes," Martin spoke up, sounding as if he'd been rehearsed about what to say, "I have my wife's pony hooked up to my cart. It only carries two adults, so perhaps your brother and nephew can just walk home?"

Now Miss Thurston's face burned bright rose-red.

"I am happy to," Mr. Lang replied, mystified. What else could he say?

Gunther favored both of them with an odd look but gestured to Johann to come with him, and the two headed down the track in the fading light of day.

Kurt took the reins of the two-wheeled cart as Martin helped Miss Thurston up onto the seat beside him. She clung to the side of the bench as Mr. Lang flicked the reins and they started down the track to town. He noticed that she sat as far from him as she could. He hoped she didn't think he'd engineered this so that he could be alone with her.

Kurt couldn't think of anything to say to her. When they were out of sight of the Steward cabin, she finally broke the silence.

"Since we've been given this opportunity to talk, just the two of us, there is something that I have wanted to discuss with you, Mr. Lang." Her voice quavered a bit on the last few words, as if she were nervous.

"Oh?" he said, hoping for enlightenment.

"After the fight at school, you kept Gunther home only one day, right? Have you been sending Gunther to school the rest of this week?"

He stiffened. "Yes, I send him. What do you mean?"

"I thought as much. He has been playing hooky."

"Hooky?" Mr. Lang turned his gaze to her.

"Sorry. *Playing hooky* means not coming to school."

Kurt wanted to explode; instead he chewed the inside

of his mouth. But he tried to stay calm for Miss Thurston's sake. "Why does he not obey me?"

"Sometimes it's not a matter of obedience," she replied, sounding hesitant.

"Then what is it about?" he asked, his cheeks burning.

"Isn't this really about whether Gunther learns more English and more about this country?" she replied in a gentle voice. "Our history and our laws? Isn't that what you want, more than his obedience?"

Her question caught him off guard. He stared at her, noticing the wind playing with the light brown curls around her face. Startled by both her question and his sudden awareness of her, his mouth opened, and then closed tightly.

Night was overtaking them. Fortunately the half-moon had risen so he could see to drive. He glanced at its silver half circle above the treetops. Then, after many quiet moments, he asked, "What am I to do with him?" He didn't try to hide his anxiety.

"Making him sit with little children won't work," she stated.

"But he must learn. And I cannot teach him." His words rung with deep feeling he couldn't conceal.

"I think private lessons would be best," she said. "I asked my cousin to invite you tonight so we could discuss this without calling attention to Gunther. If I came alone to your place..." Her voice faded.

"Private lessons?" he echoed.

"Yes. Why don't you bring him two evenings a week? I will help him improve his English, and learn American history and government. You can make sure he studies at home on the other evenings."

"That will make more work for you. I cannot pay."

She touched his forearm. "I'm the teacher here in Pepin. Whether I teach in the daytime or evening, I'm being paid." Then, seeming embarrassed, she removed her hand from his sleeve and looked away.

He wished she hadn't taken her hand away so quickly. Her long, elegant hands, covered in fine kid gloves, were beautiful. "You are good. But still, I think Gunther must not be given good for bad behavior."

"Very few sons of farmers attend school beyond eighth grade. Don't you see? It isn't normal for Gunther or good for him."

The school came into view through the opening in the forest. Kurt tried to come to grips with what Miss Thurston had suggested.

Then an unusual sound cut through the constant peeping of tree frogs. Kurt jerked the reins back, halting the pony. He peered ahead through the dark shadows.

Miss Thurston did the same. The sound came again.

A baby crying.

They looked at each other in amazement.

"It's coming from the rear of the school, near my quarters," she said, stark disbelief in her voice.

Mr. Lang slapped the reins and jolted them over the uneven schoolyard to her door. A shaft of moonlight illuminated a wooden box. The crying was coming from inside.

Without waiting for his help, Miss Thurston leaped over the side of the cart and ran to her door. She stooped down and leaned over the box.

The wailing increased in volume and urgency.

Kurt scanned the shadows around the schoolhouse as Miss Thurston called out, "Hello? Please don't leave your child! I'll help you find a home for the baby! Hello?"

No answer came. Only the crickets chirped and toads croaked in the darkness. Then he thought he glimpsed motion in the shadows. He jumped down and hurried forward a few steps but the cloaking night crowded around him. The woods were dark and thick. Perhaps he'd imagined movement.

The baby wailed as he walked toward the teacher's quarters. He joined Miss Thurston on the step, waves of cool disbelief washing through him. "*Eines kind?* A baby?"

"It seems so."

She looked as if she were drowning in confusion, staring down at the baby, a strange, faraway expression on her face. She made no move toward the child. Why didn't she pick up the child? In fact, Miss Thurston appeared unable to make any move at all.

Ellen read his expression. How to explain her reluctance? She hadn't held a child for nearly a decade, not since little William. Her baby brother.

"How does the child come to be here?" he asked, searching the surrounding darkness once more.

"I don't know." The insistent wailing finally became impossible for her to avoid. She stooped and lifted the baby, and waves of sadness and regret rolled over her.

"What is wrong?" he asked.

She fought clear of her memories and entered her quarters, Mr. Lang at her heels. She laid the baby gently on her bed and tried to think.

"Does this happen in America?"

She looked at him. "What?"

"Do women leave babies at schoolhouses?"

"No. I've never heard of this happening before."

The child burst into another round of wailing—frantic, heartfelt, urgent.

Mr. Lang surprised her by picking up the infant. "He is hungry." He grimaced. "And the child needs a clean...*windel.*"

"Windel?" she asked.

"The child is wet," he replied.

She lit her bedside candle. In the light, she noticed the child had a dark reddish discoloration showing through his baby-fine golden hair. Was it called a port-wine stain? Memories of her brother so long ago made it hard to concentrate. She could feel Kurt looking at her, most likely wondering why she was unable to take action.

"Do you have an old cloth to dry dishes?" he asked when she offered no solution. "We could use to..."

"Yes!" She hurried to the other side of the room, threw open a box of household items and grabbed a large dish towel.

Mr. Lang completely surprised her by snatching the dishcloth, laying the baby on her bed and efficiently changing him.

"You know how to change a diaper?" she asked, sounding as shocked as she felt. She couldn't help but admire his quick, deft action.

"I raised Johann from a baby. We must get milk for this one." He lifted the child. "We will go to Ashford's Store, yes?"

Glad to have direction, she blew out the candle and followed him outside. They rushed past the pony and cart and headed straight for the store. The motion of hurrying seemed to soothe the infant.

Within a few minutes, Ellen and Mr. Lang arrived at the back of the store, at the stairs to climb to the second-floor landing. Moonlight cast the stairwell in shadow so she held the railing tightly as she hurried upward. She rapped on the door, and rapped again and again. The child started wailing once more. Mr. Lang stood behind her, trying to soothe the child. She wrung her hands. What seemed like forever passed.

Then Mr. Ashford in trousers and an unbuttoned shirt opened the door. "What do you…" he began forcefully, then trailed into silence, gawking at Ellen.

"I'm so sorry, Mr. Ashford, but we need help," she said.

He stared at them yet didn't move.

"We come in, please?" Mr. Lang asked even as he pushed through the door and held it open for her. She hurried inside, again thankful for Mr. Lang's support.

Mr. Ashford fell back, keeping them by the door, still looking stunned. "Where did that baby come from?"

"We don't know," she nearly shouted with her own frustration.

"We find him on the doorstep," Mr. Lang said. "We need milk and a bottle. You have these things?" His voice became demanding on the final words.

Mrs. Ashford, tying the sash of a long, flowered robe, hurried down the hall, followed by Amanda in her long, white, flannel nightdress. The two asked in unison, "A baby? Where did it come from?"

"It is boy," Kurt said.

"We don't know," Ellen repeated, nearly hysterical herself from the baby's crying. She struggled to stay calm as memories of her little brother bombarded her. "He was left on my doorstep."

"He needs milk. And a bottle to feed. Please," Mr. Lang repeated.

Stunned silence lasted another instant and then Mrs. Ashford moved into action. "Ned, go downstairs and find that box of baby bottles. Mr. Lang, bring that baby into the kitchen. Amanda, light the kitchen lamp."

Grateful to follow the brisk orders, Ellen followed Mrs. Ashford and Mr. Lang. The lady of the house lit a fire in the woodstove while her daughter lit the oil lamp that hung from the center of the ceiling. As if he sensed that help had come, the baby stilled in Mr. Lang's arms, his breath catching in his throat.

Mrs. Ashford began rifling through her cupboard and then triumphantly brought out a tin and opened the lid. "Horlick's Malted Milk," Mrs. Ashford read the label aloud. "Artificial Infant Food. It's something new, made east of here in Racine, Wisconsin."

Standing beside Mr. Lang, Ellen's nerves were as taut as telegraph wire. In contrast, Mr. Lang looked serious and determined. Having him with her had made this so much easier.

The storekeeper entered the kitchen with a wooden box of glass bottles. With their goal in sight, Ellen slumped onto a chair at the small kitchen table. Surprising her, Mr. Lang lay the child in her arms and stepped back.

Again, holding the baby brought Ellen the waves of remembrance. Struggling against the current, she watched Amanda scrub a bottle clean while the older woman mixed the powdered milk with water and set it in a pan of water on the stove to warm. Within a few minutes, she handed Ellen the warm, wet bottle. Ellen wanted to offer the child to Mrs. Ashford, but the little boy flailed his hands toward the bottle and she quickly slipped it into his mouth. He began sucking. Bubbles frothed into the bottle.

Relief swamped Ellen.

Mrs. Ashford sat down at the table near her, watching the child eat. "He's evidently hungry."

"He has good appetite," Mr. Lang agreed, gazing down with a grin.

Ellen released a pent-up breath. She felt as if she'd run a ten-mile race.

"Where did he come from?" Amanda asked again.

"I drive Miss Thurston home from her cousin's," Mr. Lang replied. "We find the baby in a wooden box on the doorstep."

"Did you see anyone?" Mrs. Ashford asked sharply.

Ellen frowned. "I thought I saw movement in the woods. I called out but no one was there."

"I've heard of this happening," Mrs. Ashford admitted, "but I never thought I'd live to see it here. Someone has abandoned this child."

"And on Miss Thurston's doorstep," Amanda murmured.

All of them stared at the baby in her arms.

No other reason could explain the child's appearance. People didn't go around misplacing infants.

Ellen gazed down at the small face that had changed from frenzied to calm. The evidence of tears still wet on his cheeks drew her sympathy, and tenderness filled her.

Who could part with you, little one?

"How old do you think he is?" Ellen asked.

"Hard to say," Mrs. Ashford said, reaching over to

stroke the white-blond, baby-fine hair. "But not more than a month old, if that."

"Nearly newborn, then." Ellen cuddled the child closer. The tension suddenly went out of the little body. The baby released a sound of contentment, making her tuck him closer, gentler. More unbidden caring for this child blossomed within her.

"Some people are superstitious about babies born with marks like that," Mr. Ashford said, pointing at the baby's port-wine birthmark. "Maybe that's why they didn't want him."

"Yes, it's sad the poor thing's been born disfigured," Mrs. Ashford agreed.

Ellen stiffened. "On the contrary, I've heard people say birthmarks are where babies were kissed by an angel." Nonsense of course, but she had to say something in the child's defense.

Mr. Lang bent, stroked the child's fine hair and murmured some endearment in German. His tenderness with the child touched Ellen deeply.

"I can't think of anybody hereabouts who was expecting a child. Can you, Katharine?" Mr. Ashford asked.

His wife shook her head.

"But babies don't really come from cabbage patches," Amanda said reasonably, "so where did he come from?"

"That's enough about where babies come from," Mrs. Ashford snapped.

"You better go off to bed," the girl's father ordered and motioned for her to leave.

Ellen sent the girl a sympathetic glance. Some topics were never discussed in polite society. "Good night, Amanda. Thank you for your help."

The girl stifled a yawn as she left. "See you tomorrow at church, Miss Thurston."

The mention of church snapped Ellen back to reality. "I better be getting home then. Dawn will come soon enough."

The baby finished the bottle and Mrs. Ashford placed a dish towel on Ellen's shoulder.

Laying the baby on it, Ellen rose, patting his back. She prepared to leave.

The older couple looked flummoxed. "You can't mean you're going to take this baby home with you to the school?" Mrs. Ashford popped to her feet.

"I don't see that I have any other choice," Ellen said, and waited to see if she'd be contradicted.

Despite her initial misgivings, the truth had already settled deep inside her. Someone had entrusted her with this child and she would not shirk that responsibility.

Mrs. Ashford said something halfhearted about Ellen not knowing how to care for an infant in an uncertain tone that didn't fit the usually overconfident woman. Ellen hadn't appreciated the woman's comment about the child's disfigurement, and she also knew without a doubt that the Ashfords shared the common prejudice against the illegitimate, the baseborn. "I'll keep the child. I'm sure someone will realize they've made a mistake and come back for him."

"I hope so," Mr. Lang spoke up. "This is serious thing, to give up one's own blood."

His statement struck a nerve in Ellen. What had driven someone to give up their own child, their own kin?

Mrs. Ashford handed Ellen a bag of rags, three more

bottles and the tin of powdered infant food. "Just mix it with water right before you need it."

Ellen thanked them sincerely and apologized for bothering them after dark. The two had been more helpful than she would have predicted. Maybe she had judged them too harshly.

Ellen and Mr. Lang walked down the back staircase with the baby in her arms and the cloth sack of supplies over his shoulder. The toads still croaked at the nearby creek. Ellen brushed away a mosquito, protecting the baby from being bitten.

The baby had slipped into sleep. Still, his lips moved as if he were sucking the bottle. With a round face and a nice nose, he had white-gold hair that looked like duck down. His skin was so soft. She'd not felt anything so soft for a very long time.

Ellen had always told herself that she didn't care for babies much, holding herself back from contact with them. But she knew—when she allowed herself to think about it—that all stemmed from losing her infant brother. His loss had altered her life, and led her to not fulfill her accepted womanly role. This had grieved her mother.

But now everything had changed. This child—who had been given to her—needed her. She bent down and kissed his birthmark.

"William." She whispered the name that still caused such hurt.

"What?" Mr. Lang asked.

"I lost a brother by that name." She couldn't say more.

After a moment, Mr. Lang said quietly, "This baby will cause trouble."

She paused.

"People will talk."

She tilted her head as she gazed up at him tartly. "Everyone will know that this couldn't possibly be my child."

"I… Sorry," he stammered. "I do not mean that. I mean, people will not want this child here. If someone gives away a child, no one wants him."

She wanted to argue, but recalling the Ashfords' comments and attitude, she couldn't. "I will keep him, then."

Mr. Lang looked quite startled. "They will not let you."

"Why not?"

He lifted both his hands in a gesture of helplessness. "You are schoolteacher and unmarried. They will say—"

"What do *you* say, Mr. Lang?" she demanded suddenly, prodded by something she didn't yet understand.

He gazed down at her. "I say that troubled times come here. Soon."

She couldn't argue with him. But she wouldn't relinquish the child except to someone who would love him as he deserved. "Good night, Mr. Lang. Thank you."

"Good night, Miss Thurston." He paused as if he wanted to say more, but then merely waved and headed toward the cart.

She gazed down at the child as she entered her home and shut the door. She moved inside, rocking the child in her arms, humming to him. His resemblance to William, who had died before he turned one, brought back the pain and guilt over his loss, and for a moment, it snatched away her breath. Her little brother had been born when she was nearly fourteen, and he had left them so soon. And even though she didn't want to remember, to be reminded, she couldn't help herself.

She thought of Mr. Lang and how he'd helped her, how he'd also cared for a baby not his own.

"I will call you William," she whispered and kissed him again. "Sweet William."

Chapter Five

The next morning, Kurt waited, hunched forward on the last bench at the rear of the schoolroom where Sunday services were also held. When would Miss Thurston appear with the baby? He sat between a surly Gunther and an eager Johann, hoping neither his inner turmoil nor his eagerness to see her were evident.

A warm morning meant that the doors and windows had opened wide, letting in a few lazy flies. Men, women and children, seated with their families, filled the benches. Ostensibly Kurt had come to worship with the rest of the good people of Pepin. But he knew he and his brother and his nephew did not look or feel like a family in the way that the rest of those gathered today did. Their family had been fractured by his father's awful choices. Gloom settled on Kurt; he pushed it down, shied from it.

Wearing a black suit, Noah Whitmore, the preacher, stood by the teacher's desk at the front. But Kurt knew that more than worship would take place here today. The foundling child would not be taken lightly. His stomach quivered, nearly making him nauseated, and he couldn't stop turning his hat brim in his hands. He was nervous—for her.

He'd had no luck making the schoolteacher see sense last night. He didn't want to see the fine woman defeated, but to his way of thinking, she didn't have a hope. What would everyone say when they saw the baby? When they heard Miss Thurston declare she intended to keep him?

As if she'd heard his questions, the schoolteacher stepped from her quarters through the inner door, entering the crowded, buzzing schoolroom. With a polite smile, she called, "Good morning!" And then she paused near Noah, facing everyone with the baby in her arms, back straight, almost defiant.

As if hooked by the same fishing line, every face swung to gaze at her and then downward to the small baby, wrapped in the tattered blanket in her arms. Gasps, followed by stunned silence, met her greeting. Kurt had to give the lady her due. She had courage. Her eyes flashed with challenge, and Kurt could not help but notice that she looked beautiful in her very fine dress of deep brown.

She cleared her throat. "Something quite unusual happened last night. This baby was left on my doorstep."

In spite of his unsettled stomach, Kurt hid a spontaneous smile. Her tone was dignified, and when a wildfire of chatter whipped through the room, she did not flinch. Kurt could not turn his gaze from her elegant face. She blushed now, no doubt because of the attention she drew.

Recovering first from surprise, Noah cleared his throat. "Was a note left with the child?"

Everyone quieted and fixed their stares on Ellen again.

"No, the child came without any identification."

"Is it a boy or a girl?" a man Kurt didn't know asked.

"How old is he?" Martin Steward asked. His wife, Ophelia, started to rise, but Martin gently urged her to remain seated. Would Miss Thurston's family support her in her desire to keep the child?

"The infant is around a month old, Mrs. Ashford thought," the schoolteacher said. "He is a boy, and I've named him William." At that moment, William yawned very loudly. A few chuckled at the sound.

Mr. and Mrs. Ashford, in their Sunday best, hurried inside with Amanda between them. "We're sorry to be late," Mr. Ashford said, taking off his hat.

"But we lost so much sleep helping Miss Thurston with the foundling last night," Mrs. Ashford announced, proclaiming herself as an important player in this mystery. "We overslept."

Kurt watched them squeeze onto the bench in front of him, though plenty of space remained open beside Johann. The simple act scraped his tattered pride. When he noted their daughter steal a quick glance at Gunther, his tension tightened another turn. The Ashfords would never let Gunther court their daughter. That was as ridiculous as if he decided to pursue Miss Thurston himself.

This realization choked him and he tried to dismiss it.

Ellen nodded toward the rear of the room. "Yes, thank you, Mrs. Ashford. I'll need more of that Horlick's infant powder today. So far he seems to be tolerating it well."

Mrs. Ashford perched on the bench, her chin lifted knowingly.

"Well, what are we going to do about this, Noah?" a tall, young deacon named Gordy Osbourne asked, rising. Many nodded their agreement with the inquiry.

Kurt braced himself. Now unrelenting reality regarding her station in life would beat against Miss Thurston.

Noah looked troubled. "Is the child healthy, Miss Thurston?"

Before Ellen could respond, Mrs. Ashford piped up, "He appears healthy, but is disfigured by a birthmark on his head."

"He has what's called a port-wine stain on his forehead," Miss Thurston corrected, "but his hair will cover it as he grows." The lady sent a stern glance at the storekeeper's wife and held the child closer.

Why didn't she see that he'd been right? No one was going to let her keep this child. He realized he'd been mangling his hat brim and eased his grip.

"Unless the mark grows, too, and spreads," Mrs. Ashford said, sounding dour.

"I don't think that has anything to do with the baby's health," Noah commented. "A birthmark will not hurt the child."

"Maybe that's why somebody abandoned him at the teacher's door," Osbourne's wife, Nan, spoke up. "Some people don't want a child with that kind of mark."

"Unfortunately you may be right," Noah said. "But the real question is, does anyone here know of any woman in this area who was expecting a child in the past month?"

Kurt admired Noah's ability to lead the gathering. Was it because he was the preacher, or had he done something in the past to gain this position? In Europe, leadership would have to do with family standing and connections, but here, that didn't seem to matter. No town mayor or lord would make this decision. Noah Whitmore had thrown the question open for discussion—even women had spoken. This way of doing things felt odd but good to Kurt.

Noah's wife, Sunny, rose. "I think I can say that no woman *I know* in this whole area was expecting a baby last month."

"Perhaps someone from a boat left him at the schoolhouse," Miss Thurston said, "because it is the only public building in Pepin, and a little away from town. They would have been less likely to be observed leaving the child."

The congregation appeared to chew on this. Kurt stared at Miss Thurston, remembering her initial hesitation to pick up the child and her mention of a baby brother who'd died. She had known loss, too. Wealth and position could not prevent mortality and mourning. He forced his tight lungs to draw in air.

"Well, we will need a temporary home for the child—" Noah began.

"I will keep the child," Miss Thurston said, and then walked toward the benches as if the matter were settled.

Her announcement met with an instant explosion of disapproval, just as Kurt had predicted.

One woman rose. "You can't keep a baby. You're not married." Her tone was horrified.

Ellen halted. "I don't know what that has to do with my ability to care for a child. I've cared for children in the past."

"But you're the schoolmarm!" one man exclaimed. General and loud agreement followed.

Kurt didn't listen much to the crowd, but watched for the reactions of the young pastor. And Miss Thurston, who'd paused near the front row, half-turned toward the preacher, too.

The pastor's wife silenced the uproar merely by rising. "There is an orphanage in Illinois run by a daughter of our friends, the Gabriels. We might send the child there."

Murmurs of agreement began.

Miss Thurston swung to face everyone again. "I think that is a precipitate suggestion. What if the child's mother changes her mind? I don't think it's uncommon for a woman to become low in spirits soon after a birth."

A few women nodded in agreement.

"What if this woman suffered this low mood and was in unfortunate circumstances? After realizing what she's done, she might return to reclaim the child. I think it's best we wait upon events."

A man in the rear snorted and muttered loud enough for all to hear, "It's probably somebody's unwanted, baseborn child."

Noah stiffened. "I think we need to remember why we are gathered here."

That shut everyone up, suiting Kurt's idea of propriety. A child's life was not a subject for derision.

Noah gazed out at the unhappy congregation. "Miss Thurston is right, I think. A child's future depends on our making the right decision. This is something we need to pray about so we do what God wants. One thing is certain—no woman gives up her child lightly. Someone has trusted us with their own blood and we must not act rashly."

His words eased some of the tension from the room, another sign of Noah's leadership. Again, Kurt wondered about the preacher's past and how he'd come to be so respected here. Kurt's family had been respected in their village, but had lost that over his father's many sins.

"But who's going to take care of the foundling in the meantime?" Mrs. Ashford asked.

"I will," Ellen declared. "He was left on *my* doorstep."

The storekeeper's wife started, "But you'll be teaching—"

"I'm sure we can find someone who will care for the child while Miss Thurston carries out her teaching duties," Noah said, taking charge of the room. "That's something else we will pray about."

Noah raised his hands and bowed his head and began praying, effectively ending the discussion. Kurt lowered his head, too, praying that Miss Thurston wouldn't be hurt too badly when the child was taken from her. Because he was certain that that was exactly what was going to happen, one way or the other.

Ellen's face ached with the smile she'd kept in place all morning during the church service. She wished everyone would just go home and leave her alone. But the congregation lingered around the schoolhouse, around her.

Everyone wanted a good look at William and an opportunity to express their opinion of wicked people who abandoned babies. They also lauded her desire to care for the child—even if she were a schoolmarm, a woman was a woman, after all. Most voiced sympathetic-sounding, nonetheless irritating comments about William's birthmark. Noah and Sunny had helped her but underneath all the general sentiment still held that she shouldn't, wouldn't, be allowed to keep William. Ellen was nearing the end of her frayed rope.

Then Martin came to her rescue. "Cousin Ellen, you're coming home with us for Sunday dinner as planned." He smiled at everyone as he piloted her toward their wagon. When Martin helped her up onto the bench, she noted Mr. Lang and his family, who had ridden to church with the Stewards, sat in the wagon bed at the rear. This man had predicted how the community would react all too accurately. But he didn't look triumphant in the slightest, and for that, she was grateful. He nodded to her and gave her a slight smile that seemed to have some message she couldn't quite read.

As the wagon rocked along the track into the shelter of the forest, Ellen breathed out a long, pent-up sigh. She glanced at her cousin sitting beside her. "Ophelia…" She fell silent; she simply didn't have the words to go on.

Ophelia leaned against Ellen's shoulder as if in comfort. "I can't believe this happened."

Ellen rested her head against the top of Ophelia's white bonnet, murmuring, "I'm so glad you're here."

"The Whitmores are coming over after dinner so we can discuss this," Martin said. "We need to decide what to do with this child."

Ellen snapped up straight. "It has already been decided. William will stay with me."

"You can't mean you really want to keep this baby?"

Ophelia said, sounding shocked. "I don't know how I'd take care of our little one alone."

Her cousin's stunned tone wounded Ellen, stopping her from responding.

"*Ja*—yes, she does," Mr. Lang said as the wagon navigated a deep rut. "I told her last night that they will not let her."

Mr. Lang's words wounded more than all the rest. He'd been there last night, he'd experienced discovering this child with her. Why wouldn't he take her side in this matter?

She brushed the opposition aside. It didn't matter why he wouldn't support her—it didn't matter why any of them wouldn't support her. She wasn't like other women. She had goals, and now she'd added one more. If she were a weak woman, she wouldn't be here to begin with—she would be living at home under her sister-in-law's snide thumb. But she had struck out to make a life of her own, and that was exactly what she planned to do.

Those who opposed her would not win. All she had to do was come up with a convincing argument to keep this child—and her job. And frankly, she reminded herself, Mr. Kurt Lang's opinion in this matter—in all matters—was irrelevant to her.

Later, in the early dusk, Kurt walked into the Steward's clearing for the second time that day. Ever since the Stewards had dropped them off after church, he'd been worrying—about William, about Gunther, about Miss Thurston.

"Kurt, what brings you here?" called Martin, who was hitching the pony to his two-wheeled cart.

"Is Miss Thurston here still?" The fact he couldn't easily pronounce the "Th" at the beginning of her name caused him to flush with embarrassment. He tried to cast his feelings aside. He had come to talk with Miss Thurston face-to-face over Gunther's schooling. Altogether, the issue had left a sour taste in his mouth. But a decision must be made—Gunther's playing hooky had forced his hand.

"She's about done feeding the baby and then I'm taking her home," Martin said as he finished the hitching.

"I have come to offer to escort the lady home."

Martin turned to Kurt. "Oh?"

The embarrassment he'd just pushed away returned. Kurt tried to ignore his burning face. Did Martin think he was interested in Miss Thurston? "I wish to speak to her about my brother, Gunther, before school starts again tomorrow."

At that moment, the lady herself stepped out of the cabin with William in her arms. She noticed him and stopped. "Mr. Lang."

Sweeping off his hat, Kurt felt that by now his flaming face must be as red as a beetroot. "I come to take you home, Miss Thurston. And perhaps we talk about Gunther?"

She smiled then and walked toward the cart. "Yes, I want to discuss that matter with you."

They said their farewells to the Stewards, and soon Ellen sat beside him on the seat of the small cart, holding the baby whose eyelids kept drooping only to pop open again, evidently fighting sleep. Kurt turned the pony and they began the trip to town, heading toward the golden and pink sunset. Crickets sang, filling his ears. Beside him, Miss Ellen Thurston held herself up as a lady should. Only last night had he seen her usual refined composure slip. Finding the infant had shaken her. Did it have something to do with the little brother she'd mentioned?

Kurt chewed his lower lip, trying to figure out how to begin the conversation about his brother. "I still don't agree with what you have said about Gunther," he grumbled at last.

"But yet you are here, talking to me" was all she replied.

A sound of frustration escaped his lips. "Gunther..." He didn't know what he wanted to say, or could say. He would never speak about the real cause of Gunther's rebelliousness. He would never want Miss Thurston to know the extent of his family's shame. His father's gambling had been enough to wound them all. What had driven him even further to such a disgraceful end?

Kurt struggled with himself, with what to do about his brother. Gunther needed to face life and go on, despite what had happened. Would his giving in weaken his brother more?

"Your brother is at a difficult age—not a boy, not fully a man," she said.

If that were the only problem, Kurt would count himself fortunate. So much more had wounded his brother, and at a tender age. A woodpecker pounded a hollow tree nearby, an empty, lonely sound.

"Gunther and Johann are all I have left." He hadn't planned to say that, and shame shuddered deep inside his chest.

"I know how you feel."

No, she didn't, but he wouldn't correct her. "Do you still think to teach Gunther in the evenings?"

"Yes. As you know, you can send him to school, but you cannot make him learn if he's shut his mind to it. Private lessons would be best."

Kurt chewed on this bitter pill and then swallowed it. "He will have the lessons, then."

"Will you be able to help him with his studies on the evenings when I am not working with him?"

"I will."

"Then bring him after supper on Tuesday." Miss Thurston looked down at the child in her arms and smiled so sweetly—Kurt could tell just from her expression that she had a tender heart. Something about her smile affected him deeply and he had to look away.

She glanced up at him and asked, "Have you told Gunther about this?"

"I tell him soon," he said.

"Good." She sounded relieved.

He, however, was anything but relieved. His fears for Gunther clamored within. They had come to this new country for a new start. He wanted Gunther to make the most of this, not end up like their father had.

They reached the downward stretch onto the flat of the riverside. He directed the pony cart onto the trail to the school. Again, he was bringing her home in Martin's cart and again someone was waiting on her doorstep. This time a woman rose to greet them. What now?

Kurt helped Miss Thurston down. She moved so gracefully as a shaft of sunset shone through the trees, gilding her hair. He forced himself not to stop and enjoy the sight. Instead, he accompanied her to greet the woman.

"Good evening," Miss Thurston said, cradling the sleeping baby in her arms.

The other woman replied, "I am Mrs. Brawley. My husband and I are homesteading just north of town."

"Yes?" Miss Thurston encouraged the woman.

"I have one child and I heard the preacher say this morning that you needed someone to care for the baby." The woman gazed at the child, sleeping in the lady's arms.

"I take it that you may be interested in doing that?" the schoolteacher asked.

"Yes, miss. I could take care of two as well as one."

"May I visit your home tomorrow after supper and discuss it then?"

"Yes, yes, please come." The woman gave directions to her homestead, which lay about a mile and a half north of town. They bid her good-night and she hurried away in the lowering light of day.

"Well, I hope this will solve the problem of William's care during the schooldays."

Her single-mindedness scraped Kurt's calm veneer. "You think still they will let you keep the child?"

She had mounted the step and now turned toward him. "Perhaps you are one of those who think a woman who does not wish to marry cannot love a child, and is unnatural. That is the common *wisdom.*"

Her cold words, especially the final ones, startled him. "No. That is foolish."

Her face softened. "Thank you, Mr. Lang."

He tried to figure out why anybody would think that. Then her words played again in his head. "You do not wish to marry?"

"No, I don't wish to marry."

Her attitude left him dumbfounded. "I thought every woman wished to marry."

She shook her head, one corner of her mouth lifting. "No, not every woman. Good night, Mr. Lang. I'll see you Tuesday evening."

"Guten nacht," he said, lapsing into German without meaning to. He turned the pony cart around and headed toward the Stewards' to return it. Thoughts about Miss Thurston and William chased each other around in his mind. Very simply, he hated the thought of seeing her disappointed. What if she became more deeply attached to William and the town forced her to give the child away in the end?

Why wouldn't she face the fact that the town would not let her keep William? He wouldn't press her about this, but in fact, the town *shouldn't* let her keep him. The question wasn't whether Miss Thurston was capable of rearing the child. But didn't he know that raising a child alone was difficult, lonely, worrying? Didn't he know it better than anyone here?

Chapter Six

On Monday morning, Ellen inhaled deeply, preparing to face teaching school with William in the room. With any luck, tomorrow he would be with Mrs. Brawley. But until then, she'd have to make do.

She entered the still-empty schoolroom and set William in his basket on her desk. She gazed down at him as he slept, his little fists clutching the blanket. Every time she looked at him or held him, the feelings she had for him deepened, coiling tighter around her heart.

She walked outside into the air that still held no fall crispness, and rang the bell. The children stopped playing and ran toward her, jostling for their spots in the line. They filed in, taking their seats row by row. When all were seated, she shut the door with satisfaction at their orderliness and returned to stand by her desk.

"You still have the baby," Amanda said and then colored. "I'm sorry, Miss Thurston. I didn't mean to talk out of turn."

Ellen nodded her forgiveness. "It is an unusual situation but until his mother returns—" Ellen's heart clamped tight "—or I find someone to care for William, he will have to come to school. Now, I will begin with our youngest grade. Slates out, please. The rest of you, please take out your readers and begin reading silently where we left off on Friday."

All went well till in the midst of listening to the fifth graders recite their times tables, William woke with a whimper and then a full-scale cry. The sound raced up her spine. But she reminded herself that she already had a plan for this situation.

Every child stopped and turned their attention to the basket on her desk.

Johann popped up. "Miss Thurston, the baby is crying."

The other students laughed, and Johann looked abashed and sat down with a plump.

Ellen smiled at him. "I think you may be right, Johann." She lifted the child and checked his diaper. "Amanda, would you be kind enough to take William to my room and change his diaper? I left everything on the table for you. And mix him another bottle of Horlick's. That's all laid out, too."

Amanda beamed and hurried forward to carry William's basket through the door behind Ellen. Ellen motioned for the fifth grader, who had been interrupted, to begin his times tables again. She listened to the boy with one ear and to the sounds of Amanda crooning to William in the next room with the other.

Ellen could make this work—she knew she could. All she had to do now was prove it to everyone else.

After supper, Ellen left the Ashfords and began walking to the Brawley's claim with William in her arms. As she walked, an unread letter from home clamored to be taken out of her pocket. Mr. Ashford, the postmaster, had given it to her before supper.

But she didn't have the strength to face it yet. She would never admit it to anyone, but rising to feed William at least twice each night had exhausted her, flattened her somehow. And she was not sure she could handle what the letter might hold. She would have to prepare herself for the ordeal of reading it.

Walking steadily, she had no trouble finding the newly built log cabin and she called out the familiar frontier greeting, "Hello, the house!"

Mrs. Brawley came outside to welcome her. "You came!" The petite dark-haired woman, who looked barely twenty, sounded relieved.

Ellen noted that she wore a fresh apron and held her own child, who looked to be a few months older than William. Behind her loomed the young man of the house. He did not seem very happy to see Ellen. Nevertheless, she stepped inside and greeted him, offering her hand.

He shook it, all the while grimacing as if he had a toothache. "I want to make it clear—my wife does not need to work for anybody. I'm able to provide for my family."

Mrs. Brawley blushed and lowered her eyes.

Ellen realized she should have anticipated this. "I understand that, Mr. Brawley. I thought it kind of your wife to help me out in this unusual situation."

He looked somewhat mollified. "I just don't want anybody getting the wrong idea."

"If your good wife and I come to an agreement, I'll make certain everyone knows she is doing it out of the goodness of her heart, and that I'm beholden to her kindness." Ellen scanned the room and found what she'd hoped for—a clean, orderly house.

"Okay, then," he said gruffly, offering what passed for a placatory grin. "I got animals to see to. I'll leave you womenfolk to thrash this out." Pulling on his hat from a peg by the door, he left them.

"Won't you sit down, miss?" The woman motioned toward one of the chairs at the table.

Drawing in a deep breath, Ellen agreed. "Where are you and your husband from?" Ellen asked, thinking how touchy the man's pride had been.

"We grew up west of Chicago, but my husband wanted his own farm so we headed north." The woman sounded as if she'd rather not have come to the frontier.

Ellen had chosen to come to Pepin for her own reasons, not a husband's. "I'm from Galena myself," Ellen said, keeping the conversation going, and soon they were chatting about leaving one's family. The letter in Ellen's pocket reminded her of her own.

"Now, you don't mind taking care of an orphan?" Ellen asked.

"Oh, no, it's not the child's fault," Mrs. Brawley replied quickly. "And I'll treat him just like my own." As they talked more, Ellen noted the woman's ease with William and the excellent attention she gave her own child. When Ellen was satisfied Mrs. Brawley had no prejudice against a foundling, they agreed upon both wage and plan. Mrs. Brawley would pick the child up each morning before school and Ellen would come fetch William each day after school. They shook hands and Ellen left, feeling as if everything were neatly taken care of.

Except for the unread letter from her sister sitting like a hot potato in her pocket.

The letter presented another fiery trial Ellen must endure. Could she bear to read about Cissy and her new husband? After she'd put William down later that night, Ellen finally faced her trepidation. With sure fingers, she opened the letter and began reading.

August 23, 1870

Dear Ellen, dearest sister,
Why did you leave before we returned from our honeymoon? Randolph said something about your wanting to spend a long visit with Ophelia before the school year started. I didn't realize that you'd made the decision to take the teaching position in Pepin definite. Was I so involved in my own affairs that I ignored this?

I know that we've been through a difficult time, losing Mother and Father. But then Holton came into my life and I thought it would make a happy new beginning for all of us...

Ellen could read no further, her heart squeezing so tight she felt strangled. She folded the letter and slid it into her music box's secret door. Her fingers trembled and she forced back tears. She gazed around at her one room with its few familiar possessions—the music box, the quilt her grandmother had sewn for her, a sampler her great-grandmother had stitched as a girl in Massachusetts. She clung to these as Holton's betrayal wounded her afresh with every memory of home. *I'll read more tomorrow when I can handle it.* She could no longer hold back the tears, and they ran down her cheeks. *I'm glad you're happy, Cissy.*

On Monday evening, Kurt waited till Johann had gone to bed early as usual. Then he found his brother sitting outside on the bench by the door, gazing at the surrounding forest, the last of the sun's bronzed rays sifting through the trees and branches. Kurt sat down beside him and Gunther made room for him.

Kurt understood Gunther's fascination with the forest. At home in Germany very few forests had been preserved. Had Germany looked like this once—a vast forest with little villages, overshadowed by the brooding evergreen trees and tall maples? But the beautiful surroundings didn't distract him from his purpose. He'd argued with himself over whether the schoolteacher was right till he was ragged inside. Now he must speak. Tomorrow Miss Thurston would be expecting Gunther for his first private lesson.

"I know you have not been going to school," Kurt said flatly and without preamble.

Gunther started and swung to face him, instantly fired up. "I am too old—"

"Ja, you are too old."

This halted Gunther's words. He stared at Kurt.

Kurt inhaled deeply. "But there is still much you need to learn."

Gunther looked unhappy but didn't reply.

"How will you learn about this country without school?"

Kurt asked to force Gunther to deal with the problem as an adult. If he wished to be treated as an adult, he'd have to start acting like one.

There was a pause; cricket song filled their silence and then Gunther suggested, "I could read books."

"Is your English good enough to understand those books?"

"My English is better all the time," Gunther said, some of the edge seeping back into his tone.

Kurt stared at his boots. This still felt like giving in, like letting Gunther get his own way, making him weak.

"Miss Thurston has offered private lessons two evenings a week, starting tomorrow. Do you want them?"

Gunther sent him a look laden with suspicion and folded his arms. "Private lessons? Can we afford that?"

"She says she is the teacher for Pepin and will teach anybody who wants to learn whenever they can come. Do you want to learn, Gunther?"

Gunther eyed him as if he didn't trust him.

"You did not set Johann a very good example," Kurt scolded, frowning, and felt the frown lowering his own mood.

"I couldn't get you to listen to me," Gunther objected.

Kurt bent forward and folded his hands. Their relationship was not the usual between brothers. It never had been. Their father had never "fathered" Gunther.

Gunther rose. "So I go to school tomorrow after supper?"

"We'll go with you," Kurt said. "Maybe I can learn, too."

This thought obviously startled Gunther. Then the lad grinned. "We go to school together—you and me?"

Kurt shook his head, standing. "Go to bed."

Gunther chuckled and went inside.

Kurt stared at the last of the sunset and thought of Miss Thurston, so pretty and so caring. But she was going to be hurt over this baby and there was nothing he could do to help her.

On Tuesday evening, Ellen stood in the doorway of the school, waiting for Gunther to arrive. Would he? Or would he skip evening school, too?

As she waited, she tried not to think of the contents of her sister's letter, which she'd finished reading before she went to retrieve William from the Brawley's. The letter's contents still upset her stomach and played through her mind. She'd thought she'd left matters in the best way she could, but evidently that had changed for the worse.

She sighed. The autumn days still lingered in a long twilight. Then she saw a trio of shadows approaching. Apparently Gunther was not arriving on his own.

Holding Johann's hand, Gunther walked beside Mr. Lang, who marched toward her as if someone behind him had a rifle aimed at his back. The man, whose good looks still caused her some unease, had very definite ideas. Gunther's head was lowered in obvious uncertainty. She hoped this solution would work for the boy.

Even as she tried to focus on the important task at hand, her unruly mind kept drifting back to phrases from her sister's letter.

I know you couldn't possibly live with our brother and his wife. It seems to me that Alice brings out all the worst in Randolph. Shouldn't love bring out the best in a person?

A very good question, Ellen thought. Was this evidence that her sister was maturing?

"Good evening, Miss Thurston." Mr. Lang greeted her as always, with that distinctive European style, making his respect for her plain. She noted that his blond hair waved around his ears, and he needed a haircut.

She forced a smile, reminding herself that Gunther needed her to make this work. "I see you've brought Johann, too."

"Yes." Mr. Lang looked stressed. "I thought he could help me watch the child while Gunther takes his lessons."

This surprised Ellen, but it shouldn't have. She recalled how Mr. Lang had pitched in and taken care of William that night they'd found him. Because of that, she had expected Mr. Lang to side with her about keeping William. But he hadn't. Now, here he was offering her help, not lecturing her about her campaign to keep William.

An unusual and complicated man.

"A good idea," she replied.

As she looked at Mr. Lang and was reminded yet again of Holton, more of Cissy's words played in her mind. *I must say that I've been surprised by some of our oldest friends. They don't seem to welcome Holton as they should. Holton dismisses it as just small-town clannishness, but it hurts me all the same.*

Ellen hoped no one would tell Cissy the plain truth. Initially, when others noticed Holton switching his attentions from her to Cissy, she'd crafted excuses. She'd done it foremost to save face but then to protect her sister.

But maybe I shouldn't have. Perhaps I should have

*told Cissy the truth. But would she have believed me?
Or put it down as jealousy?*

Ellen forced herself back to the present. "Gunther, I
thought we'd do our lessons in my quarters. Come in."

Soon she sat at the table with Gunther, and Mr. Lang
settled in the rocking chair holding William. Johann
played with a carved wooden horse, tapping its hooves
on the half-log floor. Accustomed to being here alone
every evening, Ellen noticed a difference. The room felt
as if it was happy to be filled with more than just her
and William. *Foolishness,* she chided herself.

"Gunther, I am not going to be teaching you as a
child, but as an adult student." She had given this a lot
of thought and had rehearsed this speech in her mind.
She looked directly into the young man's blue eyes, so
like his handsome brother's. No wonder he'd gained
Amanda's attention.

"Gunther," she began, "you have much to learn about
English and American history and government if you
are to be a knowledgeable American citizen. But I'm
only going to teach you if you are interested in bettering yourself, preparing yourself to vote intelligently in
the future. Do you want to learn?"

Gunther looked surprised. "I thought it had been
decided already."

"I can present lessons," she said, "but I can't make
you learn."

Gunther glanced at his brother, then lowered his gaze
to the tabletop. Ellen waited while Gunther thought, and
her mind drifted back to the letter.

*Please write soon and tell me you're happy up there
in the wilderness. If you aren't, we can bring you home
where you belong.*

Home where I belong. Holton's duplicity had robbed her of her home forever. Her emotions tumbled downward. Despair gripped her, but she wrenched herself from its grasp.

"What do you say, Gunther?" she asked more sharply than she'd intended.

The young man raised his eyes to her.

"Yes, I want to learn about this country's history, its government and I want to get better at English." Gunther's words tumbled out in a rush.

Relief rolled through her. "Yes, I can help you with speaking English, and also with reading and writing proficiently. And I will teach you American government and history—"

"That will not take long," Mr. Lang interjected, an edge to his voice. "This country is not a century old, even. Germany's history goes back over a thousand years."

Ellen heard the wounded pride in Mr. Lang's tone. He'd left his country behind. As a stranger in this new place, he was counted as less than others.

Gunther snapped, "I don't care about Germany. I want to be American. You brought us here. This is where I will live." Jabbing his chest with his thumb, he added, "Where I will take a wife."

Ellen thought of the Ashfords' low opinion of Gunther. Obviously Gunther hoped that gaining education would help change their minds. She hoped so, too. "Then shall we begin?"

Gunther nodded to her. "Yes, please." His tone no longer was angry.

"Since you mentioned it, I think we'll start with help-

ing you improve your pronunciation of English sounds."
She began with the difficult "th" sound.

As she helped Gunther learn to position his tongue
between his teeth to make this sound, she noted from
the corner of her eye Mr. Lang and Johann silently mimicking her. So she would be teaching three, not one.

A strange feeling came over her, and she realized
that sitting in her quarters and helping Mr. Lang and
Johann and Gunther while Mr. Lang held William was
close to how she felt when with Ophelia and Martin.
This was a disturbing thought, which triggered a disturbing sentence from Cissy's letter.

*You must plan to come home for a visit at Christ-
mas. Holton and I will meet you at Moline and bring
you home in our carriage.*

She lost track of what she was saying to Gunther
as the words rang in her mind. *Home,* Cissy had written. But she felt she would never go home again. She'd
lost her parents to typhoid a year ago; her brother to
his mean-spirited, pretentious wife and now her little
sister to Holton.

Despair over these injuries weighed like lead shot
in her midsection.

Then William gurgled in Mr. Lang's arms. The man
smiled down at her child, and his expression touched
her heart. She would leave the past behind and make
her own family here. With William.

Oh, God, please make that come true.

Chapter Seven

Removing his hat, Kurt hesitated at the school door. Today after Sunday worship, everyone had shared a potluck picnic on the school grounds. Now the school board was going to hold a school dedication, an event new to him.

He found himself looking for Miss Thurston, as he'd been doing all day. And all day he'd overheard bits of conversations about her and William. No one approved of her keeping the child. Had Miss Thurston heard them, too?

Holding Johann's hand, Kurt entered the school and sat on their usual half-log bench at the back of the room. Johann was excited about something but when Kurt asked, the lad had just grinned. Kurt noted that the three men who'd been elected to the board—Mr. Ashford and Martin Steward and another man he didn't know—sat in the first row along with their families.

Miss Thurston, dressed as fine as a fashion plate, sat at her desk. She wore a stylish dress of some shiny dark blue material. With her bearing both graceful and striking, she overshadowed the other women in the room.

He tried not to stare at the lovely picture she presented, something he found he was doing more and more these days.

On her desk perched the basket with the napping child. He watched as people kept looking at it and then looking away.

An air of expectancy hummed in the room, the scent of pine and cedar emanating from the newly cut, rough log walls. He liked that. How different the village school he'd attended had been, which had stood for centuries before he entered it.

He glanced around and glimpsed his brother sitting on the other side of the door. He noted a subtle change in Gunther. The boy still didn't sit up as straight as Kurt would have liked, but he didn't slouch quite as much, either. However, he was still gazing at the storekeeper's daughter. Kurt shook his head, wishing he could spare the boy the pain of coming rejection.

Mr. Ashford cleared his throat. "I'd like to welcome you all to the formal dedication of Pepin's first school."

Applause and foot-stamping broke out amid the crowd. Kurt sensed the pride the young town was feeling. They had worked hard and contributed much to see this school finished. Johann sat very straight beside him, still appearing eager about something.

Noah Whitmore asked everyone to stand and pray with him. The prayer came straight from the man's heart, asking God's blessing on the building, on the teacher, on the children and their families. At the end, a solemn and hearty "Amen!" swept the gathering.

At Mr. Ashford's request, Miss Thurston rose. She looked very elegant yet commanding. Her back straight, her chin lifted, but not so high as to challenge others.

And he noted that she also wore a stylish hat with a feather today, not a bonnet like the other women.

"I have asked Miss Thurston to say a few words today," Mr. Ashford said.

The teacher turned to face the filled schoolroom. "Instead of speaking myself, my students have prepared a recitation for you in honor of this special day. Students," she said, "come forward as we rehearsed."

Her students—including Johann—leaped to their feet and hurried forward where, with a little jostling, they assembled in age order, the youngest students in the front.

"Johann," Miss Thurston said, "will you announce our recitation, please?"

"Yes, Miss Thurston," he replied in a loud voice, stepping forward. "We, the students of Pepin Community School, will recite the Preamble to the United States Constitution." Red-faced but proud, Johann moved back in line.

Noting that Johann had spoken with almost no accent, Kurt wondered if he'd been carefully rehearsed by the teacher. He also noted that he didn't know what "preamble" meant. He leaned slightly forward to hear it.

"We the People of the United States—" Miss Thurston started the students in a clear, strong voice and then let the children go on without her "—in Order to form a more perfect Union, establish Justice, insure domestic Tranquility, provide for the common defence, promote the general Welfare, and secure the Blessings of Liberty to ourselves and our Posterity, do ordain and establish this Constitution for the United States of America."

Excitement and wonder raced down Kurt's spine, a tingling—an awakening. *We, the People.* Not the princes, not the lords, not the gentry—*the people* ordained and established. In some unseen way, he felt himself expanding, becoming more than he had considered himself before hearing these words. He inhaled deeply, letting this sensation sink in. He couldn't take his gaze from Miss Thurston as she stood so tall and so brave, without a bowed head or a voice of deference. *I love this country.*

A moment of silence and then everyone surged to their feet and applauded, some holding their hands high. The applause went on for over a minute, the parents glowing with pride. Kurt joined in. That Miss Thurston had chosen his nephew, the scorned immigrant, to introduce the recitation was not lost on him. How kind of her. How good.

No doubt awakened by the applause, William began to cry. Miss Thurston swiftly lifted him from his basket and he calmed immediately. Again, Kurt noticed everyone eyeing the teacher and the child.

"Well recited, students," Mr. Ashford pronounced, also with a sidelong glance at the teacher.

Kurt wished William hadn't called everyone's attention to himself. He knew how this would end but he wanted nothing to hurry along what would inevitably happen.

"Miss Thurston," Mr. Ashford said, "will you tell us if there is anything you need to do your job as teacher of Pepin Community School?"

Miss Thurston inclined her head. "I'd like the parents to ask their children each evening to share what they learned in school that day."

The parents around Kurt nodded in agreement and looked more pleased with each word the teacher said.

"Also, I ask that each child bring their own cup for water," Miss Thurston added. "I've studied modern sanitation and it is becoming accepted that using the communal cup, which hangs by the pump, is a way of spreading contagions."

The parents bent their heads together and discussed this startling announcement, seemingly impressed by Miss Thurston's knowledge. And when she thanked the parents for doing such a good job preparing the children to come to school, they all beamed at her praise. She was absolutely winning them over as their teacher. Kurt only wished that she could win them over in all matters, for her sake.

Mr. Ashford thanked the community for coming, and everyone applauded, rising to gather their families and head home. For some reason, Kurt found he couldn't leave. Johann had left his side to talk to friends outside and finally only he and Miss Thurston remained. She walked toward him, one brow lifted as if questioning him.

He could not provide a single, sensible reason for lingering. How could he say that he'd found it impossible to leave without speaking to her?

"Did you need something, Mr. Lang?"

Like an ocean swell, an answer came to him. He needed only to speak a few words to Miss Thurston. He had denied his growing interest in her, which was both inappropriate and doomed. But being in her presence, and speaking with her, had become a pleasure he couldn't deny himself.

"A very good dedication," he managed to say. "I had not heard that before. The preamble."

She gazed at him. "Thank you. I think the children

did a good job. Did you notice how well your nephew pronounced his part?"

Kurt found his mouth had gone dry. "Yes. *Danke*—thank you." Since he couldn't trust his tongue, he simply smiled and bowed, and then took his leave as quickly as he could.

Outside, he called Johann and soon the three of them were walking home together. As he listened to Johann's chatter, Kurt sternly took himself to task for giving in to his foolishness with regard to his feelings. Just as Gunther had no hope of gaining Amanda, Kurt had no hope of attracting Miss Thurston. The old wound twisted inside him like a sharp knife. The woman he'd proposed to had rejected him and at the worst possible moment, just after his father had lost almost everything and decided to take the coward's way out. In the end, that had pushed him to leave Germany.

Just as well. Just as well, he thought. And no one here must ever find out.

At school late on Tuesday afternoon, Ellen listened to the eldest students as they alternated reading portions of Longfellow's poem, "The Song of Hiawatha," aloud. The day had turned sultry, and she dabbed her face with one of her mother's delicate lace-edged handkerchiefs, one that she'd hidden from her sister-in-law, Alice. Alice thought that all of Mother's possessions should go to the wife of the eldest son, and the daughters should get nothing.

Ellen didn't like the way her thoughts stirred up irritation. Why was she thinking of Alice—of all people—now?

When the tall form of a man appeared in the doorway of the school, she thought one of the fathers had come early to take a child home. The sun shining behind him cast him in shadow.

"Yes?" she asked, shading her eyes to see.

"Ellen?"

It was her brother's voice! "Randolph?" She ran to him, and he opened his arms and let her hug him.

"What are you doing here?" Fear lanced through her. "Has anything happened—" She couldn't finish her question.

"No, nothing dire has happened."

Then why had her brother traveled three days north to see her?

She waited for him to continue, but he didn't. She stepped back from him and showed him in. He looked more and more like their father all the time—slender with wavy, dark hair and a distinguished face.

When she realized that all the children were gawking at Randolph, she mastered herself and said, "Students, this is my brother, Randolph Thurston. Please stand and say, 'Welcome to our school, sir.'"

The children rose as one and a slightly out-of-unison welcome rang through the schoolroom.

Randolph bowed slightly. "Thank you, children."

She glanced at the large wall clock. "Randolph, I still have some lessons to finish before the end of the school day. If you go through that door, you can wait in my quarters."

"Of course. I don't want to interrupt the children's studies." With a friendly wave, he strode up the aisle past her and through the door.

However, the children were distracted. She didn't blame them since she was distracted, as well. Finally she decided to let them go home early. Nothing was being learned and she found her agitation over her brother's presence growing moment by moment. Though she was glad to see him, she didn't want him to find out about William—at least not from anyone else.

After the last student hurried outside, she shut the school door and walked to the entrance to her room. To brace herself, she drew in a deep breath, crafted a smile and went through to her room. "Well, Randolph, this is a surprise."

He rose from the rocker. "Yes, I decided to come and see how you were situated myself. I left my overnight bag at the general store. The proprietor invited me to stay the night and directed me here."

Was this really a visit to make sure she was happy here? The brother she'd known before he'd married Alice would have done so, but not the man he'd become since.

"Well, how do you like my quarters?" She motioned with some pride toward her cozy room.

"It is simple compared to what you were accustomed to."

"Yes, but I like its simplicity." *And that it is my own place, with no one here to snipe at me.* She tried to push away the volumes of hurt and anger Alice had created and which she still carried, thinking that she needed to get over Alice, forgive Alice her unkindness. "I'm not unhappy to see you, Randolph, but you must have a reason for coming."

"I came to see how you were faring here in the wilderness," he repeated, his evasion so clear that a first grader could have perceived it. "You've only written once since you left home," he scolded gently.

"And if my memory serves, dear brother, you didn't answer that one letter. Alice did," she teased him lightly in return.

"I've been very busy with business."

I moved to another state and began a new career, but I'm just a woman, therefore, what I'm busy with is not as important as what a man is busy with.

She decided not to voice this, knowing she didn't need to keep pestering him. Eventually he would have to tell her. This avoiding something he didn't want to do was so like Randolph that somehow it reassured her.

And she couldn't prevent him from meeting William. *Might as well face it.* She claimed her bonnet from the peg by the door and pulled on cotton gloves, determined to face the situation head-on.

"There is something I need to pick up just north of here. Will you accompany me?"

As she led her brother through town, she introduced him to everyone who came out to meet him. Finally they left town behind them and headed up the track toward the Brawley claim.

"What are you picking up?" he asked again.

"You'll see," she said, delaying. Better to be with the Brawleys when the truth came out. Their presence might temper Randolph's reaction.

Soon they approached the Brawley cabin. "Hello, the house!" Ellen called out.

Mrs. Brawley walked out with William in her arms. The woman's usual friendly greeting died on her lips at the sight of Randolph. Confronted by an unexpected guest, Mrs. Brawley automatically smoothed her hair.

"Mrs. Brawley, may I introduce my brother, Randolph Thurston? Randolph, this is Mrs. Anson Brawley."

Looking puzzled, Randolph slightly bowed and greeted the woman.

The moment of revelation had come.

"I wanted to surprise you, Randolph." Ellen lifted William from Mrs. Brawley's arms. "This is William. I'm adopting him."

Watching Randolph's shock rise through him like a geyser chafed her nerves. He would probably have much to say, like everyone else. Yet what could he do?

While Randolph silently grappled with her news, she chatted a few moments with Mrs. Brawley about how William's day had gone. All was well. Ellen thanked the woman. She shouldered William's sack of baby things but her brother gruffly told her to give the sack to him to carry. Was it just good manners or did it show concern for her? She pondered this as she led Randolph toward town.

As soon as they were out of sight from the claim, Randolph exploded. "What is this all about, Ellen Elizabeth Thurston?"

She drew in a deep breath. "The infant was left on my doorstep last week."

"What?"

She repeated the sentence.

"Surely someone else will take the child?"

"I am keeping him." Ellen kissed William's forehead.

"Nonsense."

"Did you notice what I named him?" she asked, hoping he would understand.

That shut him up. "William," he said finally.

"Yes, William."

They walked on in silence. Was Randolph remembering how he'd helped her care for their little brother? How they'd wept together when they'd laid him to rest?

Suddenly another thought intruded. Gunther would come for his session this evening, and Randolph probably wouldn't like that, either. After supper at the Ashfords, she would try to persuade him not to come back to her quarters with her. She wanted to avoid the unpleasantness over her associating with "rude, ignorant immigrants," as she had heard her brother once say.

Mr. Lang was as far from rude and ignorant as a man could possibly be. And even in Gunther's angrier moments, he wasn't exactly rude. And Johann, well, he was a smart and charming boy.

She sighed, feeling frustrated that Randolph had intruded on the life she had built for herself. And still more worrying, she didn't know why Randolph had come.

Whatever the reason, she had a feeling that Randolph's visit was going to be a complicated one and might end with a confrontation—if he thought she was returning to Illinois.

Uneasy, Kurt stood by while Gunther knocked on the door of the schoolteacher's quarters. Though they'd all washed up before coming, he felt the effects of the uncomfortable heat, even this late in the day. When would cool autumn come?

Miss Thurston opened the door and motioned them inside.

"I brought you flowers, miss." Grinning, Johann shoved a handful of wilted brown-eyed Susans into her hand.

"Oh, Johann, thank you." She quickly put them in a jar of water and placed them on the table.

And then Kurt glimpsed a well-dressed man sitting in the rocker—where Kurt usually sat. This must be Miss Thurston's brother, the one Johann had mentioned. Was this a good visit with family or had the man brought bad news?

"*Guten abend,* Miss Thurston." Irritation with himself rushed through him, hot and uncomfortable. Why had he greeted her in German?

The schoolteacher introduced Kurt to her brother. Kurt stepped forward and shook his hand, feeling the lack of calluses—this man didn't work with his hands. Though they stood eye to eye in height, the man managed to look down on him.

"Randolph, Gunther is an adult student of mine. He's bettering his English and preparing for American citizenship. I'll be busy an hour or more tutoring him. Perhaps you would prefer to go back to the Ashford's, after all?"

Her brother responded with a brief and disapproving smile. "I'll stay. Do you entertain students—" her brother eyed Mr. Lang up and down "—alone in your quarters often?"

Kurt felt a twinge of anger. Was the man insinuating that this was improper? Kurt nearly said something in her defense but contented himself with a pointed look at her brother. Surely he should know his sister would never do anything dishonorable or even questionable.

"So far only Gunther needs adult instruction," she replied stiffly. "Now we must begin so they can return home while some light still lingers."

Kurt caught the discontented tone in her voice. Her

brother's visit evidently did not please Miss Thurston. Had Mrs. Steward, her cousin, written to her brother about the child and now he had come to forbid her to adopt William? No, there hadn't been time for a letter to reach Illinois.

Miss Thurston motioned for Gunther to take his seat at the table as usual. "Mr. Lang, why don't you bring my desk chair in from the schoolroom and be comfortable?" Then she began speaking to Gunther and looking at the assignments he'd done since their last session.

Gunther replied in a strained voice, no doubt unsettled at having a stranger present during his lesson. The lad had tried to hide his pride at successfully completing all his assignments. Kurt had praised him, and had been looking forward to thanking Miss Thurston for suggesting this teaching arrangement. The brother's presence had ruined the evening.

But Kurt obeyed her suggestion and brought the chair into the room, sitting opposite her brother and meeting the man's disapproving gaze, face-to-face.

Johann dragged his wooden horse from his pocket and approached the man. "My uncle made this for me."

The brother barely glanced at it. "Very nice." Then he returned his gaze to Kurt. "How long have you and your wife lived here?"

Kurt knew immediately what prompted this question. Another twinge of anger. "I am not married. Gunther is my brother. Johann is my nephew. That is our family now."

The man looked more chagrined.

"Miss Thurston told us she is from Galena. Are you from Galena, too?" Johann said.

Kurt savored how easily Johann pronounced that pesky "th" sound now.

"Yes, I am" was all the man said.

Kurt tried to think of some topic of conversation, but realized he was content to sit in silence with the man rather than have to make conversation with someone who so clearly did not like immigrants. He listened to Johann tapping his horse's hooves on the wooden floor, and Gunther and Miss Thurston discussing his writing lesson.

Finally, Randolph Thurston fidgeted in the rocker and then rose. "Ellen, I am tired from my journey. I think it best I take your advice and return to the Ashford's since I accepted their hospitality for the night."

Miss Thurston swiveled to face her brother. "I'm sure you are tired. Get some rest. Mr. Lang lives close to Martin and Ophelia—I was going to have him tell them you are in town and invite ourselves to supper tomorrow after school. It wouldn't do not to see them while you're here."

"Good. I want to see their place, too." Mr. Thurston nodded toward Kurt. "Nice meeting you and your family. Good night."

Kurt heard the last sentence and did not believe it for one moment.

"I'll see you tomorrow then, Randolph." Miss Thurston dismissed him with a wave of her hand and turned back to Gunther.

The man left quickly.

Kurt heard the baby stirring in the basket. He went over and picked him up to find the child needed a fresh diaper. As he changed the child, he wondered not only what had brought Randolph Thurston to Pepin, but what it was about the man's presence that seemed to agitate Miss Thurston.

After the lesson ended, Miss Thurston rose and said, "You two go on. Mr. Lang will join you soon. I want to have a few words with him."

Kurt paused in the middle of her room. As the lads left, Johann chattering as usual, Gunther cast a quizzical look over his shoulder.

"Miss Thurston?"

She looked distressed. "I hope you weren't offended by my brother's…coolness. He is always a bit formal, but—"

"It is fine," he said, bending the truth.

"Very well, then." Her smile looked strained. "I will see you Thursday if not sooner."

After the long day, the schoolteacher's hair was beginning to slip from its pins. He found he was clenching his hands to keep from reaching out to touch the silken threads of gold that the summer sun had gilded in her light brown hair. The impulse caught him off guard and hurried him to the door.

"Yes, Thursday." He nodded, swiping his hat from the peg and heading outside. "Good night."

As he rushed to catch up with his brother and nephew, many thoughts swirled in his mind. Why had the brother come? Perhaps he'd come to persuade Miss Thurston to leave?

The thought of her being removed from their town felt like someone slamming a door inside him. The school had become the center of their community and Miss Thurston had brought such life to Pepin. He remembered the lift he'd felt when Johann and the other children recited the preamble, and thought of the change he'd already seen in Gunther after just a few lessons with the teacher.

Kurt, however, refused to contemplate just how much she'd added to *his* life. He must not think such thoughts. Even if, by some circumstance, he felt he could pursue her, he would simply cause trouble for her. Her brother's obvious disdain made that clear.

The thought hit him like acid, burning into his heart. The truth was, he was no good for Miss Thurston. And there was very little he could do about that.

Chapter Eight

Before supper that evening, Martin took Randolph outside to show him all he'd done on his land over the past year, leaving Ellen alone with Ophelia. As soon as the men were out of earshot, Ophelia exclaimed, "Did you know Randolph was coming?"

"No." Ellen held William and rocked the cradle with Ophelia's baby with her foot.

"Why is he here?" Ophelia was making gravy and busily stirred the contents of a large cast-iron skillet.

"I wish I knew."

"Do you think someone told him about…" Ophelia nodded toward William.

"The post doesn't move that fast and if you didn't write him, who would?"

"Well, you know I wouldn't have written a word to Galena about all this. I hope my mother doesn't get wind of it." Ophelia sounded really worried.

"Even if she does hear of it, she wouldn't dare say anything against my character," Ellen said, trying to sound convincing.

"Humph," Ophelia made the sound. "You witnessed

the scene she enacted when she visited here only last year. Do you think your brother's worried about Cissy? I mean do you think there's some trouble concerning her and Holton?"

Since this unwelcome thought had occurred to her, Ellen frowned. "Cissy did say that some people were less than welcoming to Holton."

"I wonder why…" Ophelia turned her attention to her gravy.

Ellen shrugged, leaning down to kiss William's forehead. The truth was she missed him during the long school days apart. She didn't need to burden her cousin with the truth about Holton or discuss Alice. Ophelia knew Alice all too well already.

"Remember when Randy got too big for his britches," Ophelia asked, using her brother's childhood nickname, "and we all called him 'Boss' and played pranks on him?"

Ellen thought of her brother's disapproval of her choice to live here and teach school and felt that he probably still thought of himself as boss.

Ellen sat beside Randolph as he drove the wagon they'd borrowed from the blacksmith, with William asleep in the basket at her feet. They were on their way home. During dinner with Ophelia and Martin, Randolph repeated his excuse to their cousins for coming to Pepin. But tomorrow Randolph would head back to Galena and he still hadn't told her why he'd really come. By now, Ellen's nerves had been stretched tight enough to snap.

Finally in the dying light of day, she and Randolph approached the schoolhouse. He helped her down and lifted the basket, then followed her to her door.

She opened the door and inside, lit a lamp on the table. Then she turned to her brother. "Perhaps, Randolph, the time has come for the truth. You must have wanted something to come all this way and for such a short stay. What is it?"

After setting the basket down by her bed, Randolph put his hands together and worked them. She sat in the rocker and waited, listening to the crickets and cicadas outside.

He finally cleared his throat. "Ellen, it's time for you to give up this nonsense and come home where you belong."

His words sounded prepared and practiced, and Ellen heard Alice's voice in them. "My home is here now," Ellen said, keeping her tone light. "Please come to the point."

"Alice is expecting." He paused as if waiting for a response.

Looking her brother in the eye, Ellen said the only words she could. "I felicitate you."

"My wife needs family—needs you—home in this time of stress." Randolph dropped his hands.

They both fell silent.

"Is she having a difficult pregnancy?" Ellen finally asked.

"The doctor says she is merely suffering the usual discomforts."

"Then I fail to see why I am needed." Ellen waited.

Randolph's jaw worked as he evidently prepared to come to the point. "I'm afraid that Alice is having trouble keeping house help. The Irish girls can't seem to come up to the mark anymore. And with her feeling so badly... Ellen, it's your duty to come home and help out. Alice isn't strong enough to—"

"Alice is as strong as an ox," Ellen said blandly and rose. "I would suggest Alice learn to treat the Irish girls better and then she'll have no trouble keeping house help. Let me be clear, Randolph. I will not come home to keep house for Alice."

I have no intention of returning to Galena. Ever.

"Alice said you'd be difficult," he said, obviously disgruntled. "She wrote this note for me to give you." He handed her the letter, but wouldn't make eye contact.

She unfolded it.

Dear Ellen,
I'm sure you will refuse to come back, even though it is your duty as the unmarried sister to help your family. So let me just say this. Gossip is buzzing about Cissy and Holton. I don't know why people waited so long to begin commenting about Holton switching his attentions from you to your younger and much prettier sister, but they did. I think your leaving town prompted a resurgence of the gossip. Cissy is finding all this talk distressing. I have done my best to put a good face upon the business. However, if you don't come home, I'm afraid I won't be able to carry this off. If you love your sister, you will come home and save her embarrassment.
Sincerely,
Alice

The letter and its veiled threat left Ellen aghast. She looked into Randolph's face, shadowed in the lamplight.

The letter was dreadful but it might serve a purpose. Cissy had said it well—Alice brought out the worst in their brother. Maybe the time for revelation had arrived.

"Do you know what Alice has written me?"

"No."

She handed the note to him. "Here. Read it."

He accepted it reluctantly and then glanced down. Barely a minute passed as he read it. His face reddened in the low light.

"Randolph, you are my brother and I love you. But I don't think you realize that your wife shows a very different face to you than she does to me or even Cissy. Or the Irish girls who've left your employ."

Halfheartedly, he began, "You're reading something in this note that isn't—"

"No, Randolph, you and I both perceive the meaning plainly. And in your heart, you know that trying to bring me home now is selfish on Alice's part. That's why you've delayed and delayed telling me why you came."

Her brother sank onto the bench by her table, staring at the single page in his hand.

Ellen waited.

"I haven't wanted to admit it to myself," he said, not looking up. "But when you left so abruptly, Alice and I had an argument. A neighbor woman had said something sharp to me about Alice knowing why you'd left."

Ellen didn't reply. Randolph must work this out for himself.

"What am I going to do, Nell?" he at last asked. His use of her childhood nickname touched her. "After reading this, I can't deny it any longer. I've married a vain, selfish woman."

"I don't know what you can do except stand up to her. By ignoring it, you've been condoning her behavior."

He nodded slowly. "I'm sorry I didn't speak up when I first sensed matters weren't right between you and Alice."

"You are in a difficult position."

"And you are, too," her brother said, his voice becoming stronger.

"What?"

"What about this foreigner, this Mr. Lang?"

Ellen felt herself starch up on the outside and soften on the inside, an odd combination. "What about Mr. Lang?"

"I'd have to be blind not to notice how *friendly* the two of you are."

Ellen sent her brother a repressive look. "If you are implying that there is anything between us other than friendship—"

"Perhaps on your part, it's only friendship. I am a man and I know when a man is interested in a woman. Mr. Lang is interested in you."

Ellen half-turned from him. "Then he will be disappointed. I have no interest in romance now."

Her brother grumbled. "I know who's responsible for that."

"I don't want to speak of Holton—"

Randolph changed subjects. "You shouldn't have gone so far away, Nell."

"I am happy here. And now I have William."

"Martin told me that the town is against your keeping this foundling."

Her heart lurched but she answered calmly, "The town will get used to it."

Randolph sat a few more moments before he rose to leave. "My boat is expected early in the morning. I will write you when I get home. And don't worry about Cissy. I'll take care of everything." He turned.

She rose and threw her arms around him. "You can handle this, Boss." She used the old name to try to lift his mood. "Give my love to Cissy...and Alice."

He hugged her close. "We lost our parents too soon. Perhaps if they'd still been here..."

She choked back sudden tears. "I wish you traveling mercies."

After their farewells, she watched him drive up the track toward town in the moonlight.

Dear God, help my brother. He will need it to succeed.

Chapter Nine

Ellen stood by the school door, smiling as she watched the children enjoy their afternoon recess. She swallowed a yawn and leaned against the doorjamb, hoping William would soon sleep the night through. A stiff breeze played with the fringe on her shawl and her bonnet shaded her from the bright sunshine.

The first cool morning had come. A few leaves on the tallest maple trees had suddenly been trimmed in scarlet. The unusually long summer appeared to finally bow its head to autumn. She would have to start knitting warm socks and buntings for William.

"They're gonna take that baby away from the teacher," a boy's voice said.

The words, coming from around the corner of the schoolhouse, startled Ellen from her reverie.

"I don't know why. What's wrong with a teacher having a baby?" asked a girl.

"'Cause teachers don't have babies. Or husbands. Only single ladies—old maids, like Miss Thurston—get to teach school."

"Oh, what do you know? Miss Thurston's not an old maid. She's too pretty—"

Ellen rang the bell, smiling as she shook inside. She understood all too well that children merely mimicked what their parents said at home.

From all over the schoolyard, the children ran to her as usual. She had recognized the voices she'd overheard but tried to forget who they were. Children weren't responsible for their parents' prejudice.

One thing was clear: it was time for Ellen to come up with a plan, or else risk losing William.

And that was something she had no intention of doing.

The school board meeting took place on the third Sunday afternoon of the month as usual. Sitting on the front bench in the schoolroom, Ellen had devised a way to distract everyone from William's presence in her life by giving them something else to talk about. It wasn't the best plan, but it was the only one she had at the moment.

At the front of the schoolroom facing the benches, the three men on the school board—her cousin's husband, the old preacher's son Micah and Mr. Ashford—had arranged themselves in a row. A few men and women clustered toward the back of the room to observe, but most people had gone home to enjoy a quiet Sunday.

Mr. Lang had not stayed for the meeting. Ellen found herself wishing that he had. She sat alone on the front bench facing the board, maintaining a calm expression and confident manner. Unfortunately, both were a facade. Her stomach swirled unevenly.

Martin, the board's secretary, was reading the min-

utes from the last meeting. "Miss Ellen Thurston asked
the board to consider purchasing a wall map for the
school. The suggestion was discussed. A motion…"

Listening, or trying to appear as if she were listening, Ellen waited for Mr. Ashford to ask if there was
any new business. Then she heard William begin to
cry in her quarters. Her jaw tightened. All three men
on the board turned toward the door behind them. *Oh,
please, not now, William.*

She'd hired Amanda to watch him so he wouldn't
disrupt the meeting—she didn't want to call any attention to William right now. When he stopped crying
abruptly, she found herself able to take a deep breath.
Thank you, Amanda.

The board resumed their deliberations with Martin's
notes being accepted unanimously. Next, Micah presented the treasurer's report. Then Mr. Ashford asked,
as if merely a formality, "Is there any new business to
discuss?"

Some people began to move, perhaps preparing to
leave. In her room, William was fussing and the sound
knotted the back of Ellen's neck. People stopped gathering themselves and looked askance toward the door
to her quarters. Mr. Lang in contrast appeared at the
door and took his place in the last bench.

His arrival and the negative expressions on the others' faces pushed her to her feet. "I have some new business to discuss with the board, if I may?"

The board members looked at each other and Mr.
Ashford cleared his throat. "Yes, Miss Thurston, what
is it?"

"I have come up with an idea I think will encourage
our students to excel in their studies."

Those attendees who'd risen sat down again.

"What is it?" Martin asked.

"I propose our school prepare for and host a regional spelling bee here next April."

An astounded silence met her proposal. Unfortunately, Amanda's voice, as she tried to soothe William, filled it.

She pressed on, feigning a lightness far from what she felt. "I know that there are schools in Lake City, Downsville and Bear Lake. All three are within an easy driving distance for a midday gathering here. I would write to the teachers of those schools and invite them to prepare their students for the spelling bee."

She took a deep breath and prepared to speak louder in order to cover William's continued whimpering.

"Then in April on the appointed day, the teachers and their students who have excelled in spelling will come here to compete with our best spellers. Also, I think two levels would give students in all the grades a chance to qualify to represent their schools. We could ask for a small donation from each school that participates to defray the cost of plaques for the winners."

She found herself breathless. Finally, William had quieted.

The board no longer looked surprised that she had spoken in the meeting; they looked pleased. Mr. Ashford glanced at the other board members.

"This sounds very interesting, Miss Thurston," Micah said.

"I can see that this would prompt all our students to work harder on their spelling lists," Mr. Ashford agreed.

"I also think it will add some zest to the school year, giving us a goal to work toward," Ellen replied. From 'the corner of her eye, she glimpsed Mr. Lang nodding in approval. That lifted her spirit more than anything else. She tried to temper this but couldn't.

"Do we need further discussion?" Mr. Ashford asked.

The other board members shook their heads no.

"I make a motion that Miss Thurston contact the schools nearest Pepin and invite them to a regional spelling bee to be held in April, 1871 at Pepin Community School," Micah proposed.

"I second that," Martin chimed in.

"All in favor, say aye," Mr. Ashford said. After hearing the response, he said, "Motion passed unanimously."

A smattering of applause followed this.

"If that's all, I will entertain a motion to adjourn this meeting," Mr. Ashford said, starting to rise.

"Hold up!" A man in the rear stood. "I want to know when the board is going to deal with this baby left at the school."

Ellen froze where she stood. Her plan to distract everyone from William had just dissolved.

Mr. Ashford looked irritated. "That is not on the agenda for today."

"Well, the spelling bee wasn't, either," the man shot back. "Now, what are people from those other schools going to say when they come here and find that our schoolteacher has a baby? It won't look right."

"It's just not fittin'," another man agreed. "Schoolteachers are supposed to be single ladies of good reputation."

Ellen straightened and turned to face her accusers.

Before she could speak, Martin rose. "I hope no one in this town is casting aspersions on my wife's cousin.

Miss Ellen Thurston's character and reputation are spotless here and in Galena." Martin's aggressive tone charged the room with tension. "My cousin has even been received by the Grants in their own home."

A heavy and tense silence ensued.

"I wasn't castin' aspersions," the second man said in a calmer tone. "Everybody knows Miss Thurston is a fine lady. But it just isn't done."

The first man nodded emphatically. "He's right. Everybody says so and something must be done. We think it's mighty sweet that the schoolteacher wants to take care of the foundling. But it's just not fitting."

"I move that we table this discussion and hold a special school board meeting next Sunday," Martin said quickly.

"I second," Micah added.

"Ayes?" Mr. Ashford asked. Both men said aye and the school board meeting ended.

Shaken, Ellen turned and managed to smile at the school board members.

"Miss Thurston, the idea for a spelling bee is excellent," Micah said. She accepted this with a nod.

Amanda appeared in the doorway with William in her arms. "He wants you, Miss Thurston."

Ellen hurried forward and accepted the baby. She smiled down at the child who, for the first time, smiled back at her. Tears sprang to her eyes and she blinked them away. "Thank you, Amanda."

But Mr. Lang left without speaking to her and that stung.

Finally, only Martin remained. He followed her into her quarters. "Ellen, we know how much keeping this child means to you. Ophelia and I have talked it over, and we'll take the baby in. That way you can see him and be in his life."

Ellen was quite astonished by her cousin's offer, but Ophelia already had enough to do, caring for her own child. "That's very kind of you. But I plan to keep William. I don't think there is any law saying that I can't."

"It may not be against the law, Ellen, but you might have to choose between William and your job here. People apparently have very set ideas about single schoolteachers raising orphans."

Ellen held her tongue. She longed to refute what he said but couldn't. "I hope it won't come to that."

Martin patted her shoulder. "We'll see you Wednesday for supper, then?"

"Yes, thank you, Martin." Ellen saw him to her door. When he had gone, she sat in the rocker and gazed at the little child who had been entrusted to her.

She had a small inheritance in a bank in Galena, earning interest for the years far ahead when she retired from teaching. So while she wasn't penniless, she wasn't of independent means, either. She must work to provide for herself and William. She might be forced to choose between Pepin and William. She didn't like to think of moving and trying to come up with another way to make a living.

The thought of leaving tightened into a hard knot of pain. The school children had already become so dear to her, and she truly loved her work. The prejudice against her keeping William angered her, and she felt she might have a tiny glimpse into how Mr. Lang felt on a daily basis. She wondered why he'd come to the meeting and why he'd left without speaking to her. Her brother's words played in her mind. Was Mr. Lang interested in her? She hoped he wasn't but a tiny part of her hoped he was. She pushed this puzzle aside.

Why can't I keep this baby and teach? How can I fight this foolish prejudice against a teacher raising a child alone?

While Miss Thurston taught Gunther, Kurt sat glumly on the doorstep outside her quarters, thinking about what had happened at the school board meeting. The difference of opinion over the baby between Miss Thurston and the town didn't appear to be lessening.

He wanted to help her, and he didn't want to see this fine woman hurt. Perhaps he should be trying to persuade her to give in.

Beside him, the cause of all the commotion, William, lay kicking his feet and cooing in the cradle that Noah Whitmore had made as a gift. In the schoolyard beyond, Johann was swinging on one of two wooden rope swings Kurt had recently hung from trees, one for the girls and one for the boys. As Johann swung, the rope rasped against the tree branch, creaking.

Miss Thurston stepped outside and sat down beside him, a shawl around her. Coolness edged the evening air. He half rose and then sat again. As usual, she was dressed in a very fine manner with lace edging her high collar and cuffs. She looked completely at ease, as if she had no notion of the controversy piling up around her.

"Have you heard about the special school board meeting?" she asked abruptly.

Yes, he had, and hearing about it had made his stomach sick. *"Ja."*

"I hear in your tone that you think they will make me give William up."

He turned his gaze to her. *"Ja."*

She glanced down for a moment. "I honestly don't understand why anyone should care if I adopt William. He has not interfered with my school teaching at all."

"Yes."

"That's your third *yes*. You can't say it again without losing two points," she teased, suddenly grinning.

Her joke caught him off guard. He chuckled and shook his head. She was an unusual woman. "You make a joke but I do think they will make you give up William."

"If they make me choose between the school and William, I will choose William. I will leave Pepin."

"No." Kurt felt as if the word had been wrenched from deep inside him. "No."

She smiled with a bittersweet charm. "You've switched from *yes* to *no*."

He ignored her sally. "Where would you go?"

"Sunny Whitmore has told me of an orphanage south of here on the Illinois shore of the Mississippi. I might go there and see if they have need of another matron. It would be a good fit for me and William."

Kurt felt as if he had been caught between the jaws of some mighty animal and was being crushed. He nearly said no again, but stopped himself. He knew he never could be more than a neighbor to Miss Ellen Thurston, but that was better—much better—than losing her bright presence altogether.

He must try to persuade her. "Miss Thurston, I know better than you how it is to raise children alone. I have been father to Gunther since we lost our mother. I adopted Johann when my sister, Maria, died. Being father and mother to two boys—" He drew in a deep breath. "It is hard."

"I'm sure it is. But William was left at *my* door. I don't think it was random. I think someone wanted me to have him, to raise him."

Kurt watched Johann pumping his legs, swinging higher and higher. He loved the boy and wouldn't be parted from him. From behind, he heard Gunther softly reading aloud the Bill of Rights of the U.S. Constitution. Things had changed for the better between his brother and him, and Miss Thurston had achieved that. He was beholden to her.

Therefore, he must make her see the truth.

"You are a woman alone. A boy needs a father to learn how to be a man."

"I had hoped you were on my side, Mr. Lang." When he didn't answer, she continued, "A boy needs a mother to learn about women." She lifted her hands palm up. "How many children are raised in perfect homes?"

He snorted in derision. *I was not.*

"I had wonderful parents. But even with their guidance, life has taken unexpected twists and turns for my brother, my sister and me."

He thought about Randolph Thurston. The man had not liked Kurt being around his sister—Kurt understood that. But her brother had not appeared happy in himself, either.

As his thoughts drifted, he noticed the fragrance of rosewater drifting on the breeze, and realized the lovely scent was Miss Thurston's perfume.

Kurt looked into the distance at the darkening horizon. Seeing that they'd stayed too long jerked him back to practicality. "Boys!" he called, standing up quickly.

"We must go now. The sun is nearly set." He turned and gripped her hand. "Thank you again." He wanted to say more but he couldn't—what he had to say would be too personal.

Miss Thurston looked puzzled by his sudden departure but she said a polite good-night and then reached for the baby.

Soon the three of them were hurrying fast toward home. As darkness began to overtake them, the parting image of Miss Thurston holding William in her arms wouldn't leave Kurt. The terrible sensation of being forced to accept her fate pressed down on him.

I cannot let her leave Pepin, he thought. *Not after all the good she has done Gunther and the other students. This is about my duty to this community. It is not about how I may feel about Miss Thurston.*

Kurt turned his attention to the boys before he could acknowledge that he wasn't being entirely honest with himself.

Chapter Ten

Ellen had dressed with care for the special board meeting with a delicate balance in mind. She'd chosen a sober yet stylish dress of navy; she wanted to impress but not appear ostentatious.

As she looked around the room, she noticed Mr. Lang had not yet come in. Would he desert her? She cast this concern aside. She'd told Randolph she wasn't interested in romance and a thought like that was not appropriate. Whether he was here or not had little bearing on the issue at hand.

She'd chosen not to try to hide William this time. He napped in his cradle at her feet while she sat beside her desk before the schoolroom packed with citizens of Pepin, all of whom had come to address whether she could keep both William and her job.

She'd prayed about this, but her tension had not lessened. When Mr. Lang entered at last, she breathed a sigh of relief despite herself. He sat on the rear bench beside Old Saul in his wheelchair.

She had begun to know and like some of the people of Pepin. She recalled how hard it had been to come here to start a new life, and she was not anxious to venture into the unknown again. The very thought hollowed her out like seeding a melon.

Mr. Ashford looked at the clock and then at his own pocket watch. He loosened the tight collar around his throat and then he brought the meeting to order. After Noah Whitmore prayed for wisdom and guidance, Mr. Ashford rose and stepped to the front. "We have come here at the request of many parents and citizens to discuss whether our schoolteacher, Miss Thurston, should be able to keep the foundling and remain our teacher or not."

Ellen did not like the expressions of most of the men and many of the women. They telegraphed an aggravation with her as if she had affronted them in some way. She wondered where that came from, as it was a far cry from the warm welcome she'd initially received. Only Mr. Lang and Old Saul looked sympathetic.

Ellen rose and stood beside the storekeeper. She decided to be direct. "I would like to know why my taking in a foundling is a matter of public discussion."

"He just told you," a man from the middle said pugnaciously. "You're a teacher. You're not supposed to have a baby."

Mr. Ashford raised both his hands. "This is a school board meeting and there are rules to keep order. You can't just up and start talking. You must rise, say your name and then ask to speak."

Conceding this, Ellen nodded agreement and returned to her seat.

Another man, the father of twin girls she'd found precocious, rose. "I'm Isaac Welton and I'd like to say a few words, please."

Mr. Ashford nodded assent.

"We, my wife and I, think Miss Thurston is a bang-up teacher. Our girls love to go to school and at the supper table, can't wait to tell us all they'd learned. I just want Miss Thurston to know that our disapproval of her keeping this foundling has nothing to do with our respect for her as a lady and a teacher. That's all I—we—" he glanced at his wife "—got to say."

The man's words touched Ellen's heart. "Thank you, Mr. Welton." Her eyes sought Mr. Lang. He returned her gaze, not revealing anything. She looked away.

Another man rose. "I'm Jesse Canton."

Ashford nodded for the man to speak.

"Everyone knows Miss Thurston does a good job. But the thing is, a schoolteacher having a baby around, it just doesn't look right. I mean people, strangers, might get the wrong idea." The man looked uncomfortable. "If you know what I mean." Most everyone in the room nodded in agreement with his sentiment.

Ellen took a deep breath and rose. "I think I should reply to these comments, Mr. Ashford."

The storekeeper looked doubtful but nodded. "You have a right to a say." He sat down.

Already girded for battle, Ellen faced the room of disapproving faces. Her mind was made up, and she knew what she was going to do. She found herself looking to Mr. Lang again, and the kindness she saw in his eyes, even though it was a sad kindness, somehow gave her an extra bit of strength and courage to say what needed to be said.

Kurt had the sensation of the roof slowly lowering on him, closing him in, a feeling of imminent loss and pain. He'd known how this would go, but had no way of preventing or even slowing what was about to happen, and this helplessness was unbearable.

But Miss Thurston spoke evenly and forcefully, impressing him yet again.

"So far the only reasons given here have been that a schoolteacher doesn't usually have a child, and that when strangers see the town's schoolteacher with a child, they might get the wrong idea of this community. But we live in America. We, as a nation, do things that others have not done before. I think the only question should be this—whether or not caring for this child prevents me or hinders me from doing my job well."

Another man near Kurt rose. "Joe Connolly." When he'd been acknowledged, he continued, "Those are not the only considerations. A child needs a ma and a pa. Everybody knows that. This child won't have a pa." He sat down among approving murmurs.

Kurt, having already tried this argument and failed, knew exactly what she was going to say.

"I agree that having a mother and a father is the ideal situation," the schoolteacher replied. "However, how many children are fortunate enough to reach adulthood still having both parents? I myself lost both parents to typhoid. And where will this child go if I don't care for him? Mrs. Whitmore has suggested that orphanage south of here. Yet if we send William there, he will have neither father *nor* mother."

A man stood, red-faced. "But a schoolteacher isn't supposed to be married or have children. It isn't done!"

"Why?" Miss Thurston asked, eyeing the man.

Mr. Ashford sent a warning glance to the man for

not following procedure. He sat down, grumbling to himself.

Kurt had to keep his lips pressed together. He wanted to stand up and tell them all to be quiet or they might lose this fine woman. And then where would the town of Pepin be? They had no idea what a treasure they'd be losing.

Martin Steward rose. "I really think this meeting has gone on long enough. Ophelia and I have offered to take the child and raise him as our own. There is no need for this public upset."

Kurt hadn't known that. The perfect solution. The tension in the room ebbed amid murmuring.

Miss Thurston turned to him. "Martin, I appreciate the offer, but as I've already said, I'm keeping William. He was entrusted to me. And if the town doesn't want the two of us—"

Kurt's heart thudded against his breastbone. She was going to go through with it. She was going to tell them she would be leaving.

Miss Thurston faced the crowd. "If I can't keep this child and remain your teacher, then I plan to—"

"I am Kurt Lang," he said, surging to his feet before he even recognized what he was doing. His mind scrambled for words. Now more than ever it was important that he spoke correctly. He had to, for her sake. "I am new in this country." He swallowed down his nerves. "Many things here are different than in the old country. This is a free land. I see more than you, you who are born here. Why can't a teacher raise a child alone? Isn't every mother a teacher? And every teacher a mother?"

Everyone had turned to him, gawking.

Sweat trickled down his back as he continued, forcing his voice to sound strong and sure. "My mother taught me much. And I am both father and mother to my nephew, Johann. Would you take him from me because I am not married? Should a farmer be allowed to raise a boy by himself?" He took a breath, one final thing to say coming from deep within. "Miss Thurston is a good person. William will be lucky to have her as a mother."

He sat down abruptly. He wanted desperately to wipe his perspiring forehead with his handkerchief but felt it best to continue to look his surprised neighbors in the eye. And then he looked at Ellen, and saw a combination of shock and gratitude on her lovely face.

The people had been silenced.

Probably they couldn't believe that he—a man who spoke with an accent and wasn't even a citizen—had spoken up in a public meeting. He could hardly believe it himself.

The old pastor touched his arm. "Will you push my chair to the front?"

When Kurt complied, everyone turned at the sound of the wheelchair. A few men who had risen—no doubt to contest what Kurt had said—slowly sank back to their seats. When he reached the front, Kurt turned the chair so that the older man faced the gathering.

"I have listened to all the opinions voiced here this evening," Old Saul said. "And I can see merit in all of them. But in this case, what mere men think doesn't amount to much. Yes, a child should be blessed with a mother and father. Yes, it is unusual for an unmarried schoolteacher to raise a foundling alone. Yes, no doubt people who visit here may think it out of the ordinary. However, only one fact matters."

Everyone sat forward, listening carefully so as not to miss a word.

"I don't believe the child was left on Miss Thurston's doorstep by accident. I think William's mother meant the lady to have him. And more important, God meant for Miss Thurston to have this child. I have prayed about this, as I'm sure Noah has." Old Saul glanced at Noah, who nodded solemnly. "And each time, I have received peace about Miss Thurston keeping the child."

Kurt swallowed, trying to grasp what the man's opinion could mean for Miss Thurston's future.

"I don't think we should meddle in this." The older man's voice strengthened. "William was given to Miss Thurston, not anybody else. He is being well cared for and the children in school are being well taught by a fine woman. We should be satisfied, don't you think?"

Uneasy silence filled several moments, then Noah spoke, "I thank Mr. Lang and Old Saul for clarifying this situation." He nodded to each in turn.

"I must agree with Old Saul. And I'll add that I was pleased when Mrs. Brawley stepped forward to help with William, and when Martin and Ophelia offered their help. In a way, this child has been given to all of us."

This last statement seemed to affect everyone in the room. No one rose to counter Noah.

Mr. Ashford talked quietly with Micah and Martin, then stood beside Noah and Old Saul. "If no one else has anything further to say, I think Noah should close with prayer and we can all go home."

Kurt bowed his head during the prayer. The crisis had passed and had left him dumbfounded. He'd been sure Miss Thurston was going to leave him…leave their town, that is. But there had been a complete turnaround. And he had helped make it happen.

A welter of emotions cannonaded within him. Had he done right to defend her? What would people think? More important, what would *she* think?

Mr. Lang had turned the tide in her favor. Why? Ellen hadn't expected that at all and was even more surprised when many people came forward to shake her hand and peer down at William, who'd slept through it all. She now knew what the Bible meant about going through the crucible and being refined by fire. She felt as if that was exactly what had just happened to her.

The town's attitude toward her and William had changed in just a few moments. What had prompted Mr. Lang, who had been concerned about her desire to keep William since the very night they'd found him, to speak on her behalf? She couldn't help but stare at him from across the room, where she was pleased to see people speaking to him. She hadn't realized until this very moment that usually he was ignored. Her heart seemed to swell for him.

Had the world tilted on its axis?

"Well, you won," Ophelia said, giving her elbow a squeeze. "But raising a child alone won't be easy. You know that, right?"

Ellen wrenched her gaze from Mr. Lang. "I don't expect it to be easy, Ophelia. But I do expect that we can help each other over the coming years."

Ophelia threw her arms around Ellen. "You are truly my dearest cousin." Then Ophelia lowered her voice. "Did Randolph ever tell you why he'd come here?"

"He did," she said, as she stepped out of their hug. "I will tell you about that another time."

Ellen saw that Noah had taken the handles of Old Saul's wheelchair and was preparing to leave. She hurried forward, offering her hands. "Thank you, sir."

He grasped her hands with his, which were gnarled and wrinkled. "God has entrusted you with a child. I will pray you are given the grace to carry this forth."

His words brought unexpected tears. She couldn't speak so she squeezed his hands and then stepped back so his son could push the old preacher outside.

People moved around her, offering their farewells, and she replied politely. But as she waited for Mr. Lang to come and speak to her, she realized that he had left without a word. A lost feeling filled her that she couldn't quite explain.

When she was finally alone again, she shut the school door and secured it. Then she dragged the cradle into her quarters. William, as if on cue, stirred and began whimpering.

"Right on time, young man." She mixed the Horlick's for him and then carried him to the rocker where she hummed to him as he took his night bottle. Suddenly, fatigue overwhelmed her. "We'll sleep well tonight, William."

She closed her eyes and once again saw Mr. Lang rise to his feet in her defense. What had changed his mind? Warmth for him welled up within her but she took herself firmly in hand. Her path had been set.

She had always resolved to pursue an education, not marriage, as most women did. But Holton had somehow weakened or made her forget that for a brief time. Perhaps after losing her parents she had been vulnerable. But now she was herself again. She taught school in Pepin, and a child had been entrusted to her. Therefore, she shouldn't, and wouldn't, interpret Mr. Lang's defense of her as anything more than a change of mind expressed by a caring and sympathetic man. Because she would never be foolish over a man again.

Once had proven to be quite enough, thank you.

Chapter Eleven

In the quiet amber of twilight, Kurt and Johann stood over the outdoor wash basin, cleaning the supper dishes. As they worked, Kurt wrestled with a question: Should he and Johann go with Gunther to the school this evening or not? What did Miss Thurston think of his speaking up for her after he'd held the opposite view to hers? How would she react toward him? Would she want an explanation?

When he recalled his speaking in Miss Thurston's defense at the meeting, his heart flipped up and down like a hooked fish. He'd tried to convince himself that he'd spoken up for her, but in reality, he had to admit that he'd done it because he didn't want Miss Thurston to leave.

The feelings he had for Miss Thurston brought back memories of his broken engagement with Brigitte, making him recall the cause of their breakup. He and Brigitte had been childhood sweethearts. His father's gambling had turned her family against him, but she had remained true.

But when his father had lost everything and then

taken the easy way out, the shame had been too great. Like a metal file, the memories scraped against his peace, shredding it fragment by fragment, leaving him raw and bleeding.

He was becoming enamored of Miss Thurston, though he knew he had no business forming any attachment—spoken or unspoken—to a woman so far above him. Overhead a crow cawed, mocking him.

I must remember who I am here and what I am now.

But even as he thought this, something chafed at him, something that wouldn't let him consider the matter settled. He was a newcomer here, a foreigner, but this land with all its freedom was loosening the old ways of thinking in him.

Gunther stepped outside. "Are you done with the dishes?"

Kurt noted with pride and some apprehension how carefully Gunther was speaking each word. His brother's motivation could not have been more transparent—he wanted to be accepted here, wanted to be American. He wanted to court Amanda Ashford.

Kurt had tried many times to warn Gunther against this distant hope. But why? Maybe Gunther was young enough to lose his accent, to become acceptable to the Americans, to win the Ashfords' approval. What was possible for Gunther might not be possible for him.

"Gunther," Kurt said, his decision made. "I have things to do this evening. I will not go with you." Kurt looked down at Johann, denying the cold loss this brought him. "Will you go to help with little William? Can I trust you to know what to do?"

Johann stood very straight. "I can take care of William. I know how to rock him and hold the bottle." He pulled his wooden horse from his pocket. "And he likes my horse, too."

Kurt let the corners of his mouth rise, let his tension ease. He had two good lads. He looked to Gunther. "You don't need me there, do you?"

"No, but I thought you liked to go with me." Gunther looked puzzled.

Kurt studied his brother's face. Had Gunther noticed his preference for Miss Thurston?

He shrugged as if the matter was of no importance. "I have worked hard today. I need to sharpen my tools." He forced himself to sound convincing. "You are young. It is long walk. You have more energy."

Gunther still looked puzzled but merely lowered his head as if bowing to his brother's decision.

Johann quickly dried the final pan and hurried to Gunther, who had secured his books on a strap hung over his shoulder and was waiting to leave. Kurt watched them go down the path. Part of him strained like a horse at the starting line, strained to follow them. He clamped his lips tight so he didn't call out he'd changed his mind.

Instead, he dragged out a chair and began doing what he'd told Gunther he would do. He began sharpening his tools. The shrill noise of the small grindstone filled his ears and grated his nerves. He suddenly saw himself sitting at home in his village using this same grindstone.

Home…

A sorrow he could never voice seized him tightly and twisted him, as if wringing him. An image he would never be able to banish flashed in his mind, his father's lifeless body, hanging in their barn. He rubbed his eyes, willing the pain away. Would a time come when thinking of home didn't bring piercing, wrenching pain?

The answer rushed to him. When he was with Miss Thurston, the pain was forgotten. Her sweet voice soothed him like no other. The temptation to be with her was a dangerous one. He must be wary or spoil the delicate balance of their friendship. And they were friends. If anything he did or said hinted at courtship, she would withdraw from him. He must watch himself, his words, his manner when with her. But to deny himself the pleasure of being with her was impossible.

"The colonists had no representation, no member in Parliament," Gunther explained earnestly, sitting at the table in Ellen's quarters. "They believed they shouldn't have to pay the taxes England demanded."

Across from him, Ellen tried to keep her mind on Gunther as he explained taxation without representation. Behind her, Johann knelt by the cradle, entertaining William with a stream of chatter about the wooden horse. But neither Gunther nor Johann seemed able to command her complete attention. Why had Mr. Lang stayed away this evening? She'd been so looking forward to thanking him properly for what he'd done.

Had she offended him? Did he regret defending her? Why did his absence bother her?

Mr. Lang's excuse of being tired and needing to stay home was perfectly natural and understandable. But now she was forced to confront the fact that she had begun to look forward to their evenings together.

I cannot allow myself to slip again. I miss seeing Mr. Lang because we've been thrown together so much, that's all.

A jumble of emotions rioted within as she calmly

asked Gunther, "And how did England respond to the colonists' argument?"

"Parliament, the English congress," Gunther replied with an eagerness she loved, "said that the colonists had virtual representation, that Parliament represented all of England and its territories."

Gunther's English had improved so much in such a short time. Though she knew he was not pleased that his accent lingered, his progress lifted her mood. "Exactly right, Gunther. Do you think that made sense?"

Gunther paused to prepare an answer as her mind went back to the question of Mr. Lang. Was her disappointment actually about his absence? Or was it merely that after dealing with children all day, she looked forward to adult conversation? Of course, she spoke with the Ashfords at supper each evening, but she didn't exactly count them as friends.

Mr. Lang is my friend. A startling idea.

"No, it didn't make sense," Gunther answered finally. "I think it was just a way to make a good-sounding excuse. I don't think the men in Parliament thought much about the colonies. They were so far away."

As she nodded in agreement, she wondered, could she consider a man a friend? Single women rarely had men who were friends, not suitors.

But why couldn't she consider Mr. Lang a friend? Just because they were both unmarried didn't mean they couldn't be friends, did it?

Somewhere in the back of her consciousness, a warning bell faintly rang. She ignored it.

On Saturday morning, Martin had come with his pony cart and fetched Ellen and William so Ellen could help Ophelia with the fall canning. Ellen had worn her oldest dress and an older apron. Now Ophelia and she were outside in the quickly warming morning. With a large, long-handled, slotted spoon in hand, Ophelia was dipping tomatoes into a pot of boiling water and setting them to cool on the table outside. Ellen was coring the stems and then slipping the skins off the warm scalded tomatoes and then dropping them into a large pot in preparation for making catsup.

Several feet away on the wild grass, Johann entertained William, who lay on a blanket, kicking his feet vigorously. Johann also kept Ophelia's cheerful toddler, Nathan, from crawling too far away with the help of the Steward's dog. Johann had walked over by himself as planned.

Ellen found herself about to ask her cousin if Mr. Lang would be coming over, too, but she nipped off the thought. Mr. Lang had his own work to do.

"I'm so glad you offered to help," Ophelia repeated, perspiring as she leaned over the boiling water.

"I can see why you needed me." Ellen glanced at the bushels of ripe tomatoes sitting around them. The sight inspired Ellen with a desire to lie down and nap.

"I know it's a lot of tomatoes." Ophelia smiled tartly as she had when they were girls together and up to some mischief. "But I have a bumper crop this year and that might have to stretch over two years. One never knows," she said airily, "what the next harvest will bring. We might have a drought and no tomatoes."

Though grinning, Ellen smothered a sigh. For some reason she couldn't identify, her normal zest for life had diminished over the past week. Everything she did seemed heavy like a chore.

"Ellen, are you all right? You seem down in the dumps." Ophelia slid another two tomatoes into the boiling water and watched them closely.

Ellen tilted her head. She could fool everyone but Ophelia. "You know me too well."

"I would think you would be happy now that it's been decided you can keep William." Ophelia turned the tomatoes and then scooped one up, letting water drain through the spoon.

"I would think so, too." Ellen didn't look up from the basin in her lap where the red skins fell. "Sometimes I can't believe I won. I don't know. Maybe it's the letdown after all the turmoil over my effort to keep him."

Maybe it's because you haven't seen Mr. Lang since the meeting, a voice whispered in her mind.

Ellen ignored it and forged ahead. "Does that make sense? Perhaps a reaction to all that stress?"

"Perhaps." Ophelia flexed her shoulders but didn't look up. "You never told me why Randolph came north."

Yellow-and-black finches twittered and flew from branch to branch, as if gossiping about the two women. "You guessed, didn't you, that Alice sent him?"

Ophelia glanced at Ellen, her face twisted with apprehension. "What did Alice want?"

"Me. She's expecting and has managed to get such a bad reputation that no Irish girl will work for her."

Ophelia made a hissing sound of irritation. "That woman. So you told him no?"

"Of course I did." Ellen went on to reveal how Alice had tried to blackmail her into returning to Galena.

Ophelia was suitably shocked and aggravated. "That woman! Makes me remember why we would never play with her when we were kids. Spoiled crybaby."

Ellen agreed with a nod and then shooed away a fly. "Well, I haven't heard anything since from my brother so we'll just have to wait and see."

At that moment, Johann made a neighing sound as he held his wooden horse above William's face, and the baby gurgled in excitement. As Ellen watched the two, her question about Mr. Lang simply slipped right out of her mouth, as if she had no say in the matter. "Johann, what's your uncle doing today?"

"Harvesting corn with Gunther, miss," Johann called politely while running after Nathan, who was crawling fast toward the surrounding forest.

Of course Mr. Lang was harvesting corn—every man and many women were. She vented her irritation at herself on the tomato in her hand, squeezing it until it spit seeds up onto her cheek.

Ophelia chuckled and handed her a clean rag. "What's that? The tomato's revenge?" she said.

Grinning ruefully, Ellen wiped her cheek and shook her head, frustrated at her foolishness. She remembered such foolishness all too well from when she'd allowed feelings for Holton. She wanted no part of it now.

But the trouble was, it seemed that she no longer had any say in the matter. Mr. Lang refused to leave her mind.

As the morning wore on, the women continued their work. A few times the Stewards' dog rose to its feet and barked. Once it started to head toward the fields, but halted when Ophelia told him to stay. He whimpered on and off, staring toward the distant field where Martin was picking corn. Maybe he just missed his master.

When the first batch of tomatoes was finally simmering outdoors in a large pot, Ophelia glanced at the sun directly overhead.

"I wonder why Martin hasn't come for lunch. He knew I'd be serving a cold meal." She turned to Johann. "Will you run and tell Mr. Steward that I'm going to put out our lunch?"

Johann nodded and jogged away, the dog racing after him.

"He's such a nice boy," Ophelia said, leaning backward, stretching her spine.

Ellen tried not to let her mind drift to his uncle, who was nice, too. She had barely washed her hands and taken off her tomato-smeared apron when Johann came running back.

"Mrs. Steward! Your husband needs you. He can't get up!"

Ellen flew to William, and snatched him from the blanket as Ophelia scooped up Nathan. The two women pelted after Johann toward the farthest edge of the cornfield.

Martin was lying at the end of a row, flat on his back. A large muslin bag filled with corn lay beside him, its contents scattered.

Despite the noon-high sun blazing on her shoulders, the sight of Martin on the ground chilled Ellen.

Ophelia dropped to her knees beside him. "What's wrong? What happened?"

Martin panted. "I don't know. I was picking corn. I heard a noise and turned too fast, I guess. Something snapped in my back. The pain… I couldn't stay on my feet. I fell. I must have lost consciousness. When I came to, I tried to get up, but I can't get up by myself, Ophelia." Fear shuddered in each of the last few words. "I tried to call out but couldn't."

"I will get my uncle!" Johann called over his shoulder, already running back toward the cabin and the trail beyond.

Ellen took charge of both children while Ophelia ran to get thirsty Martin some water to drink. The dog lay next to Martin, his large brown eyes worried. Fear rattled Ellen as she pressed William to her and talked nonsense to Nathan who crawled to his father and sat, patting him.

Then Ophelia appeared with a dipper and a bucket of cold spring water. She knelt beside her husband and gently lifted his head and helped him drink. Then they waited.

Both women were relieved to hear the sounds of men running through the field sometime later. Johann appeared with Mr. Lang and Gunther, and Ellen felt her fear and tensions relax, giving way all at once at the sight of Mr. Lang.

She knew he would be able to help. He was that kind of man.

"Martin is hurt? How?" Kurt asked, panting from running. He focused on Martin, not Miss Thurston, schooling his eyes to obey him with effort.

"I did something stupid," Martin replied, sounding as if merely forcing out each word caused him pain. "I had a full sack of corn. I heard something and twisted. I must have passed out—I came to on my back. Kurt, I tried to get up but the pain…"

Kurt dropped to his knees beside Martin, ignoring

the nearness of Miss Thurston, who stood within a few feet of him. "Can you move your hands and feet?"

Martin complied, gasping as if the movements caused him pain.

Kurt rested a hand on the man's shoulder. "This is good, Martin. You have not caused injury to your spine. You have only pulled a muscle, I think. It will heal with time."

"Listen to Mr. Lang, Martin," Miss Thurston murmured, just behind Kurt. Her voice so close shivered through him. He quelled his quick reaction, forbidding himself even a glance at her.

Martin moaned, sounding both upset and in pain. "But it's harvest. I can't be laid up, flat on my back."

"You do not worry," Kurt said. "Right now we need to get you to your cabin. You cannot spend the rest of the day lying here in the sun."

Martin tried to get up but failed, stifling a groan.

"No," Kurt commanded sharply. "You must stay still or hurt yourself more. We will move you." Kurt looked to Mrs. Steward. "I need a strong blanket."

Ophelia leaped to her feet and ran toward the house.

"I'm so glad you came, Mr. Lang," Miss Thurston said. "There was nothing we could do for him."

"I am glad to help." Kurt rose but did not look at her. He had stayed away from her this week as if doing a penance. He'd hoped his pleasure at being near her would ebb with distance and time, but as he lifted his eyes to hers, he knew that it hadn't. Seeing her now awakened him as if he'd only been half-alive while away from her.

He just hoped it didn't show.

Mrs. Steward ran toward them with a folded navy blue wool blanket in her arms.

Gratefully, he turned away from Miss Thurston to the task at hand. With quick directions, he and Gunther lifted Martin onto the blanket. Using it as a stretcher, they carried him through the cornfield to the cabin.

Inside, Kurt eyed the rope bed. "I think he will be better on the hard floor on a few thick blankets." Ophelia quickly arranged a pallet of blankets and then he and Gunther lowered Martin to the floor.

Martin's face had gone from white to gray, probably from the pain of being moved. "Thank you," he said, panting. His wife dropped to her knees beside him and wrung her hands. Kurt hated to see her so distressed. "You are not to worry, Martin. We will harvest your corn."

Miss Thurston moved closer to him. He wanted to distance himself from her, but couldn't. Everyone had gathered into a circle around the stricken man. The dog lay down again beside his master, whining with what sounded like sympathy.

"How long do you think Martin will be laid up?" Mrs. Steward asked Kurt.

Kurt remembered himself and drew off his hat. "Maybe a week, two weeks."

Martin groaned. "Who will take care of the animals?"

"I will come and stay here," Gunther announced.

"Gunther!" Miss Thurston exclaimed with obvious surprise. Kurt and everyone else turned to look at him, startled.

Gunther reddened at the attention. "Mrs. Steward will need help with her husband. I can lift him and I can do his chores," Gunther said in a tone that announced he would not be deterred.

"Oh, Gunther," Mrs. Steward said, springing to her feet to clasp Gunther's hand. "Thank you. Thank you."

Kurt couldn't press down the pride rising in him. Gunther had been changing over the past weeks and now the difference was unmistakable. His brother had lost the chip on his shoulder, and Kurt and Gunther both had Miss Thurston to thank for that.

"That's very good of you, Gunther," Miss Thurston said with a look of obvious approval. Kurt couldn't help but smile at her then, and she smiled back. Gunther was turning into a fine young man. The fact that Miss Thurston saw it, too, was nearly overwhelming for Kurt.

Miss Thurston moved toward the door, asking Johann to come with her to watch the children. "I must keep working on the catsup. Everything will spoil and be wasted if I don't."

"Ellen, as soon as I see to Martin, I'll bring out the lunch. Mr. Lang, I have enough for all of us."

Kurt watched as Miss Thurston laid William in the cradle outside and Johann set Nathan down on the grass. For a brief moment he watched her stirring the simmering tomatoes and let himself imagine what it would be like if she were…his wife. And a mother to Johann, and even Gunther.

He shook his head to clear his thoughts. He had much work to do and he wasn't needed here. "Can I help?" Kurt asked, saying exactly what he hadn't intended to.

Miss Thurston looked surprised. "What?"

"I am the cook in our house," he said. "Perhaps I can help?"

I should leave now. He didn't move.

She dipped the thermometer into the simmering tomatoes. "It's the right temperature. We need to ladle the sauce into the Mason jars." She gestured toward the line of clean jars covered with clean dishcloths on a bench near the cabin.

He nodded. "I will hold the pot, you will ladle the sauce and seal the jars."

Soon the two of them were working side by side. As they wiped the jar rims with clean rags and then capped them with lids, he was careful not to accidentally brush against her or touch her hands. This trying to keep apart tortured him. Mrs. Steward soon came outside, carrying a tray of sandwiches. Miss Thurston hurried to her side. "How is he?"

"Resting." The wife set the tray on the table and sat on a bench as if the action had taken the last of her strength. She bent her head into her hands. "We didn't need this."

The woman's morose tone moved Kurt. He knew how unexpected disaster dashed hope.

Miss Thurston patted her cousin's back. "We will manage. Gunther has offered to stay and help you. Mr. Lang will harvest your corn. I'll come every evening to do what I can. You're not alone, Ophelia."

When Kurt realized Mrs. Steward was weeping quietly, he stepped away to give her privacy. As he looked at the Steward's cabin, Kurt had to acknowledge that though he had planned to distance himself from Miss Thurston, circumstances had thrown them together once again.

What could this mean? Was he being tested to see if he could keep within the boundaries that separated them? What would happen if he couldn't?

* * *

After the long day of labor at the Steward's had been completed, once more Kurt held out his hand to help Miss Thurston onto Martin's pony cart to take her home. He didn't know what to say so he slapped the reins and started down the path. Darkness cloaked them, though a nearly full moon lit their way. Turmoil over sitting beside her again unsettled him.

William lay asleep in his cradle in the back. Exhausted to his marrow, Kurt wished he could lie down and sleep, too. In addition to helping with canning what they called catsup, jars and jars of the red sauce, he'd shown Gunther how to help Martin move, and he'd brought in several bags of corn and stored it in the corn crib to dry, all after working since dawn.

Crickets chattered, unseen. A mourning dove cooed overhead. Yet the human silence stretching between Kurt and the schoolteacher wasn't the pleasant kind they had begun to share during Gunther's lessons. Tension vibrated between them.

"I can't believe this has happened," Miss Thurston finally said. "Right in the midst of harvest. Martin kept trying to move till you insisted he was making his condition worse, not better. Thank you." She glanced at him sideways. "Thank you, Mr. Lang, for all you have done today."

"Gunther and I will get Martin's crop in. You need not worry."

"I promised Ophelia I'd dig potatoes next Saturday." She sighed, exhaustion in her voice.

"You would dig potatoes?" he asked with surprise.

"My mother always had a kitchen garden. I used to help her with it. I like growing things and picking things. I've never dug potatoes, though. But since I'll probably be invited to eat many of the potatoes Martin has grown, I better be ready to dig some," she added, evidently trying to lighten the mood.

He tried to make the image of Miss Thurston digging potatoes fit, but couldn't. "America is a strange country."

"Why do you say that?"

He shook his head, still baffled. "In Germany, no lady digs potatoes."

She glanced at him, but the low light merely cast her elegant profile in stark shadow. "I am considered a lady because I am of good reputation, nothing more. Ophelia is a lady, Mrs. Whitmore is a lady. If they can dig potatoes, why can't I?"

He shrugged, unable and unwilling to voice his discomfort with this idea. "I hope I am not seen as pretentious," she added. Her tone had stiffened.

"What does that word mean?" he asked cautiously, afraid he had offended her.

"*Pretentious* describes a person who is self-important, a show-off."

"No, you are not pretentious," he said, sounding out the word new to him. "But you are a lady—a fine lady."

She appeared to give thought to his words. "I think I see what you're trying to say. But this is America. That very first day, when you drove me home, you and I talked about the Grants. Remember?"

"I remember." *How could I forget that day?*

"In the past, Mrs. Grant was the wife of a man who ran a leather shop with his father. Now she is the wife of the president. Here, people aren't constrained by society to stay in one place or one rank. We can occupy many different stations in one life. What matters is what we can do, what difference we make in this world."

He didn't respond, torn between the hope that her startling words, this new idea, ignited in him, and the conviction that they did not apply to him. *Maybe that is true of Americans, Miss Thurston, but they will never think of me as anything but a foreigner.*

"You are new here and people look down on you because of that." He sensed her leaning forward a bit to see him better. "But it won't always be that way."

Swinging around to face her, he voiced a sound of disbelief. "No?" Even he was surprised by the sarcasm that laced the word, trickling sourly through him.

"No," she repeated with emphasis, ignoring his tone. "Look at Abraham Lincoln. He was born in a log cabin, worked as a farmer, then a lawyer, then became president. So you weren't born in this country—so what?"

"You are kind, but that I was born in another county will never be forgotten."

"You are building your reputation here in this country every day, Mr. Lang," Miss Thurston said, sitting straighter. "Don't you see that? You've been given a brand-new start."

He'd left Germany exactly for that purpose, yet somehow, inside, he had yet to change, heal. He looked at Miss Thurston beside him, and for a brief moment, he actually considered telling her about what had happened at home, what had driven him to leave his country.

But he knew he could not. She would never look at him the same way again.

He faced forward again and fell silent. The hope that had been warring inside him with despair folded inward, unequal to the contest. Hope only set one up for pain.

Chapter Twelve

Sunday morning had come. Ellen's back and arms ached from the day of making catsup. She finished dressing William in a baby shift Ophelia had made for him and looked at herself in the mirror to check that she was presentable. She felt a pang over how tired she looked, and found herself thinking of what Mr. Lang would see when he looked at her.

She turned hastily away from the mirror and walked into the schoolroom for worship. There, she paused. She usually sat with the Stewards, and now realized everyone would notice their absence. She must be tired, or else she would have considered that already. Would she be the one to give the bad news?

She couldn't resist glancing toward the back to see whether Kurt and Johann had arrived this morning. Perhaps they stayed home to help Gunther with the Stewards. Or perhaps she had somehow offended Mr. Lang last night.

She approached Noah Whitmore as he prepared for the service. "Are you aware of Martin's accident?" she asked in a low voice. At his dismayed denial, she told him what had happened yesterday.

Noah looked shocked. "I'll ask for prayer. Thank you for telling me, Miss Thurston." Then he glanced at the wall clock. "I need to begin."

Ellen settled down beside Sunny Whitmore, who had obviously overheard Ellen. But she said nothing to Ellen as her husband opened the worship service.

Unhappy over Mr. Lang's absence, Ellen let William nap on her lap. She patted him, noticing how he was becoming chubby. For a moment, her heart sang with silent thanksgiving for him. She held in all the blessing of being given this wonder, this child.

The service progressed to the end, when at last Noah opened the time for intercessory prayer. He announced the news about Martin and a collective sound of dismay went through the congregation.

"What can we do to help?" Gordy Osbourne, the church deacon, asked.

"He'll need help getting in his crop," Noah began.

Ellen rose. "Pastor, Kurt Lang has already volunteered to bring in Martin's crop. Since he is the nearest neighbor, he's the one who came to help us with Martin."

An odd silence followed, a prickly momentary pause as Ellen sat again. Then Gordy brought up another need. "Ophelia, that is Mrs. Steward, will need help with chores and such."

Ellen raised her hand, her mood lifting. "Gunther Lang volunteered to stay with the Stewards and do Martin's chores, as well as help with his care. I think the Langs must all be at the Steward's now, helping my cousins. That's most likely why they are not here this morning."

Another pause came, filled with some ominous meaning Ellen couldn't read.

"I'm glad to hear that," Noah said. "The Langs are the closest neighbors to the Stewards—"

"But they're foreigners," a man in the back objected. "Do the Stewards want them around?"

Anger ignited and blazed within Ellen, nearly consuming her, tying her throat into a knot. She was astounded. And yet, given the conversation she and Mr. Lang had had just last night, she should not have been. In fact, she should have expected this.

Noah looked distressed, his head tilting down with disfavor. "The Langs have always been good neighbors to the Stewards and I don't know what being foreign has to do with one Christian helping another. The Langs have never missed a Sunday at worship until today. In fact, Kurt helped build this very school that you are sitting in now," Noah said, gesturing to the walls around them. "I think as we pray today we need to remember that in God, there is no Greek or Jew, slave or free, man or woman. To him, we are all loved and valued the same. He sees no difference between us." He held up both hands. "Let's pray for the Stewards and the others who can't be with us today."

The fire of Ellen's anger began to die down, thanks to Noah. She hoped his words would give the good people of Pepin something to think about. Because their words had certainly given her something to think about.

She'd told Mr. Lang the community would come to accept him. Now she hoped she'd told him the truth.

* * *

Sitting at the Ashford's table for Sunday dinner, Ellen tried to keep her mind from wondering how Ophelia and Martin were faring today. After the meal, she intended to walk out and see for herself. Maybe Amanda would watch William for her. Right now her little one lay on a blanket nearby, trying to roll over.

Mrs. Ashford finished loading the table with dishes and removed her apron. The delicious aromas of bacon in the green beans and butter melting on corn bread started Ellen's mouth watering. Mr. Ashford said grace, and then his wife motioned for him to start passing the bowls. She glanced at Ellen.

"I'm so sorry to hear about Martin's unfortunate accident. But I was surprised to hear the Stewards had become thick with the Dutch."

Ellen's fork stilled as she stared at the storekeeper's wife.

"Miss Thurston, I'm glad you told everyone about Gunther volunteering to help the Stewards," Amanda said, glancing sideways at each parent in turn. "People are so mean to him just because he wasn't born here. What does that matter?"

Both Amanda's parents reacted with deep disapproving frowns. Mrs. Ashford shook her head, her nose elevated. Something snapped inside Ellen.

"Yes, Amanda, and they're mean to Mr. Lang and Johann, too. Why? Just because they speak with an accent?"

Mrs. Ashford replied stiffly, "It's because they aren't Americans."

"Gunther is going to become an American citizen,"

Amanda piped up. "He's studying with Miss Thurston so he'll be ready to take the test to be a citizen."

Both her parents looked at Amanda with startled disapproval.

Ellen's heart beat faster for the girl. To distract the parents, Ellen rushed on, "My great-grandfather, Patrick, came from Ireland as an indentured servant just before the Revolution. I'm sure he faced the same prejudice as immigrants now. But we are not ashamed of him."

"You're part Irish?" Mrs. Ashford said, sounding surprised. The unchanging prejudice against the Irish was particularly sharp.

"Yes, I am." Ellen had lost her appetite but she forced herself to begin eating.

"But he was your great-grandfather," Mr. Ashford pointed out. "That's a long time ago."

Ellen sighed inwardly. Maybe she had indeed misinformed Mr. Lang last night when she suggested that the people of Pepin would come to accept him. Would these people ever give Mr. Lang or Gunther or Johann a chance, or would the Langs carry the burden of this unreasonable bias for the rest of their lives?

She wanted nothing more than to find a way to help the community see how sweet Johann was, and how Gunther was growing into a fine young man…

…and what a wonderful, generous person Mr. Kurt Lang was. As she thought of him, his handsome face came to mind, wearing one of his endearing smiles. She thought of how when she'd walked through town with William recently, people hadn't frowned at her as before but they hadn't come up and cooed over him like they did over the other babies in town. But Mr. Lang always greeted her and tickled William's chin to make him grin. His kind nature always came through to her.

Mr. Lang and his family didn't deserve the shoddy treatment they usually received. Perhaps it was time she came up with a plan.

Several days later, Ellen stood at the front of the schoolroom, a tad buoyant. She had some good news for her students that she couldn't wait to share.

"Children, do you remember when I told you about my desire to have a spelling bee in the spring? Well, I have received a letter from the school at Bear Lake." She held it up. "The teacher writes that their school will participate in our spelling bee."

The children applauded, and their excitement cheered her.

"Since we now have one school committed to the spring spelling bee, today we will formally begin practicing. To prepare us for competition, we will form two teams and spell against each other. Starting with Amanda, count off by twos, please."

Amanda announced, "One!"

The boy beside her counted off, "Two." The separating count ended with the first row where Johann sat among the first graders.

"Now number ones go to my right and number twos go to my left. Stand against the opposite walls." She motioned with her hands. As the children went to their places, Ellen overheard one boy say to another. "Bad luck. We got the Dutch kid on our team. You watch. We'll lose."

The words hit her and she experienced the strange feeling of being drawn back like stone in a slingshot.

She opened her mouth to reprimand the boy, but telling people how they should think or feel never worked well. A better idea quickly came to mind, which would send a strong message without her having to say a word to him.

"The captain of team one will be Amanda Ashford. The captain of team two will be Johann Lang."

A few members of team two groaned. She cast them a wordless scold and they lowered their chins, and then gazed directly at the boy who had made the rude comment about Johann. He, too, looked at the floor.

She opened her copy of *Webster's American Spelling Book* as she explained the rules. "If a team member misspells a word, he or she will sit down. The team with the last person standing wins. I'll begin with team one. Amanda, step forward, repeat the word I give you, then spell it, and repeat the word, please. Your word is *zeal*."

Amanda stepped forward, standing very straight. "Zeal. *Z-e-a-l*. Zeal."

"Correct! You may shift to the end of your row." Ellen smiled and tried to look cheerful and not too serious. This should be fun, too. She turned to Johann. "Your first word is *kin*."

Johann chewed his lower lip. Finally the girl standing next to him shoved him forward. "Kin," Johann parroted, staring at the floor. "*K...i...n*. Kin."

Ellen's heart lifted with pride as well as relief. Johann's face beamed. "Correct! Please move as Amanda did," she said, trying to sound as neutral as possible.

She noticed that many in Johann's row looked startled. *We'll show them, Johann.* How she wished Kurt— Mr. Lang—were here to see his nephew's victory. She could practically hear his deep musical voice congratulating Johann.

Unable to stop from smiling, she turned to the next student in team one and pronounced the next word as she wondered if perhaps this spelling bee had even more potential than she realized.

On Saturday, Kurt paused where he stood on Martin's land, listening to the voices around him. Miss Thurston had indeed come to dig potatoes. Since just after noon, he had been picking Martin's corn and stewing over what he must say to Miss Thurston.

Nearby, Johann and Mrs. Steward also dug potatoes. The storekeeper's daughter had brought lunch and then stayed to care for the children. She sat on a blanket with the babies in the shade, close to where Gunther was picking corn. Kurt hadn't missed their frequent exchange of glances. Or the girl's innocent blushes.

Fleetingly he recalled being a child, so carefree, so unaware of tragedy. An innocent time in life. Or it should be. He thought of Johann, who faced challenges here that Kurt had never had to face. And he was concerned that Johann being captain of a spelling bee team was only going to make things harder for him.

Kurt had hoped for a few moments to speak to Miss Thurston but no opportunity had presented itself. He twisted off another rough cob of corn and dropped it in his nearly full sack. When could he get her to himself for a moment?

Then his wish was granted. Gunther excused himself to go check on Martin. When Mrs. Steward rose to go along with him, Amanda called Johann to watch the children while she prepared a bottle for William. Johann ran to the shady spot, eager to play. Kurt saw his opportunity and forced himself to walk over to Miss Thurston.

She sat back on her heels and looked up. "Mr. Lang, what can I do for you?"

She had a smudge of dirt on her nose and across one cheek. In spite of this, and though wearing an old dress and apron, she appeared as elegant as ever. He wrapped up all his foolish feelings and put them away.

"Miss Thurston, I am glad you choose Johann to be captain, but…"

"But?" she prompted.

"Maybe people will not like this and make trouble for Johann."

She rose to face him, a militant gleam in her eye. "What kind of trouble?"

His inability to put his thoughts into words chafed his nerves. Or perhaps it was merely the nearness of her. "They will call him names" was the best he could mutter.

She tilted her head and considered him. He felt his face warm.

"Mr. Lang, that will only happen if he does a poor job spelling. If he does a good job, quite the opposite will happen. He will rise in their estimation. I suggest you go over his weekly spelling list every evening. I know this is harvest but before bed—"

"We do already," he said somewhat gruffly. Why did he have to notice how her hair had slipped down the back of her neck, and how, from her working in the sun, two tiny golden freckles had popped up on her nose?

"Then I don't think you have anything to worry about." She smiled. "Johann is doing quite well."

Evidently she was unaware that Johann doing well

might only make others sharpen their claws. He didn't want to point this out, spoil her faith in her students. Without another word to her, he turned to carry his bag of corn to the corn crib near the cabin.

His head was full of worry for Johann—till he heard a girl's giggle. Uneasy, he halted at the point where the cornfield gave way to the clearing and scanned his surroundings.

To his right, just in the cover of the surrounding forest stood Gunther and the storekeeper's daughter. She pressed her back against the tree and Gunther rested a hand above her head, leaning toward her.

Aggravation and alarm vied within Kurt. He had ordered Gunther to put Amanda Ashford out of his mind. He was too young, and her parents would make a big noise if they heard about their daughter and that "Dutch" boy. Kurt nearly called out to Gunther, but something stopped him.

Things with Gunther had been much better at home. Did he want to risk this new harmony just because Gunther was stealing a moment with Amanda?

At that instant, Mrs. Steward solved the problem by coming around the cabin toward the fields. She waved to him. "I'm bringing water for us!"

He walked to meet her. Out of the corner of his eye, he noted the young couple separate and disappear, probably to reappear far from each other in a few moments. "Good. I will just add this to the crib and be right back."

Mrs. Steward halted and poured him a cup of water. "Wait. After you dump the corn, would you drop in on Martin? I think he'd like a man to talk to."

Kurt downed the cold water in a single draft and, refreshed, handed her back the cup. Though he wanted to make every working minute count—who knew when rain would come and make the fields muddy and the corn wet?—he nodded to her request. He understood loneliness, since he lived with it daily. The least he could do was go talk to Martin.

He dumped his sack of corn into the crib and then secured its door against scavengers. He walked to the cabin, his muscles still warm from the work. Sitting down would feel good.

He stopped in the open doorway, sorting through his thoughts, choosing something safe to discuss with Martin.

"Kurt," Martin greeted him with evident pleasure. "How is the harvest coming?"

An easy subject. "I think you have a fine yield. The soil is good here."

Martin grinned, moved slightly and grimaced. "I'm sorry to make double work for you."

"It is no trouble. You would do the same for me."

Martin nodded. "How's Ellen?"

"Ellen?" Why had Martin asked him that? "She is digging potatoes."

"I see. That's all you have to say about my wife's pretty cousin?"

Kurt stared at Martin.

"You think Ophelia and I haven't seen how you look at her sometimes when you think nobody is looking?"

Kurt tried to deny this but his tongue tangled up and nothing to the purpose came out.

"Don't be so shy. I know Ellen has declared that she isn't interested in marriage, but…"

When Martin's voice trailed off, Kurt studied him. "But?" he prompted finally.

"Sometimes a woman gets swept off her feet by a man with a glib tongue," Martin said, not enlightening Kurt very much. "I think Ellen is getting over…something like that. I probably shouldn't be saying anything. It's her business, not mine." Martin appeared pained by his suggestion.

A man with a glib tongue? That gave Kurt some idea of why Ellen held herself aloof sometimes. "I understand," Kurt said, though of course he really didn't. "I think another two days and I'll have your corn in."

Martin looked relieved at the switch back to farm talk.

Soon Kurt excused himself and headed back to the cornfield, turning over in his mind Martin's words about his cousin. Kurt had thought Martin would be against his interest in Miss Thurston, but he hadn't sounded unsympathetic. What should Kurt make of that?

Why did life have to be so complicated? All he wanted was to raise Gunther and Johann and live a quiet life, free of gossip and conflict. What was wrong with that?

Well, to start with, in all honesty, that *wasn't* all he wanted.

Before turning his attention to getting in Martin's corn, he looked across the field to where Miss Thurston was digging, giving in to bittersweet temptation.

Chapter Thirteen

The Sunday worship had finished and outside people were chatting, or climbing into wagons and carts to head home. Kurt had brought Mrs. Steward and little Nathan with him, and now he waited for them alone beside his wagon. After the closing prayer, Mrs. Steward had been surrounded by people who wanted a firsthand and detailed report on her husband's recovery.

Johann mingled with the other children. Since today was the Sabbath, none of them could run or play or swing but they could talk and tease quietly. Kurt couldn't see Gunther, which of course made him think that Gunther was with Amanda.

"I wonder why Miss Thurston doesn't put that Dutchman in his place." A woman's sharp voice from the other side of his wagon hit Kurt like an arrow through his heart.

"Maybe she doesn't realize that he's making up to her," said another woman.

"Humph. No woman is that naive. You heard him speak up about that baby she'd taken in. I think she encouraged him. Why else would he have done that?"

Kurt cringed. What he had most feared was happening. His association with Miss Thurston was harming her reputation.

"I wonder if that's why she chose his nephew to head up one of the spelling teams at school."

"Maybe that's just for practice, not the competition. I'm sure she wouldn't put a foreigner forward at the big spelling bee in the spring, would she?"

The other woman sighed. "Who knows what she would do."

For a moment, Kurt hoped they wouldn't see him as they came around the side of his wagon. But as they came abreast of him, they glanced his way and shock registered on their faces. In return, anger boiled up inside him. Covering this, he nodded slowly at the women, touching the brim of his hat as their faces reddened. They flashed him false smiles and gathered their skirts to hurry toward their husbands and their wagons.

His body radiated heat like a torch. *People are talking about me and the schoolteacher.* Hadn't he been flogged enough by gossip and whispering in Germany? Must he also endure it here?

He'd been right to be concerned that people would gossip about Johann being chosen as captain. And he was right to fear that Gunther's infatuation with Amanda would soon be noticed and spark more gossip. But never in his worst nightmares had he thought people would link him with Miss Thurston in a romantic way. Being coupled with him would surely do her no favors.

As Miss Thurston approached him with William in her arms, Kurt suddenly felt as if every eye around the clearing was on him.

"I'm going home with Ophelia," she said.

He knew Miss Thurston was waiting for him to help her up onto the bench yet he found he couldn't touch her.

"Let me get Johann," he said sharply, stepping away from her. He hated himself for such a display of poor manners, but he had no idea how else to save her reputation.

"Johann," he said as he approached the boy, "it is time we leave."

Johann looked unhappy but, waving to his friends, he joined Kurt. "My team is studying spelling. We are going to win again."

Kurt glanced at his nephew's shining face.

My team. We are.

Dismay and gratitude warred in his heart. Was it possible Miss Thurston was right, and that Johann was being accepted? *And I left her standing by the wagon.*

They arrived back at the wagon and found Mrs. Steward and Miss Thurston already seated on the wagon bench. Gunther sent Kurt a confused look. "I helped the ladies up."

"*Danke.* Thank you, Gunther." Kurt walked around and got himself up on the bench without looking at the women while Johann climbed in back with Gunther. Kurt untied the reins and started the team off toward home.

As he drove, he couldn't help but wonder if the two women he'd overheard were saying what everybody else in town was already whispering. He swiped at his perspiring forehead with his sleeve. He knew exactly what he must do to silence the gossips. He hated the very thought of it, but he'd been left with no recourse but to gently distance himself from Miss Thurston.

He owed her that much.

* * *

On Tuesday afternoon, Ellen was standing at the front of her classroom, listening to the second graders reading aloud from *McGuffey's Reader,* so happy for just another routine day. Then Mrs. Ashford burst through the school doors.

"We need Johann!" she shouted. She grabbed the boy by the hand and yanked him to his feet, dragging him behind her like a kite tail. "It's an emergency!"

Half the students also jumped to their feet.

"What is it?" Ellen called to the woman's back, her pulse racing suddenly.

Mrs. Ashford didn't reply, holding on to Johann and running outside.

"Amanda!" Ellen said, halting the girl who looked ready to follow her mother. "Come forward! Children, stay where you are and do whatever Amanda tells you to. Disobedience will not be tolerated." Ellen swished past as the girl moved quickly to the front of the class.

What could possibly cause Mrs. Ashford to require Johann? Ellen reached the town's street within minutes. A Conestoga wagon sat in the middle of the street, oxen drinking at the water trough in front of the General Store.

The blacksmith and Mr. Ashford stood beside the wagon looking troubled. Ellen approached them, trying to calm her breathing. "What's wrong?"

"It's a bad business," Mr. Ashford replied. "We've sent for the preacher, but you go on inside and help my wife, please. The…woman is distraught."

The woman? And why the hesitation? She tried to peer into the wagon, but Mr. Ashford forestalled her with a raised hand. "Don't look."

His words pushed her back as if he'd shoved her. He was clearly shielding her from something he thought unfit for a lady. She hurried inside and found Mrs. Ashford sitting by the cold stove, patting a weeping woman's hand. Three boys like stair steps huddled behind the weeping woman.

Johann was in the center of it all, speaking to the stranger in German.

Ellen tried to still her qualms and sat in the chair opposite the woman. "Mrs. Ashford, what's happened?"

"I'm afraid that this poor woman stopped for help. Her husband was ill. Mr. Ashford couldn't understand her but she took his hand and drew him outside. When he climbed into the wagon, he found that the poor man had already expired."

From what she'd seen outside, Ellen had anticipated something like this but still couldn't hold back a gasp. "She doesn't speak English?"

"Barely any. That's why I came for the Dutch…for Johann. I didn't know how to tell her."

Ellen hated that a seven-year-old boy had been given the task of informing a woman that her husband had succumbed to death. But necessity often forced youngsters to accept responsibilities they were too young to carry. How was the boy?

Ellen noted his unusual crestfallen expression. She touched his arm. "Johann, tell the woman that the town will help her. Mr. Ashford has sent someone to fetch our pastor."

"Yes, indeed. We must help her," Mrs. Ashford agreed, wiping her own eyes.

Ellen realized that the storekeeper's wife was feeling

the woman's suffering. Some things cut across the barriers of language and nationality. "What is her name?"

"She is Mrs. Bollinger," Johann said, "Marta Bollinger from Switzerland."

"Where was she bound?" Ellen asked.

Johann asked the woman and then replied, "New Glarus."

"Why, that's way southeast of us," Mrs. Ashford exclaimed. "They should have gone east when they reached the Wisconsin River."

Johann translated this. The widow sobbed, rocking in her misery. Her children huddled closer to her.

"Johann, I think it's better not to ask her any more questions," Ellen instructed. "Mrs. Ashford, I think some chamomile tea might calm the lady."

"Of course!" The storekeeper's wife leaped to her feet. "And I'll bring some food down, too. Won't take me a moment."

Ellen was glad she'd come. She would make sure no one said anything unfeeling or unkind to the poor woman. Johann talked gently to the children in German, but the three boys said little in return. The eldest looked to be only around the same age as Johann. Moving nearer, Ellen patted the woman's back, praying for her.

Soon Mrs. Ashford bustled in with a large tray of tea, thick slices of fresh bread, pale butter and golden honey for the family.

"Danke" was all the woman said, tears still washing down her face. She tried to nibble at the food. The boys murmured their thanks, too, and they ate as if starved. Mrs. Ashford had just returned with another tray with sliced apple cake when Noah Whitmore arrived.

And Kurt Lang, just behind him.

Ellen's heart leaped at the sight of him. Kurt would be able to comfort the woman.

"Is this the new widow?" Noah asked gravely, doffing his hat.

"Yes," Mrs. Ashford said, looking truly saddened. "You brought Mr. Lang with you."

Ellen was pleased to hear the obvious relief in Mrs. Ashford's voice.

"Kurt says he will translate for me. I think it's better to have an adult address this sensitive situation."

"Of course." Mrs. Ashford wiped away a tear herself. "It's just so sad."

At this moment, a woman with a basket over her arm entered the store, jingling the bell, startling them. Mrs. Ashford hurried to steer the customer away from the knot around the cold stove. Ellen stepped back also but stayed nearby because she didn't want the woman to be surrounded only by men. Johann moved to stand with the three little boys.

Noah sat on one side of the widow and Kurt on the other. "Has she been told her husband is dead?" Noah asked Johann.

"No," Johann said, sounding scared. "I thought it better for my uncle to tell her. He would know what to say. Her name is *Frau* Marta Bollinger."

Ellen looked at Kurt. When he met her gaze, she wanted to reach out and comfort him. The task before him was an dreadful one. But she knew he had the strength and heart to do it. And apparently, so did other people in Pepin.

Kurt nodded to Johann and then grasped the woman's hand. "*Frau* Bollinger, my name is Kurt Lang," he said in German. "I came to live here this spring. This man is Noah Whitmore. He is the pastor here. I am very sorry but I'm afraid your husband is dead."

The woman bent her head into her hands, sobbing. *"Nein, nein..."*

Noah gently claimed her other hand. "Tell her we'll take care of everything. And she isn't to fear being in want. She has our deepest sympathy."

Kurt translated this and patted the woman's hand. He was aware of Miss Thurston hovering nearby, her sympathy evident in her expression. He wished he could turn to her to help him comfort this stranger. She would know just what to say. But he had promised himself he would not do anything to add to the gossip about them.

"What will we do now?" *Frau* Bollinger asked Kurt, near hysteria. "I have no idea how..." She shut her mouth, obviously trying to stay in control.

Kurt did not know how a burial was handled here. He knew how death was dealt with when one had a church and a churchyard, a home and a family. He turned to Noah. After Noah reassured Kurt that all would be done as it should be, he rose and went out to talk to Mr. Ashford. Miss Thurston took Noah's place beside the woman, her pretty face drawn in deep concern. She murmured soft, comforting words to *Frau* Bollinger.

To witness Miss Thurston being so kind to this woman reminded him that he must keep his distance from her. Kindness could move any heart and he needed to keep his own far from Miss Thurston. He focused his attention on the widow as they began to help her calm herself to face her husband's final resting. Bad memories of funerals flowed through Kurt's mind, stirring up a pain too deep for words. He noticed behind him that even Mrs. Ashford spoke to the customer in hushed tones. His sympathy went out to this woman, a stranger in a strange land.

After all that had taken place since Mrs. Ashford had come running into her school, Ellen felt dazed. Noah and the Ashfords had sent for people, and the poor man had been laid out and buried on land Mr. Lang offered. Now Ellen, the Ashfords, the Langs, the Stewards, the Whitmores with the Bollingers stood on the gentle green hillside where they had laid Joachim Bollinger to rest. Around them the maples blazed scarlet, bright spots amid the sorrow.

Ellen had already decided what she would do, and now was the time to announce it. "I'll take Mrs. Bollinger and her sons home with me."

Everyone turned toward her.

"But you don't speak their language," Mrs. Ashford objected.

"I was hoping that Mr. Lang would permit Johann to stay with me to translate. That would make it easier for her sons, too."

As everyone simply stared at her in disbelief, a host of melancholy black birds swooped skyward, their strident calls filling the air.

"I'm offering," Ellen said, raising her voice, "because staying with someone unmarried will be easier for her, and because I have plenty of room." This was true since most families lived in one-room cabins with a loft; adding another family would crowd any host family.

Ellen glanced to Mr. Lang but he looked away. This cost her more than she wanted to acknowledge. She suddenly realized that throughout this trying incident, he'd kept his distance. She wondered why, and was this just because of this situation or something else?

"Well," Noah said, "in light of the language barrier, if Mr. Lang was married, I would suggest he host them. But yes, I think you're right." He paused, probably to see if there were any other offers. None came. "Kurt, would you tell the widow that Miss Thurston has offered her a place to stay. Unless she has some objection."

The woman, looking only half-alive, listened to Mr. Lang. She merely nodded and murmured, *"Danke."*

Ellen moved closer and gripped her hand, trying to comfort her without words. *God, help this woman.*

In worship that Sunday, Ellen didn't sit in her usual place beside her cousin. She sat with her houseguests, the widow and her children, wanting to help them through this crucible of being on display. All too well she recalled her first few weeks here when she endured being the center of attention. Not a pleasant memory.

With William asleep on her lap, Ellen sat on one side of Marta Bollinger and Mr. Lang sat on the other. Gunther sat on the other side of Ellen, then Marta's three sons and finally Johann. People continued to gawk at the widow and her sons. Ellen wished people here would behave in a more mannerly way. Didn't they know staring was impolite?

Marta had donned mourning, and the black of her dress set off her very fair skin and flaxen hair. Several times over the past few days, the woman's beauty had overwhelmed Ellen. For some reason, Marta's beauty pinched at her, and Ellen was not proud of that.

From the front of the room, Noah brought his sermon to its end. Then he glanced toward the rear bench.

"I'm sure you've all heard about the widow and her sons. Miss Thurston has told me of the many kindnesses shown this bereaved family. I want to thank everyone who has brought food to the schoolhouse for them. And a special thanks to the Ashfords, and to Miss Thurston."

Mr. Lang translated what Noah said to Marta, who whispered back to him. Mr. Lang rose. "Mrs. Bollinger says thank you everyone for your kindness in her loss. She told me her husband has a cousin in New Glarus. That was where they were headed. She still wants to go there. I think she will need someone to go with her." Mr. Lang sat down.

The thought that he might volunteer stung Ellen, and she wrestled her feelings under control.

"Thank you, Mr. Lang. Please tell Mrs. Bollinger we'll figure out who will go with her—"

Gunther surprised Ellen by rising. "I can take her. I speak her language." The young man reddened as he spoke.

"Thank you for offering," Noah said. "We will discuss this with Mr. Lang and Mrs. Bollinger. Let's pray."

Soon everyone had spilled out into the schoolyard to enjoy the sunny October day and to tender their condolences to Marta. Ellen stood near the widow. She couldn't stop herself from watching Kurt translating for Marta. The two stood so close. Ellen tried to quiet her edginess. What was it she was feeling? Could it possibly be…jealousy?

Finally, everyone finished offering sympathy through Mr. Lang. The Ashfords had invited Ellen and her guests to Sunday dinner. Kurt and Gunther headed home. Though stung over Kurt leaving without speaking directly to her, Ellen walked with her guests to the General Store and up the familiar back staircase.

When they entered the upstairs quarters, Mrs. Ashford called for Ellen to help her. Ellen left Johann with the Bollingers and entered the kitchen. "How can I be of help?"

Mrs. Ashford motioned for her to come close and whispered into her ear, "I have come up with the perfect solution for Mrs. Bollinger and her sons."

"Oh?" Ellen whispered, too.

"Mr. Lang should propose to her."

Ellen gasped, shards of surprise shooting through her. Her first instinct was to insist that it was a terrible, terrible idea. But she found she could not utter a word.

"I know it's not the usual. But just think—when will another Dutch woman come to Pepin? Mr. Lang would have a wife who understands him and three more sons to help with the work."

Ellen, reeling from this unpleasant shock, turned her back to Mrs. Ashford. She knew it was rude but without a word, she went to the dining table and sat.

The meal went by in a blur. Ellen struggled against the ugly undertow of jealousy, her cheeks flushed and warm. She'd experienced this same resentment and shock the first time Holton had come calling and taken Cissy out for a stroll instead of her. And now she faced it again.

Why am I feeling this way? I don't intend to marry. Mr. Lang has made no advances toward me. This is too foolish for words. I refuse to feel this way.

Her turbulent emotions paid absolutely no heed.

"Did you notice how Gunther offered to help Mrs. Bollinger?" Amanda asked.

Ellen came back fully into the flow of conversation. Amanda's parents had pokered up so Ellen replied, "Yes, Gunther is very thoughtful."

"Yes, he is," Amanda stated with emphasis.

Then Marta spoke to Johann, and Johann turned to everyone and said, "Mrs. Bollinger would like to know if there is any way she could travel south on the river with her wagon and team. It would be quicker and safer than by land. I can tell," Johann added, "she wants to go to her family soon."

"That's understandable," Mr. Ashford said. "Tell her that barges dock here sometimes. She must be packed and ready."

"Does she have funds for the fare?" Mrs. Ashford asked.

The widow replied that she had some funds left.

The rest of the dinner passed with conversation about the weather, the rising prices, the news of unrest in the South between blacks and whites. Would the trouble between North and South ever end? Ellen tried to participate in a normal fashion but couldn't concentrate. Images of Mr. Lang leaning close to Marta bedeviled her.

Afterward, Johann and the boys went outside to wade in the shallows near shore, looking for shells. Claiming William, Marta settled into the rocking chair—holding the baby seemed to soothe her sorrow. And Ellen saw Amanda slip away, having a good idea of whom she was going to meet. Gunther.

As Ellen helped Mrs. Ashford by drying the dishes, the storekeeper's wife wore a deep frown. Ellen surmised she was worried about Amanda and Gunther, too. But her next words took Ellen by surprise.

"I know you think my idea of Mr. Lang marrying this widow is foolish, but it isn't."

Ellen nearly dropped the gilt-edged china plate she was drying. "Why would you think she would remarry so soon?"

"I know she is recently bereaved but marriages of convenience happen all the time. I mean, when will another Dutch woman come through for Mr. Lang to marry?"

Ellen startled herself by speaking her mind. "You think then that no English-speaking woman would marry Mr. Lang?" Heat flashed through Ellen at her own words. *Why did I say that?*

"Well, most American women don't want to marry foreigners."

Ellen struggled, holding back words.

"I mean, yes, he is very good-looking, but that accent." Mrs. Ashford shook her head as she scrubbed another dish within an inch of its life.

"I don't think Marta has any desire to marry anybody." In the midst of her own upheaval, Ellen tried to say the words as unemotionally as she could.

"Well, I will tell you my mother's story. She was orphaned at only thirteen when both her parents died," Mrs. Ashford said. "She had three younger brothers to provide for. When a neighbor much older than she offered marriage and a home for her brothers, she accepted. Sometimes a woman does what she must for her family."

Ellen heard the fierceness in Mrs. Ashford's voice. "She was very brave."

"Yes, and the marriage turned out to be a good one.

I loved my father and my older uncles. You may think I'm unfeeling but life isn't always pretty and polite."

Ellen touched the woman's shoulder. "You're right, of course. Life throws us surprises, both pleasant and unpleasant." The words vibrated in Ellen's mind.

"I just hope that Amanda comes to her senses. Ned and I see how she moons over that Dutch boy."

"His name is Gunther." Ellen maintained a calm tone. "And don't girls fall in and out of calf love many times? She's only fourteen. Surely you've seen how Gunther is turning into a fine young man."

Mrs. Ashford paused in her scrubbing. "I hope you're right."

Ellen bit back all she wanted to say in favor of Gunther. She knew that telling people what they should think and how they should feel never prospered. Besides, given all the turmoil she was experiencing herself this afternoon, she was in no position to lecture anyone.

She wondered what Mr. Lang would think of the possibility of a marriage of convenience with Marta Bollinger. She closed her eyes in denial. The very thought of it caused her stomach to clench.

Chapter Fourteen

For late October, the Monday was golden and balmy. Ellen even had a few of the school windows open. So unfortunately for her state of mind, she could hear Mr. Lang and Marta speaking German as he helped her load the wagon with her belongings. The sound of them chatting in a language she couldn't understand grated on her nerves. She hated this evidence of weakness and worked hard not to reveal it. After everything that Mrs. Bollinger had been through, she deserved kindness, not jealousy.

She brought her attention back to the third graders, who were practicing adding and carrying over on their slates. "Add 12 plus 19," Ellen instructed. "Raise your hand when you have the answer." Johann coughed and then sneezed in the first-grade row.

Tomorrow morning, early, Gunther and one of Old Saul's grandsons would travel with the Bollingers to New Glarus. With the weather getting colder, Marta had decided not to wait upon the chance of a barge arriving. Ellen was furious with herself for being glad that the widow was leaving. Jealousy was such a lowering emotion.

Johann coughed again.

"Dorcas, please tell us the answer." Ellen glanced out the window as Mr. Lang and Marta, both smiling, tried to fit one more thing on the wagon. They were smiling. She swallowed down her unworthy response.

"31?" Dorcas, the daughter of the new homesteading family replied.

"Yes. Now, children, 27 plus 18." The sound of chalk on slates gave sound to the irritation she was experiencing over Mr. Lang helping Marta.

Johann coughed a third time, and she glanced his way and paused. He appeared flushed. She didn't want to call attention to him, but a faint worry nudged her. "Johann, come here, please."

He obeyed.

She touched his forehead with the back of her wrist and felt heat. "Johann, you may have a fever. Did you feel warm this morning?"

He shook his head. "No, miss." He coughed again.

She was irritated with herself. *If I had not been concentrating on my own ridiculous emotions, I would have noticed this earlier.* "Go sit on the far side of the room, please."

"Did I do something wrong?" he asked.

"No, Johann, but you may be contagious."

He looked confused, but went to sit on one of the empty benches. The children in the room became restless. Ellen decided to assess the situation. She went from child to child, touching their foreheads. Three other children, including Marta's oldest son, also felt warm. A presentiment of coming trouble draped itself over her mind.

All the students looked worried now, glancing to brothers and sisters.

To avoid igniting fear, she must be firm. "Children, I need to take the temperatures of these students. Please work quietly on the assignments I gave your class for this evening."

The sound of worried whispering followed her as she walked swiftly into her quarters. From her trunk, she brought out a large, leather-bound book, a medical dictionary of symptoms and treatments. She located her medical kit and turned back toward the schoolroom.

"Miss Thurston?" Mr. Lang had halted just outside the door to her quarters. "Is something wrong? You look worried."

She gazed at him, wishing he had spoken to her not only because she must look fearful. When had he stopped talking to her as a friend? She pushed down this reaction and her alarm. "I'm not quite sure yet." She moved swiftly back into the classroom, acting as if she weren't aware that Mr. Lang had followed her to the connecting doorway. On her desk she set up the thermometer and poured alcohol into a glass vial in a metal stand.

She spoke to the isolated children. "I am going to take your temperatures. Have any of you seen a thermometer before?" She held it aloft.

All heads swiveled to see it.

"What does it do, miss?" Johann asked, sounding fearful.

"First of all, a thermometer tells what a person's body temperature is. If a person's temperature is above 98.6, that means a fever. Now, I am going to slip the glass cylinder into your mouth and under your tongue and wait five minutes. It doesn't hurt. Just make sure you don't bite it."

"I should go home," Dorcas said, rising. "My mama told me to come right home if anybody got sick in school. I don't want to catch anything—"

"Sit down!" Ellen ordered as others rose, too. "I am merely taking temperatures. There will be order here."

The children sat down, but the atmosphere became agitated with worry.

Ellen proceeded to take Johann's temperature, watching the wall clock tick toward a full five minutes. She forced herself not to glance toward Kurt, still standing in the connecting doorway, silently observing her every move.

After the longest five minutes in her recent history, she withdrew the glass stick and read the rainbowlike mercury—100.2 degrees. Not allowing her dismay to show, she shook down the thermometer, immersed it in the vial of alcohol, and then went to the next child.

By the time she'd finished, she'd become completely and dreadfully certain that some contagion had invaded her classroom. She forced her lungs to inhale and exhale evenly. Yet she couldn't regulate her galloping heart.

She looked at all of the feverish children. They were coughing, had runny noses and inflamed eyes. Could this be just the common cold? She moved to her desk and opened the large medical dictionary she'd brought with her. The near silence magnified the dry ruffling sound turning each page caused.

She opened to the section of childhood illnesses and read quickly through the various collections of symptoms. Mr. Lang moved into the room just behind her and stood watching the children, supporting her decree for order.

After reading, she walked back to the isolated children. "Johann, will you open your mouth, please?"

Small red spots dotted the inside of Johann's mouth, and the mouths of the others. Dread sent gooseflesh up her arms.

Measles.

There was no doctor in this town. And even if there had been, no cure for measles existed. She tried to make her worried mind focus. What should she do next?

"What is it?" Mr. Lang from the front of the room asked.

"I'm afraid that we have an outbreak of measles," she said as unemotionally as she could.

Dorcas popped up from her seat and ran toward the door.

"Stop!" Ellen commanded, racing after the girl. She caught her shoulder just before she escaped.

"Mama told me if any sickness came to school, to run home," Dorcas insisted once more, trying to pull free.

"Dorcas, everyone here has already been exposed to measles. If you run home, you might give it to your parents and your two little brothers. Now come back and sit down."

"Mama said!" The little girl pulled away and dashed through the door.

Ellen tried to catch her but the child escaped. Feeling her pulse throbbing in her temples, Ellen stood at the door to prevent more children from fleeing. Mr. Lang had moved to guard the other doorway. He looked very concerned, just as she must.

Her head spun with all the questions. The children had all been exposed to the disease but it might take days for symptoms to appear. "Children, if I let you go home, you might spread the infection to your families. You could bring hurt to them," she explained to the strained faces beseeching her.

"Will we be in quarantine?" Amanda asked, sounding frightened.

Quarantine, a terrifying word. How could she quarantine all these children here? She couldn't care for a roomful of sick children by herself. Her petty concern over Mr. Lang and Marta shamed her.

I should have been concentrating on my students. Did I miss something this morning that I should have caught? Dear Lord, what should I do?

"Miss Thurston," Kurt said after several moments of heavy yet restless silence, "I will go tell Noah Whitmore and Mr. Ashford. They will help."

The schoolteacher looked at him, her hands clasped tightly together. "Thank you, Mr. Lang. An excellent suggestion." The relief evident in her voice commanded his sympathy.

"I come back soon." He turned and shut the door, hurrying through her quarters and then outside. Briefly he told Mrs. Bollinger what had happened. She exclaimed and, shutting the tailgate of the wagon, hurried inside, saying she would help the kind teacher.

Kurt went straight to the Ashford's store. He burst inside and found the proprietor helping two women he recognized vaguely from church. His agitation spurred him but should he speak in front of others?

He removed his hat and nodded politely to the ladies.

"Mr. Ashford, may I speak with you a moment, please? The matter is urgent."

The two women gave him a look as if he'd spoken out of turn, and moved to look at fabric together. Kurt ignored them and strode forward and motioned to the storekeeper to come closer.

"What is it, Lang?" Mr. Ashford was clearly annoyed that Kurt had interrupted a sale.

Kurt lowered his voice. "I have come from school. There is sickness. Miss Thurston needs help."

"Sickness? What kind?"

"The teacher says maybe measles." Kurt didn't know the German word for this illness but Miss Thurston had looked as if it were a bad disease.

Ashford's face fell and he whispered, "Measles can be deadly, or cause blindness. It is very dangerous."

Kurt's insides turned to ice and a roaring swelled in his ears. Johann could die?

The storekeeper turned and said, "Ladies, you must finish your purchases and then I'm closing up."

The women turned to the proprietor in surprise.

"Miss Thurston thinks there has been an outbreak of measles at the school," the man explained.

The women gasped. Kurt was frankly surprised that Mr. Ashford had been so plainspoken about the situation.

"Mr. Lang and I will head over to the preacher's to decide whether quarantine is necessary. I will be closed for the rest of the day."

The transactions were tied up quickly. The ladies held handkerchiefs over their noses and mouths as they rushed from the store.

Ashford locked the door and flipped the sign to read

"Closed." "We'll borrow the blacksmith's nag and cart. Let's go!"

He paused, then hurried to the bottom of the rear staircase. Quickly he shouted the facts to his wife. "Go to the school and help Miss Thurston! I'll get Noah Whitmore!"

Within a few minutes, they were heading as fast as the rough trail would allow them, soon rounding the bend to the Whitmore place. Kurt recalled Miss Thurston's grave expression and how the women in the store had gasped and hurried away.

What *was* measles? Was Gunther in danger as well as Johann?

And what about Miss Thurston? The thought of anything happening to her was more than Kurt could bear. He snapped the reins, encouraging the horse to go faster.

By the time Ellen glimpsed Kurt, Noah and Mr. Ashford coming through the trees, a few parents already had gathered outside the school door. Had Dorcas told everyone she met? Regardless, the word had spread.

They had to decide whether to quarantine the students or not. She was grateful to see the others arrive. She didn't feel up to making that decision alone. Mrs. Ashford stood beside her in quiet support.

Noah hurried forward. "Miss Thurston, are you sure your students have measles?"

Grateful for his calm tone, she held up the hefty medical dictionary. "I brought this so I would be prepared for the inevitable. Wherever children gather, contagion can spread. According to this, it certainly sounds as if they have measles."

"Then our main priority is deciding how to handle this outbreak. Ordinarily we would quarantine any child who showed symptoms. Miss Thurston, does that book tell how long it takes for symptoms to show?"

"Ten to fourteen days. And the disease usually takes the same time to run its course. Also, stricken children should be kept away from the sun or bright light to protect their eyes." Ellen clasped the heavy book to her as a shield. Mrs. Ashford patted her arm.

"We want to take our children home," one mother spoke up. "If they stay here with the sick children, they *will* get it."

Noah's deep concern and uncertainty showed on his face. Ellen had the sudden urge to weep. Evidently the panic around her was seeping into her own emotions. Or was it something more? Images from the past...a fevered baby in her arms, struggling for breath...

No, no. That is in the past. She wrenched herself back to the present, forcing herself to gain control. She, like everyone else, waited to hear what Noah would say.

"I think each family should decide for themselves whether to leave their child here at school or take the child home," Noah said at last.

"No!" Ellen objected. "Each parent should consider their younger children. The younger the child, the more chance of..." Fear clogged her throat. She couldn't go on. When she looked at the faces around her, she realized she didn't need to say more.

"But you cannot care for so many alone," Mr. Lang protested.

"Kurt is right," Noah said. "If anyone decides to leave a child here at the school in quarantine, one of the parents or an older sibling must stay to nurse that child."

"And I suggest we close the school for regular classes till this has run its course," Mr. Ashford said. "Personally, I've had the measles so I will keep my store open, but only come if you are in real need of something."

Noah and the other men nodded solemnly. And then Ellen heard, "That's what we get for letting foreigners into our town."

Ellen recognized the speaker as one of the men who had opposed her keeping William. She knew people would think what he had just said, though she'd hoped no one would say it aloud.

"We live in a river community," Noah said in an even tone. "We may never know how this disease came here."

"Well I for one think it's clear how the disease came here," the man said, staring at Mr. Lang. Ellen watched as he met the man's gaze dead-on.

"Mr. Lang," she said. "Will you get William for me?" She sensed a ripple move through the assembled crowd. Even Kurt himself looked surprised that she would make such a request after what the man had just said. "He has already been exposed. Tell Mrs. Brawley what's happened and that I'll be keeping William home for the foreseeable future. Tell her I'm sorry." Her voice died in her throat. The thought that she might have infected the Brawley baby crushed her.

The sympathy on Mr. Lang's face nearly brought her to tears. "Miss Thurston, you are not to blame for any of this," he said.

She couldn't trust herself to respond to his kind words.

"I will get William and supplies then return to be with my nephew. Noah, please tell Gunther to stay home."

Ellen heard the anxiety in his voice. She wished she could reassure him, offer him hope. But she could not mouth false platitudes in the face of this thing that had come against them all.

"Those of you with no children at school should go home now and stay there," Noah said. "Don't come into town until this is passed. Miss Thurston, if you need me, send for me." Then he began to pray aloud. "Heavenly Father, help us. Preserve the lives and sight of our children. All of us. Amen."

"I'm taking Amanda home," Mrs. Ashford said. "But I'll bring food and medicine by suppertime."

Ellen nodded but she was more aware of Kurt as he hurried off to bring William home to her. She was touched by his willingness to help others—to help her.

Given permission to claim their children and take them home, people milled in front of the door and consulted one another. The unclaimed children fidgeted inside the schoolroom, looking out the door and windows, waiting while their parents decided what to do.

Their worry flared palpably. If they decided the mother would stay, the parting of husband and wife and child at the schoolroom door touched Ellen's heart. Especially heartbreaking to watch fathers say goodbye without touching their children.

Ellen struggled against cold waves of fear coursing through her. She tried to pray but no words came.

Chapter Fifteen

Word continued to spread and by evening, all children had either been taken home or remained in quarantine with their mothers. Kurt watched as families dealt with the crisis and tried to face it as bravely as they could.

The quarantined group at the school included Marta's children, Johann, little William and three mothers who stayed with their children in hopes of protecting their toddlers, staying safely at home. An unnatural hush hung over the school.

As the sun set, Kurt helped these women make pallets on the opposite side of the schoolroom floor from those who were already ill. He pumped and carried water in for tea and washing. All the while he tracked Miss Thurston, aware of the fear she masked.

He wanted nothing more than to offer her comfort, but he knew he must keep his distance, especially in such close quarters. His mind kept going back to the way she'd stepped in when one of the townspeople had all but accused him of bringing measles to Pepin. She was an extraordinary woman. There was no doubt.

Standing outside Miss Thurston's door, Mrs. Ashford

handed him a large kettle of pork and beans, and one of thin oatmeal for the sick children. Amanda handed in a pot of hot willow bark tea for the fevered.

For once, Mrs. Ashford didn't have much to say and she and Amanda left quickly.

Just before dark, Kurt brought in more wood to keep the low fire burning in Miss Thurston's fireplace and in the large Franklin stove that sat against the wall between the schoolroom and teacher's quarters. Eventually, once everyone was settled for the night, he took a seat at Miss Thurston's desk.

He woke in the dark with a start sometime later. What had wakened him? How long had he been asleep?

The school door stood open, letting in a wedge of moonlight. Cool air rushed in. One glance told Kurt that only Johann's pallet was empty.

Kurt moved quickly to the open door. Looking outside, he glimpsed nothing but the trees surrounding the school. Fear grabbed the back of his neck. He shut the door and raced to Miss Thurston's room to see if Johann had gone there. He leaned inside.

Miss Thurston looked up from the rocking chair. "What is it?" she asked softly, urgently.

"Johann. He isn't inside."

She leaped to her feet, laying her child in his cradle. She hurried to him and clutched his arms. "We must find him. The night air will do him harm."

She whipped on her shawl, lit a lantern and let herself out her door. He hurried after her, closing the door silently behind him. In the midst of the schoolyard, she stood in a shaft of moonlight, turning her head slowly, scanning the woods. The wind ruffled the leaves, but he could hear no other sound.

Dear God, help us find him. Johann could have wandered anywhere. If they didn't find him…

Terror for his little nephew turned his empty stomach. He swallowed down dry heaves.

Miss Thurston picked up her lantern and began searching the circle of trees around the clearing. She halted and motioned for him to follow her.

"Do you see him?" he asked, keeping up with her.

"No, but this is the path the children sometimes take to the creek that leads to the river. I think he might go this way out of habit."

He hadn't thought of that danger. The Mississippi River was so near.

Miss Thurston began nearly running and he edged in front of her. *God, help. God, help.* With each step, his mind chanted this.

The trees thinned so near the river flats. Ahead, Johann's white shirt glimmered in the creek. "Johann!" Kurt thundered.

Miss Thurston grabbed his elbow. "He's delirious. Don't agitate him. He's not really awake."

The boy mumbled something as Kurt waded into the creek, shivering from the cold water. Panic surged within him, a bellows being pumped hard and fast. He lifted Johann and carried him out of the creek, dripping cold water.

"Is he breathing?" Miss Thurston asked, hurrying to him.

"I don't know." He couldn't think.

She leaned close, putting her cheek next to Johann's mouth. "He's breathing. Let's get him inside. Quickly!"

The two of them raced back to the school. The

schoolteacher reached the side door first and swung it open wide. He ducked inside.

"Lay him in front of my hearth and strip him," she whispered. "I'll find something for him to change into." She went to her trunk and began rummaging.

Kneeling, Kurt stripped off Johann's clothing, tossing the sopping wet pieces to the floor.

Then she was at his side again, pushing a dry towel into his hands. "Dry him." She used another towel on Johann's face and hair. "Rub his skin as you dry him. It will bring the blood to the surface."

He did as she said, grateful to see the white skin turn ruddy under the friction. Finally, they had him dry and dressed and wrapped in a blanket.

"Was ist los?" Marta had risen from the bed.

Kurt explained what had happened as he laid Johann on the floor in front of the hearth.

Marta exclaimed her distress, picking up the sodden clothing and hurrying outside, saying she would wring them out and hang them on the clothesline.

Kurt knelt beside his nephew. "Why did he do it?"

Miss Thurston pressed her wrist to Johann's forehead. "Sometimes a high fever causes delirium. Or he might have instinctively sought the water to cool his fever. He likes the creek. He goes there during recess often."

"But being chilled could kill him." Just saying the words shook Kurt.

"His fever is down," Miss Thurston said calmly. "We will just keep him warm and hope this hasn't made matters worse." She laid a warm brick at Johann's feet to ward off the chill.

"I shouldn't have fallen asleep." He rested his forehead in his hand. *"Dummkopf."*

She gently took his hand away from his head, and he was forced to look at her. "You fell asleep because you were exhausted. You woke and we found him. We are only human."

"I can't lose him." *I can't bear to lose anyone else.* His mind went to Gunther. How was he? Was he sick and alone?

"Don't worry about Gunther," Miss Thurston said as if reading his mind. "Ophelia and the Whitmores will check on him. Now strip off your wet shoes and socks before you come down with this, too."

He wanted to argue but he knew Miss Thurston was right. He eased back and did what she'd asked. A shiver shook him and he didn't know if it was from his sodden shoes and socks or from terror. He was too frozen even to pray.

Two days of nursing the children passed in a blur.

Night had fallen once more and most of the sick were dozing restlessly. Two of the children who had remained had come down with the illness, and one more child had come with her mother to enter the quarantined school.

In her quarters, Ellen sat in the rocker, nearly paralyzed with fear. William, so small and helpless, lay on her lap. Last night he'd begun sneezing and she'd discovered the telltale red spots in his tiny mouth.

I could lose him, this child who was entrusted to me for safekeeping, this child I love.

The fire burned low and William's fever burned higher. By firelight, she saw how hard the tiny infant fought for each breath. She'd been afraid to give him the

willow bark tea Mrs. Ashford had brought over which
sat on the table nearby. Would it help or hurt such a
small child?

Since she'd first noticed William's symptoms, this
fear had been trying to wrap itself around her lungs
and choke her. She'd held it at bay, but now the terror
conquered her.

Why did I think I could raise a child?

She began to weep, each sob wrenching her.

Then, before her eyes, William began to convulse.
Her little brother had seized like this before he died.
All those years ago, Dr. Litchfield had said that no one
could have saved him. Remembering her brother only
increased her suffering. Instantly ice went through her
in horrifying waves. She rose and cried out wordlessly.

Please, God, help. Help my William.

Unable to fall back asleep, Kurt was sitting in Miss
Thurston's chair again, keeping watch over the sleeping children and mothers, when someone cried out. He
peered into the gray moonlit room, listening. The sound
had come from behind him.

Ellen.

Panic sliced his heart. William—was he worse?

Hoping not to disturb the others, Kurt rose and raced
on tiptoe to her quarters. Ellen sat in her rocking chair
holding William, horror on her face.

He moved swiftly to her. "What is it?" he whispered.

She looked up, tears spilling from her eyes. She tried
to speak but could only weep. Kurt knelt beside her. In
a shaft of moonlight from the window, he saw the child
flushed with fever and breathing with difficulty. Then
the child shook violently and gagged.

Instinctively, Kurt snatched up the infant into his arms and turned him on his side. The thought of the child choking shot like lightning through his mind. He unwound the blanket and ran to the door. He stepped outside into the cooler air.

The child convulsed once more, then lay quiet, lying over Kurt's arm, panting.

Ellen hovered beside him. "Won't the night air harm him?"

Kurt found he was panting, too, the emotional reaction causing him to feel as if he'd just sprinted across a finish line. Finally he managed to say, "Perhaps not. Just a few minutes. We let him cool down and see."

When William appeared to cuddle closer as if seeking warmth, Kurt turned and gently urged Ellen inside. He silently shut the door behind them and halted by the fireplace. Ellen stood opposite him, gazing down at the child. Everything else receded from Kurt's mind. There was only Ellen, the child and him.

"You are worried," he whispered so inadequately.

She nodded, shaking with renewed but silent weeping.

He had no more words. He laid William in the cradle at her feet. Then, not letting himself pause to consider, he did what he felt compelled to do. He drew Ellen into his arms.

"You must not fear so," he whispered into her ear. "He is sick but I think the bad part is done."

They shared the same fear. This evening, Johann had been so feverish he had not recognized Kurt.

At first, she stood straight and stiff in his arms, and then she gave way, leaning into him. "I should have let them take William from me. He wouldn't have become sick, then," she murmured brokenly.

"You don't know that," he replied. "You cannot know that."

"I can't stop remembering losing my baby brother. He could barely breathe." She sobbed against him, not making a sound as she shook in his arms. "He shook like that, too. And then…"

"This child will live," he whispered, forcing certainty into his voice.

She shook her head no against his chest. "My baby brother died in my arms."

At these heartbreaking words, he wrapped his arms tightly around her and let her hushed sobs beat against him. He absorbed her anguish as best he could. But Ellen's desperate state ignited his own alarm. He'd survived what had happened in Germany. *He would not see Gunther and Johann taken from him now.*

He realized those words were whistling in the dark, as death hovered at their elbows, always ready to snatch life from them. But he would give in to this despair, nor would he let Ellen.

He focused on the sweet woman in his arms. Here, in this dark room while all slept, he could comfort her. Had he ever known a woman with a kinder, more caring heart? He buried his face in her soft hair, allowing himself to breathe in her natural scent and a trace of lavender.

Minutes passed. He let himself float, without thought or worry, just holding her close. Comforting her comforted him. Was that wrong? He knew in his heart it was not.

Finally, she drew a long, shuddering breath and straightened herself. "I'm sorry I gave in like that," she whispered.

He tried to think of words but none came to mind. Then, as if someone else were in control of him, he leaned forward and kissed her forehead. "William will not die."

She tried to smile but failed, her lips quivering with more sobs. She bent and lifted the baby out of the cradle and back into her arms.

Kurt waited there, not sure what to do. He knew he shouldn't have held her like that, but it was done now. And if he was honest with himself, he didn't regret it.

"Do you think I should try some of the willow bark tea?" she asked.

"I do not think a spoonful will hurt," he said. "I'll get it."

He poured out a spoonful of the tepid brew, and then tickled William's chin, waking the child. He trickled the tea into the baby's mouth. When he was done, he gave Ellen a smile and turned to go back to his uncomfortable chair.

"Kurt," she murmured, "thank you."

She said my given name.

Kurt didn't turn, afraid for her to glimpse his reaction. *"Guten nacht,"* he murmured and walked softly back to the classroom, trying to ignore the thrill he was feeling at the sound of his name on her lips.

He moved to the pallet where Johann tossed and turned, mumbling in his fevered sleep. With the inside of his wrist, Kurt tested his nephew's forehead. Would the fever never break? Kurt didn't even have the energy to walk back to the desk and sit. Instead, he lay down beside Johann on the bare half-log floor and fell asleep almost instantly, the last thought in his head of Miss Ellen Thurston and how right she had felt in his arms.

Chapter Sixteen

Standing outside the school in the chill morning air, Kurt felt as if he'd aged a decade over the past two weeks. The worst of the measles outbreak had passed. A few children remained at home, still recovering from the illness. But after today's thorough cleaning had been done, the school would no longer serve as a hospital, but return to its true purpose. He hoped people would come to help them get it ready, but it was possible that they might still be afraid to come.

He rubbed his eyes with both hands. After two weeks of little sleep, he wondered if he'd ever feel rested or normal again.

Pale and thinner, Johann came outside and leaned against him. Kurt patted his bony shoulder. "Tonight, we go home."

"Good. I want to see my kid," Johann said, referring to his beloved pet, a baby goat. "Do you think he missed me?"

"I'm sure he missed you." An image of Johann, delirious and floating in the cold creek, flashed through Kurt's mind. *That night I thought I'd lose you, little one.*

Movement at the edge of the trees snagged Kurt's attention. Gunther appeared in the clearing. Kurt's heart clenched and then expanded. One glance and the young man raced to them. Throwing down a bucket, he wrapped his arms around Johann and lifted him off his feet.

Kurt didn't know how it happened, but soon they were hugging each other as they never had before. Then he realized Gunther was crying hard, wetting Kurt's shirt. He held his brother close. In a way he couldn't understand, Gunther's tears were washing away the fear and cleansing him, too.

Finally, Gunther drew back and lowered Johann to his feet. "I missed you, little guy."

Kurt had expected Gunther to speak in German as they usually did when no one else was near. But he'd spoken in English and with so faint an accent that he'd almost sounded like someone else. For the first time, the knowledge that his baby brother would soon be a man lodged solidly inside Kurt.

"I missed you, too, Gunther," Johann said.

From inside the school, a child called to Johann.

"Be right back," Johann said, leaving them.

The two brothers gazed at each other. "I thought we might lose him," Gunther admitted and then swiped his wrist over his moist eyes.

Kurt couldn't speak. He hadn't thought Gunther would fear what he feared. *He is growing up fast, too fast.*

"I thought I might lose you, too." Gunther looked down then, not meeting Kurt's eyes.

Kurt could think of no reply to this. When trying to keep Johann from succumbing after his cold night swim, he'd given little thought to his own vulnerability to illness.

"We had a rough time in Germany." Gunther leaned back and folded his arms. "But here we have a new chance."

Kurt drank in each of Gunther's words of hope. "Life is getting better," he said. Kurt thought of Miss Thurston, of how deeply he'd allowed her into his mind, his heart.

Gunther stared down at the step. Finally, he just nodded.

As if Kurt had summoned her merely by thinking of her, Miss Thurston stepped outside. "Did you come to help us sanitize the school, Gunther?" Her words were warm and her smile also.

All too well, Kurt recalled the sensation of holding this lovely lady close. Now, every time he saw her, he had to fight the urge to put his arm around her and draw her near. Not a wise idea.

"Yes, I brought cleaning things," Gunther said, picking up the bucket he'd dropped and rattling the contents.

"Good." Before she could say more, a wagon rocked into sight. The old preacher's daughter-in-law, Lavina, sat beside her younger son, Isaac, who was close to Gunther in age. She waved, announcing, "We brought my laundry tub to boil water for the cleaning!"

And then more wagons jostled into the schoolyard. Kurt was relieved to see that at least some people had turned out to help, after all.

Kurt helped move the benches and all the other furniture in the school and Ellen's quarters outside. Though he kept busy, Ellen would not leave his mind.

I will do the work here and then I will go home and I will not think of her.

An inner voice replied, "Not think of her? Who do you think are you fooling?"

Ellen welcomed those who'd come to help disinfect the school with pure joy. The fact that the town of Pepin had made it through the measles and not lost a soul was surely something to feel good about.

Soon she was sweeping out the schoolroom while outside others filled the laundry tub to begin heating water. Kurt seemed to be everywhere she looked, helping everyone with everything. She tried to stop herself from noticing him, from responding to the sound of his deep, sure voice. But since the night when he'd comforted her with such tenderness, she seemed to have no control over herself. The man had lodged in her mind. And her heart. She had not a clue what to do about him.

People on their hands and knees began scrubbing the floor and walls with the hot water and lye soap. Marta was polishing the windows with pungent vinegar water and newspaper. The potent mix of odors made Ellen's eyes water. She decided to work outside, away from the fumes and away from Kurt Lang.

There, with a stiff-bristled brush in hand, she scrubbed down the benches. Amanda, recovered now from her own bout with measles, watched the children—including a healthy, happy William—outside in the sun. Ellen noticed that except for Lavina, the Whitmores and her cousins, those working to disinfect the school were those whose children had recovered from measles.

Evidently, much of the population would steer clear

of the school building for a time. She couldn't blame them. But it brought her a worry. She wished most of all the Brawleys had come to help today. How had they weathered the measles outbreak? No one had mentioned them yet.

Mrs. Ashford worked nearby. Something about the dejected way the storekeeper's wife moved and sighed again and again put Ellen on alert. Finally, Ellen asked in an undertone, "I think you should sit down for a while. You've helped so much already, bringing food even after Amanda came down with the measles."

Mrs. Ashford's face crumpled. Ellen drew the woman to sit on a more private bench behind her quarters. "What's wrong?"

The woman continued to cry. Finally, with a hiccup, she asked, "Have you seen Amanda's face?"

Ellen stopped to think. "From a distance. What's happened?"

"Her eye, her right eyelid droops," the woman said in a hushed, hopeless tone. "It makes her look squinty."

Ellen considered this. "That's a possible aftereffect from measles, I think. Yes, the medical dictionary warned that could happen. The muscles in the eyelid are weakened."

Mrs. Ashford muffled a wail in a handkerchief pressed to her mouth. "It gives her a very off appearance. How will we ever find her a decent husband?"

The words sent anger flaring through Ellen. She called on her self-control, not letting out any of the words rushing through her mind. When she could command herself, she said, "Amanda is intelligent, kind and hardworking. Any man with sense at all would find in her a wonderful wife."

Mrs. Ashford sniffed. "You're sweet to say that, but men always want a pretty wife."

"Some men make that mistake," Ellen said, recalling how much prettier her younger sister was than she. "But others look under the surface. Besides, Amanda always presents herself well. What is a droopy eyelid after all is said and done?"

"Ned says it could have been worse. She could have caught small pox and been dreadfully pockmarked."

Or she could have died.

Ellen patted the woman's arm. "Why don't we leave Amanda's future husband up to God?"

Mrs. Ashford rose with a pronounced sigh. "Of course, you're right. I don't know why I'm being so foolish."

Before the measles outbreak, Ellen knew she would have responded inwardly that this woman *was* foolish. But Mrs. Ashford had worked tirelessly to help Ellen and the other mothers tend their sick children, and Ellen saw her differently now. She patted the woman's back, trying to comfort her. "Let's go back and finish those benches."

As they rounded the corner, Ellen saw that the yard had emptied of workers except for Amanda, who was watching toddlers near the swings. And Gunther.

Gunther leaned forward and tenderly kissed Amanda's right eye.

As she heard Mrs. Ashford's sharp intake of breath, Ellen braced herself, awaiting in dread for the onslaught of scolding. But she waited in vain.

Mrs. Ashford took Ellen's elbow and hurried her back to where they had been.

Ellen obeyed the silent prompt not to let the young

couple know they'd been observed, but was confused. Hadn't Mrs. Ashford seen Gunther kiss Amanda's eye? If she had, why hadn't she reacted in her usual manner? Ellen sent her companion a questioning look.

"I didn't want to embarrass my daughter," the woman confided, obviously touched by the tenderness she'd just witnessed. "It seems you were right about Gunther, Miss Thurston. Perhaps he is a fine young man after all."

Astounded by Mrs. Ashford's change of heart, Ellen looked back at the young couple. For a moment, her mind recreated the image she'd just seen. Only this time, she—not Amanda—sat with William in her arms, and Kurt was kissing her, starting a warm current swirling through her.

Red-faced, Ellen quickly turned away from Mrs. Ashford as if the woman could somehow know what she was thinking.

By the first week of November, Kurt was once again helping work with Marta outside the lady teacher's quarters. Once again they were packing up the Bollinger's possessions for their impending trip to New Glarus. School had resumed now, and the horror of the town's measles epidemic was behind them.

Because all the windows were shut tight against the advancing cold, Kurt could hear Miss Thurston's voice inside the school but he couldn't make out individual words. Still, he couldn't stop himself from listening.

Since the night he'd held her, the feelings he had for her had become harder—much harder—to conceal. He'd been trying to keep his distance from her, but it had done him no good. In some ways, it had probably made the situation worse. Absence did make the heart grow fonder.

Marta carried out the final box and set it into the rear of the wagon. "That is all except for the bedding." The woman sighed and leaned against the lowered tailgate. "Why are you alone?" she asked him suddenly.

Her question startled him. "What?"

"Why aren't you married?"

He couldn't hide how shocked he was. "I have Gunther and Johann to care for."

"You should have brought a wife with you."

The memory of Brigitte's horrified face flew into his mind. His father's act had horrified everyone at home, and with the horror had come repulsion. No one wanted even to look at Kurt or Gunther or Johann. Bitterness choked him, his heart hardening.

"I would never have come here unless my Gus wanted us to. And now he will never see New Glarus." Marta appeared to be fighting tears, her lips quivering. "I don't understand why this has happened. Every step of the way we prayed and now I'm here alone to raise our sons."

Pushing aside his own tragedy, Kurt rested a hand on her shoulder. "You have suffered. But God hasn't forgotten you. Gus died but your son didn't succumb to the measles."

"I know. I don't want to sound ungrateful. I'm just speaking what's in my heart to the only adult here who can understand me."

He comprehended that, too. So many times he had felt left out when people spoke rapidly or when they addressed him as if he were hard of hearing. And he was unable to express himself as clearly, as thoroughly in

English as he could in German. Talking to Marta was a relief in that way. But she wasn't the one he really wanted to speak to.

"Why don't you come with us to New Glarus?"

Her question startled him so, he jerked backward. "Leave?"

"Yes, New Glarus is Swiss but we are German-speaking Swiss. You would be with people who understand you and know Europe, not just this lonely, raw land." She cast a glance about her.

"Leave?" he repeated, taken aback.

"Yes, you would be among those who are like us, not these people who think they are better than we."

All the rude words and misconceptions that had been hurled at him over the past months streamed through his mind, sparking a fire in him. He hadn't realized that he'd stored them up.

This woman only spoke the truth. But he didn't know what to say in reply.

"You think about it," she urged him. "I could delay leaving to give you time to gather—"

"No," he said, speaking more sharply than he wanted. "I have worked too hard to leave. Gunther is doing better and Johann has a good school with a good teacher."

Marta shook her head at him. "I see how you look at the schoolteacher. But if you think she will marry you, *a foreigner*—" she said the word in English "—you are deluding yourself."

Kurt's insides twisted with denial and shock. "I am not so unwise." He swung away from her.

Marta caught his arm and stopped him. "I'm sorry. I just don't want you to be…"

He turned back, his hot anger dwindling by the second. "I know." He held up a hand as if to make peace. "Gunther and I will come just after breakfast tomorrow to start your journey."

Marta murmured her thanks and released him.

Kurt was glad he'd walked to town. He had more than two miles home to work off his spleen.

The idea Marta had planted resisted his efforts to uproot it. Life would be easier if he went to a German-speaking village.

But my home is here.

And of course, Miss Thurston was here, too. The thought of never again seeing her elegant features or hearing her gentle, cultured voice left him bereft as if a dark veil descended over his heart.

For that reason alone, he should leave with Marta.

In the crisp November dawn, Ellen carried William as she and Kurt walked to town with Marta. It was not lost on Ellen that Marta walked between her and Kurt. Ellen was grateful for the distance, and she also resented the distance. Both reactions irritated her.

Dawn gold still hung in the eastern sky. Behind them, Gunther, with her three boys jabbering excitedly to him in German, was driving Marta's wagon into town. There he would pick up the old trading road along the Mississippi and head south. Marta had preferred to walk into town.

Ellen worried about William and the Brawleys. The husband hadn't wanted William in the first place. And in the days after the outbreak ended, Mrs. Brawley hadn't come for William. Letting the uneasy matter lie, Ellen had accepted Marta's offer to watch him during school hours. But today with Marta leaving, Ellen had to go through town on her way to leave William for the day.

Marta said something in German to Kurt, pausing in front of the store. Ellen only caught "Mrs. Ashford." She looked to Kurt for the translation.

"She would like to thank the Ashfords," he replied to her unspoken question, and then turned toward the store.

But before he could enter, Mrs. Ashford came out, followed by her husband. "I thought you'd be leaving early," the wife said.

Marta hurried forward, speaking in heartfelt German as Kurt translated. "Thank you, Mrs. Ashford, for all you and your husband have done for my family. We were strangers and you fed us. We were sick and you helped us. You are true Christians. Thank you."

Marta curtsied.

Mrs. Ashford blushed at the praise. Her husband replied, "Mr. Lang, you tell Mrs. Bollinger we were happy to help. And that we hope she and her sons will prosper in New Glarus."

Marta shook hands with both Ashfords as Amanda came around the side of the store and approached Gunther. The lad tied up the reins and climbed down to meet her.

Ellen was watching the Ashfords observe the young couple, wishing each other farewell. Marta came to her and tearfully shook her hand. *"Danke. Danke."*

Ellen drew Marta close and pressed her cheek to hers. The woman had become a friend and now they must part. "God be with you, Marta."

Kurt helped Marta up onto the wagon bench next to Gunther. Her three boys sat at the back of the wagon, looking out over the raised tailgate and waving their farewells.

"You stay safe, Gunther!" Mrs. Ashford called out.

The lad looked shocked, but responded with a polite bow of his head, "Yes, ma'am, I will."

Ellen maintained a straight face. Mrs. Ashford constantly presented yet another facet of human nature. Though Ellen sincerely doubted a drooping eyelid would keep Amanda from marrying, Mrs. Ashford obviously was not going to risk alienating a possible suitor.

In Ellen's arms William fussed a little as if he were aware that friends were leaving. Ellen rocked him close and hummed to him as she stood beside Kurt. Together, they watched the wagon turn and head southward along the trail that followed the Mississippi, that mighty river, all the way south to the delta at New Orleans.

When she could no longer see the wagon, Ellen started walking toward the Brawleys. Kurt fell into step beside her. She didn't understand why Kurt was walking with her, but she was glad of his company. Each step weighed upon her. She hadn't heard anything from the Brawleys since the measles outbreak.

It was difficult for her to admit it, but having Kurt by her side made her cares easier to bear. He was the kind of man who could help solve any problem, any issue. In that way, he was invaluable.

Actually, she was beginning to realize that Kurt Lang was invaluable to her in many ways. The question was, what was she going to do about it?

"You are worried?" Kurt said, unable to keep the words back. After the wagon had disappeared around a bend, he'd also been unable to make himself turn and walk home as he should. This morning, Ellen had some magnetic force he couldn't break free from. Which, to be honest, was no different from any other morning in his recent memory.

"I am worried," she admitted.

"Tell me."

She shook her head. "A waste of words. And most of what we worry about never happens."

He chewed on this idea, appreciating how she did not give in to worry, an unusual trait. Crows, fat with pilfered corn, sat in the bare trees and mocked the two of them. Overhead, geese flew in a long V against the gray sky. Crumpled red and amber leaves and golden pine needles littered the path beneath their feet. Somehow walking beside this special woman heightened his wonder at the beauty all around them and gave him a simple joy.

As they approached the Brawley cabin, Kurt noted that Ellen straightened as if she were bracing for something.

When Mr. Brawley stepped outside the cabin and folded his arms, she didn't seem surprised.

However, Kurt didn't like the man's hostile stance.

"Miss Thurston, I'm sorry but my wife won't be watching your foundling anymore. We can't take the chance of you bringing disease from the school to our house."

Kurt bristled at the man's tone. This was not how he should speak to a lady like Miss Thurston. He took a step forward then halted. Ellen would not want him to make a scene.

Ellen stopped short. "I understand. Give my regards to your wife."

Kurt sent the man a disgruntled look and turned with Miss Thurston, impressed with her aplomb.

When they were out of sight of the cabin, she looked at Kurt. "Unfortunately, my worry proved to be warranted this time. What am I going to do with William during the school days?"

He wanted to say, *I'll keep him.* But of course, he couldn't. He, too, had work to do, and more than usual with Gunther gone for at least a week. "I will take him to Mrs. Steward today. She will watch him."

Ellen let out a long sigh. "Thank you, Kurt. I can always count on you."

She had said his given name again. Delight shimmered over him and then caution rattled a warning. He recalled Marta's words about how Ellen would never choose to be with a *foreigner.* He refused to allow himself to consider what her use of his given name meant, pushing his joy away.

In front of the General Store, they paused.

"I'll walk Johann home after school," she said. "Please tell Ophelia I'll come and pick up William then." She transferred William and his sack of necessaries to Kurt. "Thank you so much."

Kurt nodded and turned with a wave. He strode down the path toward the Stewards', troubled by thoughts he had no right to be thinking. And all because she'd called him by his given name, an act that had much more meaning to him than she could possibly know.

For a brief moment, Kurt allowed himself the pleasure of wondering what it would be like to be able to talk to Miss Thurston exactly as he really wished to, to tell her what he thought of her, not to hold back anything. He wished he could just walk with her in an evening, just the two of them…and as more than friends. He thought of brushing her pale cheek with the back of his hand and burying his face once more in her fragrant silken hair. He tamped down the feelings these errant ideas sparked. Oh, Ellen…

Chapter Seventeen

Weary, Ellen sat at the table in Ophelia and Martin's cabin, trying to think of someone to replace Mrs. Brawley. She sipped her tepid coffee and rested her elbow on the table, not caring that it was unladylike, as little Nathan crawled around William's basket, chattering baby talk.

Ophelia was washing the supper dishes in a tin tub on the table. Ellen drained her cup and handed it to her. "I really appreciated your watching William today. Are you sure you can care for him tomorrow?" Ellen asked.

"Yes, and I'm going to keep him here tonight," Ophelia insisted, shaking out the damp dish towel. "You need one night of completely uninterrupted sleep. I see how dragged out you are. And pale."

If you only knew, Ellen thought.

This afternoon, as she was teaching, the realization had dawned on her that she had begun thinking of Mr. Lang as Kurt. She'd even accidentally referred to him as Kurt several times, and wondered if he had noticed. She tried to convince herself that this was merely a sign of their growing friendship but she was too honest to let herself get away with that fib. Kurt Lang had become special to her, very special. And she tried not to make more of this than she should. Memories of Holton had faded. Holton and Kurt were cut from very different cloth, very different men.

Then she heard Kurt's voice outside, greeting Martin, who was finally up and about, and able to tend to his animals.

"I'm glad when Kurt brought William this morning, he offered to drive you back in our cart to save you the long walk home. You look exhausted."

Ellen didn't have the strength to argue with her. Something beside her fatigue was weighing her down. But what? Kurt's handsome face flickered in her mind. She closed her eyes as if this would make the image go away.

"Miss Thurston?" Kurt entered, his hat in hand. "I am ready to drive you home."

His voice sent chills up her arms, a feeling she hadn't ever experienced before, not even with Holton. She rose with a practiced smile in place, spent a moment smoothing William's bedding and whispering good-night and then donned her bonnet and shawl. The evenings became cooler and cooler. Winter would come all too soon, she feared.

Ophelia stepped outside to wave goodbye, shutting the door behind her to keep their cabin warm.

As she took her place on the seat of the cart, Ellen's arms felt empty. For a moment she almost jumped down to run back for William. But she gripped the hard bench under her, hanging on as Kurt started the pony up the rutted, bumpy trail.

For a moment, she had the impulse to lean her tired head on the broad, substantial shoulder just inches away. She sighed at herself. *I'm merely exhausted, not just physically but mentally. That's what this is all about.*

But tonight, because of Ophelia's kind offer, she would be able to sleep and begin to recover from the stress of the past few weeks. Her mind returned to the first time she'd sat beside Kurt on this pony cart. He had driven her home and they'd found William in a wooden box on her doorstep. Could that only be a few months ago?

Neither of them spoke as amber evening turned to black-velvet night. A chilling half-moon lit their way. She snuggled deeper into her wool shawl and felt her chin bobbing. She tried to open her eyes wide but it was too much work. She sighed, letting the veil of sleep soothe her.

A bump jolted her and she woke with a start and realized she'd fallen asleep on Kurt's broad shoulder. "Oh," she breathed.

"No worry. You were sleepy. It is all right."

She blushed and was grateful for the shadows cast over them from the moonlight. Better to say no more. She straightened herself and faced forward, letting herself enjoy sitting near this man, even enjoying the rocking over the ruts in the rough road as they made her slide closer still. She nearly rested her head on his shoulder again.

And then Kurt turned from the trail to the narrow track into the schoolyard, and Ellen sat up straighter.

Someone had lit a lamp in her quarters.

Kurt jerked up sharply on the reins. He glanced sideways, the shadows hiding his expression from her.

"You are expecting someone?" he asked. When she shook her head, he said, "I will come to the door with you," and started the wagon on its way again.

Ellen didn't demur. With strong hands, he helped her down from the cart and they walked together to the door. She paused there.

Who was waiting for her? Had Randolph come again, bringing bad news from home?

She refused to let fear get a toehold. She turned the knob and pushed the door open, but pausing, not entering immediately.

Cissy turned to her, the glow from the lamp and low fire lighting her pretty face and strawberry-blond curls.

"Cissy!" Ellen ran forward. She had no other words to say.

"Oh, Nell," her sister wailed and threw herself into Ellen's arms.

Kurt cleared his throat. "I will go now. After school tomorrow, I will bring William when I pick up Johann."

Ellen gently nudged her sister away. "Thank you, Kurt—Mr. Lang." She blushed over the slip of her tongue. She must not call this man by his given name. "Please tell Ophelia that my sister has come for a visit."

"I will. Good night." He bowed himself out and shut the door behind him.

"Who is that?"

Her thoughtlessness pained Ellen. Why hadn't she made a proper introduction? Now Kurt probably felt that she didn't think he was worthy of meeting her sister. "I'll introduce you tomorrow. That's Mr. Kurt Lang. He's a close neighbor to Martin and Ophelia. I ate supper with them and he drove me home." She heard herself babbling, but couldn't stop. Her mind was racing, streaming with questions she couldn't put into words.

But it seemed that Cissy wasn't quite listening. She sat in a straight chair and looked away from Ellen. She was the picture of dejection.

Ellen covered her eyes with her hands and tried to rub away the tiredness. She sank into a rocking chair. After many moments of silence, she said, "I'm happy to see you, Cissy. But you are obviously distressed. Why have you come?"

Cissy buried her face in her hands and began weeping.

The sound buffeted Ellen, as if a straw broom were slapping her, trying to break her thin, protective shell. In her haze of exhaustion, Ellen missed the signs of hysteria until Cissy began to have trouble breathing.

Ellen leaped up and pulled her sister to her feet. "Cissy! Cissy!"

Her sister slumped against her as if she couldn't get her breath. Ellen reached past her to the pitcher of water on the table and managed to fill a dipper half-full. She splashed it into Cissy's face.

Her sister gasped and then collapsed against her, shaking.

Ellen realized two things simultaneously. Her sister had worked herself up to a state beyond reason, and she herself was too tired to do anything about it.

She half-dragged Cissy over to her bed, letting her down gently. Then she removed her sister's shoes and loosened her corset stays and covered her. Ellen dressed for sleep, blew out the lamp and slid in on the other side of the bed.

Her last thoughts were selfish ones. She had felt so happy riding with Kurt. And now this. Why did her sister have to come now? *I can't face another crisis.*

Kurt drove slowly home in the nearly complete darkness. The precious moments alone with Ellen had affected him. When she'd fallen asleep on his shoulder, he'd felt as if it were the most natural thing in the world. But he'd hated to see how upset Ellen seemed upon finding her sister waiting in her quarters. He knew the shock had made her forget to introduce him. Perhaps it was just as well. Would this sister trouble them as that brother had? Her family obviously didn't bring happiness to Ellen. Why couldn't they stay in Illinois where they belonged?

Drowsy morning dawned after a restless night. Ellen lay in bed, not wanting to open her eyes, to wake completely. Cissy was lying beside her like they had at home as girls. However, they were no longer girls.

If she opened her eyes, she'd have to face another crisis, one that most likely involved Holton. Unfortunately, waking to the sensation of phantom bricks stacked upon her chest had become all too familiar. What had happened to cause Cissy to come north, and more important, alone?

Her sister suddenly jolted upright. "Holton, no!"

Ellen sprang upward herself, and caught her sister. "Cissy, you're fine. You're here with me."

Her sister fell back, breathing hard.

Ellen took her hand. "Cissy, what's wrong?"

Her sister rolled away from her. "Everything."

Glancing at the small bedside table, Ellen glimpsed her pendant watch. The dial read 8:37 a.m. Could that be right?

She threw back the covers and leaped out of bed. "I must get up! My students will be here in less than a half hour. You rest more, and I'll make us some tea."

Soon she was dressed and brushing the tangles out of her hair. She'd been too tired to brush and braid it last night. All the while, she watched her sister lying in bed, staring at the fire. She prepared tea and set a cup on the table. "Cissy, come and drink your tea."

"I'm not hungry." Cissy sat up slowly as if she were ninety years or more.

Ellen decided kindness was not working. "I know you're very upset but not eating will help nothing. Get dressed and make yourself some toast." She heard voices outside. "The children are arriving and I must begin my day. We'll see Ophelia later and you'll meet my little William." To soften her words, she went over and kissed her sister's forehead. "And then you can tell me what's happened."

Cissy accepted the kiss but said nothing.

Ellen crossed to the door and then halted abruptly, what she'd seen catching up with her. When she'd leaned close to her sister, she'd glimpsed a yellowish tinge around her left eye. As if the eye had been bruised.

Memories of an Irish maid who'd been beaten by a boyfriend bubbled up in her mind. She turned and looked back at her sister who had not moved from the bed.

"Cissy, is there anything wrong?" Ellen asked tentatively. "Anything you need to tell me?"

"No," Cissy replied, not turning to look at her.

The reply did not satisfy Ellen, but what could she do now?

And she realized then as much as she wanted to know, she wasn't sure she could handle it. Too much had happened over the past year in her life—grieving her parents, losing Holton, defending William, battling the measles. How much more could she take?

Though she knew she should go back to her sister, the sounds of more children arriving in the schoolyard propelled her forward. *Oh, Lord, what has caused my sister to run to me?*

That evening, Martin, Ophelia, Ellen and Cissy sat around the table in the Steward's cabin, outwardly calm, inwardly tense. The reason for Cissy's unexpected visit had yet to be broached, though Ellen knew she was not the only one who'd noticed the slight bruise on her sister's face.

As usual, Nathan crawled under the table. William, still thin after his bout with measles, lay in Ellen's lap as she sipped her coffee. She patted him and savored the last bite of the sweet yet tart apple brown betty with fresh whipped cream Ophelia had made.

"You're really becoming a good cook," she complimented her cousin, trying to put some life into the anxious mood of the room.

"Yes," Cissy agreed in such a dispirited tone that even Martin noticed.

He rose and kissed Ophelia on the forehead. "An-

other outstanding meal by my lovely wife. I have to see
to the stock for the night." And he escaped the danger
of impending feminine emotions.

"All right," Ophelia said, taking this pretty bull by
the horns, "what's wrong, Cissy?"

Cissy shook her head.

The time for hesitation ceased in Ellen's opinion.
"How did you bruise your eye?"

One sob escaped her sister's mouth. "Holton struck
me."

Despite the fact that Ellen had already suspected
this in her heart, she gasped so hard she almost choked.

Ophelia leaped to her feet, hurried over to Cissy and
put her arm around her. "No. Oh, no."

Ellen found she couldn't move or say a word." It was
the last straw," Cissy declared. "As soon as I was sure
I could hide it, I packed up and left him."

"Why didn't you go to Randolph's?" Ophelia asked.
"It's his place to deal with your husband. A woman's
family protects her, if necessary."

Cissy shook her head and sent a searing look toward Ellen.

Ellen's initial shock was wearing off. She recalled
how her sister could hold on to a wrong, how hard it
was to break its hold over her. "What, Cissy? What happened? What led up to this?" *What aren't you telling us?*

Cissy sprang to her feet. "You dare to ask me that?
After what you did?"

Ellen's mouth dropped open and she gaped at her
sister. *After what I did?*

Before Ellen could respond, the door opened and
Kurt and Martin came in. Ellen found herself wishing

she could simply leave with Kurt before she had to hear Cissy's answer to her question. She wanted to sit beside him and draw strength from his presence.

"I can take you ladies home now, Miss Thurston," Kurt offered, his hat in hand.

Gazing at him warmed her, steadied her. "Cissy, this is Mr. Kurt Lang, a good neighbor. Mr. Lang, this is my sister, Mrs. Holton Rogers."

Kurt bowed his head to Cissy, "Mrs. Rogers."

Cissy merely nodded, lifting her chin with a touch of haughtiness. Ellen knew that Cissy was taking her grudge against Ellen out on Kurt. She wished they were girls again—she'd pinch Cissy.

Martin helped Cissy with her shawl as Ellen wrapped William up in a warm blanket to go home. Ophelia forestalled her, taking William into her arms. "I think I'll keep him one more night. We'll be coming in the morning for the workday at school. You need sleep." And she covertly nodded at Cissy as if to say to Ellen, *Find out what's wrong with her.*

Ellen wanted to object. Watching William sleep had become one of her sweetest pleasures, but she knew Ophelia was right. "Thank you." Ellen kissed her cousin's cheek.

Kurt helped her with her shawl, his strong hands brushing against her. Then he opened the door and she and Cissy walked into the chill early-autumn twilight. She tightened the shawl around her. Kurt paused at the two-wheeled cart. It only sat two on the bench, and the driver had to get on first and balance it.

"I'll ride in the back," Cissy said, giving Ellen an unreadable sidelong glance.

Ellen didn't try to decipher it. She waited while Kurt took his seat and Cissy settled herself in the rear. Then he reached down and pulled Ellen up beside him. The desire to keep her hand in his swept through her. Instead, she moved her grip to the bench. "Hold on, Cissy."

Kurt agreed as he turned the cart and headed toward the sinking sun, its rays filtering through the golden trees and evergreens.

Martin waved and went inside. And envy swept through Ellen. Ophelia had married wisely and now she had a snug cabin, a baby, a busy happy life with a good man.

Were those things within her reach? She'd been so certain when she'd come here of what she wanted, now she wasn't so sure.

As the cart rocked over the bumpy trail, Ellen experienced the strangest sensation. It was as if invisible bands connected her to Kurt, tugging her toward him. She fought against the pull, but soon she found herself sliding closer to his solid, comforting body, inch by inch. Only her most rigorous effort at control prevented her from leaning against him.

The world around her receded till she only perceived the two of them. In the lowering light, she studied his hands gripping the reins, the golden stubble on his chin, the way his hair curled around his ears. She forced her gaze forward, trying and failing to stop looking at him, very aware that her sister sat only inches behind them.

All too soon they reached the schoolhouse and her door. "Don't get down," Ellen told him. She slid from the bench. "Thank you, Kurt."

Cissy hopped off the back without a word.

"Good night, ladies." He touched the brim of his hat. "I will wait till you are safe inside. Mrs. Rogers, it was very nice to meet you."

Cissy did not acknowledge that Kurt had spoken to her as she made her way to the door. Ellen sighed and gave Kurt an apologetic smile before she hurried after her sister, the chill nipping at her heels.

"Kurt?" Cissy asked archly before Ellen could even close the door, her hands on her hips. "You called that Dutchman Kurt?"

"I believe we have more pressing matters to discuss than Kurt Lang, Cissy," Ellen said, feeling her face redden. "Would you care to tell me what you meant at Ophelia's?"

"I'm tired, Ellen," Cissy replied. She turned her back on her sister and began preparing for bed.

Ellen warmed bricks on the hearth and then with only light from the low fire on the hearth, dressed herself for sleep and slipped into the warmed bed beside Cissy. She would eventually get the whole story from her sister. Cissy was hiding more than being struck, though that was bad enough. Cissy was nursing another wrong in her heart, something her little sister was prone to do, her one character flaw in Ellen's opinion.

But Ellen found that she was having a difficult time being as sympathetic to her sister's plight as she thought she should have been. Perhaps it was the fact that she'd lashed out at Ellen earlier. But more likely, it was the way she'd treated Kurt, as if he were not worthy of common courtesy.

Ellen couldn't think of a man more worthy of common courtesy than Kurt Lang.

Tomorrow was another day. She would put aside her anger and insist her sister tell her the truth, and get to the bottom of whatever had happened with Holton. Holton had hurt her, but she didn't see him as a man who would hit his wife. But Cissy wouldn't have told them a lie. Regardless, something was not the way it should be between her sister and her husband.

Please, Father, help me to be the sister that Cissy needs.

Chapter Eighteen

On Saturday, the next morning, Ellen sat in the knitting circle on benches inside the schoolroom with her sister. She realized she was biting her lower lip, her sister's moody presence casting a pall over her. Cissy sat to her right, occasionally stitching on a quilt square while Ellen knitted a pair of mittens, her wooden needles clicking.

Everyone in the circle had welcomed Cissy, and her sister had risen to the occasion and appeared fine to the casual observer. Ellen was not a casual observer, however. And she was dreading hearing the rest of the story from her sister, guessing that her sister held Ellen responsible for some portion in her problem. She found it impossible to relax.

The women of the community had come together to knit, quilt and sew today while the men built the school's woodshed. Outside, the men were enlarging the school clearing by cutting down trees and then chopping the wood to stack and dry. Winter was coming—the brisk wind that buffeted the windows announced that.

Ellen's stomach knitted itself into knots. The news

that Holton might have struck Cissy was not the only cause. She knew there was more, and since it was being held back, Ellen was certain it would be worse. Although what could possibly be worse?

"I'm so grateful to everyone for donating yarn and for knitting socks, hats and mittens. My son Isaiah will be so happy," Lavina said, sitting across the circle from Ellen. Her son helped at the Ojibwa reservation in far northern Wisconsin, and they were knitting items to donate to his mission work.

"I thought he'd come home for good by now," Mrs. Ashford said. "He's been up there with those Indians almost a year."

"He is needed at the mission. And he loves it," Lavina said mildly.

Ellen could hear the men's voices outside over the noise of saws, hammers and axes, and she realized she was actually listening for Kurt's voice. This caused her to blush, and she bowed her head over her work so no one would notice.

"So have President and Mrs. Grant been home to Galena, Mrs. Rogers?" Mrs. Ashford asked Cissy.

"No," Cissy said, not looking up from her quilt square. "I believe they are quite busy in Washington."

Mrs. Ashford waited for more of a reply, but none came. Ellen's neck muscles knit themselves tightly together. Her sister seemed to have drifted back into her sullen rudeness. Ellen felt she needed to make some excuse for her, but didn't quite know how.

"What do you think of your sister taking in a foundling?" The archly asked question came from one of the women whom Ellen didn't know well.

Cissy looked at William lying in his cradle at Ellen's feet, exercising his legs and arms and gurgling as toddlers crawled around him playing with blocks and clacking jar rims. "My sister has a tender heart—too tender sometimes."

"Everyone knows how sweet your sister is," Sunny Whitmore agreed.

"Yes, Ellen is *always* thinking of others," Cissy replied with an ironic edge to her voice.

Ellen pricked up her ears and gave her sister a sharp look. What on earth was she referring to? As soon as the knitting circle was finished, Ellen intended to get to the bottom of it. She couldn't put it off any longer.

As Kurt entered the schoolhouse behind Martin, he couldn't stop himself from immediately directing his attention to Ellen. To him, she stood out from all the other women. He tried to not let this show. But he couldn't help responding in kind to the welcoming smile she sent him.

"It's lunchtime, isn't it?" Martin asked, taking off his leather gloves as the other men began coming in, clapping their chilled hands together.

The women rose from their handwork and the men began moving the benches into rows and noisily setting up the rectangular folding tables Noah Whitmore and Gordy Osbourne had built. The women set out the food on the table in the teacher's quarters. Soon Noah had blessed the food and the work the community had come together to do, and everyone settled down to good food and to enjoy the gathering.

Kurt found himself sitting beside Ellen, across from the Ashfords. The teacher's sister sat beside Mrs. Ashford, not talking to anyone. He'd gotten the impression she didn't like having an immigrant nearby. However, he wasn't about to leave Ellen's side. He'd realized that Ellen, under her smile, did not look happy and he suspected her sister was the reason.

Just then, the door opened and Gunther walked inside. "Hello! I see I arrived in time for a good meal!"

Amanda leaped up as if to go to him, but instead she remained beside her father, smiling and clasping her hands together.

Kurt was surprised and pleased by the warm welcome Gunther received. People called out, "Welcome home!" A few of the men even rose and slapped him on the back.

Soon, Gunther sat near Kurt with a heaping plate of food, telling everyone about the trip to New Glarus. "Mrs. Bollinger's cousin has a fine farm at New Glarus and he welcomed her," Gunther said between bites. "Of course, everyone was sad about her husband's death, but her cousin will look after her. It was odd to be someplace where everyone was speaking German." He shook his head. "I've gotten used to English."

Amanda smiled at him and he grinned back.

"Amanda," Mrs. Ashford said, "why don't you go to the dessert table and choose something for Gunther? The desserts are nearly picked over."

Amanda looked startled, but moved to obey.

Kurt was also quite surprised by Mrs. Ashford's instruction to Amanda. Then he felt the lightest touch glance his hand under the table. Looking sideways, he caught the briefest smile as it flickered over Ellen's face. The intimacy of this wordless communication nearly withdrew all the air from him. He struggled to appear normal while his heart did somersaults.

"I think I'll go, too," Ellen said, rising. "May I get you something, Mr. Lang?"

"Yes, thank you, Miss Thurston," he replied, sounding much more normal than he actually felt.

When Amanda and Ellen returned with desserts in hand and set them in front of Gunther and Kurt, Ellen's sister got up, her chin lifted defiantly. "Ellen, I have one of my headaches. I'm going to lie down." Then she left, walking stiffly through the crowded room as if she'd been offended somehow, looking neither right nor left.

"I am sorry your sister does not feel good," Kurt said.

"Me, too," Ellen murmured, sounding worried.

"We should remove what's left of the food from your quarters," Mrs. Ashford said, "so we don't disturb her."

Ellen rose and the two of them disappeared through the connecting door. Amanda asked Mr. Ashford's permission to go outside with Gunther to "talk."

Kurt watched in amazement as the man nodded his permission. After the young people left, Mr. Ashford looked at him. "I'll admit, Mr. Lang, that we didn't have a very good opinion of your brother at first. He seemed to have a chip on his shoulder. But he has helped many without being asked. And Amanda tells us he is studying hard and plans to become a citizen when he's able."

"Yes," Kurt said, astonished by both the burst of pride within him and Mr. Ashford's words.

"You're doing a good job with your charges."

Kurt nodded, dry-mouthed. *"Danke."* In a daze, he got up and went to help the ladies move the food out of the teacher's quarters. When Mrs. Ashford left the room with her hands full, he leaned over to whisper in Ellen's ear. "What has happened with the Ashfords?"

Ellen merely looked him in the eye and raised both eyebrows, giving him a pleased smile.

"So, Ellen," Cissy snapped, reminding him that they were not alone. "You left me behind with Holton and are already interested in someone else. A foreigner, to boot."

Ellen turned to her sister, appearing incredulous.

Kurt mumbled a few quick parting words and hurried outside, shutting the side door behind him. What was going on? Who was Holton? His head spun with questions.

He quickly donned his jacket, went outside and picked up where his work had stopped along with the other men congregating around the finished wood shed. Swinging an ax to make firewood would be easier than trying to figure out what was happening inside between the two sisters.

Ellen gaped at her sister. "Now? With the whole town in the next room, you decide to tell me what's going on *now?*"

"Yes, now!" Cissy exploded. "Why didn't you tell me the truth about him, Ellen?"

Surprise buzzed up Ellen's spine. "About whom?"

"I'm not a child! Why do you keep treating me like one, Ellen?" Cissy jumped to her feet.

Reeling, Ellen sat down on the stool by the hearth. "I have no idea what you are talking about."

Cissy glared at her. The expression brought back memories of trying times with Cissy as a stubborn little girl and the times when Cissy had behaved like Ophelia's mother, making something small into a crisis. All drama.

Two women came in to retrieve the last of the plates, and the dish tub and towels. One glance at the sisters and they vanished within a minute, shutting the door behind them.

"I'm ready to listen," Ellen said evenly.

Cissy sank to the side of the bed. "Why didn't you tell me about you and Holton?"

Hearing the question out loud—the question she'd avoided even thinking about. Now she was unsure of what to say, of how to handle the situation.

"Why didn't you tell me he was making up to you before I came home from school?" Cissy stamped her foot, angry again.

Finally, Ellen came to herself. Now, when she recalled her brief interest in Holton, she didn't feel the same hurt she'd felt before. Why was that? Could it be, perhaps, that her feelings for Kurt had shown her what she had really been looking for when she'd allowed Holton to become part of her days? She nearly blushed, just thinking of what it would be like to have Kurt call upon her and treat her as someone special.

"Holton did take me out walking and escorted me to a few functions before you came home last summer." Ellen didn't add anything about his flattery and marked attention and the way he'd kissed her hand at each farewell.

"Why didn't you tell me?" Cissy demanded.

"I… I…" How could she say the truth?

"Because I'm your little sister and you didn't want to hurt me?" Cissy asked with withering disdain.

Ellen gave her sister an apologetic shrug. "Because I love you and you were so taken with him and happy."

"Oh, Ellen," Cissy said, the starch going out of her.

"Was that really a kindness? How could you let me fall in love with a man you thought untrustworthy?"

Cissy's words struck Ellen like lightning. "I never thought that. I just thought that like most men, he wanted you because you...because he preferred you. I didn't think him untrustworthy...not as far as you were concerned."

Men always want a pretty wife, Mrs. Ashford's voice echoed in her mind, recoiling from them.

"I wrote you about the gossip after you left," Cissy continued. "I didn't believe it at first, but then Alice told me it was true and that you left because you couldn't bear to live in town with me and Holton together. Then Ophelia's mother had to come and enact one of her scenes in my parlor about how I'd stolen Holton from my own sister." Cissy's tone had become dramatic as if mimicking Aunt Prudence.

"Oh, dear," Ellen said with real sympathy, neglecting to mention that Cissy's recent behavior had put her in mind of Aunt Prudence.

The two sisters sat, mute. Ellen didn't know what to say. *What was I thinking?* And why had Holton struck Cissy? He'd never seemed that kind of man. *Did I unwittingly cause my sister to marry an unworthy man?* The possibility devastated her.

"Cissy, I need to know how you got that bruise. How did it happen?" Ellen insisted.

"I told you. Holton struck me." Cissy's tone was pouty and she turned away.

Ellen wanted to press the issue but knew this could only stir her sister to more melodrama. And most of the town was still so near them. *The truth will out,* she told herself, *in time.*

* * *

There was only one person Ellen wanted to go to—Kurt. She realized he couldn't change anything. He didn't even know about Holton and her and Cissy. Still, at the end of the day, Kurt had lingered after everyone else had left. Was he hoping to speak with her?

Wrapping her shawl close around her, Ellen stepped outside, leaving Cissy to mope alone. At the far side of the clearing, Johann was gathering woodchips into a sack for kindling. Kurt was working on the new wood-shed, testing the swing of the double doors. She approached him. "Kurt?"

He turned, startled. "Ellen."

Every fiber of her being drew her closer and before she could talk herself out of it, she was resting her head against his chest. Oh, the comfort of being near him.

After a moment's pause, his arms closed around her. "You are upset, *ja?*"

"Ja," she whispered.

"Your sister has troubles?"

She nodded against him.

He patted her back and murmured, *"Liebschen."*

She didn't know what the word meant, but it sounded nice. "I don't know what to do."

"You are wise. You will sort it out."

She shook her head against him, again feeling the thick flannel of his shirt rub against her cheek. She had thought when she'd kept quiet over Holton's sudden interest in Cissy that she had acted in Cissy's best interest.

Now she might have let her sister be swept into a possibly disastrous marriage. She felt this guilt pulling at her.

Was that true? She wanted to lie down on the cold

ground and weep until she ceased to think. "Kurt, sometimes I just want to pack up William, get on a riverboat and run away." Even as she said the words, she knew they weren't entirely true.

She didn't want to leave this man.

Unable to lie to herself any longer, she pulled away from him and looked into his eyes. *I have feelings for this man, deep feelings.*

The thought stunned her.

"I know how that feels, but we both ran away already. Didn't we?" Kurt asked gently.

Over Kurt's shoulder, she glimpsed a familiar figure entering the clearing. Ellen wanted to pick up her skirts and run. "Evidently, I didn't move far enough," she said with an ironic twist.

"What?" Kurt turned.

Ellen's brother was striding toward them.

Instant irritation swept away Ellen's low mood. Did the whole family have to troop to her door?

Randolph strode toward them. "Ellen! Is Cissy with you?"

Ellen recognized that tone of voice. It was Randolph's "I'm the big brother; I know best" tone. "Yes, Cissy arrived yesterday."

"Where is she?"

"In my quarters." She motioned toward the door behind her.

Randolph paused to kiss her forehead. He turned to Kurt and raised an eyebrow. "You're that Dutchman who lives near Ophelia?"

"My name is Kurt Lang, Mr. Thurston," Kurt replied formally. Neither man extended his hand in greeting.

Randolph looked back and forth between Ellen and

Kurt, his silent questioning what Kurt was doing alone with his sister plain.

Ellen forced a smile. "Cissy's inside. Please go in quietly. William is napping."

Randolph lingered another few moments, eyeing Kurt, and then her brother marched to the door and went inside.

"*You* may have moved far enough from home," she muttered to Kurt, "but I am still just a few days away by boat." She sighed. "Thank you…" What could she say—*thank you for comforting me, for understanding… for holding me?*

"You do not owe me any thanks," Kurt said to her gently. Then he called to Johann, who started to run to him.

Ellen knew she should move away, but she couldn't.

Johann reached them and held open the bulging cloth sack. "See all the kindling I picked up?"

She smiled and complimented him on his hard work.

After a pause, Johann looked back and forth between them, evidently sensing something.

Finally, Kurt smiled and said, "Good day, Miss Thurston." He pulled at the brim of his hat, and he and Johann walked away.

Ellen waited till they had disappeared around a bend. She'd hoped he would turn for one last look her way, but he didn't. She stood there, feeling again his strong arms around her, wishing she hadn't been forced from his embrace.

"Ellen?" Cissy called from the doorway. "Aren't you coming in?"

Ellen stifled her desire to make a run for it and turned back toward her door. "Yes, Cissy, I'm coming."

Hoping to soothe everyone's nerves, Ellen made a pot of coffee and set out cake that had been left for her while Randolph paced and Cissy sat gloomily on the side of the bed. William woke and Ellen changed his diaper and prepared him a bottle. Then she sat in the rocking chair with him.

A log crumbled on the hearth, bringing Ellen back to waiting for Randolph to come to the point. Perhaps she would now finally understand what had happened to Cissy.

Randolph poured himself a cup of coffee and cut a thick slice of the brown sugar cake. He sat down and ate hungrily. "The food on the boat was atrocious."

"Did you come alone, Randolph?" Cissy asked.

Ellen sincerely hoped so.

"Yes. Alice is expecting and Holton couldn't leave the bank. I told everyone that Ellen had invited us to visit before winter set in and the river froze." Randolph looked directly at Cissy. "What were you thinking, running away like this? Do you want to plunge our family into scandal?"

Cissy stood with fury on her face. "Did you know that Holton made up to Ellen before I came home?"

"The whole of Galena knew, Cissy," Randolph said, taking another bite of cake and washing it down with coffee. "No one was surprised that he changed his mind. You're prettier than Ellen and younger."

Ellen gasped.

"No offense, Ellen, but it's the truth, so why deny it?" Randolph continued chewing in between words.

Ellen steamed in silence.

"Then why didn't anybody tell me?" Cissy demanded.

"No one wanted to hurt your feelings," Randolph said. "Why are you making such a fuss? After my last visit here, I insisted Alice stop fueling that bit of gossip. Now you've managed to stir everything up again."

Ellen decided it was time to get to the gist of the matter and leave her part out of this. "Randolph, Cissy says Holton struck her. Are you aware of that?"

Randolph's cup hung in midair. "What? You can't be serious. No man of consideration hits his wife."

"Cissy's eye was still faintly bruised when she arrived," Ellen said.

"Is this true, Cissy?" Randolph demanded, his jaw jutting forward.

Cissy burst into tears.

"The truth, Cissy," Randolph insisted.

It wasn't until Randolph addressed their sister so sternly that it occurred to Ellen that Cissy might be lying. She began to feel angry before her sister even answered.

"Oh, very well. Holton and I were arguing. I tried to push past him. He stopped me and I stumbled and bumped my head against the molding."

So Holton hadn't struck Cissy. It had been just an accident.

"Cissy, how could you—" Then she stopped before her anger got the better of her. "Why would you mislead me about something as serious as that?"

"Cissy, you *married* Holton," Randolph said. "He isn't perfect. No one is," Randolph admitted. "If Holton ever does intentionally harm you, you are to come to me immediately and I will deal with him. But I fail to see why you've made a big fuss and started people talking again for nothing."

"It wasn't nice to find out from Alice that the gossip about Holton and Ellen was true," Cissy said resentfully.

"That's why you're acting this way?" Ellen asked.

"Alice told you that, did she?" Randolph looked displeased. "We'll deal with that when we return home."

Ellen gazed down at her child, wishing her siblings could return home immediately. Her life was here now, not with them. She wished them well but she did not care about gossip in Galena. She busied herself burping William.

At that moment, Randolph turned to Ellen. "As for you, Ellen, I think you're getting too thick with that Dutchman." Before Ellen could reply, he went on, "Cissy, I will accompany you home tomorrow. Another boat is expected to dock after breakfast. River traffic is humming before the Mississippi freezes. I will go to the General Store now. They offered to put me up again for the night." He kissed them both on the forehead. "I'll see you in town no later than eight o'clock in the morning." With that, he left.

Ellen went to the door and latched it firmly. She turned and faced her sister. "Celeste—I think it's time you started using your full given name—you are a married woman and yes, Holton squired me around town before you came home. But he chose you over me." Ellen was startled to realize that saying this aloud no longer held any pain for her. "Now you must be a wife to him, and not go around telling horrible lies about the way he treats you. After all, you chose him, as well."

And I choose Kurt.

The thought almost literally rocked Ellen back on her heels.

"Ellen, are you all right?" Cissy asked.

"I'm fine," Ellen said, sitting down slowly, suddenly imagining the family she and Kurt could make, with William, and Johann and Gunther. Her heart shivered with the thought.

I choose Kurt Lang. I'm in love with him, and I want to marry him.

Was there any chance he felt the same way?

Chapter Nineteen

Just after dawn, Kurt was in the barn milking the cows when he heard a man's voice call out, "Hello! Is this the Lang place?"

Kurt got up and looked out his partially open barn door. He was not surprised to see Ellen's brother in the clearing, looking around. After the disgruntled expression the man had turned on him yesterday, he figured this conversation was coming sooner or later.

He sighed and walked to the open door. "What can I do for you?"

The man marched over to him. "I'm Randolph Thurston, Miss Thurston's brother."

"*Ja,* I remember." The cow bellowed behind Kurt. "I am milking. You can come in." Kurt turned and went back to his stool, leaving the man no choice.

Randolph followed him inside. Kurt continued his work, not interested in making this conversation easy for Ellen's brother. "I have little time so I'll come right to the point."

"That will be best for both of us." The streams of milk hit the metal pail loudly, rhythmically.

"Every time I come to town, I find my sister Ellen in your company," Randolph said in a stiff, constricted tone.

"It is small town. People help each other when they can."

"The Ashfords say that you and she have people talking."

Kurt lost patience and rose. "What have you come to say?"

Ellen's brother glared but stood his ground. "Do I have to spell it out?"

Kurt leaned toward Randolph. "*Ja*, I'm just a stupid Dutchman. Spell it out."

"My sister's educated and has been raised to a higher standard—"

"Your sister is a fine woman—educated, kind and good. And I am not courting her." Kurt wanted to slam his fist into the man's face. He restrained himself. "That is your concern, yes?"

Randolph looked as if he were chewing cud like the cows.

"I am busy working. Do you need to say anything more?" Kurt asked.

"No. I just wanted to clear the air." Randolph turned and left with no further words.

Kurt clenched and unclenched his hands and then shook them out so he could continue his chore. He couldn't take his anger out on the cows.

He spent a moment gazing around the snug barn where his plow horse, two black-and-white Holstein cows and two brown goats would winter. When he'd come here, he'd lived in a tent. Now he had a good-size cabin, a barn, a full corn crib and root cellar. If Randolph Thurston had come to an empty piece of land this spring, would he have accomplished as much?

The cow lowed as if scolding him to get on with it. Kurt sat back down on the stool and began again, milking.

I am not courting Ellen. But I would like to.

There was no point in denying the truth. The memory of Ellen leaning against him last night rolled through him. *Ellen, dear Ellen.* But while the Ashfords had begun to view Gunther as acceptable, Randolph had made it clear that Kurt was not.

And although Kurt didn't care what Randolph Thurston thought one way or the other, he would never, ever want to make trouble for Ellen. That was exactly what he'd been trying to avoid since the very first moment he had found he liked her.

Sitting at the Ashford table after breakfast, Ellen let Amanda take William from her. An unusual lassitude gripped Ellen today. Breathing and speaking seemed to take great energy. In fact, it had since her revelation about Kurt Lang and her feelings for him.

"We'd best be getting ready for worship," Mrs. Ashford said.

Ellen nodded and leaned her head in her hand.

"You seem down, Ellen. Are you missing your sister and brother already?"

Ellen recalled the stiff farewells she'd exchanged with her siblings at the dock earlier, and shook her head.

"It's a shame they had to leave when Thanksgiving is just next week," Mrs. Ashford continued. "I'd invite you to eat with us but you'll probably be joining your cousin and her family, won't you?"

Ellen barely nodded.

"What *is* the matter?" The storekeeper's wife leaned across the table and touched Ellen's hand.

"I'm sorry," Ellen said, trying to come up with an explanation for her behavior that she could offer Mrs. Ashford. "I was actually trying to think of someone who could watch William during the schooldays. I need someone close, especially for the coming winter."

Mrs. Ashford looked thoughtful. "Maybe it's time Amanda quit school and started putting money away and filling her hope chest in earnest."

Dismay filled Ellen, galvanizing her. "Oh, no, she's the captain of one of the spelling teams. And she's doing so well. I'd hate for her to miss the spelling bee in the spring."

This halted Mrs. Ashford's counterargument. Evidently this woman wanted to see her daughter at the regional spelling bee—as did most parents. Spelling had become one of her students' favorite and most studied subjects.

"And you wouldn't want her to miss eighth-grade graduation," Ellen said, improvising. "I'm going to ask my uncle to come from Illinois to address our graduates."

"Your uncle who sits in the state legislature?" Mrs. Ashford asked with excitement in her voice.

Ellen nodded. "I plan on writing him soon."

"Oh, that would be wonderful!"

Ellen breathed a sigh of relief. It seemed Amanda would be allowed to finish the eighth grade after all.

Suddenly Mrs. Ashford sat back as if startled. "Why don't I care for William during the day?"

"Oh, Mrs. Ashford, do you have the time?" This possibility hadn't occurred to Ellen.

"Why not? I've raised ten children. They've all married and scattered. Our son went all the way to California, so I am left with no grandchildren near. And your William is a good baby. He never fusses. Why, he'd be company for me during the long winter days."

Ellen gazed at the woman who had once called William disfigured. However, after watching Mrs. Ashford during the measles outbreak, Ellen had no hesitation. "I can't think of anyone who would take better care of him. I will pay you, just as I've paid you to take my dinners here." She let out a huge sigh. "Oh, thank you. That relieves me of such a worry."

As she discussed terms with Mrs. Ashford, Mr. Ashford came back from outside chores, rubbing his chilled hands together. "Time we were setting off to the school for worship. It's nearly ten o'clock."

The ladies quickly donned shawls and hats, and Ellen claimed William and they walked together through the barren trees to the schoolhouse. As they arrived, Old Saul was being helped down from his wagon. Smiling, he waved to her as he leaned on his son's arm. At his welcome, a feeling of gratitude suffused Ellen.

This had become her town. She was very aware that the school had become the center of the community, bringing people together, helping them help each other. She realized that she was important to this town, as the schoolmarm, the woman who would prepare the children for their future, for the town's future.

Since the measles outbreak, the town had been a bit divided and nervous, with some people even expressing concern again about Ellen raising William, a baby who seemed to appear out of thin air and could have come from anywhere. It was simply fear, that's all it was. Perhaps holiday cheer would bring the community back together again.

Then Ellen realized that, as the schoolteacher, she was in the perfect position to help the community re-unite. And she had an idea.

She hurried through the gathering to Noah Whit-more and motioned to him that she wanted a private word. She murmured her idea to him and he instantly agreed. As she joined her family in their usual "pew," she glanced over her shoulder and noted Kurt, Gun-ther and Johann taking the bench in the rear that they seemed to favor. She waited to try to catch Kurt's atten-tion, but he seemed very focused on the floor.

Ellen listened carefully to Noah's sermon on loving one's neighbor as one's self, a theme that her idea dove-tailed with quite nicely. At the end of the sermon, he paused before the final prayer. "Miss Thurston spoke to me before service today. She asked me to announce that this Wednesday, the day before Thanksgiving, the chil-dren will put on a brief program to commemorate the First Thanksgiving. Everyone is invited at two o'clock in the afternoon."

A buzz greeted this announcement—a happy buzz to Ellen's ear. She was already drawing up the program in her mind, which would emphasize gratitude to God and their common heritage as Americans.

And perhaps she'd remind people that pilgrims had been foreigners, too. She hoped she'd have a moment to talk to Kurt.

The hum of happy voices lifted Ellen's burden. A few mothers stopped her on their way out to tell her about the fun they were having learning the weekly spelling lists with their children. As she spoke with them, she could pick out Kurt's voice amid the many voices behind her. She soon realized she'd actually been seeking it.

"I did see him, yes," Kurt was saying to Martin.

"I tried to head him off," Martin said, sounding apologetic, "but he wouldn't take my word for it. He has this idea that you and his sister are…" Martin shrugged in an embarrassed way.

"Do not worry, Martin. He didn't say anything I didn't know already." Kurt turned then and suddenly she and Kurt were facing each other. A new awareness of him shimmered over her.

The ladies bid her good-day and she stepped toward him, but he turned and headed for the door.

What had Martin been talking about with Kurt? A sense of urgency pushed her to follow him outside. "Kurt," she said, "Wait."

He didn't pause.

Then she did something she had never done—she pursued a man. She hurried after him into the nearly empty clearing. Very few people had come outside, as most wanted to finish their social time in the warm schoolroom.

Kurt finally halted by his wagon.

"Why didn't you stop?" she asked, holding her shawl tightly around her.

Kurt looked irritated. "You will catch cold—"

"Randolph visited you this morning and was rude to you, wasn't he?"

Kurt looked her in the eye. "It doesn't matter, Miss Thurston."

She could tell that whatever her brother had said had hurt Kurt, and she fumed. "I wish my family would learn to mind its own business."

Kurt said nothing, but Ellen could see the pain on his face and it nearly broke her heart.

"If you saw whom my brother married, you would see how silly it is for him to object to…" Suddenly she realized where her tongue was taking her, and she halted, swallowing words that should not now or perhaps ever be spoken aloud.

"Miss Thurston," Johann said, appearing at her elbow, "what kind of program will we be having? And what is Thanksgiving about?"

She drew her gaze from Kurt to the child. "I will tell you all about it in the morning."

"Let us go, Johann," Kurt said abruptly. "Say farewell to Miss Thurston. You will see her tomorrow."

Ellen watched as Kurt led his nephew away. It was not lost on her that he had not said farewell to her himself, nor was it lost on her that she had almost said, *If you saw whom my brother married, you would see how silly it is for him to object to my wanting to marry you.*

Shock tingled through all her nerves. She had almost told Kurt Lang that she wanted to marry him! But based on the interaction they'd just had, she got the impression that her brother had upset what had been growing between her and Kurt. She didn't know whether to do or say something. What could she say?

On Wednesday afternoon, Ellen stood at the front of the packed schoolroom, hopeful that this program would bring back the community's spirit of unity. The women and smaller children filled the benches while the men lined the walls. The standing-room-only attendance pleased her. Nonetheless, she glanced again at the door, wanting to see one particular face.

Mrs. Ashford sat in the front row, holding William and doting on him. Every parent and most everyone else in town had come to see the program. Except for Kurt. Why hadn't he come to see Johann recite his piece?

From what she'd overheard between Martin and Kurt on Sunday, her brother must have asked Kurt to keep his distance from her. Would Kurt have agreed to such a request, such interference? Yet as a man of honor, he would never do anything that he thought might harm her reputation and Randolph might well have suggested this. The very thought of Randolph's interfering in her life made her want to growl. He had no room to be giving her advice.

Rising above her irritation, she forced herself to focus on the task at hand, and at her signal, Noah Whitmore stood at the front. "We will open with prayer."

Ellen listened to Noah's calm voice, his words setting the tone with a message of love and community. The tightness around her lungs loosened a notch. But she couldn't ignore her disappointment at Kurt's absence.

Then Noah was sitting down and she walked to center stage. "Welcome to the First Annual Thanksgiving Program at Pepin Community School."

Polite applause and some whistling followed her greeting.

"The students have worked very hard and I am proud of their efforts," Ellen said.

The back door opened and Ellen saw Kurt and Gunther slip inside and edge in beside the men who were leaning against the back wall. Joy surged through her, followed by trepidation. She cleared her throat. "We will begin by singing, 'We Gather Together.'"

The children filed out from her quarters and formed ranks, the oldest in the rear and the youngest in front. A few of the children forgot themselves and waved to their families.

Lavina came forward and led the hymn. Soon the schoolroom was filled with the heartfelt song, full of thanks for the bounty of the harvest, and praise for the Lord.

When the hymn ended, a pleasant sense of expectation expanded around Ellen.

The younger children sat down on the floor in a semicircle at the front, and Amanda stepped forward and began to read.

"'One hundred and two pilgrims left Plymouth, England, in 1620 and sailed to the new world.'" As she read, three fourth graders donned paper hats in the style of the seventeenth century. "'They settled near Cape Cod. There they met Squanto, an Indian of the Wampanoag or Massasoit tribe.'"

A fifth-grade boy with feathers in a band around his head walked over to the fourth graders and raised his hand in greeting. "'Squanto had been kidnapped as a young boy by a sea captain and taken to Europe. He could speak English. He taught the pilgrims how to grow maize, beans and squash.'"

As the program continued, the door at the rear opened and a woman—a stranger—stepped in, scanning the room as if searching for someone. Ellen wondered who she was.

Amanda handed the book to another eighth grader who began reading, but the boy's voice trailed off as heads turned to watch the stranger. The woman was walking slowly up the center aisle, rudely studying the people in each row. People glared at her for disturbing the program. Ellen prompted the lad to start reading again.

"There he is!" the strange woman exclaimed and ran to Mrs. Ashford. The woman snatched William from Mrs. Ashford's arms, igniting an instant uproar. Ellen leaped forward and tried to wrest William from the woman's arms. "Take your hands off my son!"

With angry voices, people surged to their feet and converged on the woman and Ellen.

Kurt reached her first and wrenched William from the stranger. "What do you think you are doing?" he demanded. "This child belongs to Miss Thurston!"

The woman burst into loud tears. There was something false about her—Ellen did not think for a moment the weeping was real. "Who are you?" she demanded.

"I am the poor woman who was forced to leave my baby on your doorstep," the woman wailed.

Everyone quieted, watchful.

"Forced?" Noah pushed to the front. "Who forced you to abandon your child?"

The woman buried her face in a handkerchief and wept louder, as if she couldn't bear to tell her tale.

Ellen examined the woman from head to toe. She looked to be a few years older than Ellen, dressed in worn and not too clean clothing. A torn cuff caught Ellen's eye.

"Fate has been cruel to me," the woman said. "I'm a poor widow who lost her husband before my child was born. And then he was born disfigured so." She wept copiously.

Ellen gritted her teeth, holding back her words, letting the woman tell her story. She tried to remain calm, for nothing so far had registered in her mind to give any credence to the woman's claim.

"I found a man who would marry me, but I didn't think he'd want my baby, too, so I left him here."

More wailing and tears followed.

Ellen reached the end of her short rope. Seething, she scanned the faces crowding around. Did they believe this woman?

Those who hadn't wanted this *disfigured* foundling in their town in the first place were nodding as if they did believe her. Ellen held her tongue, knowing anything she would say would be discounted.

But how could she put a stop to this?

"So," Noah Whitmore said, "you say that your husband died before your child was born, and since you wanted to find a new husband right away—before a proper year of mourning—you abandoned your child on Miss Thurston's doorstep?"

Ellen took heart. When the pastor put the situation in plain terms without all the weeping and histrionics, anybody could see that the story proved to be as thin as broth and did the woman no credit.

But the woman nodded, silently agreeing to these dreadful facts, her face still buried in her handkerchief.

"Do you have any proof?" Noah asked.

"Proof?" the woman replied with surprise, looking up. "What proof could I give?"

"*Ja,* a very good question," Kurt spoke at last.

"You don't sound like an American," the woman snapped. "What do you know about anything?"

Ellen swallowed a sharp retort, trusting Noah to handle this. Kurt merely gazed at the woman, holding William securely in his arms.

"Before we could give you this child, we'd have to have something more to go on," Noah pronounced. "We know that Miss Thurston is giving the child good care, but we don't know you."

"Well!" the woman declared. "You can't prove that I'm not the baby's mother."

"Ma'am," Noah said, "the burden of proof lies with you. Bring someone or something to back you up and—"

The woman sent a scathing glance at Kurt and Ellen and then pushed through the crowd. When she reached the door, she turned dramatically and called, "I'll be back! You haven't heard the last of me. That's my child and I won't be denied!" With that, she swept out and slammed the door behind her.

"She didn't even say what her name was," Mrs. Ashford said in the quiet after the storm.

"Nor did she tell us where she's from, for instance, and how she got here to leave William in the first place…if she did," Noah added.

"The dustup about the foundling with a birthmark left on the Pepin schoolteacher's doorstep has become common knowledge up and down the river," Mrs. Ashford said. "People would come in and ask Ned and me whether it was true or not."

Old Saul cleared his throat. "Noah, I have grave doubts about this woman's story—grave doubts. But time will tell. I will pray for clarity in this. I hope everyone will. Not every person is to be trusted."

Ellen heartily agreed with this but decided it best not

to say anything. The truth will out, Shakespeare had said, and Ellen did not doubt him.

"Everyone," Ellen said finally in her best teacher voice, "the children haven't finished their program. Please be seated so all their hard work won't go for naught."

The crowd returned to their places, but the good feeling of the community coming together to give thanks had been spoiled, broken. At the end the children all bowed together and everyone applauded, but the zest had left the room.

Afterward, people milled around in groups, talking in low tones about the woman, not beaming and bragging over the children's program as Ellen had hoped. She roiled with frustration. Her plan to bring the community together again had been demolished by a woman she didn't believe for a moment.

The only bright spot came when she remembered that Kurt has wrested William from the woman and had defended her. But the way he would not look at her before he departed left her feeling even worse. Was this because of her brother's meddling?

Chapter Twenty

Wearing her best day dress of figured amber silk in honor of Thanksgiving at Martin and Ophelia's, Ellen wished she could get into the holiday spirit. She sat at the Steward's table watching Nathan and William, unable to tear her thoughts from yesterday's unexpected interruption at the school play.

The one person she wanted to talk to was Kurt. Also invited for the holiday, he and the boys were due to arrive at any moment. However, yesterday after the school program, he had made it clear that he did not want to speak to her. In some ways, she understood—it would have fueled the gossip about them even more.

Her only hope was that Kurt would drive her home from the Stewards'. Perhaps then, when they were alone, she'd have an opportunity to talk to him about William, and also find out what was bothering him.

Ophelia glanced at a list she had on the mantel and checked one more item off with her pencil. "Everything is done." She exhaled with satisfaction and untied her spattered apron.

Ellen smiled, but only with her lips; her heart remained weighed down. Would she be forced to take William away from here in order to keep him? Would she have to leave this place that had become home? Would she have to leave Kurt?

A knock sounded. Martin called out, "Come in!"

Kurt, Gunther and Johann entered, letting in the late November cold. The next few moments were taken up with exchanging greetings and hanging up coats and scarves. Ellen made a point to send Kurt a special smile. He merely nodded and then looked away.

Her spirits plummeted lower.

"It's getting cold. Maybe we get snow soon," red-cheeked Johann announced happily and then made a beeline to William, who was napping in his cradle.

Soon the seven of them sat around a table laden with bowls, one each of potatoes with a pool of melted butter, corn, dressing and a basket of yeast rolls. And a platter of wild turkey, Kurt's contribution to the feast.

Though the meal was wonderful, Ellen's appetite eluded her. She tried to keep all her anxiety inside. Tried but failed.

"Ellen, I know you're worried about William," Ophelia said finally.

Ellen felt ashamed for casting a shadow over the holiday meal Ophelia had worked so hard to prepare. "I'm so sorry."

"Nothing to be sorry about," Martin said. "If that woman is William's mother, I'll eat my hat—and Kurt's, too."

"Why would she say he's her son if it isn't true?" Gunther asked, his face twisted with puzzlement.

Ellen had tried to come up with reasons but couldn't. She also tried to gauge Kurt's reaction but his expression had become shuttered as if he'd put up a wall between them. Why? And why did she feel empty, frail because of it?

"I don't know why that woman would claim William was hers," Martin said. "But it's just too fishy. Her husband dies and she immediately starts looking for another one? What kind of wife does that?"

"A wife who's left destitute," Ellen said. "Sometimes women don't have a choice."

They all looked to Ellen in surprise.

"But give up her own blood?" Gunther interposed. "That's not right."

Ellen listened to the arguments, all of which had already streamed through her mind over and over. Still, Kurt was silent.

"What will you do, Ellen?" Ophelia asked.

Ellen paused for a moment, and then said, "Maybe I should just go home to Galena. I have family and friends there who will support me," she said.

Kurt swallowed a sound of surprise.

At this, silence fell. Martin and Ophelia stepped into the breach and began talking about their plans for a quick visit home before the Mississippi froze. "We haven't been home since we came north," Ophelia said. "Mother wants to see her first grandchild again."

"When do you leave?" Ellen asked.

"Tomorrow morning," Martin said.

This news surprised Ellen. "So soon? You didn't say anything."

"Mr. Ashford told us the river captains expect the icing over within the next month," Martin said. "It might come sooner, and we don't want to get stuck in

Galena. A trip home by land in the cold isn't what I want for my wife and child."

Ellen got his point. Travel over land in the cold could endanger little Nathan. And with the threat of the imminent freezing of the Mississippi, the visit would be a short one, which they preferred.

"I will take care of your stock," Kurt offered.

"Thanks. I was hoping you would," Martin said, sounding distinctly relieved.

"Then we'll leave you the leftovers," Ophelia said. "I don't want the food to go to waste."

"I think I should come and stay here," Gunther suggested. "An empty cabin is not good."

"You're right," Martin said, giving Gunther a friendly slap on the shoulder. "We would be better off with someone staying here. Not just in case of a thief, but with all the hibernating animals foraging, a bear might break in easily and rip everything apart."

Kurt nodded, looking grateful. "You are thinking, Gunther."

Recognizing Kurt's pride in his brother, Ellen felt a pang. She missed talking to him about Gunther, about Johann. *I'll feel better after we talk on the way home.* Her ragged spirit yearned to be near him and she looked forward to sitting beside him on the journey home. She could bring up Randolph and somehow take the sting from his words. Or she could try.

But it did not turn out the way she'd hoped.

When the meal was finished and the dishes begun, the men went out to get wood. When they came back in, letting in a cold draft, Martin shed his coat and gloves but Kurt kept his on.

"Mrs. Steward, thank you for the wonderful meal.

I must go home now. One of my cows is not well and I want to keep close watch on her."

His announcement hit Ellen right between her eyes.

Obviously startled, Gunther looked up from washing the large roasting pan.

"Yes, of course," Martin said, looking back and forth between Kurt and Ellen, and making it obvious that he, too, had expected Kurt to drive her home.

A few awkward moments passed. Ellen endured them, feeling discarded.

"I'll drive Miss Thurston home," Gunther offered, drying the last pan and setting it upside down on the table. "Johann can ride along with William in the rear. He'll enjoy it."

Kurt bid everyone goodbye without any special word or even a glance toward Ellen, and then shut the door hard behind him.

Soon, in the darkening afternoon, Ellen and William were bundled up for their chilly ride home. Johann carried the baby and Gunther got up on the cart bench first.

Martin and Ophelia walked Ellen outside. "You must have faith," Ophelia murmured close to Ellen's ear. "William will not be taken from you. That woman will have no proof. She didn't even give us her name. That's telling."

Ellen didn't say what she was thinking, which was that many in the community still would pressure her to give up William if it came down to it. But she found, as Martin helped her up onto the two-wheeled cart, that the sinking feeling dragging her down was not about the stranger who was lying about William.

Kurt, why have you turned away from me? This is more than Randolph's interference. It must be.

Then Martin leaned forward and said to Ellen, "I think you will be as happy as we are to have the river freeze."

Ophelia turned to her husband. "What do you mean, Martin?"

"Before he left, Randolph stopped by to have a few words with Kurt."

"You didn't tell me that," Ophelia protested. She looked to Ellen, and Ellen nodded, letting on that she'd guessed.

"Perhaps that has something to do with Kurt's demeanor today?" Ophelia asked.

Ellen found she couldn't even answer her cousin. Her brother's meddling could not be the cause of Kurt's distancing himself from her. She couldn't imagine him bowing to such pressure.

Martin put his arm around his wife, calling out a final farewell as Gunther turned the cart and headed away in the early autumn twilight. Ellen clung to the rocking bench, trying to understand what had gone so terribly wrong. On the way home, Ellen couldn't decide if she were colder inside from her distress or outside from the chill. Wind buffeted them and swayed the treetops. Dry oak leaves clung to the branches above and the sky stretched overhead, bleak gray.

"Miss Thurston," Gunther began, "I have finished reading the American history book you loaned me. Can we start our evening lessons again? I'll understand if you—"

Ellen was momentarily ashamed of herself for wallowing in her problems. "No. I want to help you keep up your studies. Do you want to come this weekend or wait till next week?"

"May I come Saturday afternoon?"

"Yes, we'll start learning more American geography. You can help me mount the new wall maps that just arrived."

"I'll be glad to help." The young man again fell silent.

Ellen tried to think of another topic of conversation, but all she could think was that Kurt had told Martin he'd expected Randolph's disapproval. Something else was at work here.

In the silence, Ellen remembered the many times Kurt had taken her home in this cart, and she'd rested against him. Had the sweet connection she'd felt with him ended? The bleak gray sky slipped inside her as angry words for her interfering brother flowed through her mind.

She had to find the courage to talk to Kurt…and let him know her heart.

Chapter Twenty-One

Saturday afternoon came, cold and clear, and Ellen welcomed Gunther and Johann. As she watched Kurt drive away in the cart without so much as a wave, loneliness welled up within.

Kurt's avoidance of her made her feel as cold as the December nights. He could easily have come in with Gunther today as he had in the weeks before Marta appeared and measles broke out. *If I don't know what's changed, what can I do to reach Kurt?* When he came back to pick up the boys, she must find a way to speak with him privately.

After shedding coats and mittens by the door, Gunther and Johann went straight to the fireplace to warm their hands. "I wonder how much colder Wisconsin will be this winter," Gunther commented, shivering.

Ellen considered this. "I think the weather might be a bit colder here than my hometown. But it's nothing we can't handle." Memories of a few past blizzards came to mind and she added, "I should draw up guidelines for parents to follow when deciding whether to let their children walk to school or not. Frostbite and getting lost in a snowstorm are possible."

Even as she smiled to reassure the boys, her gaze shifted toward the door as if she expected Kurt to appear.

Johann hurried over to William, who lay on his back on a blanket in front of the fire, kicking his legs and trying to roll over. "Hey, William. I brought my horse and look, now I have a goat, too." The boy proudly displayed his carved toys above the baby's face.

Gunther suffered one more whole body shiver and then pulled a book from his pocket. "I read it, and learned so much. Is it true that Abraham Lincoln was born in a log cabin like we live in?"

Ellen smiled slightly. "Yes."

"Is that why the Ashfords have changed their opinion about me? Is it because they are giving me a chance to prove what I can do? That I could accomplish much, too?"

Ellen paused to consider her answer. "In a way. They are seeing what you do and how you behave."

"And that makes up for me being a foreigner?"

Ellen sighed. "Some people will always hold that against you, I'm afraid. But not all. When I first met you, you were very unhappy and it showed in your attitude and behavior. That has all changed now."

Gunther nodded seriously.

Ellen thought back to when Gunther had been so unhappy. Did it have anything to do with Kurt? She knew she shouldn't ask this of Gunther but she was tempted, especially since their conversation the other night, after the Thanksgiving meal.

Taking herself in hand, Ellen donned her shawl and

led Gunther with his coat on into the chilly schoolroom. When school was not in session, she only heated her quarters. The next half hour went quickly as she and Gunther hung the maps of the United States and the world. On his pad of paper, Gunther sketched a crude map of the thirty-seven states and ten territories plus Oklahoma, Indian territory and the newly purchased Alaska. Then, the lesson finished and the two of them, very chilled by now, hurried back into her warm room.

"Look!" Johann exclaimed, pointing at William.

William grunted and rolled over, and crowed with his victory. Ellen clapped her hands and Johann sang an impromptu song, "William can roll oooooover! Oooover!"

She and Johann cooed over the baby, and Ellen was filled with joy at William's accomplishment. Then she looked at Gunther's face, which was dark with some murky emotion she could not identify.

Before she could say anything, he got up, buttoning up his coat. "I will bring in more wood." After snagging his hat, he was gone.

Ellen didn't hesitate. She tightened her shawl and pulled on wool mittens. "I'll be right back, Johann."

She found Gunther bent forward in front of the woodshed, pressing both hands flat against its door, his distress obvious. "Gunther?"

He swung around.

She saw tears in his eyes and took another step forward.

He held up a hand, fighting for control. She waited, shivering.

"Bad things," he began when he could command his voice, "happened to us in Germany."

Ice crackled around Ellen's heart. She tried to think

of what to say, some comfort to offer. But she desperately wanted to know what kind of bad things he was talking about. Did these bad things have anything to do with how Kurt had pulled away from her?

Gunther wiped his face with the back of one hand and folded his arm, tucking his hands under. He leaned against the woodshed doors. "When we watched William roll over, I remembered when Johann's mother died. He had just learned to roll over." The young man's voice broke on the last word.

"My parents both died last year," Ellen said, trying to say: *I know how you feel.*

"Then last year my father died and that was the worst—"

"Gunther!"

At Kurt's shout, Ellen jumped and swung around.

Kurt leaped down from Martin's pony cart, his chest heaving as if he'd been running.

"We go home *now!*" Kurt barked. "Where is Johann?"

"He's inside with William," Ellen said as calmly as she could, hoping her tone would help soothe Kurt.

"I'm getting more wood for Miss Thurston," Gunther said combatively, opening the shed door.

Kurt walked past Ellen as if she weren't there and called out, "Johann! Time to go home! *Now!*"

Ellen didn't budge as Kurt disappeared into her quarters. Moments later, he returned with Johann behind him. "Hurry and put that wood inside," he said to Gunther, who had come out of the shed with an armload of wood. "We go home now."

Gunther halted. "I'm not going home with you, remember? I'm staying at the Stewards' place. And before going there, I'm expected to help Mr. Ashford around the store this afternoon and take supper with them. Then I'll go back to the Stewards' and do the milking. I will ride to church with you tomorrow."

Gunther's polite but firm tone impressed Ellen. He no longer was the surly teenage boy she'd met only months ago. She turned her attention to Kurt, whose face registered a storm of anger. He turned and marched toward the cart.

"See you tomorrow, Miss Thurston! Goodbye, Gunther!" Johann called as he ran to catch up with his uncle.

Ellen held open the door for Gunther. She wanted to ask him to finish telling her what had happened in Germany, but neither of them spoke as he knelt and stacked the wood neatly by the door.

"Thank you, Gunther."

"You're welcome, miss." He looked at her. "My uncle is still sad."

Ellen nodded, unable to speak.

"I will see you later at supper with the Ashfords."

After Gunther left, she slowly unwrapped her shawl and hung everything neatly on the pegs by the door. Then she prepared a bottle for William and fed him. She looked down at the chubby, happy face, her heart aching for the man she loved. "Kurt is very sad," she told William. "What hurt him, little one? What awful thing happened in Germany to force him to run all the way here to Pepin to escape it?"

On Sunday morning, Kurt stood in the schoolroom, singing along with the hymn. But the peace he'd begun to feel in this room on previous Sundays had vanished without a trace.

"There is a balm in Gilead
To make the wounded whole..."

Gunther sat with him and Johann, but anyone could see his brother wanted to sit with the Ashfords. The boy thought himself in love.

In love. Bile rose in Kurt's throat.

Did love really exist in this dark, hurtful world? His traitorous eyes sought out Ellen, who stood alone toward the front of the room.

What had Gunther told Miss Thurston about what had befallen their family? The heat of shame rolled through him in waves.

He alone carried the full weight of the past. Johann and Gunther's youth protected them. *I'm so tired, Lord.*

"There is a balm in Gilead
To heal the sin-sick soul..."

Even as Kurt sang, he was sure there was no balm in Gilead for him. He would carry this weight till he died. Only then could he lay it down.

His mind rebelled at this curse, remembering the joy of holding Ellen close, of breathing in her floral scent and cradling her softness within his arms. That had been a balm to his wounded heart. But that could never happen again. She didn't need a wounded soul like his.

Noah prayed, and the service ended.

"Come," Kurt told the boys. "We go."

People gathering to speak to the pastor on their way out blocked the doorway. Wanting to escape before Ellen came anywhere near him, Kurt chafed. But he waited till he and the lads could make their way into the aisle and then approached Noah. As usual, Kurt said, "Thank you for the good sermon."

Noah gripped Kurt's hand but didn't relinquish it.

"We appreciate how Gunther has pitched in to keep things safe at the Steward's while they're gone."

"Ja." Kurt nodded, extracting his hand from the pastor's grip.

"Do you need any help putting up enough wood for the winter? Gordy and I are going to clear another field before the first good snow and could use you and Gunther. You'd get a share of the wood." Noah searched his eyes as if reading his heart.

Kurt edged a step away, nodding. "Thank you."

"Come over later or tomorrow morning and we'll talk it over."

Kurt hurried his two boys through the door into the chill wind. And then he felt a hand claim his sleeve.

Ellen Thurston stood before him. "May I have a word with you?"

"It is cold and we must get home," he replied and turned away.

"It is cold indeed when a friend turns his back," she said.

He swung around, aware of people all around them, hurrying to their wagons or heading home on foot. "What do you need?"

"To talk to you."

"We have nothing to say to each other."

"I have much to say to you," she said plainly, her beautiful eyes beseeching him.

It hurt just to look at her. "I have no time for talk."

Kurt turned and climbed up onto his wagon bench. Johann looked shocked, his mouth hanging open. "Get into the back, Johann." Kurt untied the reins. "Come on, Gunther. It's cold."

Gunther sent Miss Thurston a sympathetic look and then glared at Kurt, but he climbed up on the bench.

Kurt slapped the reins and without a backward glance turned his wagon and started up the track. Against his will his mind replayed the hymn. *There is a balm in Gilead to make the wounded whole...*

When they arrived at their cabin, both Johann and Gunther wordlessly got off the wagon. Kurt unhitched the team, rubbed them down and put them out to graze the dry grass. He looked at his barn and cabin, and thought that what he'd been told about America had proven true so far—there was free land, and a hard-working man could make a place for himself.

A few feet from the cabin door, Kurt halted. His unruly imagination drew up an image of Ellen in a crisp, white apron, standing in his doorway, telling him to hurry inside where warmth and a good meal awaited him. The imagined picture beckoned and then mocked him. Searing pain made him gasp and bend over, resting his hands on his knees. How could mere emotions hurt so much?

Finally, he straightened and went inside where he and Gunther ate lunch in an unfriendly silence. Johann looked worried but said nothing until he asked to be excused to go out and play. Kurt nodded.

The moment the door shut behind Johann, Kurt and Gunther faced each other.

"Why did you act like that today? Rushing us off?" Gunther asked.

Kurt ignored this. "What did you tell Miss Thurston about what happened in Germany?" Nausea rolled through Kurt.

"I only told her bad things happened there," Gunther said with a defiant edge to his voice. "You heard me, didn't you? And why shouldn't I tell her that?"

"Why?" Kurt thundered in German. "Why don't I want everyone here to know what happened at home? Are you crazy?"

Gunther stared at him. "Even if I told Miss Thurston, do you think she would repeat it to anybody else? Don't you know what kind of lady Miss Thurston is by now?" Gunther struck the table with his fist. "Are you the child here or am I?"

Kurt leaped to his feet, breathing fast and hard. "You will not talk to me like that."

Gunther rose and gazed at his brother with pity. "I am living in the here and now. I am Gunther Lang," he pronounced the words the American way. "I am learning to be an American. I will never return to Europe. Nothing we left behind would draw me back there. And nothing that happened *there* can touch me *here*."

Gunther's words ricocheted in Kurt's mind, and he could not reply.

"We watched little William roll over yesterday by Miss Thurston's fireplace and it reminded me of losing Maria." The lad stopped and obviously swallowed down his emotion. "Because Johann had just rolled over for the first time the day Maria died. She was too ill to see Johann that day. The fever had already taken her husband and she was leaving us, too." Gunther bent his head for a moment, struggling visibly for control. "I can never talk to you about what happened because you don't want to talk about it, won't talk about it. But it happened to me and Johann, too. It didn't just happen to you."

Kurt silently admitted the truth of that. His throat shut tight. Sweat dotted his forehead.

I can't bear to talk about it.

"I don't take pleasure in talking about it. But if I had told Miss Thurston all that happened to us—losing Maria and her husband, the way our father lived… and how he died—she would say nothing to anybody about it. She is not the kind of lady who gossips. I trust her. Why don't you?"

Kurt swallowed and tried to come up with words but couldn't. Stark, uncompromising shame and loss riddled him.

"I've made up my mind," Gunther said. "I am going to court Amanda for the next two years till I'm eighteen and can stake my own homestead. Then I will ask Amanda to marry me. *I* am not going to let the past ruin my future."

The two of them stared at each other for a moment. Then Gunther went to the pegs by the door, drew on his coat and left.

Kurt felt ill, exhausted. He slumped into his chair and buried his face into his hands. As he thought of Gunther's words, the scene with Miss Thurston outside the school played in his mind.

I am unworthy of her, and not just because of her money or her uncle who sits in the Illinois congress.

The way his father died had stained Kurt and nothing would ever wash him clean. With a sinking sensation, he recalled the look on Brigitte's face when he'd told her about his father's death. She had jilted him then, just one week after the public announcement of their betrothal.

Sometimes he thought his father had planned everything to hurt Kurt and Gunther in the worst possible way.

Sometimes he wished his father lived again so he could pummel him, hurl abuse at him for what he had done. Kurt shook with a sudden rage, shocking himself.

Why, Father, why did you do that to us—after everything else you'd done?

Sitting alone in her quarters, Ellen had barely moved in the hours following her public scene with Kurt. Most likely people were gossiping about her brazen behavior over cups of coffee, laughing about the schoolteacher throwing herself at the Dutchman. No doubt they thought her pathetic.

It's fitting—I feel a little pathetic.

Ellen had declined Sunday dinner with the Ashfords and spent the rest of the gray day alone, caring for William—holding him close and rocking him soothed her battered heart. She pondered her feelings for Kurt, acknowledging that what she felt for Kurt was nothing like what she'd felt for Holton. She hadn't fallen in love with Kurt because of his handsome face, though he certainly was handsome. She'd fallen in love with him because he was working hard to help his brother become a man and to raise a motherless nephew. And Kurt had come to her aid so many times—when the community had tried to force her to give up William, and when William had convulsed and she'd been afraid of losing the baby. Hardworking, unassuming, caring Kurt had stolen her heart. Would she ever get the chance to tell him?

Ellen rose and laid William in his cradle. The sun had sunk below the horizon—winter nights came early now. She struck a match and lit the oil lamp, setting the glass cover in place just as a knock came at the door.

Startled, Ellen swung around. She'd heard no wagon arrive. No one had called out to her. So who had come out in the cold night to knock on her door? She reached the door and twisted the knob.

Chapter Twenty-Two

Ellen opened the door, letting in a gust of cold wind. A woman cloaked within a black shawl huddled at her door.

"Hello?" Ellen said hesitantly. Could it be that strange woman who might come a second time to try to wrest William from her?

The woman, hiding most of her face, glanced around in a furtive manner. Then she stepped forward, gently forcing her way inside. "You don't want me to be seen standing here. Please."

Ellen didn't recognize the woman's voice but her words surprised Ellen and she gave way, allowing her inside. Then she shut the door to keep out the cold. "How may I help you?"

The woman walked to the fireplace and stood before it.

Then Ellen noticed that under the shawl the woman wore a shiny red dress with a scandalously short skirt and black silk stockings.

Ellen was speechless.

A woman of easy virtue had come from the saloon

to her door. In all her life, she had barely glimpsed—
and certainly never spoken—to a woman outside her
chaste world. The line separating decent from indecent
women was sharp and vast, unable to be breached. Ever.

"I know I don't belong here," the woman said as if
reading Ellen's mind. "But when I heard, I had to come.
I reckon you can guess I come from the saloon. They
call me Lila."

Not 'My name is Lila.' 'They call me Lila.' "I'm Ellen
Thurston."

"I know all about you. Men talk at the saloon, you
know…"

The woman trailed off. Ellen didn't know she'd been
the topic of discussion at the saloon. The thought bog-
gled her mind.

Lila rushed to reassure her. "I don't want you to get
the wrong idea. Everyone said that you are a fine lady,
smart and real kind to the kids—I mean, schoolchil-
dren."

Ellen nodded, trying to figure out what had brought
Lila to her fire.

"Well, and that's why I—" Lila began.

At that moment, William rolled over on the blanket
and gurgled happily. He made a few attempts at pushing
up with his arms, then gave up and swam with his legs.

Lila fixed her gaze on William, unmoving.

Ellen suddenly couldn't breathe.

"He's grown so much in just a few months," Lila
whispered.

Ellen gasped silently. This couldn't be happening.

Lila dropped to her knees and reached for William.
Just as Ellen was about to panic, Lila pulled back and
began to weep silently.

Ellen could not think what to do but she couldn't bear the woman's distress. "Please, please don't cry."

Lila sniffed back tears and rose. "I saw you in town once, and you had such a sweet face and such fine manners. I knew you'd make a good mother."

"William…he's your child?" Ellen asked.

Lila nodded, gazing downward.

"Why are you here?" Ellen felt the earth giving way beneath her. *Do you want him back?*

"I don't want him back," Lila blurted out, as if she'd heard Ellen's anguish. "I hear some woman came and wants to take him from you."

Ellen's mind had slowed so that it moved with the speed of cold honey dribbling down the side of a jar. She couldn't sort out everything that was happening.

"You can't let that lyin' woman take him." Lila's voice got stronger. "You can't let nobody take him. I gave my baby to you. I wanted *you* to have him, *you* to raise him, don't you see?"

The woman's fervent plea woke Ellen up, her tension easing. "I do see, Lila. And I promise I will never let anyone take William from me. I might have to leave and go to my hometown, Galena, however. There I have family and backing. My uncle is a judge."

"Good. Good," Lila said. "You do what you have to for…for William, all right? And you can't let anybody know he was born upstairs at the saloon. No one must ever know." Lila raised both hands as if in supplication.

"But many have guessed he might—"

"Guessin' ain't the same as knowing," Lila insisted. "If people know, he'll never live it down. That's why I just up and left him on your doorstep so no one would ever know where he come from." Lila stepped close to

Ellen. "You got to promise me. No one must ever know he was born upstairs at a saloon or his life will be a misery." Lila leaned toward her.

Ellen got the impression that the woman would have taken her hand but feared to breach the division that separated them.

This woman entrusted me with her child. Gratitude carried Ellen forward.

She grasped both the woman's hands in hers. "No one will ever know from me, Lila. I promise. I am so grateful. I didn't think I would make a good mother..." Emotion clogged Ellen's throat.

"Oh, no, I saw right away that you would be a sweet mother. I knew you'd know just how to take care of my...him."

Then Lila tugged her hands free and rearranged her shawl to hide within it. "Peek out and see if there's anybody around. I don't want nobody to see me."

Ellen obeyed and as she expected no one had come to her clearing. She motioned for Lila to come to the door.

Lila slipped past Ellen. "Thank you."

"Thank *you*. You've given me the most wonderful gift..." Ellen couldn't find more words to say.

"You give me the best gift. You love my son and you'll give him a chance for a good life." Then Lila slipped away, disappearing into the dark among the trees.

Ellen closed the door and rested against it. The facts that had just been revealed poured through her like a waterfall. Now she knew who had given up William and chosen her to have him and why. But she would never let anyone use it against him.

She knew what she must do.

Even if it cost her Kurt.

* * *

Sunday afternoon brought the first real snowfall. Ellen left Amanda in charge of William in her quarters and prepared to attend the school board meeting. She'd made her decision and would carry it out today. The Mississippi was freezing and she must take action now.

While the school board members followed the agenda, Ellen sat very straight beside Mrs. Ashford near the front of the crowded schoolroom.

The men who had worked on the woodshed and had cut wood for the school had been invited to attend to receive public recognition. Ellen was very aware that though Kurt was part of this group, he had not come. Over the past few days, he had continued avoiding her. This made what she had to do both easier and harder.

Just before the board began the brief ceremony to thank the men, the door opened behind her. She didn't have to look back. She heard a few quiet accented words and knew Gunther and Kurt had arrived. Her stomach quivered like jelly.

"Miss Thurston, you said you had something to address," Noah said from the front of the room, sitting beside Mr. Ashford.

Ellen rose on trembling legs. She had decided that she must protect William at all costs, even if it cost her the only man she'd ever loved. "I am afraid that I must tender my resignation—"

Suddenly Amanda's panicked voice came from the next room. "No! No! Help! Help!"

Kurt was on his feet immediately, dashing toward the connecting door, just a few steps behind Gunther. As he passed Ellen, he grabbed her hand, pulling her along with him. The other men leaped to their feet and raced forward, too.

They entered the teacher's quarters to find Gunther standing with his back to Amanda, protecting her, his fists raised. Amanda held William close and tight.

Kurt turned to see who Gunther was confronting and thundered, "You again! What are you here for?"

The woman who'd come earlier to claim William as hers stood in Ellen's quarters with a man who looked to be related to her.

"I am not letting you take William," Ellen declared, stepping to Amanda's side and putting an arm around the girl.

"Well, I brought my brother," the woman said, her chin reared up toward Ellen. "He'll tell you the baby is mine."

Kurt knew they were lying. He didn't know how, he just knew.

"If the baby is yours, why were you sneaking in here then?" Amanda asked accusingly. "You didn't even knock, just you came at me and tried to take William out of my arms!"

"You're lying," the brother said.

"Amanda doesn't lie," Gunther barked. "If she says it, it's the truth." Gunther clenched his fists and kept them raised.

"That's right," Mr. Ashford agreed from just inside the connecting door. "My girl doesn't lie."

The woman buried her face in her shawl. "Oh, everyone is against a poor widow!" she shrilled.

Kurt knew in his gut the woman was lying. How could he convince others of this? And what had Ellen said right before Amanda cried out? *I am afraid that I must tender my resignation...* She was going to leave Pepin. She had said before she might go home to Galena to enlist the support of her family to keep William. And now she was going to go through with it.

At this realization, Kurt's heart raced so fast, sweat beaded on his forehead. Then he looked at Ellen and it was as if his heart stopped. In her eyes, he saw the same anguish he'd seen only once before in his life—in his sister's eyes, at the moment she realized she was dying and would leave her tiny Johann an orphan. The memory twisted inside Kurt, nearly forcing out a groan.

In that instant, Kurt knew he couldn't let Ellen lose William; he couldn't allow her to be wounded so deeply that something in her might die. But what could he do?

God, help.

Noah shouldered forward. "Let us all go into the schoolroom and discuss this civilly."

Along with everyone else, the two strangers moved with reluctance into the schoolroom. Gunther stayed protectively at Amanda's side and Kurt joined him, hovering near Ellen. He racked his brain. How could he protect William from this deceiving woman?

People encircled the main participants, not sitting. A sense of watchfulness, wariness hung over them all.

Suddenly, before he knew he landed on a plan, Kurt found the words to say. "If you are this child's mother, you must prove it."

Every face turned toward him, most looking shocked.

"That's true," Noah agreed, "but how?"

Kurt glanced at William, and more words came to him somehow. "Everyone can see one of the child's birthmarks, but his mother would know where his *other* birthmark is."

Every face swung to the woman, who appeared perplexed, chewing her lower lip and frowning. The silent tension in the room rose higher, tighter. The expressions around the woman hardened.

"Well?" Noah asked.

She blurted out, "On his back."

With Amanda still holding him, Ellen lifted William's baby dress, revealing his smooth, unmarked back.

A growling swept through the crowd. Kurt felt it within himself. He clenched his fists and stepped toward the man and woman.

"Why have you lied?" Noah demanded.

The woman began weeping, but others took up Noah's question, insisting on the truth.

Kurt waited, moving closer still to Ellen.

"I heard about the child left on the doorstep here," the woman said tearfully. "I'm not able to bear children. I just wanted to give this child a good home."

Rank disbelief met this. Anger and outrage at being lied to was expressed by a spontaneous hissing from the crowd.

"My new husband is expected to return any day to take us to a homestead in Kansas," the woman continued, trying to justify herself. "We would make a home for the babe."

When this speech met with no sympathy, the woman's brother blurted out, "She's got to have this baby or he'll know she wasn't—"

She hushed him sharply, guiltily.

Noah stepped forward then and asked, "How can we believe anything you say? First you say you bore this child and left him on the doorstep to look for a new husband. Now you say your new husband expects to see you with a child. None of this holds together."

"I've heard of women," Mrs. Ashford announced, "who tell men about to leave for the West that they are pregnant. But it's just a ruse to induce the man into marriage before he leaves. And then when he returns, what happens if there's no baby?"

More hissing followed this suggestion. Kurt began to wonder if the crowd might attack these two, who edged toward the rear doorway.

Noah addressed the town. "Lying, and attempting to steal a child does not recommend you to our community. In any case, God chose Ellen Thurston to raise William."

The pastor's words swayed popular opinion. Every head was nodding, scowling at the woman and her brother.

"If you'd been honest, matters could have ended differently," one of Ellen's most vocal critics said, glaring, disgusted.

Amid the crowd, a path to the schoolroom doors opened as if directing the disgraced twosome to leave.

"This isn't right," the woman said, raising a fist. "This isn't the last you'll hear of me," she blustered as she and her brother left.

One of the men slammed the door closed after them. "Good riddance," he pronounced.

Noah held up both hands to quiet the room. "Would everyone be seated, please?" The crowd moved to sit. "I think that we must put to rest this idea that Miss Thurston cannot keep this child. Did you hear her say she was going to tender her resignation?" Noah scanned the faces before him. "If you can't accept this child as hers, you will lose Miss Thurston from our school, our community. Is that what you want?"

"No," Kurt said aloud, along with many others. Ellen gazed at him with such gratitude in her eyes that he had to look away.

"Miss Thurston," Noah said, "you were going to go home to better defend your claim to William, weren't you?"

"Yes, Ophelia's father is a judge. He would have given me his support," Ellen said, rising.

"Old Saul said that God had given William into this lady's care," Noah said. "We must let this matter rest there."

A man stood. "I been against the teacher keepin' the foundling. But I see today that was wrong of me. Those two were as shifty a pair as I ever seen. Don't you worry any more, Miss Thurston. You'll keep that child or I'll know the reason why."

Many added their agreement to this. Finally, Kurt began to breathe easier.

Noah proceeded with the public thanks to those who helped build the woodshed and the meeting ended on a positive note.

During the social period after the meeting, many men who'd never spoken to Kurt came up to him, surprising him with their congratulations and thanks for exposing the lying woman. They even shook his hand. He knew he'd always be "the Dutchman" in their minds, but something had shifted for them—he could see it in their eyes. Perhaps something had shifted inside him, too.

Finally, only Kurt, Gunther, the Ashfords and Miss Thurston remained. Mrs. Ashford sent Kurt an appraising look and said, "I think Amanda and Gunther and William should come home with us now. It's time you two had a talk," she said sternly.

And with that, Ellen and Kurt were left alone.

Without a word, Ellen led Kurt into her quarters. In front of the fire, she turned to face him. Her gratitude to him for saving William was tempered by a need to know, to come to an understanding of what had broken them apart. "You were wonderful," she said simply.

The words released something in Kurt, and before he could stop himself he had taken her into his arms. He held her, whispering, *"Liebschen."*

Ellen leaned back and looked up at him. "Why have you been avoiding me, Kurt? Was it Randolph?"

"He told me to stay away from you. That you're too good for me." At the time, the words had been very painful to hear, but Kurt said them now as if they were nothing—and they were.

Ellen didn't know whether to be relieved or infuriated. "But that is not what has kept you away, is it?" she pressed him.

Kurt exhaled loudly. "It wasn't just your brother. I already knew he didn't think me good enough for you."

"Then what?" She rested a hand against the mantel.

The light from the fire cast her in a glow, highlighting the golden strands in her light brown hair. She was so lovely. He must speak now, tell her everything. It was time.

"Ellen, it was because I did not *feel* good enough for you." The old sorrow hung around his neck, threatening to weigh him down. But he reeled himself in, and focused on her. "Bad things happened to us in Germany."

"That's what Gunther said. But can't you tell me what happened there? Don't you trust me?"

"With my life," he said, resting a palm against her soft cheek for just a moment. Then he leaned forward and braced his hands against the mantel, gazing down at the low fire. "After a wasted life, my father gambled away our farm and then hanged himself in the barn."

Ellen gasped and then wrapped her arms around Kurt's shoulders as best she could, resting her head against his as he continued to stare into the fire. "Oh, Kurt, how awful for you."

Her words, spoken with heartfelt sympathy, released the pain in him. Tears flowed and he couldn't stanch them. They washed down his face, cleansing him.

"I found him. I will never forget the sight. And after...no one would speak to us. Or even look at us. Because he was a suicide, we couldn't bury him in the churchyard. My fiancée ended our engagement with a note tacked on my door. Gunther and Johann and I were left with just enough to pay for our fares and some money to start over. We left the week after."

Kurt straightened without breaking their connection. He held her close and breathed in her sweet scent. "Ellen, my sweet Ellen."

"Yes," she murmured, "I am your Ellen. And you are my Kurt. I love you and will not let you go, no matter what," she said with all the fierceness she felt. "No one here needs to know what happened over there, Kurt. It wasn't your fault. When my little brother died, for years I blamed myself deep within. But it was false guilt, as is yours. There is no way you could have stopped your father. A son can't control a father."

Kurt received her words as absolution—at last. "You're right."

"God must think we're slow. We've blamed ourselves for losses we had no hand in. That isn't what He wants for us."

Kurt nodded against her.

They held each other a long, silent time and Ellen reveled in his strength and the very handsomeness that had at first made him suspect. With a lighter heart, she tousled his golden curls. "Kurt, you're too handsome to marry the old maid schoolmarm."

"Foolishness. You are a beauty. But you must know that I will always be *that Dutchman*," he said.

"And I'll always love *that Dutchman*," she said, stroking his cheek with her soft palm.

He clasped her to him again, thanking God for this woman, this special gift. He lowered his mouth to hers and kissed her as he had wanted to for so long.

Ellen drew his breath in and reveled in his gentle yet demanding kiss. She had never been kissed like this and with such love in all her life.

"Will you be my wife, *Liebschen?*"

Words she had thought she never wanted to hear. How foolish. Of course, what really mattered was the man who said them. "Yes, Kurt, I will be your wife." Joy enveloped her. She wanted to stand on tiptoe and sing.

Kurt laughed aloud as if he also couldn't contain his joy at this special moment.

She now knew the difference between calf love and real love. Kurt was her real McCoy.

Snow fell thick and fast on Sunday morning. It was almost time for worship to begin. Ellen dressed with care, wanting to look her best on this very special day. She finished getting William ready and then carried him into the schoolroom.

Martin and Ophelia had returned from Galena. They sat in their usual place but this time Kurt, Gunther and Johann had joined them, no longer sitting in the back. Already, people stared at this new arrangement, whispering to each other. But they had smiles on their faces, as if they were anticipating something. Ellen, unable to keep from smiling herself, walked over to the Stewards and the Langs. Kurt rose and lifted William into his arms. Then she sat beside him, feeling all eyes on her back. For the first time since she'd come to Pepin, the feeling was not a bad one.

Noah cleared his throat and everyone sat down, looking expectantly toward him. "Before we begin today, I think that Martin Steward has an announcement to make."

Martin stood and turned to face the congregation. "It is my distinct pleasure to announce the engagement of Kurt Lang to our cousin Miss Ellen Thurston—"

Clapping and whistles drowned out Martin's last words. "When's the weddin'?" someone called out.

Kurt stood and beamed. "In May next year. Right after school ends."

"That means we have to find a new teacher for next year," Mr. Ashford said, sounding surprisingly pleased.

Mrs. Ashford was weeping into a lace handkerchief. "I'm so happy. So happy."

Old Saul tapped his son, who then rolled the wheelchair down the aisle to Kurt. "I told you the day I met you that God had a plan for your life, a good one."

Kurt shook the large but frail hand. "You were right."

"'A man who finds a wife finds a good thing,'" Old Saul quoted with a twinkle in his eye. "And you found a very fine one. God bless you both."

Ellen took Old Saul's other hand and the three of them formed a circle of unity as Noah asked everyone to bow for a prayer of thanksgiving. At the end of the prayer, Old Saul said, "May God richly bless you with a love that grows and a family to love."

And everyone called out, "Amen!"

Kurt pulled Ellen closer to him, too proud for words. She smiled at him and whispered, "I love you."

He bent close to her ear. "I love you, *Liebschen*."

Epilogue

April 18, 1871

The crowd sat on benches and in wagons that parked around the schoolyard clearing, watching Martin intently as he prepared to read the next word at the long-anticipated Pepin spelling bee. An especially lovely spring day cheered everyone, blessing the exciting event. Three other schools had arrived in midmorning to compete and now, after over two hours of spelling, only three students still stood on the makeshift platform in the schoolyard.

"Dorcas, you have won the spelling bee in the primary grade class," Martin said. "Please be seated until we have a winner for the advanced class."

People applauded as Dorcas sat down.

Both dressed in their Sunday best, Amanda and a boy from the Bear Lake School, Samuel Tarkington, still remained standing nervously on the platform.

Ellen held hands with Kurt as they sat on the first row of benches. She wanted to get up and shout, "You can do it, Amanda!" But she worked hard to hold herself with dignity, as a lady should. Johann sat with his fellow first graders, watching closely. Ophelia sat on Ellen's other side, jiggling Nathan, who was squirming on her knee.

"The word is *dichotomy*," Martin read from the approved list.

"Dichotomy," Amanda repeated. "*D-i-c-h-o-t-o-m-y.* Dichotomy."

"Correct," Martin said,

A burst of applause.

Martin turned to the boy. "The word is *euphonious*."

Samuel looked very white. Tension filled the school clearing. His family leaned forward. "Euphonious. *E-u-p-h-o-n-i-o-u-s.* Euphonious."

"Correct!" Martin said.

Excited applause from Samuel's school broke out.

"Hauteur," Martin said to Amanda.

"Hauteur," Amanda repeated, visibly trembling. "*H-a-u-t-u-e-r.* Hauteur."

"I'm sorry, Amanda," Martin said, sounding sorry. "That is incorrect."

A gasp went through the crowd. Ellen tightened her grip on Kurt's hand. Amanda stepped to the side of the stage, waiting to see if Samuel would miss the word. She looked shaken.

Gunther rose from the bench, catching her eye.

She smiled tremulously back at him.

"Samuel, spell *hauteur*," Martin said.

The boy cleared his voice. "Hauteur. *H-a-u-t-e-u-r.* Hauteur."

"That is correct," Martin announced with enthusiasm. "Samuel Tarkington, representing Bear Lake School, is the winner in the advanced category and the last speller standing in the First Annual Southwest Wisconsin Spelling Bee."

Everyone rose and applauded, no matter what school they'd come to support. The applause went on and on till Mr. Ashford and three other men mounted the platform. Mr. Ashford held up his hands and the crowd settled down to listen.

"We are so happy that three other schools joined us in this first annual spelling bee." He shook hands with the other men who represented the three other school boards. "We intend to do this again next year and hope even more schools will be able to attend."

Then Mr. Ashford invited Samuel, his parents and teacher to come up to receive the large winning plaque. "Each year this plaque will be awarded to the winning school, engraved with the name of the winning speller, their grade, and the year."

The crowd applauded as Samuel accepted the plaque with a big grin.

"The top three spellers will receive ribbons." Mr. Ashford waved up Amanda and Dorcas, and hung a blue ribbon around Samuel's neck, a red one around Amanda's and a yellow one around Dorcas's. "Let's applaud all the teachers, parents and students who worked so hard to make this spelling bee a rousing success!"

The crowd rose as one, applauding, whistling and stomping their feet.

Ellen felt nearly lifted into the air.

Mr. Ashford continued, nearly shouting over the crowd, "I want to also announce that our teacher, Miss Ellen Thurston, was the person who came up with the idea for this spelling bee. Next month, she is going to marry Kurt Lang, one of our prominent citizens."

Not expecting Mr. Ashford to announce this so publicly, Ellen blushed. But at Kurt's insistence, she waved and smiled at everyone. Then Noah closed with prayer and Mr. Ashford invited everyone to partake of the potluck refreshments on the school grounds.

Ellen and Kurt stood together, receiving best wishes and compliments on the spelling bee. Finally, they walked together toward the food tables. "Prominent citizen," she murmured to Kurt with a smile.

Kurt chuckled, and pointed at Amanda and Gunther already sitting at a nearby table with the Ashfords. "He thinks we will be related."

Ellen laughed. "I think he's right."

Noah and his wife, Sunny, came up behind them in line. "We're so glad for both of you," Sunny said, with a smile that radiated joy.

Noah agreed, adding, "We've just received good news. My cousin Rachel Woolsey is coming from Pennsylvania in June. It will be good to have family nearby. Rachel is a wonderful girl."

Mr. Ashford overheard what Noah was saying, and he came over and asked, "Do you think she'd be qualified to teach?"

Noah shook his head. "No, Rachel is a notable cook and baker. She intends to start her own bake shop here."

Mr. Ashford looked surprised and many around them put their heads together to discuss this startling announcement. Ellen already knew all too well the challenges this unconventional woman was going to face in Pepin, but if the community could rise to the occasion for her, they could do it again for Miss Woolsey.

She looked up into Kurt's blue eyes and her love

for him nearly overwhelmed her as he drew her hand
to his lips.

"*Liebschen.*"

Then they made their way through the line, chatting
with neighbors and filling their plates, just as their lives—
soon to be joined together—had been filled with love.

* * * * *

SPECIAL EXCERPT FROM

🍃

LOVE INSPIRED
INSPIRATIONAL ROMANCE

*What happens when a beautiful foster mom claims an
Oklahoma rancher as her fake fiancé?*

Read on for a sneak preview of
The Rancher's Holiday Arrangement
by Brenda Minton.

"I am so sorry," Daisy told Joe as they walked down the sidewalk together.

The sun had come out and it was warm. The kind of day that made her long for spring.

"I don't know that I need an apology," Joe told her. "But an explanation would be a good start."

She shook her head. "I saw you sitting with your family, and I knew how I'd feel. Ambushed."

"I could have handled it. Now I'm engaged." He tossed her a dimpled grin. "What am I supposed to tell them when I don't have a wedding?"

"I got tired of your smug attitude and left you at the altar?" she asked, half teasing. "Where are we walking to?"

"I'm not sure. I guess the park."

"The park it is," she told him.

Daisy smiled down at the stroller. Myra and Miriam belonged with their mother, Lindsey. Daisy got to love them for a short time and hoped that she'd made a difference.

"It'll be hard to let them go," Joe said.

"It will be," Daisy admitted. "I think they'll go home after New Year's."

"That's pretty soon."

"It is. We have a court date next week."

"I'm sorry," Joe said, reaching for her hand and giving it a light squeeze.

"None of that has anything to do with what I've done to your life. I've complicated things. I'm sorry. You can tell your parents I lost my mind for a few minutes. Tell them I have a horrible sense of humor and that we aren't even friends. Tell them I wanted to make your life difficult."

"Which one is true?" he asked.

"Maybe a combination," she answered. "I *do* have a horrible sense of humor. I *did* want to mess with you."

"And the part about us not being friends?"

"Honestly, I don't know what we are."

"I'll take friendship," he told her. "Don't worry, Daisy, I'm not holding you to this proposal."

She laughed and so did he.

"Good thing. The last thing I want is a real fiancé."

"I know I'm not the most handsome guy, but I'm a decent catch," he said.

She ignored the comment about his looks. The last thing she wanted to admit was that when he smiled, she forgot herself just a little.

Don't miss
The Rancher's Holiday Arrangement *by Brenda Minton,*
available November 2020 wherever
Love Inspired books and ebooks are sold.

LoveInspired.com

LIEXP1120

LOVE INSPIRED

INSPIRATIONAL ROMANCE

UPLIFTING STORIES OF FAITH, FORGIVENESS AND HOPE.

Join our social communities to connect with other readers who share your love!

Sign up for the Love Inspired newsletter at **LoveInspired.com** to be the first to find out about upcoming titles, special promotions and exclusive content.

CONNECT WITH US AT:

 Facebook.com/LoveInspiredBooks

 Twitter.com/LoveInspiredBks

Facebook.com/groups/HarlequinConnection

Get 4 **FREE REWARDS!**

We'll send you 2 FREE Books <u>plus</u> 2 FREE Mystery Gifts.

Love Inspired books feature uplifting stories where faith helps guide you through life's challenges and discover the promise of a new beginning.

FREE
Value Over
$20
